# The Land of Is

*The Land of Is*

Published by The Conrad Press Ltd. in the United Kingdom 2022

Tel: +44(0)1227 472 874

www.theconradpress.com

info@theconradpress.com

ISBN 978-1-915494-01-6

Typesetting and Cover Design by: Charlotte Mouncey, www.bookstyle.co.uk
The Conrad Press logo was designed by Maria Priestley.

Printed and bound in Great Britain by Clays Ltd, Elcograf S.p.A.

# The Land of Is

Vian Andrews

To my children and my children's children
and their children too

I never hear the word 'Escape'
Without a quicker blood,
A sudden expectation –
A flying attitude!

I never hear of prisons broad
By soldiers battered down,
But I tug childish at my bars
Only to fail again!

Emily Dickinson

# Song 1

My minders have grown bored over the years, getting older just as I have, all of us set in the routines that were designed to assure the public the dowager me is as well-tended as the wide lawns that run right to the edge of the cliffs above the river. Mostly, I am quiet and seemly, but these minders know my temper - not the crankiness of a privileged old woman irritated by spilt milk - but a hard, low-voiced, growling bitch of the first order, made more masculine than most on the road to perdition. They leave me alone to ponder my sins, not knowing that I have ways and means to write this record.

I have now completed this history of your father and me, to tell you why I daggered your father's heart, murdered him in our bed at Castle Forbes. Murdered him for your sake but also for the sake of all the souls who know now how deeply they were betrayed by your father and his disciples. Sitting here in my garden, where the roses war, I don't give a damn about having anyone else's forgiveness but yours, but, yes, I will accept the thanks of all and anyone with a sense of justice.

It is a long story that starts with the woman who brought me into the world, because what I did was done to the music that Demeter played into the heart of Persephone, the secret gift of life passed from mothers to their children, one that I now share with you both. But don't expect to go on a sentimental journey. Ours was a hard one, taken over the landscape of horrible truths, which, now that you have inherited your father's empire, you have a duty to take.

My mother's name was Merri Weer. Once she had been set in motion, she never stopped. She was born in Chicago in 2026. July, she said. Her mother and father were still together on that joyous day, but barely. The heat of that summer shrivelled the last of the tenuous cocoon their teenage passions had spun around them, so her father wriggled free and went off on a wing and a prayer, out of the squalid, crumbling, dangerous city to someplace else, where my grandma's bitching and my mother's baby howling went silent behind the batting of time.

Merri did not talk about her Chicago childhood, or the prolonged death by a painful cancer of her mother when Merri was in her late teens. I can tell you almost nothing of those days because Merri recounted almost nothing. But she got some schooling there, so she could read and write very well, but not nearly as well as she could deal with numbers. For her, arithmetic and mathematics were a constant revelation of the forces of nature, including human nature, and they accorded well with the practical, no-nonsense, persevering formula of her own character.

A few months after Merri's mother died, the long awaited 'big one' hit the west coast, a vicious quake that killed tens of thousands in an instant as the entirety of the man-made world in which they worked and ate and fucked and slept, came crashing down on their disbelieving selves. The tsunami that swept-in moments later ground the heads and limbs off thousands more. What was left of LA and the other towns and cities along the Pacific littoral after years of inundation from a rising sea, was left in a wet and pulverized ruin upon which were strewn the dazed and drenched survivors drying under a killing sun. The quake's vibrations carried their calls for help eastward like ripples through a pond.

Merri and a few dozen other young people in Chicago answered the call. Pulling together what they could – medical supplies, potable water, blankets, clothes and other necessities – they formed a long caravan of trucks and cars and headed west, letting the AutoWay take them as far as it could before, about thirty miles from blue water, the highway itself became a broken and undulating heap of fragments and busted bridges that would take two decades for the bankrupt government of the United States of America to stitch back together. Sort of.

The story of the rescue and recovery efforts has been told elsewhere, so no need for me to repeat what is already known. Besides, mother never told me what she herself did there, although even years later, people we encountered on the road (people she would quickly hush if she caught them admiring her a little too much) told me that in the disorganization and chaos of those days on the coast, Merri's anger at the incompetence, arrogance and punctiliousness of those who purported to be running things, caused her take charge of the crews working in her area.

Intuitively knowing what needed to be done, she barked orders, lashed the indolent with a fierce tongue, breathed new energy into the devastated, and though exhausted in her bones, got things done. Hundreds were saved who otherwise would have perished. Even though she was a mere girl at the time, I don't doubt it for a minute.

Merri never went back to Chicago to live and, in fact, apart from brief stints here and there, she never lived anywhere again. Not anywhere you might call a place. Instead, she drove her life, and her life drove her, down the broken highways of our broken country, doing as much good as she could, bartering with womenfolk of all kinds, keeping men at a distance, surviving on a little food and a love of song. When she died, it was on the highways of the east. Had it been up to me I would have buried her by the side of a western road that she, and later I, had travelled on, but it was not to be.

Many weeks after the quake, she and one of the men of her crew, were tasked to take one of the huge rescue vans that were put into service by the feds to return to Chicago for desperately needed supplies. The AutoWay was choked with traffic in both directions, so they decided to cut across the south on whatever roads and highways were still driveable, using an ancient road atlas for navigation because the GPS in the van was telling lies. Virtually all the beacon and guide systems that had been installed along these roads in days gone by had been ripped out of their housings and sold by hungry locals for parts.

There was no way to put the van into selfdrive, so off they went, taking turns at the wheel. Keep in mind that Merri was only seventeen or eighteen, beautiful in her bones, raven-haired, high spirited, intelligent, open minded, ready with a laugh, given to touching those who came into her circle without ever realizing that her touch could ignite in others a deep, reciprocal affection, or envy or insecurity or love or lust. You can see for yourself in the 3Ds. Here she is standing on the step of that van at a recharging station near some pass-by town, put into leering focus by, what was his name? Eddington, I think. Yes, Eddington. There he is in those other pix, striking the mistaken pose of a boyfriend, not a colleague.

By this time, 2040 or so, people everywhere, but especially

in the parched and increasingly barren regions of the west, had begun to adjust their lives to avoid the pernicious effects of sunlight beating down on earth through the thinnest of those ozone filters that one time had kept humanity safe. The ritualized chants and supplications of ancient priests glorifying the sun from the high tops of slave-built stone piles, to Ra, Helios, Kinich Ahau and dozens of others, could not escape the blistered lips of modern men and women. They hated it, for too much exposure to the sun could kill.

Those of us who chanced to come outside in daylight hours, if on foot, kept to the shadows, moving quickly from one to the other, or we conveyed ourselves in window-tinted self-drives from one covered lot to another. Most of us worked and played at night, from dusk to dawn, illuminated by a ubiquity of diodic lights that nearly eliminated shadow altogether. We lived in night's black and white glare and made our way into the over-exposed dimensions of day only when necessary.

Merri and Ed drove all day and night, making good time, one at the wheel, one in the rear sleeping, brewing coffee, scrolling their vice for news, consulting maps and clocks, and, when their bellies growled, preparing both a traveler's meal. Merri liked to have the radio on as she drove, fiddling with the dash tuner if a signal waivered, or if a song disappointed, or if the DJ took too long spouting nonsense before cueing another tune.

Ed drove with the radio off, so Merri often kicked back with her headset on, lost in the sanctuary of her favorite music, not realizing that Ed did not turn off the radio because he preferred silence, but because he loved to hear Merri's *a capella* voice, singing as she listened. It stirred him, so as the vehicle rolled from place-to-place, he gathered a love of Merri like a clinging moss. The non-stop friction of wheels on the roadbed transmuted into a sexual yearning with an increasing kinetic force, but only for him, not Merri's oblivious and singing self.

It was only later over the course of years the highway, by then a simulacrum of the deep rut of her exhausted mind, that Merri came to deeply know the country through which she and Ed then moved with such purpose. On that journey, with the heaped-up, bleeding ruins of LA fresh in mind, as the repurposed rescue van she and Eddington drove pushed at speed past the villages, towns and cities that hung on the necklace of the highway, Merri allowed herself to be distracted. The solace of the music pouring into her ears out of the workings of some take-for-granted skygod made her blind to the ruination that was all around her, in every direction as far as the eye could see. As blind to it as to her companion's agitations.

Eddington, however, while sitting in the driver's seat, saw things that made him shout out holy-smokes, and my-god-did-you-see-that when his eye caught the remains of some new and as yet unseen calamity that had earlier befallen his fellow man or woman. However, his there-but-for-the-grace-of-God-go-I nonchalance made him uncurious about what horror might have happened, so he passed by them as one passes by pictures on a wall. Besides, Merri was unstoppably Chicago-bound, and he had every intention of pleasing her.

In subsequent years, Merri allowed a retroactive shame to attach itself to her memories of that trip. Shame about not seeing what was so plainly in front of her as she and he steered the van down the wretched highway, through the destruction, havoc and exploded clutter everywhere in evidence. Not shame for what she did to Ed, though. That always made her smile.

East of Amarillo, while Ed was in the driver's seat, Merri decided to shower-off the dust and fatigue that was clinging to her. Once done, she came out of the shower stall, a towel wrapped around her, the swell of her breasts rosy from the heat, hair wet, skin of her neck and shoulders gleaming. She did not see Ed's eyes in the rear-view mirror where he was framing her, seized on her loosely wrapped, beautiful body as though it were possessable.

She did not think his sudden, holy smokes exclamation was for her, but thought some on-road mangle made him pump the brakes and bring the van to a stop. She moved toward the front windows to see what was going on. He rose from the driver's seat and turned toward her. Something in his eyes. Face red. Body tense. Breathing ragged – for her, the so far unencountered song of a man's primordial desire. In herself, quickly, her own primordial instinct, a previously unknown fear.

Merri turned away and walked toward the sleeping room at the far end of the van. Closed the door behind her. No lock. He called her name through the door. She pulled on her shorts, was about to pull on her T-shirt when the door opened. He said something. Something about love. Surely, she felt it too. He moved close, toppled her back on the bed and fell on top of her, his hard-on pressing into her pubis, hurting. One breast grabbed and squeezed. The other grazed with an unshaven cheek.

When she was telling me this story – this cautionary tale - it was at this moment her eyes closed and she went silent.

-   What happened, mother? What happened?

13

- Keep your wits about you, Wicla. That's the lesson.

- Did he rape you?

- He didn't want to rape me. I knew that. He thought I was as horny for him as he was for me.

- You let him? You consented?

- I made a date.

- What?

- I told him. I'm a virgin, Eddington. I'm a virgin. This is not the day I can give myself to you. Two days.

- He thought you had your period. Did you?

- No. But two days seemed right. Made me seem willing. Made me seem honest in the moment. I'm so sorry, Merri, he said. Delicious anticipation in his voice.

- And did you?

- In two days, we were in Springfield, Illinois. Let's stop to get a bottle of wine, I said.

- You led him on…

- This time I framed him in the mirrors. The side mirrors

of the van. I had a righteous boner of anger that had been swelling since he had affronted me. I saw him waving as I pulled out of the lot, shrinking to nothingness in the burning sun with his wilted dick. I went on to Chicago by myself, intact and proud of myself. But I also felt stirred-up in a new, strange way.

- Wow.

- Keep your wits about you when it comes to men and all their doings. That's the lesson.

In Chicago, Merri took no time at all to visit friends or old haunts. The cacophony of the city, the tired struggles of almost everyone in it, the sound of random gunfire that blew down every street and avenue on the ripping lakewind jangled her nerves and aroused no nostalgia, only a wish to be gone as soon as the van was loaded with as much cargo as it could carry, inside and on top.

The bent, gravel-voiced Black man who had supervised the loading looked her up and down again as he handed her a tablet and stylus and pointed to the place where she should sign.

- Where's the other driver? You've a long drive ahead.

- Picking him up on the way out.

- Never been to the coast. Never been out of Chi-town.

- Why?

- Don't know.

- Not too late.

- Sure it is.

She would return the same way she'd come, but this time, being alone, she would have to give herself time to sleep, so she allowed for an extra two nights along the way. Uneventful first shift. After fourteen hours of driving, she came at last to Oklahoma City. There, coming off the highway ramp, she slowed down to prowl its outer edges looking for safe harbor. But she never found a spot where her nerves weren't twitching from the apprehension of the horrible possibilities that had risen in her mind. Wherever she looked she saw furtive, gun-toting people moving in packs or heard raised voices shouting as they ordered a pack of free-roaming dogs to stop their barking. It was solid sleep she needed, not the quarter-rest of a half sleep, one ear cocked, one eye open.

She drove a couple of hours more until, just after dawn, Merri came to the outskirts of Elk City, where in the potholed expanse of the parking lot of an abandoned mall, she saw the wheeled, day-time encampment of other travelers, a cluster of motor-homes, campervans, trucks and cars recently arrived. She pulled in and took a deep breath before sidling shyly to the perimeter of circled lawn chairs where the itinerants were chatting amiably, some with bottles of beer warming in their hands.

She asked if it would be all right if she could stay the day as well. Her young age, diffidence and solitary courage aroused the protective instincts of just about everyone, so she was not only greeted warmly, but given a plate full of barbecued leftovers that she devoured with a happy ravenousness. The people there were mostly middle aged or older, but there were two or three young couples too, their youngsters lazily kicking a ball around, before everyone retreated to their beds for the rest of the day.

A few hours later, as dusk descended, Merri was awakened by a knock at the van door. She answered and, without fear, saw at the bottom of the vans steps a shaggy-headed blond woman, arms akimbo, one of the middle-aged women who had welcomed her upon her arrival at Elk City. Delmonica? Yes, Delmonica.

- Never mind the hair, dear. I'll be wrestling it into some kind of trained animal once we're back on the road. It's a daily struggle. Merri, right? If I heard you right this morning. Young woman like you all alone out here. I'll say it again, you're a brave soul. I have the coffee on. C'mon.

She led my mother between a couple of beat-up camper vans, one with an Armed to the Teeth sign in its side window, to where she and her husband had set-up, not just for the day just past, but for the past couple of weeks. Under an awing pulled down from their rig, there was a counter with a built-in stove that ran off solar batteries and a small sink full to the gunnels with unwashed utensils, dishes and cups.

- I'll tidy up later. But I'll swab out a cup for you.

- Delmonica? My mother said tentatively.

- That's right, dear. But Del is fine.

- Let me, said Merri, just as Del reached for a dirty cup.

- So, you said you were taking supplies out to the coast. I can't even imagine what those poor people must have gone through. Oh, lordy. It's OK, dear. I'll do it.

Del ran the cup under a weak stream of tepid water and swooshed the inside with two fingers, then rinsed again. She started pouring black coffee from a thermos.

- Leave enough for milk, dear?

- Yes, please.

Merri had been listening for sounds of Del's husband, Jacard, whom she assumed was in the camper, maybe sleeping off the more than a few beers he'd sucked into his vast paunch in the early hours. Not a peep. Del used the stem of a spoon to stir a dollop of boxed milk into Merri's coffee.

- Where's Jac, Del?

- Jacard, dear. He's very particular about his name. Well, that's a good question. He likes to take a walk, so out there somewhere, she said, gesturing toward the rain stained, white walls of the mall sitting glumly across the parking lot.

Merri sipped her coffee while Del kept up a constant chatter. And while she blathered, Merri realized that the rest of the camp was quieter than she would have expected. Momentarily, through the screened window of the big blue motorhome parked a short way off, she heard one of the young mothers shushing her kids.

- The government is throwing billions of dollars at the coast, aren't they. Billions. They're creatin' jobs for kids like you.

- I volunteered, said Merri.

- But it's the way it is, isn't it? If you're lucky enough to get kicked by some big, hellacious storm or an avalanche or an earthquake, you get looked after. But god forbid you just suffer disaster bit by bit all by yourself, with time itself grinding you to dust, they'll do nothing for you.

- I suppose.

- You suppose, do you? Said with bitter anger.

Del would not give Merri eye contact. She fussed with a rag wiping down a clean chair and a spotless chaise lounge. And then, turning her red, grievous face toward the kitchenette, Merri saw her pull out her vice to look at the time then look surreptitiously in the direction of Merri's van. And at that moment, Merri knew. She reached past Del, put her coffee cup down and started running, with flabby, flabbergasted

Delmonica trying to keep up under her bouncing mop of ratblond hair.

A line of men stood outside the rescue van passing the boxes Jacard tossed out the door in hand-to-hand style until the fifth man added it to their growing stack of loot. They didn't see her coming until she was upon them, and they had one foot on the lower tread of the stairs, which she used to catapult herself into the van. Once inside, she pulled the door closed and locked it. Delmonica pulled up short nearby, bending over as she gasped for breath, as she squeezed out warnings and imprecations in Merri's direction.

Inside the van, Jacard, shirtless and sweating, was picking through the cargo stacked toward the rear looking for easy-to-sell hypodermic needles. He whipped around when he felt the van sway when Merri jumped into the van. They stared at one another.

- Now, what do you think you're gonna do little, girl? He turned and took a menacing step toward her.

- You stop right there, Jac.

He stopped, but he managed a nervous laugh. Beads of hot sweat coursed down his cheeks from a set of woolly sideburns. Sweatwater beaded on top of his bald crown glistening in the light of dusk that bounced off the side view mirrors into the van's dim interior catching Jacard in their crossfire.

- Now Jac, I'm going to shoot your balls off, said Merri matter-of-factly, repeating a line of movie dialogue she had heard a couple of years ago in Chicago.

She edged over to the upholstered bench tucked in behind the driver's seat then flipped it up to reveal a storage chest below filled chock-a-block with emergency equipment – a first aid kit, dry rations, jugged water, flares, tire jack, tool kit, boxes of ammo and a loaded pistol and a semi-automatic rifle that was within easy reach. When Merri lifted the rifle out and pointed in Jacard's direction, he was already half-way out the door bellowing run, run as he tumbled down the stairs. He crashed into the humid molecules of the deepening night hard on the heels of his fellow pirates.

By the time Merri got to the door the men were gone, but Delmonica, immobile in a puddle of fear, could do nothing but stand and stare as Merri leaned the rifle against the van, then moved back and forth between the van and the looted goods reloading all except two boxes of needles that Del and Jac could turn into ready money. She understood the desperation of once honest people and wanted them to know it.

Once done, she mounted the van, pulled the door shut, then plunked herself down in the driver's seat where she started the engine and ordered the van to find the closest on-ramp to the road west. She was, she told me, fractionally older, but infinitely wiser.

- You'll always remember the names of those who betray you. Delmonica and Jacard. Probably dead now, but two of the many dead who I can name.

- And the people who did you good, mother?

- Numberless as the stars.

- Unnamed?

- Most of them, yes. Not all.

What else did she remember of that night?

Merri said that as she came up the ramp to the highway, she noticed a rusted old sign in the shape of a crest hanging from a bolt sunk into old concrete in its upper right corner: Route 66. She had not seen anything like it on the way to Chicago, but from that point on, she would see dozens more along the various roads and highways that constituted her way, and ultimately, as the years went by, she realized how those signs stitched all her experiences on that route together, not as strands in a twisted rope tying together the poles of LA and Chicago, but as the unbreakable gossamer threat that held her far-flung cosmos in one continuum where, for her, time and space were one.

Merri drove all night, stopping near Phoenix for a few hours of daytime sleep. She made it to the coast early the next morning just as the far reaches of the pewter grey Pacific were catching light from the east-rising sun. The inexplicable happiness that had gestated since she had crossed into California carried her forward, so far forward in fact that she drove past the now bare ground of the encampment where she had lived and worked before the Chicago trip.

The landscape on all sides, the collapsed and broken buildings through which she wended slowly, became unfamiliar. She turned off the music that she had just moments before been singing to. She stopped and turned back, looking for landmarks that she would know.

- I found the old depot eventually. Everyone was gone. The gate to the compound where I had lived with my team was open.

Mother hadn't seen the sign warning of unstable ground that had been hung on the gate sometime after she left for Chicago. Aftershocks had rippled through the place and torn it up. There were long, wide cracks running through the surface of the dusty ground, one of them under the spread legs of the jerry-built water tower that had defied the shaking and was still standing.

- They hadn't contacted you?

- They'd forgotten about me. Assumed I'd taken off, I guess.

- Where did everyone go?

- Don't know.

- What did you do?

- I pulled the van over to the water tower and even though there was not much left in the tank, I managed to fill all the empty jugs in the van. I'd have to boil anything I drank or cooked with, but it was a small price to pay because water was like gold in those parts. I also got enough to fill the shower cistern, so I felt like a rich woman.

- You had all those supplies from Chicago still?

- Yes, I did. But I didn't know what the hell I was going to do.

- What did you do?

- I climbed up the ladder to a platform ringing the bottom of the water tank and looked out over LA. In the few short days I had been away things had changed. The emergency part was over. The busted remains of the city were lit up by hundreds of temporary lights where crews were still digging out the dead. And even though it was a dark night, I could see a lot of Navy ships, including a couple of hospital ships, anchored offshore, with smaller boats going to and fro, ferrying people, carrying the necessaries to where they were needed, and the like. On the beaches all along the shore, huge bonfires burned the carcasses of humans and animals alike. It was a beautiful, horrible scene.

- Were you frightened? Upset?

- Me? No. I had been forgotten and the strange thing is that even though I was alone I knew I wanted to stay that way.

The girl she was cried her eyes out back in the parking lot in Elk City, but the woman who she drove into was dry-eyed.

When she left the compound for good, mother closed the gates to the compound and wired them shut, then she pulled the van in behind a hillock, so it could not be seen from the road. Then, at midnight, she stood under the high nozzle of the water tower that had been used to fill tanker trucks and pulled its chain. Naked, she stood under the moon, cold, clean and wet as a newborn in a mud made from the forgotten water in the tower and the riled, ancient dust underfoot.

*Oh, lambent light, illuminate my liquid life.*

# Song 2

On her vice, mother found the waybill she'd signed before pulling out of the depot in Chicago and read it as she peered at the labels on all the boxes piled in the van. At the end of her inventory-taking she decided the guilt that had registered in her gut because she had left two cartons of needles with Jacard and Del, was the kind that would dissipate in time. They would sell those needles to addicts, no doubt, but at least the needles were new and sterilized and would not deepen their users' miseries. Merri had three more cartons of needles that could be sold or bartered, but she could attract a good enough price from one or two hospitals or clinics along her route and be done with them.

All the remaining material was of equally high value: inside she checked off bandages and slings, thermal wraps to keep out the cold, antiseptic swabs, high nutrient bars, baby formula, water purification tablets, old-fashioned matches, ibuprofen, and several cartons of tampons and menstrual pads.

On top and tied to the back of the van under a photovoltaic tarp that produced as much power as the uncovered roof would have it if were not covered with trade goods she counted tents, camp stoves, lanterns and high intensity camp lights. She had, in other words, a small fortune in stuff - all the capital she needed to fund the start-up of her new life, a life that began as soon as she pulled out on Route 66 and headed east again.

For eleven years or so, she would travel between the Coast

and Chicago, always alone. In that time, she matured from the precocious young woman she had been into the savvy, road-wise woman she became, known to all who had dealings with her as Trader Merri Weer. During the pained fugues of her last days she circled back to those times and re-inhabited the body of the young girl she was when she first left the shores of Lake Michigan. She remembered her time on Route 66 as a series of a thousand hyphenated episodes in which she was always the hidden observer, never involved.

But, just as Merri dismissed the heroic work she had done in California as anything other than the work of two strong hands and a good back, she minimized every aspect of her life along that highway as though it were a miniature world seen from a distance.

Out of her mouth in bits and pieces came stories that were as harrowing or as joyful as you have ever heard, and so I know - and you should know - that in all the incidents she related and in the recollection of all the people who populated her tales, we find the tell-tale signs of a person whose whole being was engaged. The young, naïve but determined Chi-town girl was still in my mother, even on her last, fateful day, but my mother's truest self was the tough, cagey, careful, self-sacrificing and moral creature of her legend.

You would think that with her success on that road, with the great store of knowledge she had about the people and places along it, by sheer force of habit, that Trader Merri Weer would never leave it, but by the time I was born, mother had left Route 66 and was doing a north south route through California, Oregon and Washington. I would learn the reasons why eventually, but long before I did, when I was eleven or twelve, I remember asking my mother why she never married. I had no idea how loaded the question was for her, how fraught with pain.

- What are you looking at on that vice of yours? She asked, tightening her grip on the van's steering wheel.

She knew I was caught-up in a post-pubescent devotion to boy-girl romance programs. I hardly watched anything else.

- Didn't you ever meet a boy?

- I met a lot of boys. I never met a man, she said.

- No, really, mother. Don't you like men?

- I like them for what they're good for, which ain't much.

The melodramas that poured out of my vice involved a lot of conflict based on misunderstandings as to intention. They were all resolved when a boy and girl found their way to the necessary apologies and clarifications, followed by a shy but passionate kiss. I ached to try one. How could she not want that?

There were men everywhere we went and some of them, even to my very young self, looked good enough for my mother to kiss. Those were the men who looked good, but also had a swagger that cleared their path through the ranks of all the other, lesser men who invariably surrounded them. Or I might spy a lone man in a road-side café, with his head-down, peering into a coffee cup. I liked those thoughtful, intelligent types who seemed to ponder the secrets of the universe in the hot, dark water and I had a strong suspicion my mother would too.

I knew from watching my programs that all she had to do was give a handsome man a come-hither look and he would come over, swaggering and gregarious, or with the gentlemanly diffidence of an intellectual as the case might be. The universe may have many secrets, but surely my mother was smart enough to know the secret of catching a man's attention. If not, I was prepared to provide advice and encouragement.

- So, why did you never get married, really?

- You know what, Wicla? It's none of your business.

Why the anger in her voice? I couldn't understand why, not then.

- I have a right to know.

- Do you now?

- I must have a father, right? I'm not stupid. I know you had to do it with someone.

- Shut up. Just shut up. I'm trying to drive.

- No.

- I don't know who your father is.

- Oh, right. Sure, mother. How could you not…?

- Wicla, shut up. Just shut the hell up.

- No.

- Enough.

I was supposed to believe – not just when I was a girl – but for a long time after, that in the decade and more that she plied Route 66, she did not allow herself to look for love, to find love, to be in love. She would admit to no flirtations, to no one-night stands, to no short-term affairs that might have, if she or the man had been different, or if circumstances had been different, have evolved into something more. She would not admit to any unhappiness with the lack of love in her life, and nor would she confess an explanatory disinterest in sex, or a fear of sex, or a repugnance for sex.

I asked her one time, are you a lesbian? but she reacted so angrily that she convinced me that it was a morally reprehensible thing for a daughter to ask of a mother, and that lesbianism was a perversion that she was not prepared to talk about. And despite the fact that she knew I knew what had occurred at Folsom State Prison, she never stopped spitting-out the word lesbian in disgust. In short, she wanted you to think she was a perfectly normal, ordinary woman and that love was some kind of lucky thing that had not yet chanced to appear in her life.

But it turned out, despite the heap of silence that she had thrown on her past, that many men had done things to her that, in their accumulated effects, utterly changed her life. But she let me know it wasn't all their fault.

- If you get into bed with a man, Wicla, don't you ever turn around in a dance of regret and make believe you didn't put yourself there, because one way or another, you did.

Merri fled the time-screwed history of her life on Route 66 because she needed to put as much distance as she could between her soulsick self and all that had happened there, when drunk or sober, willing or not, she had fallen into the roused hands and under the heaving weight of men she knew and men she did not know, men whose strength shook the dignities she wrongly thought she would possess until the end of time, right out of her naked little body. She could have continued her trading along that highway, I suppose.

To keep men at bay, she could have gotten harder and meaner and uglier. But Merri had become pregnant with me, so, driving fast, she went west, changed the axis of her forward movement, and put the two of us on the road to redemption. It ran all the way to the castle room where I murdered my husband, but by that time I could hear in my mother's admonition the kind of pained self-pride that makes many women cry out we are not - will not be – victims. Not be victimized, even though the sad reflection in the mirror tells us there are times we are, men who make us so.

*A pagan poem perpetrates a prayerful paradox.*

# Song 3

Merri was in Chicago on her twenty-eighth birthday. Stricken by a twinge of nostalgic sentimentality she was pulled into its dark, rain-drenched canyons from the lot where she had parked the van, ineluctably drawn to the tenement where she had lived as a girl. The rain had not yet cleansed the streets and alleys of dirt and odor, but instead had reconstituted the dried, layered, stacked-up filth that had encrusted itself upon the city. It's pungent smells now lifted into the air by each exploding rain drop, their very molecules sent spinning into Merri's nose as she walked, collar up, supressing the nausea in her gut. But for a few wet, head-down strangers, the streets were empty, and she felt safe.

Come at last to that place that haunted her memories, the shuddermusic of pipes, the electric buzz of off-and-on power, the slamming of doors up and down the echoing hallways, songs out of radios, bowtied opinion-mashing out of table vices, the landlord's palm-slapping the door for overdue rent, but most of all the slugfest bickering of mother and father, the snapping shut of a battered valise, his frothing departure from the nest in which she could hardly make her own chirps heard.

Some years later, the sputtercoughing of a dying mother, the casket-scraping on the door jam, rough mutterings on the stairway as the bearers, casket shouldered, made the landings, with her mother's blue ghost laughing above them and above it all as they struggled through the turns. The sound off her own wings beating on new air as she lifted off and out at last through an open window, flying west to where she had found a new perch on the quaked and quaking ground of a destroyed California. A perch but not a nest. LA and Chicago were and always would be the splintered ends of the twisting highway rope.

A gust of wind off the retreated waters of Michigan Lake, a short cessation of the heavy-falling rain. Light glinting off the oily puddles that brim the deep potholes along her childhood's unhappy street. Doors open and soon voices sound from a hundred stoops where many had come out of their dry homes to smoke in the cool, clear air.

In short minutes, timed by the hoo-hah laughter barking out of some mouths, the halter top chatter of near-defeated women calming their children, by the fast feet of those descending to the sidewalks where they will make their way to bars, convenience stores, supermarkets and places of shadowy assignation, the first gunshot, the first horrible scream. The cycle of Chi-Town life begins anew, but is quickly silenced by a crack of lightening, and the beaten garbage can noise of thunder, thunder, more thunder.

More rain. And all the sudden noises of the just now reverse themselves until Merri is walking again in the embrace of a vast quiet. She walks away, finally and forever, going fast from there.

Toweling off her face and hair, sitting in the driver's seat of the van under a dim light Merri scrolls her vice and reads reports of inexorable bad weather bowling across the Great Lakes, of worse weather turning in slow motion upon the swelling Mississippi and Missouri rivers whose waters have spread to biblical proportions.

Humans on all sides are being forced into heroic struggles in which many will prove worthy and many not, where the usual few will become martyrs as they careen into oblivion over washed-out bridges and roads, or slip and slide down collapsing hillsides, or burst into flames, entangled in the snap and crackle of downed power lines. The bridge at St. Louis has been closed. In fact, all bridges south of Davenport, Iowa, on the Mississippi are closed until further notice.

Her wagon is loaded with trade goods. Merri will not stay in Chicago another night. It is her driving time. She strikes north and west to Dubuque, the one time serviceable IS 90 slow going in the rain, but the long-neglected Highway 20 that seems a faint line even on her atlas, has been treacherously ruptured by the unmitigated cycle of hard seasons and forces her to swerve dangerously around roadholes, and to slow almost to a standstill across broad cracks in the crumbled tarmac where rainwater still sifts sand from the interstices of the remaining gravel.

By morning, approaching Rockford, a near vacant shambles, a line has been crossed. She has passed through the dark, wet front encircling the Midwest and has arrived in the sunny West, singing as she drives through the ramshackle towns and villages whose citizens are now retreating as a hot sun rises in their blue skies, and then finally she comes to the western most town of Galena, Illinois, where strangers in vehicles are instructed by road signs to pass on unless one has business with its otherwise friendly people. She has no business with any of the people who peer from half-opened curtains in second floor windows, or who stand in the shadowed alleyways that intersect Galena's main thoroughfare.

Just on the other side of Galena, Merri caught a first glimpse of the topmost spires of the creaky bridge that took her into Iowa, beneath it the shrivelled ribbon of the Mississippi, which only a couple of hundred miles to the south was so mightily roiled that it is visiting terrible destruction all the way to the Gulf of Mexico.

Her plan is to find the first best route south, so she can get back to Route 66, a plan that she will execute once she and the van are fed, watered and rested. But just at the end of the bridge's long off-ramp she sees a roadblock manned by several burly men standing under a canvas shade stretched between two old brick buildings. All the men wear golden colored windbreakers, and all have sidearms hanging at their sides. Two or three cradle rifles. A few hoist mugs of coffee and josh one another as they watch the van approach. One of the men raises a hand to stop her.

- Morning ma'am.

- Good morning. What's going on?

- Where you going ma'am?

- South.

- Ma'am? This ain't south. That's south. He points.

- I thought I might get something to eat.

- But then what, Ma'am?

- I am going to keep on going.

- West?

- Just 'til I get to this old highway. She shows him the road atlas.

- The thirty-five? She's pretty rough last time I looked, which was awhile ago.

A couple of the other men sidle in behind him.

- What you got in the back?

- No fugitives if that's what you mean.

- You traveling on your own, ma'am?

- Not that it's any of your business. Yes. I am.

He sees piles of boxes stacked up behind her.

- What's all that?

- Tradeables. Things for sale.

- Like what?

- Mostly women's things.

-   Women's things? Like what?

Merri starts thinking about the mollifying commerce that might be done there in Dubuque. She's hungry and needs a hot breakfast. She's tired and needs a place to park so she can drop off the planet for a few hours. She gets up out of the driver's seat and moves to the back. The men at her window instinctively place their hands on the grips of their pistols. She opens the side door to the van and kicks the retracted stairs that unfold noisily until fully down and out.

-   Have a look for yourselves. Come on. Get out of the sun.

One of the men steps up apprehensively and steps in. He looks around then comes back to the door.

-   You gotta see this Floyd. Jimmy. C'mon up here.

A few minutes later the men come down the stairs and stroll back to the shaded barricade. Merri retakes the driver's seat. Floyd, the man who had first interrogated her, is talking animatedly into his vice as all the other men gather round listening. Then they all take their vice's out of their pockets and start making calls too, all of them just as animated and smiling.

Floyd waves to Merri and points the way to the opening in the barricade that will let her pass through into the city. He walks beside the van until she gets to the other side until she comes to a halt again.

-   Now you just make a right here on Main Street and head

into town. You'll come to Second Street. Go left. You'll see St. Raphael's. Used to be an RC cathedral but it's a general-purpose derelict at the moment. You park right out on the street in front. No one will bother you there.

- I'd like to get a hot breakfast.

- Once your parked you can find your way on foot up Bluff Street – just north of the church. Monks is probably still open. Well, it used to be Monks, but now some goddamn Spic runs the place. Good as your gonna get in this town, breakfast wise.

- Well, thank you, sir.

- Maybe we'll see you later.

Floyd pulls his forelock, big smile, slaps the side of the van, like a cowboy slapping his horse to giddyup.

Merri is awakened just after dusk by a hubbub surrounding the van, a commotion of female voices and laughter. She raises the shade on the back window where one or two women with their hands shading their eyes are peering through the dark glass.

- There she is. Get in line quick.

Merri looks out the side door window where dozens of other women are milling and chatting in clusters. Most of the women are carrying empty bags and boxes. Other containers are stacked on the sidewalk or against the church wall.

The knock on the door startles her. Not a woman's knock.

- Merri. You there? It's Floyd.

She opens. The doors to the Cathedral are swung open. There are a lot of other women inside.

- You wanna do some business? I'm sure you do. Me and Jimmy and Martinez here, we can help you shift some of your goods into the church. Let these women get a good look at what you got. Then we'll go, leave you and the ladies to your fun. You good for that?

She is more than good for it. The wives and daughters and girlfriends of these men are trapped within virtual walls by men who have erected a male democracy on the high plateau of a moral calling, the protection of the town and everyone in it. The Dubuque Vigilance Corp, gold jackets with each man's name stenciled on the back and a banana yellow badge on the right breast, mans the barricades at all the roads into the city – guarding against external insurgencies such as the raiding parties that arrived from Illinois not so long ago.

Every man belongs to one or more of the DVC's many sub-committees that together ensure that the grid of systems that keep Dubuque functioning are online at all times. The men move faster and are more sober in these hard times than even their caught-unaware fathers were when things began to fall apart across the land, and they are contemptuous of weakness in all its forms. Dissent and complaint are stifled, both in public and at home, and the jokes and jibes of DVC men make it clear that most of the noise is made by women.

Merri was not surprised by this at all because what goes in Dubuque is already par for the course in many of the places along Route 66. It's happening all over America. It's why, when she saw the East Dubuque barricade, she stopped the van for a few moments.

She needed time to put a shirt with a collar on, to comb-out her short-cropped hair, apply a bit of mascara, to put on earrings and to dab some very red lipstick on her pale lips. It's why she is doing the same now before she steps down into the crowd of women around the van and in the church.

At the barricade mother knew goddamn well that her long-necked prettiness, which she has kept despite the arduousness of her experience to date - and her put on pertness - would disarm the men, make them want to gather her into their protection.

Here on Bluff Street, once the few men who were trundling boxes into the church had gone, no woman would feel threatened by her. She'd give them all the eye contact and open-faced smiling they needed to lower their guard and then let her own made-up, young, high-breasted self, advertise the transformations that could be had were they to acquire the lipsticks and make-up, the perfumes, unguents and creams, the bras, blouses, skirts, the panties and stockings that were now laid out before them. And when they asked, with not-so-discreet embarrassment or timidity, about pads and tampons and once-a-year birth control, especially the pills, they would find she had them and that they could be had for a price.

Money passed from her customers' vices to Merri's if money was the means, and Merri made her profit out of it. But there were women and girls in the church with a look all too familiar to my mother. These women had no money, or had husbands who refused to give them any, or husbands who were so brutally parsimonious that even the least expensive thing in Merri's store could not be bought.

Knowing from her long years on the road that these women lived with keener pain than all their friends and neighbors, in houses or apartments that echoed like wells of pinched loneliness and dry resentment, Merri bartered, this for that. But she would never dicker in a way that would demean a woman with an unwanted charity.

As the day went on, everything on Merri's tables was put into the hands of the Dubuque women, while her bank account plumped-up and an assortment of jewelry, watches, gold and silverware, antiques, china, pottery, table wear, barely used appliances, unworn clothing, canned goods and preserves, and other stuff accumulated around her.

The market done, Merri boxed it all, and Floyd and the other men, squeezing past the last of the women now exiting the church, would lift the newly acquired stuff into the van, sniggering at Merri's willingness to cart away a load of crap in exchange for a myriad of new goods that would make a sizeable portion of Dubuque's womenfolk happy for quite awhile. They knew they had done a very good thing indeed, these good men of the Recreation and Fall Fair sub-committee of the Dubuque Vigilance Corp.

Would Merri come back again someday soon? wondered Floyd. She said yes, but never did.

*Ho, the mud of madness we make of our many minds.*

# Song 4

How it was that mother ended up on a back road in Nebraska somewhere west of Omaha is one of those mysteries of the uninteresting variety, but I think she was just zig-zagging her way south and west, driving under the light of a clearsky moon, stopping wherever she might dip into a pool of customers who might be interested in some of the prizes she rescued from Dubuque, parking where she felt safe enough to pass a few uninterrupted hours, allowing the daytime sun to charge the van while she slept, a pistol close at hand. Just in case.

On some old, gravelled south-traveling road lit by an infinitude of stars, humming no doubt to the inner music of her soul, she heard a rattle and bang, an unaccustomed noise coming from her beast, the van. To Merri, it is no more concerning – and no less irritating – than a loose chain is to an inveterate bicyclist. Down that road a few miles more she found an abandoned farm where she would tend to whatever it was. She pulled into its rutted drive and on into the space between a darkened house that tilted this way and a barn that tilted that. Still too exposed to passing cars on the highway, she swung in behind the barn, a few feet from a rusty water pump.

I don't know what it was about the place, about the land, but even after she fixed the engine – she was a good mechanic – she didn't get back on the road. Knowing my mother, she may have been mesmerized by the limitless expanse everywhere she turned, with her hair hardly ruffled by the thin dry breezes that carried a silence she had never heard before. And maybe she danced there. Maybe she danced naked under all those stars after washing herself in the cold water she pulled up in great gushes from the well once she'd primed the pump with bottled water bought at too high a price in Sioux City. I can see her doing that, and I can see her squishing her toes in the mud she made while dripping and turning on the hardbaked ground. Maybe she fingered the knife wound scar just above her left hip.

By this time, Merri had been traveling for more than ten years. She had endured. She was tired in her bones and it took a tract of Nebraska prairie, an uninhabited house, the dark, cowless barn and its litter of busted engines, bald truck tires, twisted wheel rims, oil containers to which old dirt was still stuck, frayed fan belts hanging from bent nails, and a pitch fork with one prong gone missing to bring her to that momentary stand still.

Within three days the turning of the earth, sunrise and sunset, arc of moon, splay of stars, had wrenched her back to the ancient cycle of human days. While the sun hung in the sky, she busied herself with her diminished inventory of trade goods, made her meals, explored the abandoned house and barn, listened for pigeon coos and fly buzz hanging in the air, stood witless while watching the murmurations of starlings, walked with long strides into the surrounding fields under a wide brimmed hat, arms sleeved, between the stubbled rows where ten foot high corn stalks once vibrated in the heat of summer, and looked for signs of life in the gigantic neighborhood her unnamed hosts once lived. No one there.

Third night, late. Propped up on her pillows she had fallen asleep with her reading light on and fallen into a dream. Something woke her. Violence in her dream? Grips the pistol. Switches off the light. All quiet outside the van, but not quiet. A creaking sound in the distance. Car door. A heavy latching as the door shuts. Nothing out the back window or the side door window. Nothing out the wind screen. She will not be trapped again.

Barefoot, holding the gun, she stepped down from the van wearing a T-shirt and shorts hastily pulled on. She closed the door quietly behind her, moved on tip toes to the corner of the barn across from the house to look down the farm drive toward the road. High stratus clouds darkened the night sky. At the end of the drive, silhouettes of poplars stood on each side at two hundred yards, give or take, between them a small black hole, a darker shape. Squeezed her eyes shut to change her focus, and when she opened them again, the shape was closer, larger. A man walked toward her stooped and limping on the median between the rutted track.

Merri backed away, walked quickly to the barn door across from where she the van is parked then stepped inside and into the shadows beside the door. Momentarily, he appeared in the open yard looking up at the house, looking up to its second-floor windows. One left shoulder is low; the body twisted to that side. He turned toward the van. His right hand cradled his left elbow. She heard him utter a soft groan. He walked slowly, dragging his stiff left leg, toward the van door. Knocked softly, waited, turned his head to look around. Knocked louder.

- I need help.

The clouds blew clear from under the moon and moonlight descends into the farmyard.

- Can you help me?

He knew he had made someone afraid. He understood. He turned and stared into the dark abyss on the other side of the barn door. Merri saw blood glistening on his high forehead, saw the disjoint in his long nose where it broke. His body thin and angular, face gaunt with a thin beard, greying moustache, raggedy sideburns.

- I'm sorry, he says.

He limped away from the van and started to make his way back to the drive.
Merri tucked the pistol into the waistband at her back and stepped out into the barnyard.

- Wait, she says.

He turned to face her.

- I am very sorry, miss.

- It's OK. I'm here.

Driving a beat-up old Tesla, too fast for a man lost in the backroads of Nebraska, he had come to the end of the road he was speeding down where it T'd with the North South Road that passed by the farm my other had stopped at. He had flown off into the field in front of him, tearing down the half-standing remains of a barbed wire fence then rolling a half dozen times before coming to rest on the passenger side, back wheels spinning, systems wheezing down to lifelessness. He got himself up and out, and once undazed, but in increasing pain, looked as deeply as he could into the inky blackness adjusting to the probability that it might be a few days before some traveler might dare to stop – stop that is, should he be alive enough to see them coming, or strong enough to raise the flag of his bloodied shirt.

It was then he saw a stream of photons emanating out of the dark somewhere just above the horizon to his south, in the otherwise uninhabited cosmos in which he was so sorely stuck. A light which drew him forth, wounded, like a brokewinged moth.

It took about a week for Merri to nurse him and the Tesla back to health. Tending to him, that first night she elicited a yelp by seizing his long nose between her thumb and forefinger and twisting it straight. She put his dislocated shoulder back into place with a warning it might hurt. She washed his face, then salved and bandaged his head gash, and finally she let him sleep alone on her bed with his left, not broken leg, splinted so he could not move the badly bruised and twisted joint of the knee. The work done on earthquake survivors all those years ago on the shaken hills of LA had not been forgotten. Could not, in fact, have been forgotten.

While he laboured to heal in uncanny sleep, she took the van out to where the Tesla still sat and used a long piece of timber she had stripped out of a corn crib in the barn to lever it from the side on which it had come to rest, so it flopped back on its wheels. She towed it back to the farm and backed it through the barn door where she could work on it in the cool of the bright barnshade by the door.

Late the next afternoon thirst and hunger, and the myriad pains that had taken up residence in his body pried him awake. He connected the dots of his day-before recollections and guessed, as he listened to the buzz of a desultory farm fly, that he must be in the van from which the woman who had bandaged and bathed him had come to his rescue. He opened the van door and looked into the farmyard where he saw the sunlit nose of the Tesla in the frame of the barndoor, now fixed and cleaned of its man-debris. A brood of invisible cicadas ratcheted their noise into the dusky air then went quiet as he stepped down and made his way to the car.

The rear driver door was open. He saw the souls of Merri's feet and assumed she had decided, with him laid out in her bed, to sleep there. He stepped closer and from that little distance saw that although her eyes were closed, her neck was arched and her stiffened body was moving just a little. He saw that her wrist and hand were tucked under the waistband of her pants, and heard finally, her soft, faraway moans.

Red faced, he tiptoed away, saw the well pump, and made his way to it. The pump's rusty squeak pulled Merri out of the dark hiding place in which a woman finds pleasure for herself and for a moment she felt the scorch of embarrassment that radiated up her neck and shoulders. Unable to put off their further meeting, she composed herself as much as she could. She walked up behind him as he cupped his hands under the spout and caught the cold, drinkable water that his last pull at the iron handle brought up from the deeps.

She told me, the story while drunk one night. Said that she did not think that he had seen her, but later, she said he had whispered into her burning ear that seeing her like that lit a fire in his balls, to which she admitted replying, that in that case they must fight fire with fire.

- Me too, she said, nodding at the water dripping from the pump.

He pumped again and the water flooded into her hands where she knelt by the spout. After they drank at the well and slapped water on their faces and necks, they went to the van where she made dinner while he talked. Mother said she tried mightily to understand the noise was that came out of his mouth but could not, for the words pouring out of the mouth of a New Jersey Jew into the ears of a midwestern loner was a very odd and indecipherable sound indeed. And yet, as he talked and laughed she knew she had rescued a dreamer, a dreamer and a planner - and for that reason he was beguiling.

The map of America that she had found in the Tesla when she was cleaning it out was falling apart at its folds, but opening it up across the hood of the car, she found vivid lines drawn in an emphatic hand joining place-to-place, and thick red circles around many towns and cities, many of them on Route 66 which made her see each of those places anew in her own mind, and X's to mark a myriad of spots in empty landscapes, and doodles of strange buildings in the margins, and a crayoned black phrase – Gates of Heaven - that made her want to turn a key to enter that place just for a moment, if such a place existed. Little did she know her wish would one day be granted.

During the next few days – really only two or three, maybe four - as she began to learn his language, and he hers, she matched his garrulousness with her reticence. Don't think for a moment, she told me, that he was so tied-up in himself that he was not interested in her. He asked her questions; wanted her to tell him of her experiences; left silence into which she could have poured any thought at all if she wished to. But she told me that her shame kept her from telling Clem her story, except in bits and pieces. Shame for what? Of what? Why? We'll come to that.

When he talked, when he laughed, when he leaned forward to tell her some secret idea, he took her out of the hard world where she was making a go of it into somewhere new and not nearly so hard. She only realized after they parted that he always bowed to the future. Clem did not go to the past any more than she did and she wondered later, if she had asked him questions about where he was from, about his parents, his upbringing, about the streets where he grew up, would he tell her.

With his fingers he drew lines and circles and marked spots in the air around her which took shape in her mind as the map of a new world, and the flow of syllables and vowels he spoke wove a tapestry that depicted a far-flung empire of strange and beautiful constructions wherein a happy people made their happy, future lives.

Walking with her through the fields one day, when he mistook her silence for the despair in which he thought she habitually abided, he asked my mother to look below the stubbled dirt, beyond the abandoned farms, past the ruin of the country through which they both traveled until their lives intersected.

- Can you not see, Merri, that we are actually in paradise?

Mother said that she could not admit to him in that moment what she believed. But she told me, that because she had danced naked, lit by the light of the Milky Way and because she had tasted cold, clear water that she herself had pulled up from the deep well below the parched ground, that because he had not breached the trust she reposed in him when he came to her door asking for help, she knew it too.

- Maybe, said Merri, but I have to live in the land of is, not was, not...

The next morning, Clem and Merri pushed his car out into the hot sunlight so it could charge up. He didn't want the battery to go completely dead – never a good thing. They talked about driving it into Omaha to get some food because Merri was running out and Clem wanted to replace it. More than replace it; fill her cupboards and fridge with good food, as much fresh stuff as they could get.

- It's too hot now. Most of the stores will be closed, said Merri.

- OK, said Clem. Let's go later.

She touched him on the arm. It was an electric moment. Strange and new.

You have to know that once she had done her nursing, she had not touched him except when it was unavoidable in their small space. Once she had removed the splint from his leg, he had slept nights in the back seat of the Tesla, its doors closed against the barn rats that scratched around once the sun went down.

During those few days Clem realized that my mother was moody and wary so even though, except for the hours of sleep, they lived in close quarters and spent every waking hour together, the distance between them was unbreachable. Merri was careful not to show any sign of desire or to give any reason for him to misinterpret her friendliness - and help - as an opening for more.

- Did he press on you mother?

- No. No, not ever.

- I don't understand why he wouldn't.

- He was shy. I don't think he had ever been with a woman. He didn't know what to do.

- Really?

- I'm almost certain.

- Were you attracted to him? Even a little bit?

- A little.

- Did you want him? Did you want him to, you know, make an effort?

- Maybe I did. When he was with me something primordial was stirring in me.

- What?

- Not what you think.

- Did it bother you that he didn't try?

- I had it coming. It was on me to change the atmosphere.

So, when she touched his arm, it was a shock to him, a spark like you get from a doorknob on a cold dry day.

- Let's have lunch, she said.

Just before dusk, she asked Clem if he would mind driving to Omaha himself to get the food. He was very happy to do anything she wanted. He made the trip, but by the time he returned, she had pulled the van back on the road and was a hundred miles south.

What had happened?

Shortly after he pulled out of the farmyard, the feeling of calm that had possessed her when she was with him began to turn into an inexplicable apprehension and foreboding. She fought against it. Always able to get busy with a task to take her mind off any anxiety that might creep in, she decided she would make a special meal for Clem and have it ready because he would be hungry when he returned. But there was nothing for her to work with. She became angry with herself for failing a simple, domestic task.

After opening and closing the near empty cupboards above the sink and stove she soon discovered the water jug in the fridge was near empty, so she decided to refill it at the well. The Tesla was gone. Of course it was. But the space it left was immense.

She walked to the well and worked the long iron handle, up and down rhythmically, caught in a sundrenched trance. She looked at the empty barn. She looked at the dead house and at the empty fields beyond. She looked down the driveway to the road. She listened for Clem's voice, for the spiral of words that floated into the ether whenever he was around and she heard nothing, and that nothing became a nothing thought and then a nothing feeling, until the water burst out of the spout and spilled down her dress then down to her shoeless feet.

The jug dropped and shattered on the concrete pad around the water pump. Merri fled to the van and pulled the door shut behind her, took to the driver's seat and gunned the van's engine. In three hours she was a hundred miles south near Junction City on Route 66, the wet lap of her dress now dry, her feet still bare. Nine months later, I was born. Until I was older than my mother was then, she would tell everyone who needed to be told that I was a child born of an immaculate conception.

You think, listening to the story that Clem, was the undisputed father, right? But what if I told you that when she got to Junction City she let two men take her to a room in some woebegone roadhouse where they drank a lot of whiskey and she let them fuck her until they were all exhausted. Who's your daddy, now?

*I drift in my deceptions 'til I drown.*

# Song 5

The Mississippi was still impassable, so even though low on goods for trade, Merri could not make it to Chicago for replenishment. But the word in the wind was that she might find all she needed in Bakersfield, which had been badly shaken by the big one, but was still standing. She had been there a few times over the years and even though the last time she went was ten years after she had decamped from LA, Bakersfield had never lost the desolate feel of a refugee camp, which, for tens of thousands, is what it had become in the aftermath of the quake and tsunami.

There was a city government, but the feds were an overwhelming force there even now because with the break down of law and order across the west – the whole country in fact – internal refugees were still streaming into Bakersfield looking for safety, respite, food and water. And they streamed out too, because the camps were no less fraught and a good deal noisier and dirtier than the places they had fled. Americans had always sought greener pastures, and there was nothing green or pastural anywhere near the metastatic sprawl of latter-day Bakersfield.

It was no longer the boom town it had been just a few years ago. The in-out traffic that characterized the city notwithstanding, it had settled into its new self, keeping low to the ground so it could not fall should the ground shake as hard as it did way back when. Bakersfield was painted in mute tones so that it blended with its dirt-beige surroundings, which, I suppose, made it difficult for the dark angels of destruction to see as they hunted in the blue skies over California for new victims to sink their fatal claws into.

The original entrepreneurs who had put up road side stalls and built ma and pa shops to sell all manner of stuff to the people had long since been displaced by a plethora of two-bit chain operators, and they, in their turn, had succumbed to the power of the big boxers whose multi-acre, low priced emporia sucked money out of the pockets of rich and poor alike for miles around. These colossi would wholesale their wares to a traveler like Merri not caring a whit that her mark-up put a dear price on even the most mundane things she packed in her van, in her case, all those kind of woman things that she had sold and bartered away in Dubuque just three weeks ago.

It had taken Merri nearly a day to get to the stores once she reached the outskirts of Bakersfield where it was bumper-to-bumper in both directions. But as tired as she was, she would not permit herself to stay in the city longer than it took to stock up. It would take the same amount of time to get out of the city and back on Sixty-Six heading east.

By the time she got to Tehachapi, a dismal, plunked-down village of crumbling ranchers and abandoned stores that had been thrown up on sunburnt ground at the end of the last century, she could only keep herself awake by slapping her face hard. Over the horizon she could see the first crack of dawn light, so she found a place to park that seemed secure enough, and then fell off the cliff of fatigue into an incoming tide of sleep.

Why is this important? Only because the next day would be

the day that her life of the last dozen years changed irrevocably. I only wanted to put you at the time and place just before and after it happened.

As dusk approached, mother woke up to a cacophony of car horns and spine shattering blasts from big rigs. She stepped out of the van and walked up to the highway where, as far as she could see in both directions along the highway, nothing was moving. Hundreds of drivers and passengers were milling around their vehicles, some reaching in through open windows or doors to deliver another blast when their angry spirits moved them to do so. Many were scrolling their vices to check for explanatory news or making calls to friends and family to announce their predicament. And then the news came. The good people of Needles had blocked the bridge across the Colorado River on the California-Arizona border, about 230 miles to the east. Why?

It doesn't matter why. Towns and cities were gating themselves, just as Dubuque had done and lately vigilantes, gang thugs and even the burghers of small towns like Needles were claiming stretches of highways as their own, charging tolls and otherwise obstructing traffic. Since the closure of the Mississippi bridges, a few short weeks ago, Route 66 had been carved-up into hotly contested fractions manned by unreasonable people espousing righteous causes, some of them wearing sheriff's badges and chains of local office.

For east moving traffic – or west moving for that matter – it was impossible to U-Turn, and Merri saw quickly that stuck drivers close to Tehachapi intersections were beginning to peel off the main highway looking for any means whatever to get somewhere.

There was no road north, so very quickly the road south would become as coagulated with cars and trucks as those on Route 66. She ran back to the van, fired it up and turned south, ending up in Ojai several hours later, and Ojai had become the refugee camp for most of the rich and famous who escaped the horrors of LA's destruction and the default site of the new Hollywood. The new Burbank, called NewB by the new locals, was close-by but tucked into a hard to see, hard to find location just to the east, straddling the road and turning it into a private highway accessible only to those authorized. What did I say about unreasonable people with righteous causes?

At any rate, Ojai and NewB were the most formidably gated communities in the west at that time, and ever since Ojai became a Hive, it is almost impenetrable except to those with the right keys. Eventually, Merri would be invited into Ojai, where she – and I - would meet the then First Husband of the United States, Paul Munro, at a swank party thrown in his honor by mother's then attorney, but she was turned away on the day she arrived from Tehachapi.

But she was not turned away at equally gated NewB because the main gate there was under the control of a formidably bulked-up and armed to the teeth Black man (a gay man she would soon learn) who was a good friend of all the other under-paid gay men and miserably paid gay and straight women who worked in the studio gulag. He was about to turn her away, but from his perch in the gatehouse, he could see a lot of stuff stacked-up in the area behind the driver's seat.

-   What have you got in their, darling?

Mother twisted around and retrieved a small box from the top of the nearest stack and showed him the label.

- As in real RiverLight lipstick? Do tell. What else?

She stood up and went further into the van and returned with another box – a little larger.

- Nancypants. Well, well. And what is it you plan to do with your cargo of delights?

- Find people who want them. Sell them. Trade for them. I'm a trader.

- So, it seems. I'm Lawrence. What's your name?

- Merri.

- Merri?

- Merri Weer.

- Dutch?

- A few centuries ago.

- Tell you what, it's close to the end of a shift. Why don't you just pull up over there and I will let it be known that trader Merri Weer has graced us with her presence. Just over there dear. Best place in the world for you, believe me when I say-

She backed-up from the gate and manoeuvred into a large, long lay-by on the side of the road. As she stacked a few boxes at the side of the van she watched Lawrence talking into his vice, laughing. A half hour later, driverless cars, taxis and small buses began pulling up to the inside of the gate, which swung open when Lawrence reached in front of him and pushed a button of some kind. Lawrence mouthed 'good luck' in Merri's direction as he supervised the flow of traffic and waved at the passengers – almost all women - urging them to pull over to where mother's van was parked.

After the last of her customers had departed, Lawrence ambled over, big smile on his face, his cheeks darkened by the day's stubble.

- I'm half sold out, Lawrence!

- Hug.

He holds out his arms.

- I'm half sold out, I can't believe it, she says clasping him around his muscular back.

- You'll sell the rest tomorrow, Merri Weer. Just be there at 6.

- What can I do to repay you? She asked.

- Come for dinner.

- I don't think that's a good idea.

- It's a very good idea, trust me. My partner and I have a place just a little way up the hill from here. He'd love to meet you, especially if you show him what you have left. You can park in our drive and get some sleep after dinner.

Lawrence and his partner, Javier, who was in charge of the scene painting shop for one of the big studios, had been given the use of a Ranger's cabin in a forgotten national park just north of Ojai. Through their civic government, the very rich people of the city had taken possession of as much of the park as they wanted, a thick swath of land on both sides of old Route 33, the Mericopa Highway that passed through the preserve. Lawrence was made the gatekeeper there too and used his formidable presence to scare away interlopers who did not carry the membership card issued by the Ojai Recreational Committee to their own.

Lawrence was a sweet, sweet man, but he could smother the natural smile on his face with a terrifying grimace, pop his neck veins and glistening muscles like a ready-to-pounce cougar, lower his voice until it filled your brain like rumbled thunder and glare at you with deep-set, red ember eyes. Oh, didn't I know it.

When I was a little girl, I shrieked when the monster Lawrence came out of nowhere, and then chased me from my hiding place in the woods to the cabin porch where Javier and my mother sat getting stewed as they talked politics, and we all laughed. Laughed and laughed. And I think their laughter must hang in the boughs of the trees surrounding the burnt ruin of that cabin even now, that their murdered ghosts still embrace in the bed where they snored so gently side-by-side all those years ago when vengeful members of the Outsider Army, the OA, who had been ordered out of the park by Lawrence earlier that day, entered through an unlocked door and killed them dead.

That first night mother visited with them, Lawrence and Javier became her very good friends, the best friends she ever had. By the time she pulled into their lot behind Lawrence's selfdrive, Javier had dinner well underway. Merri pulled a couple of bottles of not bad wine out of her stash and brought them to the immaculately renovated kitchen as Lawrence made the introductions. Javier, a foot shorter than Lawrence, saturnine in appearance but with a lighthearted, curious nature, possessed of surprising blue eyes, full lips, body like a dancer, gorgeous and intelligent. At home he was a bit of a nitpicker and a henpecker, but at work he was the demanding manager of a scene painting shop for one of the big studios, a place where everyone painted inside the lines or else.

In the course of the evening, Ojai, NewB and the cabin in the woods became the southernmost stars in mother's new firmament. They all agreed It would take months – and maybe never the way things were going - for Route 66 to become an open, toll-less highway again, at the very least, not until long after the bridges over the Mississippi were fixed and opened and the feds got the courage on to take on the dozens of local vigilantes and militias who had set up their little kingdoms along the way. They would not give up their ground without much righteous blood being shed. The feds never minded killing a few people, but at a time when they were trying to sound like a national government of the people, for the people, by the people etc etc…the PR game was tricky.

- Face it, Merri, you're fucked, said Javier. You can make it through the gauntlet, but like the rich man going through the eye of a needle, what profits a woman to use her good soul that way.

- I think you are mixing your parables, Javier, said Lawrence. But he is right, Merri.

Her new trading route, which would take her north to the Canadian border south of Vancouver and back again was crafted by the two men, who became amusingly drunk in the process. Lawrence and Javier knew people all along the old I5 route and by the time the evening was done, mother had a list of contacts, most of whom would be attached to faces and bodies in due course and become a pantheon of legendary heroes for what they did for Trader Merri Weer.

After dinner, the three went to the living room and sat together on a sofa, working on the atlas Merri had retrieved from the van. She marked the new route with black crayon and drew red crayon circles around the major towns and cities along the way in the style of a certain, not forgotten Clem.

- I could leave tomorrow. It's so exciting! But I have to stop at Bakersfield again to restock.

- You can use the Mericopa, said Javier. We'll get you a Rec card from Ojai. It's much, much faster than going 'round, even if its slow, if you know what I mean.

- Not tomorrow. No. There's something that must be done first.

Lawrence stood and started for the kitchen.

- Javier....

Javier and Merri looked at one another as Javier rose to follow. Merri heard their whispering but could not make out what they were saying, until Javier blurted out, Yes, yes, good idea! Yes! We'll do it. When they returned, Javier asked Merri to follow him and he led her into a meticulously lovely guest room with a large, quilt covered bed mounded with pillows cased in white linen.

- Towel, wash cloth and the necessaries right here, he told her, opening the bi-fold door to the en suite. Make yourself at home and sleep well.

- I can sleep in the van.

- Of course you could. But here, here you will sleep a dream of dreams. I couldn't bear it if you didn't, as lovely as your van is.

When Lawrence had tried to pour her a glass of wine at

dinner, Merri said no thanks and waived it off even though she badly wanted one, or two or three. Gentlemen that they were, neither Lawrence nor Javier asked why, but assumed she was a teetotaler. Not so, as they would discover later.

The real reason for her reluctant abstinence was that she knew by then she was pregnant with me, that, just as she had wished it would, one fervid, hard swimming spermatozoa had made it out of the salty gonadal sea that had crashed upon her in waves, on her mouth and breasts and stomach and ass and legs, but also into her exhausted, slack vagina. One of the men's seed had moved inexorably into that place where Alph the sacred river ran, that place measureless to man, where it would collapse into her perfect egg so that both mother and child could be born in the primordial embrace of a new being. She would be a mother and she would protect me with unremitting ferocity until her dying day.

*Cry out the constant care of consummated love.*

# Song 6

Merri panicked more than a little when she left the cottage early the next morning, believing Lawrence and Javier to be sleeping still. Her van was gone. Immediately, she excoriated herself, for having been so naïve and gullible as to let Lawrence and Javier con her into thinking they were friends when all they wanted was the rest of her trade goods. She bent double in her agony and anger but straightened and turned quickly toward the porch when she heard Lawrence's voice.

-   Merri. Merri. It's all good. All good.

-   Where's my van?

-   Ah! Come with me.

He locked the cabin door behind him and led her to his car and explained as the car took them to the studio lot.

-   Javier thought he would take it to the studio and wash the dust off it. I should have told you, but I didn't want to wake you.

-   You just can't do that, Lawrence. You just can't...

-   You're right. Sorry, but with a crack of smile on his lips.

\- You're laughing at me.

Lawrence's night man waived him through the gate. He took manual control of the vehicle, pulled into the lot and parked, then walked her over to the gate house where he told the night man he would return shortly. He led Merri to the scene painting shop through whose large doors she could see the back of the van, the ladder to its roof, the spare.

\- There it is. See? Looks cleaner to me.

He put his vice to his ear.

\- Javier…is it ready?

He nodded at Merri. The windowed door to the shop rolls up noisily as Javier jumped into the van.

\- Close your eyes. Tighter.

She heard the van come to a stop beside them. The side door of the van opened and Javier came down the already flopped-out stairs.

\- Open your eyes.

It took her a minute to register what she now saw clearly, large artfully done blue script on the side of the van: 'Trader Merri Weer' with a subtitle in black text, 'Whatever a woman wants and needs.'

-   Walk around Merri, Javier says.

She read the same signage on the other side and across the front above the window.

-   Showbiz, kiddo, said Lawrence.

-   You like it? Javier asked, very pleased with himself.

My mother was not sure if she did. The part of her that looked for safety in anonymity felt threatened. Part of her felt diminished; narrowed to trader only.

-   We can take it off, said Lawrence to Javier's chagrin. Really. If you don't like it.

But then Merri began to like it. The idea of it. She walked around the van again.

-   I like it.

She gave Javier, then Lawrence, a warm embrace, held on to each of them, until Lawrence spouted a few tears, quickly wiped away.

-   I've to get to work, Merri. You park over there. The shift will change in ten minutes so be ready. You'll sell the rest of your stuff.

He pinched Javier's cheek and mouthed a thank you. Javier

gave Merri a quick hug and walked back to his shop while Lawrence turned to go back to his post.

Merri sold almost all her wares to the studio women, no barter, all for money in her account and once done, she cleaned up the empty boxes and loose wrappings. She pulled up to the gate to say goodbye to Lawrence who put a key to the cabin in her hand, and then an official Ojai Rec card on the back of which he had written the code that would get her through the gates at either end of the Maricopa Highway.

- So, whaddya think? He asked. Two months?

- Maybe a little longer. Two and a half probably?

- Not a minute longer.

- Love you Lawrence. And I don't say that to many men. None that come to mind, anyway.

And off she went, first to Bakersfield where she packed the inside of the van as tightly as she could with items that would sell fast and well while leaving access to the head, the galley and the bedroom if she edged sideways down the narrow corridor she had left. She also managed to get a few tied down larger items on top - cribs, a couple of toilets, even a kitchen sink. The I-5 AutoWay was in not bad order, but Merri's business was to get to the smaller towns and communities where women couldn't get all the things that she offered, at least not easily.

The ninety-nine was not in very good shape so it was slower going, but that suited her because it intersected a lot of east west side roads that took her to out of the way places like Catheys Valley, Mariposa, Coulterville, Sonora and Copperopolis, an old mining town where the mines had become an underground town of sorts inhabited by pale people, most of them with turned down mouths and competitively bitter dispositions. There were dozens of towns and villages she couldn't make on the way north, but no matter, she had left a lot of fertile ground for the return trip.

Off to the east a few miles from these towns, she could see the higher foothills of the Sierra Nevadas and the slopes of the range itself. Old road signs pointed the way for tourists looking for the once crowded national forest reserves and parks, including Yosemite whose very name had excited her imagination when she was a little girl. She's asked a couple of women about the park when she was wrapping up the sale of a vacuum cleaner that they were going to share.

- You don't want to be going in there.

- No, you sure don't.

- Why?

- Well, for one thing, there's a lot of rock coming down on the highway.

- If a big one comes down it will kill you in a minute and you won't even know you're dead.

- And there are a few cults have taken up residence there

too. That's what I hear.

- Oh, yes, it's true enough. They worship the end of the world. Sit cross legged all day long and chant their ya-yas out.

- Praying for it.

- For the end of the world. Imagine that.

She would go in one day, Merri promised herself, and she did, although it was so long into the future, I was driving at the time.

Huge swaths of the national forest reserves had burned off, so the hills and mountains were sharply delineated with spikes of blackened tree trunks and agonized branches sticking into the bluesky background. Where conifers once stood, even giants like the legendary sequoia and redwood were tumbling out of their millennia-long history onto a ground where deeper-rooting deciduous trees were struggling to take over. There were pockets still burning, throwing an undulating, orangey glow onto the ceiling of night.

On those days when the winds off the Pacific died down, a thin miasma of acrid smoke would spread down the lower slopes and into the valleys nearly choking the dry throats of the inhabitants, young, old and in-between alike. Lots of folks were now perennial raspers and shallow breathers and many children grew up speaking their words with gravelled voices and a puff-puff cadence because it was the normal way of the valley dwellers in those parts.

Though many of the towns in California, Oregon and Washington, like those she had been through on Route 66, and in the high west towns she had traveled through not so many weeks ago, had come under the protection of citizens' committees, the feds and state police had managed to assert enough authority to prevent the capturing of highways and the levy of tolls and to keep a lid on the incipient violence so characteristic of armed men in groups.

Mother aroused no fear in anyone, so while the journey was stop and start all the way to the City of Blaine on the Canadian border where, as she explained to the barricade men once again, who she was and what she was doing to her mostly amused interlocuters, she encountered no hostility. Indeed, almost without exception, the men who stopped her at the edge of a town or city were the first to let their wives, girlfriends, mothers and daughters know that Trader Merri Weer was about to set-up shop and suggested by way of a grant of permission, that they might like to see what mother had on offer.

It was a successful first trip of nighttime work and daytime rest just as she had lived it since leaving Chi-Town. It bothered her not when, two or three weeks in, she was gripped by morning sickness because when morning came she could lay on her bed and knead her nauseated guts and stomach until she fell asleep. While her hands and fingers worked on her belly, her mind worked-out a future that included me – she said she always knew she would have a daughter – because she wanted her knowledge of the world and her little wisdom to be baked-in to my very bones. She was not talking to herself as she lay there exhausted, but to me, to the atoms that would become my little ears and my receptive brain. Already, I had become her life's companion.

By the time she got back to Ojai, her morning sickness had abated, and Merri had been seized by a vibrating happiness she had never experienced before and did not quite know what to make of. Lawrence and Javier both noticed that she was full of laughter and good spirits, more talkative than ever, but Javier was the first to notice my mother's rounder belly. When he was with her alone in the kitchen, he stopped chopping the celery in front of him and made sure she was looking at him when he spoke.

- Got something you would like to tell me, Merri?

- No. What do you mean? Not really.

- It's none of my business, I know.

- You're being silly.

- Well, if you are, it's just wonderful. Wonderful!

- Chop chop, Javier, said Merri pointing at the sacrificial stalks laying on the cutting board.

At the dinner table later.

- A glass of wine, Merri? asked Javier.

- No.

- Oh, I think we need to celebrate. Here, let me pour.

- Stop it Javier, Merri insisted putting her hand over a glass he had just put in front of her.

- Well, we should celebrate your return, don't you think? Properly.

- OK, I am. I am.

- Am what? said Lawrence, suddenly alert.

- Am. You know…

When he finally caught on, with much miming on Javier's part and tummy patting on Merri's, Lawrence fell silent and sullen, alarming her. Merri looked at Lawrence, alarmed by a sudden change of atmosphere wanting him to be as happy as she was, as Javier most evidently was, not stern and forbidding.

- What's wrong?

- You're not gay? In his deepest voice, eyes intense.

She looked at him. His eyes held his question on hers. She looked at Javier. No help there. Back at Lawrence, whose face broke at last into that wonderful smile of his, and then, as he pushed back from the table, he let loose a gigantic laugh that made her throw her bundled napkin in his face, relieved to know that her joy has just become his, and Javier's and theirs together.

- Let's dance! Music maestro!

Javier points his vice at a set of speakers set high on the wall and speaks into it. Then the cabin fills with the sound of some hundred-year-old riddle music and a song out that comes like raw silk out of the mouth of a queerly beloved man named Sinatra.

- Come along your grace. We must dance the light fantastic.

Lawrence took my mother's hand then pulled her to her feet with exaggerated courtesy, then flew her to the moon where on her tiptoes all my mother's whiskey pain evaporated in an instant.

*Oh, muse! Moor me to the truth in the river mystic.*

# Song 7

Merri did not stay long in Ojai. She went north again stopping at many places missed during the first sojourn, but this time she chanced visits to some of the bigger cities, Sacramento, Redding, Portland and Seattle among them, spending no more than a night or two in each because, despite the warm welcomes extended by friends of Lawrence and Javier, she could not shake the sense of imminent danger that collected in their ill-lit streets and unswept gutters. A dog barking in the country prayed to the moon or chorused with other dogs in the church of night, but in the city, they barked at furtive shadow-movement, to reply to gunshots, at rupturing noises out of human habitation, as counterpoint to human hollering, they barked to prove their continuing companionship to mankind even in those brutal, man-built places.

But worse, just about everyone she encountered in the cities was cynical and fatalistic, with a cast of mind so fundamentally different from my mother's, that even though she was the daughter of a meaner, much larger city, she felt like an idiot alien in their midst, a fool who could not see what these new friends saw. She was sure it was not just the way of the gay men and women she met, but typical of city people no matter what self-protecting enclave they were holed-up in. But her energetic optimism was a tonic to their souls while her road-warrior bravery filled them with shocked delight and envy.

It was difficult enough for most of them to venture out of

their ghettos, in packs, never mind alone, so to think of some woman, especially a small woman like my mother, moving around in the out-there on her own, well, it was like she was under the care of the very same gods who were punishing them. Through Trader Merri Weer, whose *bona fides* were attested to by Lawrence and Javier, they felt brushed by the kinder side of the Pantheon, especially so because Merri's swelling female belly and her plumping breasts bespoke a fecundity far removed from the godless gay aesthetic that twinkled in their lofts, ateliers, clubs and eating places. In her presence, the witty were often rendered witless.

One night she told me, when she was in Portland during that second trip, a transgendered man named Titus who had been among the very animated group she was eating with, had not said a word all night, but had stared at her the whole time. She had gone to the bathroom and was surprised – and a little frightened – to see him standing in the hallway just outside the bathroom door with his shaved head down, holding something in his hand. He spoke as she was about to walk by him.

- Miss Merri.

- Hi.

- I'm Titus.

- You have been staring at me all night, Titus.

- I know. I'm sorry. I couldn't help myself. I'm sorry.

- What's up.

- I want to give you this.

In his hand he held a wide silver bracelet, beautifully embossed with Indian motifs. She knew two things immediately: it was very expensive and it was intensely personal.

- It was my mother's.

- Then you should keep it Titus. Merri could see he was emotional. C'mon let's go sit with others, she said.

- I really want you to have it. I want you to take it with you.

- But you don't even know me…I mean…

- I want you to take it with you on the road.

- Titus…

- She wanted to travel. She wanted to see something of the world. She was very brave, Ms Merri. Very. But she never got out of the valley where we lived. My father was in a wheelchair, and, well…

- But you could…

- I won't go anywhere. I know I won't.

Titus took her right hand and slipped the bracelet on her wrist. Mother never wore jewelry – not a ring, a necklace, a brooch, nothing at all. She usually wore jeans and a white shirt, open at the neck. Hair piled on top. No makeup. In those days she didn't need any.

- OK, Titus but I'm not taking it to own it. So, if you ever want it back…

- Can I touch your belly? He did. I bet you she's a girl, he said.

Those who knew my mother in later years would not believe it when I told them there was a time when she traveled un-adorned. Titus's request – I will not call it a gift - was the start of something that as much as anything made and burnished my mother's legend. By the time I buried her, except for what Titus had put on her wrist, on any given day Merri was festooned with an ever-changing array of bracelets, pins and brooches, chains, necklaces, sashes, scarves, head bands, wild belts, even ancient time pieces that could still mark time, though hardly anyone then living could read them right. Everyone of these objects had been lent to her by someone who wanted a loved one who'd been stuck in life to go on Trader Merri Weer's journey into the great unknown. And for Merri, weighed down as she was by the awesome responsibility that was hung on her, it was a good trade, because the rattle and jangle of all that stuff kept the wolves of self doubt at bay.

At Blaine, she passed through the border into what truckers and traders called the MacAdora, a manufacturing zone tightly controlled by the Canadian government to accommodate the making of things by big companies who moved north to escape the predations and uncertainties that were endemic in the US. The warehouses there were as big – maybe bigger – than those in Bakersfield – and she could lay her hands on all the same trade goods, more in fact.

She had heard tales about Vancouver, a virtually Asian city that glittered on the shores of the Pacific not even fifty miles north of the border. It had been knocked back on its stiletto heels by the same rising sea and quakes that had destroyed LA and San Francisco, had torn into the heart of Portland, and forced Seattle to spread further and further up the slopes that surrounded its waterways. But Vancouver, like most Canadian border cities, its pockets full of gold, sprang back up and built newer, higher and better. Merri said we would pay a visit one day, but she never took time to get the tourist visa that would give us entrée to that bustling entrepot and alleged cultural mecca. Years later, I was asked to do a concert there but I sent a resentment-laden no thanks because I had no intention of being promoted as the sad-eyed lady of the lowlands to smug Canadians who had no reality to connect my songs to but still thought them charmingly poignant.

- You are making a big mistake, said Mr. Woo, my never-say-no wooer.

- It wouldn't be the first time, said I.

- Please you reconsider. Money no object, said he.

- I will sing to you alone for two million while I shower.

- That could be good, clean fun, he laughed. Call me when you want to get down and dirty.

Mother got back to California in late October, a bit more than six months fat with child as they say. She viced Javier from Bakersfield to say she wouldn't be coming down to Ojai. She wanted to make one last circuit north before giving birth. Javier had a splendidly musical ear and could hear the strains in her voice, a lot of fatigue but something else strummed his guts.

- Just a couple of nights, Merri. Just to rest up.

- You guys will kidnap me.

- Maybe. For your own good though.

- I've got women out there who are expecting Christmas goodies.

- Lawrence is going to be pissed.

- Give him a kiss for me.

- Merri…c'mon. Something is going on. I can hear it in your voice.

- I'll be back just before Christmas Eve.

- That's when you're due, Merri.

Javier knew better than to argue ad nauseum with my mother, so he let her off the hook, but held on to his uneasy feeling.

Something was going on. It was October. She was at the end of the second trimester sitting behind the steering wheel with the lump of me tumbling in her distended belly. Strong as she was, she huffed and puffed on the warehouse docks, wheezed as she pulled things out of the van to set a stage for her customers, and then again as she went up and down the metal stairs to put unsold things back again. She never regretted her pregnancy, but with the voices of a thousand women who proffered their unasked, unwanted wisdom in her head, she worried constantly about what was to come – how to fit a baby into her itinerancy, how to fit her life around this child, worried about her fitness for motherhood. Veering off the pavement to the soft shoulders of the highways she motored on, she had to call herself back from contemplations of all the things she might do, should do, would do for the sake of her daughter – she never considered she would birth a boy – in her land of is, the world where we would both, in fact, live.

As she drove north out of Bakersfield, escaping its black-hole forcefield despite the gross weight of all she carried, with dark storm clouds rising in the west and a troubling clunk-clunk emanating from the rear of the van's chassis, she opted for Route 99 again, where she would right fork east to Folsom on Route 50, go on to Placerville, and then, if the roads permitted, up to Lake Tahoe where women with money would put her well into the black. Anything sold after the always renovating, dusty-haired, paint-daubed ladies of the lake got their loot was gravy. Route 80 would get her back one way or another to Yuba, and at Yuba she could strike north again.

That was the plan, but at Alder Creek, just west of Folsom where the dribble of the near dry American River opens into a plain gravelled by rock carried by the once fast river out of its mountain redoubt, at a time when I have settled at last into a midnight snooze in behind mother's now protruding navel, at a time when on the empty road she was singing softly for the two of us, in the van's side mirrors she caught the headlight beams and the strobing red lights of a police car closing on her fast.

- Sorry, ma'am, but apparently they couldn't reach you any other way.

- They?

- The Warden's people, ma'am.

When Trader Merri Weer stopped at a town or village along whatever route she had decided on, women there would let other women in places further along know that she would be there next, or likely so if she didn't peel off in a different direction in between. As she approached the barricades or roadblock at a town's limit, the men would wave her through, sometimes tugging their forelocks or lifting their caps, sometimes with a thumbs-up, sometimes with a shake of their heads, but with no fear other than the fear of money lost to female shopping, money that could have been and should have been spent on groceries or other necessities, or for a few drinks with the boys for that matter, the only real pleasure of the menfolk. The alerted women would be waiting for her in a parking lot or way-by, cheering her arrival, and these days, more often than not, many would be carrying a hand-knitted or crafted gift for the baby in mother's belly, me.

The Warden of the once abandoned Folsom State Prison – FSP as it is called - was a woman, Lilith Morrigan, known to her prisoners and their kin as the Iron Maiden. She had been waiting for the day when Trader Merri Weer would come her way, so when she received the alert from a friend in Rosemont that Merri had arrived there earlier that evening, she mobilized.

- A lot of the gals will sure appreciate you dropping by, Ms Merri, said the cop.

- They're waiting for me?

- Sure are.

- Inside the prison? It's a men's prison.

- No ma'am. In the camp.

- Camp?

The prison did not and does not house female prisoners. In those days, Folsom held over twelve thousand men, everyone of them living in squalid and inhumane conditions. The stink of men, their sweat, piss and shit hangs in the violent air that sits on the place and never blows away. Women are housed in a tented city outside the prison walls under a different stink.

No one ever wanted to recommission FSP because once it had been closed in 2030 or so, it had been allowed to crumble and rot where it sat. It was a hellhole from day one of its new mandate and the State had no money to clean it up and ready it for humans, however lowly. But once the other prisons around the State were chockablock with jailbirds, it was put back online.

And who were those misfortunates who found themselves in FSP? Men who had no clue about where to get food and water for themselves or their families when things finally fell apart, because every grocery and convenience store in their vicinity emptied of both. Had no idea what to do when they couldn't get gas at the pump to effect an escape, or when they had no money left in their piggy banks and the great well of pogey ran dry, or when their castle homes sweltered through summer and stayed cold all winter and their lights flickered their code of despair, or when they could find no respite from the sound of crying because their distracting devices were dead and the liquor stores boarded-up and all the old drugs were almost impossible to find or too dear to buy, or when there was nothing more to risk other than one's own dignity and one's own life, when frustration and rage overwhelmed decency, when stealing the necessaries and even killing another for survival's sake made so much crazy, self-legitimizing sense.

The simple truth is the country had stopped working and when it did blood flowed through the streets of almost every city and town and through the rural counties too, and no one who lived through that time was guiltless of crimes against family, friends, neighbors or strangers. It's just that some got caught or were turned in for theft, assault, break and enter, or murder most foul. These men, and their female counterparts, were tossed into places like the Folsom State Prison upon summary conviction, where people like Warden Morrigan had been hired to manage the infrastructure of the place but not to worry too much about how the prisoners organized themselves. In the case of the men inside the bulging prisons, testosterone would do the heavy work.

Mother followed the cruiser until it stopped, but still far off from the high prison walls which she could see silhouetted against the night sky. The cruiser stopped on the top of a low rise where the cop got out of the car and beckoned her with a crooked finger. She walked up the slope to join him, aware by then of a low, rumbling din coming from the other side of the hill. As far as the eye could see on the moonlit plain below, she was astonished to see a tent city where thousands of women and children were busying themselves with their refugee lives before the sun came up.

A woman came from behind and stood beside her, the Iron Lady herself. She had not heard her car arrive.

- They belong to the men inside. They had nowhere else to go.

- It's horrible, said Merri, turning to the Warden.

- Compared to what?

- How many?

- Not sure. Never less than a couple of thousand, sometimes five or six.

- How do they…

- Survive? You're a woman. You know.

Yes, I do, my mother thought. Whatever it takes.

- I'm the Warden. Lilith Morrigan.

- Pleased to meet you Ms…

- Lilith. Lilith Morrigan. You have things I'm sure they'd like.

- They have money?

- Some. A few have things they can barter.

- These women?

- Not exactly these women. There's another area of the camp I want you to see.

Merri stepped up into the van and followed the Warden down the slope she had driven up earlier, then around to the back side of the prison complex, where, still outside the walls, they entered through a gate guarded by two men in FSP uniforms. More tents; more women, no children. She was led to an open area where they both stopped. Soon they were surrounded by a group of hollow-eyed women, most in dirty white smocks and open toed sandals.

- Prisoners? Asked Merri.

- Oh no, no, no… They work in the prison. Cleaners, kitchen workers, a few nurses, a number of them in my office, the prison library if you can call it that. Some do grounds keeping.

- Forced labor? A deep rage was forming in Merri's guts.

- No again. We pay them. Of course. And they get food from the prison commissary when there are leftovers. They're the lucky ones. All of them used to live in the main camp. I hand pick them from the applicants. But it's not too often that a position opens up. They hold on to them pretty hard.

These were the privileged few – a couple of hundred childless women who had men on the inside and energy enough for the work. They were called the Bee's as in busy as. They were paid a few bucks out of the Warden's skimpy budget, but, if they worked especially hard or innovated some labor-saving process, they might be bonused with a quick conjugal visit to their man, or more to their liking, be given a free bus pass into Folsom city and a day of freedom. None of them wanted to chance becoming pregnant.

- So, I'm a bonus?

- Put it that way, yes, said the Warden.

- No. I don't want to do this.

- Why not?

- You know why.

- You don't have enough and will never have enough for the women in the main camp, Merri, even if you give it away free and return here a thousand times.

- Still.

- Still, these women here, she said pointing at the women standing around, now impatiently, they suffer too. Look at them. Maybe not as much as the others, grant you that, but, you're here now and you have stuff to sell.

By day break, but for one box of lipsticks and all the diapers she carried in the van, she was sold out and exhausted. All cash; no barter. She pulled out of the Bee's compound just after dawn, and sheltered the vehicle in the shadow of the prison walls where she slept fitfully for a few hours. She would have to go back to Bakersfield to restock before heading north again.

On the way out of the prison grounds she found a road along the high fence surrounding the main camp and drove along watching it come alive in the dusk of another day gone by. But then she stopped and walked up to the fence, where a few women who lived in close-by tents, saw her. They walked up to the fence and looked at the sign on her van.

- You're her, one said, her dirty hands gripping the wire mesh.

- You're Trader Merri Weer, said another.

- We heard about you.

- We didn't think you was real, a real person, though. Are you real?

Merri opened the door to the van, stepped in and brought out the lipsticks. She handed them through the chain links, one to each woman standing there until the box was empty. And then mother mounted the stairs again and used it as a pitching mound to throw five boxes of diapers over the top of the fence where she watched them bounce and roll on the other side while the women clawed and screamed at one another to get hold of what they could. With the last one thrown and in the possession of its winner, the women melted back into anonymity leaving just one skinny, pre-teen boy whose stare was more lascivious than Merri wanted to believe, more than seven months pregnant as she was. Unlike the women inside, mother had meat on her bones and breasts that might feed a dozen hungry babies and that lascivious look came out of hunger, not desire.

*My pretensions are a prison most profound.*

# Song 8

At Blaine, she paid a couple of men to load the van under her barky, bloated supervision. Just beyond the canopy of the dock what had been a drizzle had turned into a drenching rain, one of a very few to visit the tinder dry northwest in recent years.

- Big storm coming, Merri, said one of the men.

- Be careful out there, said the other.

- Keep the yungun safe...

One of them bang-banged on the side of the van and sent her off into a dawn illuminated by lightening. She aimed the vehicle for the I-5, now elevated for long stretches above the slapping shoreline below. She had but three weeks and a bit to make it back to Ojai, but if she chose her route well, she would make it in good time to deliver me into the New Year, nothing left in the van but the faintly rumbled memories of the year just gone.

The clunk-clunk noise coming from beneath the van's chassis was worrisome, but she was confident the van would keep the pace as it had for every mile clocked since she had started the journey. The only thing that disturbed the rhythm of the road were the sudden kicks and elbow blows I delivered whenever I was awake. You were like a baby bird, she told me, punching at the inside of its shell to force a crack. Mother would push a knee or hand or maybe the top of my head and send me turning in the amniotic sea, but I would float back to the surface and let her have it again, make her yelp in the middle of some song she was singing or humming as she whiled away the hours.

Winds came off the Pacific and bent the rainfall from its vertical drop, bent it until it was coming at an angle that made it ricochet off the windscreen. Knowing that no one would come out in such weather even for Trader Merri Weer, she stayed on the highway until she got to Everett which was flooding. Forced on to Route 9, she would figure out a way to wriggle through the rain-pummelled countryside until she got south of Tacoma where her vice told her, the I-5 was holding up. But by the time she got there, it wasn't good, not good at all. The storm had ramped-up to hurricane strength causing the van to wobble on its wheels. She would have to stop, but where?

To the west of Olympia she thought she caught a glimpse of blue sky, and she had. The sight of it lured her on to old Route 8 where she worked her way around the hurricane damage, past downed powerlines and trees, past houses pushed off their foundations, or tilted beyond usefulness with roofs torn off, past men and women and children and dogs and cats standing in piles of rubble bewildered, looking at her hardly at all. But she was gladdened for her sake and mine by the azure sky above and by a soft wind that lofted the tattered Stars and Stripes on the staff beside the red brick offices of the local government, because such a died-down wind could harm no one.

She drove south from Montesano and made it to Raymond before the west wall of the hurricane's eye smashed into her and almost tipped the van into a water filled ditch. The rain pelting the west-facing side of the van beat a nasty tattoo into Merri's ears and filled her with dread. She said I was turning and turning insider her, spiked by her adrenalized worry, frantic to live. The wind tore at the grommets of the blue tarp that covered the trade goods tied down to the top of the van and sent it spiralling on the ropes that still held it to the other side until they too snapped and let it fly into the torrent like a howling blue dinosaur bird going to extinction. The furniture and appliances bought with hard earned money tumbled off and smashed on the roadside.

Merri spied the faint penumbra of a concrete corn silo up ahead. She found the driveway into the farm where the silo stood beside a twisted barn, in round, squat defiance of the storm. Pushed from behind, she held the van to the path of the gravel drive and took shelter behind the silo, and there, for as many hours as it took, sometimes sleeping in the rocking bed at the back of the van, sometimes, terribly awake, trying to calm the contracting hicks that seized her as she lay there in the womblike blackness of the wet night.

She awoke to a banging against the side of the van, banging and the sound of a gruff male voice and the thwump-thwump of an old gas engine.

- Ya in there? Hey! Wake up. C'mon now.

The farmer who owned the property was standing below the door, coveralls under a rubber coat, high boots.

- You were welcome to take shelter, missy, but you have

93

to get out of here now.

- Yes. Yes. Thank you.

- I'm not being inhospitable. I'm glad your safe, but this storm is pushing a surge our way.

- What?

- This land is gonna be covered in sea water in a few minutes, up to our proverbial asses. We gotta get to high ground. But stay here if you want if you want to test the theory. Your business, not mine. But fair warning.

He turned away and fast walked it to a shed behind the house, and mounted a tractor hitched to a long flatbed, where his wife and three kids sat amongst all the exposed possessions they managed to pull out of their wrecked home. She saw them turn left on the country road in front of the farm and disappear into the incessant rain.

Mother's memory was murky on all that transpired next, but she knew it took her only moments to shake off her disbelief and get us in motion. She chased after the farmer and his family but never saw them again. Driving south she watched the tidal surge pouring in under the low clouds to the west moving so fast she expected to be shoved off the road at any moment. But then the road started sloping up out of the coastal prairie under a canopy of pine trees. At last her shoulders dropped and she patted me where my head was with my ear turned to the slowing beat of her heart.

- We're ok now, baby. We're ok now, she said.

The expanding sea, driven by gusting winds and mottled with sudden smashes of hard rain, flowed across fields that a host of neophyte farmers had ploughed and tilled like small plotters in a by-gone age. They had had come out of the cities in the not-too-distant past to lands vacated in previous generations to feed themselves and give their families a chance at a good life. Pacific salt would render the fields useless for seasons to come and sting in the woeful wounds of dreamers who thought their pitchforks could keep the roiled ocean at bay.

She said she lost track of time. The post-hurricane darkness simulated both early dawn and late dusk. She found a position behind the wheel where I kept quiet, where the few-and-far-between contractions that I triggered when I kicked and rolled would not startle her to the point of endangerment on the fogged-up highway. What time was it? Did she really need to know? Want to know?

Her time-telling vice lay on the floor by the bed, and she did not want to stop to fetch it or to restack the storm-tossed boxes in the back of the van that now cluttered the narrow passage from front to back until she got somewhere where she could find safe harbor. And that vice might, if she searched the Cloud, tell her more about the ever more frequent and painful contractions now being visited on her than she wanted to know right then, might tell her that the ever-louder clunk-clunk in the guts of the van needed tending to on an urgent basis. She would get to Ojai, all her goods sold in the two weeks to come, and then deal with the fucking baby and the fucking mechanics, gripping the hands of Lawrence and Javier, Lawry and Jav,

La and Ja, La and Ja, ah-ah, ah-ah, ah-ah, ugh.

And then the highway began to rise and rise and Merri realized she was climbing up the high span of a wobbling suspension bridge. A cold sweat on her brow, doubling over the steering wheel with pain, unable to see more than a hundred yards into the blowing rain, she guessed she had come to the Columbia, and was passing out of Washington at last and into Oregon. Down below, as she would see on future trips, only the rusted crosses on the highest steeples of drowned Astoria poked up to divide the currents that swirled and bubbled where the shrunken, muddy river confronted the Pacific so full of wrath that night.

Coming down the other side, going faster than she should, she drove into a deluge that made the bridge deck almost invisible because the glare of her lights illuminated only the thick, slanting rain in front of the van. She could not stop there, not there on the perilous downslope upon which she seemed to be skating, not there where god-hurled gusts of cold wind might send the van flying into oblivion, not there when the only way she could endure the wrenching spasms in her belly and back was to grip the steering wheel and yell. Yell at those motherfucker gods.

And then, as the road flattened at the south end of the bridge the van careened off the road and crashed into the yellow barrel buffers that anticipated the arrival of the careless and misfortunate and stopped the van dead in its tracks. The Pitman Arm on the right wheel assembly had finally come apart, in case you want to know.

Strapped in behind the wheel. Dreamt. Did not dream. Woke into consciousness, rain beating on the windshield, then slipped back into the tunneled darkness. Time went by, but minutes or hours? Belly and back pain delivered her to a crying wakefulness, then subsided and tossed her back into the black surf. Rose again on what might have been a third moment or a third day. Voices heard, one close, one coming from outside. Men.

- Goddammit, Bibby, she's in here. She's breathing.

- I can get a tow line on this.

- Pull her out nice and slow. The hook 'er up…

- Give me your handkerchief. She's got a nasty cut on her forehead.

Then movement, tossing her back and forth in the loose soil of the underworld where she was rooted. Jerked to a stop, then those male voices again.

- I'll stay with her, here. Go easy. She ain't a fat woman. She's pregnant and damn close to D day.

- Fort Ketchup?

- No other choice.

- You say so.

She awoke in a small, dark room made of logs. Wooden

door just past the foot of the bedstead. Small window with orange curtains not quite together in the middle. A crack where the light got in. Sunlight. White sheets, a blue striped pillow encased in white linen, a thick wool blanket pulled up to her neck over her stomach which rose above the bones of her chest like a mountain.

On a small table beside the bed a plate littered with crumbs and a piece of crust, a glass with a bit of water in it. A feeling of calmness in the room and in her body. Outside at a distance she heard murmurs and laughter. With her right hand she grabbed her stomach and used her fingers to search for my slumbering head and found it exactly where it ought to have been. The puzzle piece of relief snapped into the peace she already felt.

Then, into her mind came the recollection of coming off a bridge, yes, yes, over the Columbia, in the sizzle of wind and rain – the tail end of that hurricane - of losing control, yes, of exploding yellow barrels gushing with water. Of nothing then, yes. But also, the possibility that the low male voice she heard were real, that the van was following behind a white wrecker whose shape was fuzzed by water, that the thick hand on her right shoulder that comforted and steadied her was also real, that she did see through the side window against which she her head was leaning a rough scrawled sign done in a thick red paint: Fort Ketchup. Clang of bell, gate opening, scurrying people.

- Why here? She's a white woman, said some shrill woman.

- For god's sake, you can't turn her away.

- We'll take her from here. Now you git! A strong, dark female voice.

Merri turned and tried to rise from the bed, to put both feet on the floor, but a sudden jab of pain in her left shoulder made her flinch and fall back. Her arm was in a sling, no longer dislocated as it had been, she will soon learn, but held in place to speed the healing. She endured the pain and swung round to sit the side of the bed.

In the armoire behind her, against the log wall, all her clothes, cleaned and pressed and hanging neat, boots with laces tucked-in underneath, polished. In the long mirror beside the armoire, her dishevelled, hair-down self in a white shift, bandaged on the forehead, huge with child, barefoot. But in this place, out of the van's steady confinement, not on the road, she succumbs to an unexpected lightness in her spirit, the blithe spirit of the saved. She remembers her father pushing her on a swing in the green park on the shore of the lake.

- Higher daddy, higher.

She stood before the door of the little room, took a deep breath, then pushed her thumb down on the black latch, and opened it, then stepped into the frame of the door while her eyes adjusted. Under the wide overhang of a building across a grassy quadrangle, three old Black women, two sitting in high backed chairs, one in a rocker, all stitching leather, doing their part to make the shoes and moccasins for which the Fort ladies became famous, mostly because of Merri's – and my - later proselytizing.

One of the women spied her before the others, then stood, and fixed a suspicious look on my mother, a look my mother returned. They kept her eyes on one another as the Black woman bee-lined it for an open door in the building behind her and disappeared into the shadow beyond. Moments later, just as Merri stepped down on to the covered wooden walk-in front of her room, a stout Black woman, her face set with an impatient scowl under a helmet of wiry grey hair, emerged into the early morning light. Soon, gaggles of other Black women came out of other doors and stood at all the edges of the quadrangle looking at mother.

Willia, known to all as Wil, saw Merri about to step off the walk into the quadrangle, but Wil held up her hand and bade her stop. Wil got about halfway across the quadrangle then came to a halt herself. Hands on hip, she turned to face the women standing around the cloistered yard. Under her gaze, some went back inside right away, but there were others whose eyes were stuck on my shivering mother.

- Go on now. Get the fuck back to what you was doin.' This ain't no sideshow.

Across from my mother, another barrel-chested older woman sat down in her chair while the others who had been stitching leather with her earlier shuffled off stage. Screen doors creaked on their hinges then banged shut. By the time all the women had gone, Wil was standing on the ground beneath my mother.

- It's fucking cold, girl. You should go back in.

Mother felt me turning in her belly.

- And you're about due to drop that poor fucking child.

Wil stepped up and took my mother's elbow and nudged her back into the room.

- Where am I? Merri asked.

- Western Oregon.

- I know. I got myself here. But what is this place.

- Fort Ketchup we call it. Now, sit yourself down.

Wil pulled the wooden chair beside the armoire and put it near the bed. Merri sat.

- Of course, it used to be known as Fort Clatsop. Don't ask me what, why or fucking wherefore, but the place was left to wrack and ruin. One of the girls had a boy child who kept calling it Fort Ketchup, and it stuck as those things do. Clatsop's an ugly fuckin name anyway. White man's idea of paying respect to the injuns who used to run wild in these parts a long fuckin' time ago.

- How long have I been here?

- Three nights.

Mother sat down on the edge of the bed.

- So, you're Merri Weer? Trader Merri Weer. Heard about you.

- I crashed.

- You did. That's a fucking fact.

- How did I...?

- A couple of local men found you. Looked to them like you were gonna give birth right then and there on the side of the fuckin' road. But that was nerves. Well, Cladine figures it so. She's the midwife. The old gal in the rocker on the other side. But you are due she says. Any minute now.

- Not 'til Christmas.

- You won't last that long missy. Guaranteed. But now that yer up and seem to be in good health we'll take you to hospital in Portland. That will be a big fuckin' relief to all of us includin' baby Jesus if that's who you planning to bring into this fucked-up old world.

- I have to get to Ojai.

- I have no goddamn idea where that's at, but if it's more than a little ways, you ain't gonna make it.

- It's in California.

Wil guffawed and shook her head.

- I can leave now. Make a start.

- And how do you propose to do that? That big old truck of yours is... Well, it's parked by a shed out back. Sorry fuckin' sight to see.

And then Wil explained that the van was in bad shape. A couple of the women with the know-how could bang out the dents, but the frontend got shoved into the motor and the front right wheel was limping like a shot-up old soldier and both required the considerable work of mechanics and parts that might be found in Portland at great cost, but not around Fort Ketchup.

The two men who had rescued her the night of the crash could tow the van to the city and she could ride up front, though she had to understand that the busted highway might jiggle the baby loose *en route*. It was going to cost money though. And it would be appreciated if she could cover her room and board, cash would be best, but some of the trade goods in the van could be taken in barter, assuming there was stuff in there useful to natural born Black women living in a tight-fisted commune. Some cash, some hard goods if that worked. Her choice.

Mother knew there was nothing free in this fucked-up old world - to use Willia's own sweet words — and it would have grieved her more not to pay than to cover her debts, moral and otherwise. She didn't want to be left with any kind of obligation that could come back to haunt her later.

That was two days after Wil and Merri first talked. It was too late to organize a trip to Portland right away. The men who had rescued her were willing to make the trip to Portland but were not available the following day.

On the second night, after the women poured out of the dining hall after breakfast and were making their way to quarters talking noisily, some giggling as they trod down the wooden walkways or across the grass, Cladine paid a visit to the small room where Merri was cussing the gods that were keeping her confined.

Cladine was a small woman, but squared-off, the trunk of an old growth tree in some cut-down forest through which new growth was sprouting on all sides. A thin white mop of cropped hair on a large round head with dark eyes deeply set beside a wide, flat nose. She was, despite her age, still vital and energetic. Out of her full mouth, when she spoke, came a lilting voice, whose gentle cadences were a drug to comfort god-cussing women like my mother.

- Oh, look at you. I know that look.

- No.

- Oh yes, dear.

- I'll go to Portland tomorrow.

- You think so?

Mother's body arched.

- How long between the contractions? Asked Cladine.

- It's nothing.

Cladine put a warm hand on her brow and counted silently to herself. Mother arched again and whimpered too.

- Two minutes. Well, it doesn't surprise me Ms Merri. You got rattled something fierce coming off that bridge. Oh, my.

- We can wait 'til I'm in Portland.

The old woman went to the door and opened it and stepped out onto the wooden walkway. Mother could hear her yelling for Willia, yelling for hot water. She came back in and looked at Merri, smiling as she waited for the last contraction to subside. She pointed at her own head with an arthritic finger and tapped it thrice.

- It's mind over matter now, girl. We ain't got nothing for the pain and this is gonna take awhile. Just remember, you ain't the first one who's had a yungun.

Cladine pulled the straight back chair near the bed and perched there, stroking mother's back while she whisper-sang old songs and muttered long lost slave prayers until I finally dropped into her waiting hands.

I was delivered at Fort Ketchup, a month early, after a labor that lasted just over twenty-five hours, into the waiting, bloody hands of ancient Cladine York who midwifed my increasingly delirious, pain-wracked, exhausted mother.

At any given time, two of the younger women took shifts to steady Merri as she knelt on the floor with her head sunk between her forearms which, with each contraction, she pushed deep into the thin mattress on the small bed where she knelt. Wil stood-by with arms crossed across her chest except when she put her hands over her ears if mother's yelps became too much.

She told me some years later, that while she watched my mother heave and push, she thanked god she had never born a child. Then, taking my hands in hers, she told me that many times since, she thanked god my mother fought all that long night to let me come into the light.

*In the labyrinth, there I lost my ludic life.*

# Song 9

I was born hollering into a late November that was colder than could be remembered by any of the old women at Fort Ketchup. But it was bright cold, and those highlit days were full of color because the gold and red leaves of October hung on the trees still and looked like they'd never lose their purchase.

Mother Merri was happy to have me suckling at her breasts, which I took to with alacrity. She loved being in the womb of that small room, whose chill she kept at bay with the thick duvet she pulled up over us. Willia sent food to the room every day, breakfast and lunch always carried by tiny, angular Erato, dinner by shy, plump Tithorea. Both girls had been born at Fort Ketchup until Will outlawed pregnancies once and for all on pain of banishment. Years later, making a guess, my mother told me that neither of the girls was more than eighteen then.

I fascinated both of them, so each in their own way strategized to stay in the room longer than it took to deliver a tray of food, tiny, angular Erato with garrulousness and cheerfully-put questions about the wider world, shy Tithy by tending to small things like straightening the curtains, or smoothing out our bed clothes while her eyes remain transfixed by newborn me especially when I sucked my mother's tit, or as I slept, swaddled in the cradle beside the bed, sometimes as my mother gently rocked it with an arm poking out from the duvet.

Tithy, the deeper thinker of the two, may have triggered the depression that enveloped mother once that first week passed.

- Lucky you bore a girl child, Miss Merri.

- I wanted a girl, Tithy. I really did.

- What I mean ma'am is, they ain't no boys here. No men at all. You ever wonder why?

- They're not welcome is all Wil said.

- That ain't the reason, Miss Merri.

Tithy stood looking down at my mother wondering whether to disclose her terrible secret.

- What is it, Tithy? said impatiently.

- You is lucky you had a girl is all.

- Yes.

- Cause if you had born a boy…

- Spit it out, Tithy.

- Cladine would have wrung its neck like a chicken. That's why Wil, why she stand watchin.' To make sure everything be alright. Otherwise, your baby would be buried out yonder at the end of the apple trees.

Tithorea knew she had said too much. She picked up the tray

of dirty dishes and left the room quickly, saying nothing more.

It wasn't true. Willia and Cladine had long ago used all means in their power, once a girl reached puberty, to warn them off the sin of sex. Until I came along, Erato and Tithy were the last children born at Fort Ketchup because, as I said, any girl or woman who got pregnant would not be able to stay at the commune. But that rule was made a few years after Wil and the original tribe of Black women had walked into the place and made it their own, fleeing Portland when it burned to the ground after the quake, fleeing the rioting, drunken, murdering men who roamed its busted streets.

A few babies had been born in the intervening years, but as it turned out they were all girl babies, so Wil never had to face the problem of dealing with a boy child. One September, everyone was picking apples in the orchard behind the fort and a couple of the adolescent girls who were running around as the women plucked the fruit off the trees stumbled on an old grave marker where they could still read the epitaph: Boy Adam, 2 months, 1 Day. R.I.P. June 4, 2025.

Two of the women saw the girls staring at the marker and walked over and answered the girls' questions by concocting a story about the fate of boys at Fort Ketchup, how Wil would break their necks, and from that time on, the myth of Adam was handed down as a cautionary tale. Wil never denied it's truth.

But the women, many of them, if not most, did have sex. Men came to the fort – on delivery, to fix things, policemen sometimes with matters interrogatory, health inspectors, CPS officials, IRS agents and other State officials and others pushed by official duty but pulled too by the musky smell of hard working black women, and especially by the scent of innocent virgins like Erato and Tithy. Almost always they were white men, but some were Black, some Asian, some Indian.

Over time, through the magic power of mutual attraction, assignations took place around the property, giving rise to the other myth, the myth of Eve, the sinning apple eater, which spread round the county to randy schoolboys and unhappily married farmers or factory workers who found ways and means of sneaking up to the periphery of the fort's property where they lay in wait like duck hunters to catch the eye of a black woman or girl out doing some chore beyond the walls of the fort.

Wil and Cladine were not naïve women, both remembered their young selves, so their countermeasures were not just mythical but scientific too. When the day came for my mother to settle accounts, any and all of the one-a-year birth control pills she carried covered most of her costs.

- We're her slaves you know, Merri Weer, said Erato out of the blue one day.

No one knew, but mother was diving into a well of despond at the time – a week or so after I was born. She had told Willia we would be leaving as soon as arrangements could be made to tow the van to Portland. Mother shifted the resentful look she was casting down upon my nursing head to look at Erato who was chattering away as usual.

- What? Sorry, Erato, what?

- Slaves. We're her slaves.

- Who?

- Wil of course. We don't get paid you know. For all the work we do.

- So, leave.

- Oh, I will. I will. I'm really a city girl. I'd like to get married and have one of those.

- You want this one.

- You got a name for her yet?

- Just a nickname.

- Do tell Miss Weer.

- Wicla. Wil and Cladine. You see…

- Now what kind of a name is that?

- A gratitude name.

- Why don't you just giver her a name, a proper name?

- I want to wait. I want to find out who she is, Erato.

- It sounds like a slave name. Like my name. I hate it.

- Change it.

- Suppose I will. Soon as I can.

But mother never did find out who I was, and so I've been Wicla all my life. It's who I became I guess, but I had to survive Merri's horrible depression first. She put a good face on things to begin with, so no one knew why I had become an incessant crier until Cladine finally pried me away from mother whose grip on me had gone rigid and mean-minded.

As Tithy stood by watching and learning the ways of the old gal, Cladine slowly cleaned the dirt from my bottom, then rocked my bony ribs with her two hands to let her know I could stop crying, then she gentled me into her bosomy possession. Tithy was left to work on Merri and to sort the little room while Cladine carried me away to safety.

During the next two months, if mother saw me it was quickly and never alone, and never more quickly than those times when mother would spring-up off her haunches where she leaned against the low part of the wall opposite the bed and fly with claws ready at whoever opened the door. Other days, she was quieter, laying in the bed or seated on the wooden chair rocking to and fro while she rubbed her hands together until both were raw. One time they let her take me in her arms, but, when they felt it was time for me to go, mother wouldn't give me up.

She folded me into her chest and turned into a corner of the room where she cried out for help - where we both cried out for help – as Wil promised holy retribution if I was not released. Alone in her room she would weep or rage, or sometimes sitting coolly on the side of her bed with her hair combed back from her blank face, promise Will she had come to her senses and was ready to leave Fort Ketchup. I'll pay, she'd yell. I'll pay anything you want. Just let me go. Let me go.

But the door to her room was not locked and the gates to the fort could easily be unlatched, so the prison she couldn't get out of was the prison of that depression, as though if she dared to leave the room Merri would be born into a place she did not want to be born into. Real motherhood perhaps, way beyond the passivity of breast feeding and the easy ritual of diaper changing.

One day in early January, Erato was sent to the van to fetch another box of diapers. As she was digging through the mess of boxes that had yet to be straightened, she heard Merri's vice ring. She followed it to its source.

- Hello.

- Merri. Is that you? Thank god. It's her. It's her.

- It ain't Merri. No sir, it ain't.

- Where is Merri? Who are you?

- Erato, sir. Merri's in the fort. I'm just getting diapers.

Lawrence and Javier were at the cabin. They had almost given up on Merri, thought she'd been killed. But every night after work Javier would dial her number while Lawrence stood beside him chewing his nails and they'd let it ring and ring until they heard Merri's recorded voice telling them sorry, the mailbox was full. Full of their messages.

- Getting diapers? Asked Javier.

- Yes, sir. For Wicla.

- Wicla?

- Merri had a baby, sir.

They asked Erato to please take the vice and give it to Merri, but Erato carried it to Wil instead and they learned all that Wil knew. And the upshot of that was that Wil and Javier negotiated time off, hired a selfdrive into which they spoke Fort Ketchup's coordinates – Fort Clatsop really - and got there two nights later. They and Willia worked out what needed to be done and all that they agreed, was done. The goods in the van could not be stuffed into the selfdrive, so Wil would keep all except what the baby needed for a few more days.

The irreparably damaged van would be junked or sold for parts or whatever by the two men who had rescued Merri. Mother and baby would return with Lawrence and Javier to Ojai and they would make sure the baby was looked after and Merri nursed back to health – a process that started happening as soon as they arrived and she heard their voices calling through the door of the little room.

And for the women at the Fort, even for Wil if she'd just

admit it, and for Cla who tried to laugh off the suggestion that she would if she could, wasn't Lawrence a sight to see; big, black, strong and possessed of some kind of superpower good humour. And Javier too, brown skinned Latino that he was, jet black hair, slim and trim and full of love and caring.

If the women gave any thought at all to the obvious knowledge that Lawrence and Javier were in love with one another, they put it out of their minds. Instead, they got busy setting-up the dining hall for the goodbye party Wil finally said they could have, and almost to a woman they thought about dancing with one man or the other and preferably several turns with both, a slow dance in a dark man's arms.

The dinner bell rang and everyone – everyone but Willia and Cladine, who were already sitting in state at the head table holding hands beneath the tablecloth – rushed to the dining hall and then to their usual places, paying no attention whatever to Wil who tried to shush them.

A moment later, Erato and Tithy, open the double doors to the hall to allow the only two men who had ever been in that sacred place to enter, with my mother on Lawrence's arm resplendent but unsteady in a long gown pulled out of someone's closet, with hair coiffed and just the right touch of makeup, and me in the crook of Javier's arm and all four of us smiling like fools as the sprinkle of January snow that had fallen on our heads as we crossed the quadrangle glistened under the lights.

The selfdrive pulled out of the fort just before Noon the following day and arrived at the cabin just after midnight. By then, Lawry and Jav knew that mother and I had not bonded, that I did not want her tit, just the bottles to which I had already been weened by Cladine, that she did not want to hold me unless it was her turn to do so.

But these three, each in their own way, were responsible people. When the love of someone or something did not inspire them, they would do what was right and necessary, even if the doing were grudging and unhappy. But unlike Lawry and Jav who let their grudges go in short order, mother would hold onto them tenaciously. I am the same way.

Within six weeks of our arrival at the cabin things were in a state of upset. The two men returned to work leaving mother with me. They were not sure that was the best thing, but what could they do? One of them might make it home for lunch, both were fast to return from work, glad from time to time that Lawrence changed shifts every couple of weeks so that at least one of them was at the cabin through more of the day.

They addressed her lack of attentiveness to me on more than one occasion and showed her through their own abundant affection that I could, if she would just connect with my bright spirit, lift her into a state of unadulterated joy. She should just give into it. But they engendered nothing but defensiveness, irritation and finally an explosion of anger that startled them. The golden light into which Merri had been invited all those months ago when she first happened upon Ojai and the NewB studios, soured and the sourness lingered like the acrid smoke from those fires that burned on nearby mountainsides and wafted toward the cabin.

One day, when Lawry and Jav were both home and I was sleeping in my crib, their bicker started to ramp into something else. Mother told them she was going for a walk and banged the door shut to let them know she had stepped out. In fact, she went around to the lower level at the back of the house where, sheltered under the deck protruding from the kitchen and living room, she eavesdropped.

- Why are you blaming this on me?

- I'm not.

- Goddamit Javier, don't tell me you aren't when you are. Yeah, I met her first.

- I never thought she would become a permanent roommate.

- You were the one who said bring her home.

- Me? Are you kidding?

- We can't just throw her and the baby out.

- She needs to get back on her feet.

- Should we offer to keep the baby?

- Are you kidding?

- She can't be trusted with her.

- She'll be fine. She just needs to have full responsibility.

Mother banged the door shut on the way back into the house too, to let them know she was back, but the bang knocked me out of my slumber and I awoke crying and hungry. Javier rushed to the crib to pick me up but Merri got there at the same time and put herself between me and him.

- I've got it, Javier.

They all sat around the kitchen island as she fitted the bottle in my mouth and let me drink my full.

- Tomorrow, guys, she said, I have to get to Bakersfield.

- Bakersfield? We're working.

- I know. I'll be taking Wicla with me, so no worries.

- You need to use my car, Merri? I can go in with Lawry.

- I've got a selfdrive coming.

- It's not a problem, Javier said.

- Maybe not, but…I've already made the arrangements, so…

Next day in Bakersfield Merri found a used van at a good price, white again, but this one had working autodrive and GPS and was configured inside with a second bedroom for me. It also had a pull-down ladder by the galley that you could use to climb to the roof top through a hatch. As with her old van, the side door was on the driver side, and beside the door there was a long side window that swung out from the bottom that could be latched to the side of the van to make a pass through.

The van was built low to the ground so there was but one step down to the pavement. The vehicle had been sitting in the sun all day, so it was fully charged by the time we drove out of the lot and headed south to the cabin with my mother singing. Turning off the van lights she rolled into the driveway into a puddle of light cast out of the living room window. She could see Lawrence and Javier cleaning up after dinner and let herself feel the twinge of her aroused conscience as she watched Javier's arm go around Lawrence's lower back when they stood in a once familiar silence by the sink.

I was asleep still, she told me as she recounted the story, so she snuck in the front door and went to our room where she changed her clothes. Then she went into the kitchen where she surprised them with her cunning. She was dressed in the vested, kerchiefed, bedecked garb of Trader Merri Weer, and with the determined look that she had lost to the hurricane winds above the Columbia all those months ago. She kissed and embraced them both in turn as thanks for their kindnesses, their generosity and patience.

- It's late. Stay the night, Merri, for god's sake.

- It's a workday for me, Javier. I'm no good in the daylight hours.

- We will see you again? Lawrence asked.

- Yep.

- Where are you going?

- First to Bakersfield to load up. Then North.

- Is Wicla going to be OK?

- I'm her mother.

- But...

- I'm her mother.

And once Lawrence and Javier had bent over my little bed in the van, cribbed on the open side by pillows, to kiss me and stroke my cheeks, off we went. But we did come back to them - every three months or so for about fifteen years, back down the Mariposa Road to the Ojai hive, back to the NewB studios where mother sold a lot of stuff every time, back into that golden light that had restored itself in their cabin. Back until that golden light and those golden men had been snuffed-out and burned-up.

*Repent ye all the ruptures of your radiant realities.*

# Song 10

The new van was never painted with Trader Merri Weer's signs, even though on more than one occasion Javier said he could have it done quickly in the studio paint shop. Merri thought it was safer to be anonymous as she plied the north-south highways and byways, and not put a target on the vehicle for those who would steal her loot, or worse, for those who might want to take advantage of a handsome woman travelling alone with her daughter. She wasn't anonymous at all, however, but became a kind of wandering spirit, uniquely gifted with the ability to pass like a wind through all the man-guarded blockades that still controlled access many of the towns, villages and communes that dotted her mental map.

Overtime, the dings and dents that had impressed them-selves on all sides of the vehicle through one mishap or another became a kind of rusted vocabulary that spoke to others – the men of the various safety committees, her customers, but also highway patrollers, fellow traders, road workers, toll takers, waiters and waitresses, those who labored in the Blaine and Bakersfield warehouses and a host of others.

Yes, we had an ordinary white van – there were many others of the very same make and model on the road – but our van had a weird charisma that was projected from the inside to the out, a way of rolling that was like Merri's gait, a speed not fast or slow, but deliberate and efficient, movement even while mother and I slept, like it too was dreaming or wrestling with pre-occupations too profound for the waking hours.

Of course, I was oblivious to everything in my babyhood, and cannot call the little fragments of sounds, smells and pictures that must have come out of my tot years, memories, not in any real sense. All that I have pieced together of those days and the days before I came along came from mother or from those whom she managed to touch, even though in many ways she herself was untouchable. Lawry and Jav loved to tell stories about Merri.

The women at Fort Ketchup, especially Wil and Cladine, but also Erato before she finally decided to brave the world, and Tithy who stayed and tried to fill Wil's and Cladine's shoes after they gave up the ghost, they all had striking, if conflicting memories of my mother. I heard a lot also from Lilith Morrigan, who became mother's friend of sorts because each in their own way were tough old broads who survived by figuring out the ways of men to supplement what they already knew about us women. You will learn the names of many more before my tale is told.

But then, you see, my own story begins to take precedence. I aged along with everyone else in this old world, and I also got a mind that can make memories and store them for purposes nefarious or necessary, as the case may be, in the up and down causes of life. Little girl memories, then adolescent memories, then the memories that flow like blood out of my teenagehood and early twenties, and then out of my true adulthood, which, at this point, is long of tooth as the saying goes. They are vivid and frightening sometimes, but also as complex as the teachings of a speechifying Christ, or as luscious and ludicrous as all the doings of the seven deadly sins. If you think it's all pain and penalty, it isn't. Therein lay all my joys and pleasures too. But I digress.

We worked at night. We rested and restored ourselves during the day when the sun did its mischief. The northwest coast had dried up, some thinking it had become a new paradise even though the ancient, green conifer forests in which their forebears had once sheltered had collapsed around them into heaps of brown splinters.

People loved the usual good weather even though occasionally the land underfoot would shake and shimmy with the tectonic slip-slide that bedevilled the entire rim of the Pacific, and even though from time-to-time Washington and Oregon crouched and cowered under the mad blows of hurricanes quite indifferent to the works of man.

The California coast, reconfigured by earthquakes and tsunamis had become wetter, at least from Mendocino south. Both sides of the mountain cordilleras that snaked down from the Canadian border, lost their glaciers, lost their snow caps, kept for themselves most of the little water they shook out of the heavens and so they yielded less and less to the contributaries and riverways that once bubbled and frothed with a life-giving surfeit that flowed into the mouths of downstream people and animals on both sides. The news that dripped out of our vices told us of widening deserts in the heart of America, deserts that engulfed many of the places that were among Merri's regular stops on Route 66 when she shuttled between LA and Chi-Town as a girl-woman.

The world east of the Mississippi seemed to people in the west like a different planet, the Federal government an abstraction, or sometimes, like a nattering ghost in the machine of immediate time and space. However, to be fair, their invisible hands were busy repairing the interstate Autodrives or building new ones, fixing systems that had broken down or replacing them, clearing out the rubble and clutter of the broken and destroyed, making potable water out of the salty ocean, doing their best to re-establish law and order, even when they drew blood from those whose firepower, at the end of the day, could not match those of the soldiers who came to enforce orders from on high.

Name the President? Some could. Identify more than a couple of cabinet Secretaries? Hardy anyone could pop a name let alone put a face with it. Fly the flag? Out of some old habit maybe. Vote in elections? If the weather was good and some bone was stuck in your craw. The national government was doing its best to keep some idea of a country alive, but it was hard going in a population where just about everyone, like my mother was fending for themselves and their family, if they still had one.

When I was a baby, mother pushed forward but always with a heavy sack of fatigue on her shoulders because I was a fitful sleeper and always hungry. My mother thought I woke for milk, but I think for her affection and attention too. I was cribbed most of the time, as she drove from place to place, as she herself attempted to sleep for just a couple of hours at a stretch, as she restocked, as she dickered and bartered with the women who flocked around the van wherever she stopped. But sometimes, when Merri was doing business, I would squawk and holler, so she'd bring me out and make a smiling show of her little girl, but always looking for a mothering sort to whom she would hand me over for cuddles and even bottle feeding if that is what was required to plug my noise. In this way did I, little Wicla, also become imprinted into the mythology of

Trader Merri Weer, making her seem more brave than when she was single, more beset by the travails of the road, more of a woman, really, softer than her hardening look actually suggested about her interior life.

As a tot, I slept longer so Merri did too, but I still wasn't much use to her, if I can use that word, except now I offered the amusements that a talkative, sing-songy child can, sometimes sitting on the passenger seat next to her instead of whiling away the hours on the still railed bed at the back of the van. Somewhere along the line she had purchased or traded for a tablet vice that pulled down a continuous stream of kiddie songs and vids, and she would sing along with me as she drove, correcting my mispronounced words and making sure I got the stories of the songs straight. It was one of the only things that delighted her but, of course, one of us would weary of the play and her irritated silence would fill the vehicle.

Now when we got to a place for trade, Merri might stand me on a couple of boxes stacked beside the van and cajole me to sing one of our songs to the gaggle of clapping, warmed-up, cash-carrying women. Often her customers would bring their own kids so I would be set down to play in their midst, but only to watch them go when their mothers had gotten what they wanted.

I never knew mother to carry on a conversation with any of these women, so as far as I know she never made a friend out there, although she had a good memory for names and faces, who was married, who was suffering in marriage, who had lost a loved one, whose kid had won a prize, whose husband had just been taken to jail or returned and the myriad other events and incidents that constitute the landmarks of a changing life. The mood she set was always good natured and full of fun. Even if she were in a foul mood when we pulled into a parking lot or some other way-by, by the time she swung the van door open her whole body and face would change into that of a happy and gregarious midway performer and do a little ta-da to elicit applause, cheers and whistles from the ladies gathered round.

Because mother was so buoyant and full of jovial vinegar, many of them thought the Merri in Trader Merri Weer, was actually merry. But in that case it was really merry Merri quite contrary. None of them would guess that out of their company she could be sullen and brutal. That was for me to know. Oh, yes, they might be witness to a moment of anger.

She didn't like people to rummage through boxes or bags of stuff that she was not ready to open to all. She didn't like it when women snuck in behind her to take a peek inside the van. She didn't like looky-loos with no money in their pockets, she didn't want to be bargained with to the last dollar. She didn't like anyone who presumed to give advice, especially advice about the raising and education of little me.

Her crankiness about such things, her barky reproaches, her finger wagging and sharp 'hands off sister,' were usually packaged in a joke or a wink, which mitigated the effects that a more bald-faced reaction would have produced. So, really, it was much easier to conclude that she was a pleasant, good-natured woman with a touch of road-weary salt in her veins than an angry woman who could be pleasant when the occasion required.

Schooling? I was going to read and write, I would learn arithmetic, learn how to think, and that was that. Practical. And I did, for when it came to make sure I came into possession of those skills, Merri put in the time. She found stuff in the Cloud that she would pull down into my tablet and take me systematically up and down the scales of the alphabet, of numbers, of basic arithmetic, making me learn all by rote, testing me until, should she herself make a mistake, I would correct her. She'd bang her knee with the palm of her hand and howl at that, make me giggle and register the hurt of a small joy, memorable as xyz and 123.

- Aren't you the smartypants? She'd say, clenching my left thigh with her right hand until I begged for mercy.

And, of course, we sang, and when mother said you know you have a nice voice, kiddo, I wanted my voice to be more than nice, just for her. Maybe that would let her stop hitting my face with the back of her hand when she thought I was being lippy and I wasn't. Maybe she'd do a little less screaming at me when I was being obstreperous whatever that meant. Maybe she wouldn't let me go hungry just because of some spat with me, or because somebody else shut down her appetite and roused the beast of punishment in her tightened belly.

I think I was a pretty good kid. For a mother like her I was. Even when I was as young as four or five I became a bit more useful, coming back to that word. I knew what was in inventory as mother called all the stuff piled up inside the van. Knew how she liked to stack things and pile things, knew where things were should she call me to fetch something quick, which happened a lot. I just became more efficient and astute as I moved toward and past my adolescence. I could anticipate what she might need just from the way her shoulders moved if a woman asked for something not set out on the ground by the vehicle.

More often than not I would use the pass-through window - like I was dishing out hot tamales from a food truck, then I would stay close by listening to the non-stop chatter outside awaiting the next order. In my middle teens, when I first realized that Merri was slowing down, it didn't matter much in terms of the business because I was now doing more and more to compensate.

I was just past sixteen when, for the first time, mother came down with a horrible flu. We were in western Washington, parked in the lot of an abandoned gas station on the outskirts of a small town that used to be called Chewelah – Indian country as Merri called it. It's probably still there, somnambulant under a sweltering sky. She couldn't get out of bed.

By dusk, a gaggle of women who knew us from previous visits had found their way to us expecting to buy or barter. In a small town like that, barter was more usual than purchase and some of those women made incredible crafts adored by city folk, and there was one woman, Keefer George, who was a bona fide artist, a painter, who was always willing to swap a painting for things she could add to her eccentric wardrobe. Before she fell asleep, mother said, no, no. No business today.

Working around her slumbering body, I moved goods out to the sales ground as Merri called it and did brisk business all evening. Everyone was sorry that mother was sick, but they were happy to hear I could talk – I was usually quiet while mother did her work – and they wanted to know where my beaky nose and dark hair came from because they certainly hadn't come from Trader Merri Weer. I didn't know, so I couldn't provide the answer.

The last customer was taken care of just before midnight, so

I tidied up, then went into the van where I wiped mother's hot face and dry lips with a cool, wet cloth before retiring to my bed, energized by the success of my work, measured in dollars earned, goods moved and the satisfactions of contact with all those curious women, all of whom had known one another since childhood, treating themselves to something new.

I did what I did most nights, I took up my latest tablet and hunted for one-off music stations that played human music, not the algorithmic crap the big stations flushed into the ears of the tuneless, and I let myself go to sleep under a blanket of notes and lyrics whose ultimate meanings so far escaped me.

Next morning, a still sick but warlike Merri shook me awake and fed me a breakfast of indecipherable screaming.

- For god's sake mother, what?

I swung my legs out from my covers and stood up to her.

- What now?

She backed up a little, brought up short by my sudden assertiveness.

- I said no.

- They were waiting for us.

- They could have waited until tonight.

- Everything went well, mother. Really well, actually.

She recovered her dominating self and moved closer.

- I am Trader Merri Weer. Me. Not you.

- Check your accounts.

- That's not the point.

- If that's not the point, what is?

I pushed by her.

- What do you think you're doing?

I turned the burner of the stove on and reached for the kettle.

- I'll make the coffee.

Later that day, while driving south to Spokane, I spoke up from the couch behind the driver's seat.

- Teach me to drive.

Long pause, after reflecting further than she had already reflected that afternoon.

- OK.

*We wend our way in the wilderness of why.*

# Song 11

I wanted to blame Lilith Morrigan for injecting booze into the veins of Merri's life – and mine. But that's not fair. It's not fair either to say mother overcame her scruples about doing business with the Bees at the women's camp at Folsom State Prison because the trade was good. We could have gone to any of a dozen places and done as much trade - or more - as we did there among the privileged few at FSP. But my mother and Lilith liked one another. Kindred spirits.

It became my job to conduct our business while Merri went off to Lilith's private quarters for a long gab – mother's word - over three finger drinks of scotch, scotch that Lilith insisted she buy from our stock, always over mother's ritual objections.

Long before I began sharing the driving, mother would moderate because she didn't want to take the wheel and put little me or our cargo at risk. But now that I was, they would disappear for longer stretches of time and when mother re-appeared, usually in the pre-dawn hours, she was drunk. Happy and drunk. When she returned, I would still be up, usually reading, sometimes writing in my journal or listening to music while I tried to figure out how a song works. I would put mother to bed, then drive off to a place on the other side of the prison that Lilith said was a lot quieter and shut everything down for the day.

For a long time, I didn't know their friendship had blossomed into an affair. Well, maybe affair is the wrong word because that implies at least a bit of mutual love to frame a lot of mutual lust. Put it this way: it was, for Merri, an affair of the heart and it was her heart that was made happy in blonde Lilith's strong and fleshy arms, the rub and tickle of their love-making just part of that.

Later on, once I had a bit more experience myself, I wondered what it was Lilith saw in my mother, what about my mother raised her temperature. It must have been, I concluded, the strand of neediness that was knitted into Merri's chain-mail bravado; her sinewy, always hard and lithe body, her muscled ass, her coconut breasts.

Lilith was the only human being Merri was intimate with until the day she died. Though we only got back to Folsom every six months or so, mother used to say those months were of a clock, not a calendar, each month seeming to last but five minutes, the days like seconds. Once we got within a hundred miles of the place, mother would take the wheel and push hard to the thump-thump beat of some old tune she pulled out of the cloud, a beat that belonged really to a long-gone America.

Full throated, the both of us, as the miles ahead grew fewer than those we left behind, for when my mother was floating on that cloud she would call me out from the back of the van to join in. On the last leg of those journeys to Folsom, I could not resist leaving my refuge, for it was mainly my refuge from her morose self, but I didn't need a refuge to protect me from her joy. Or my own.

In the intervening months, life on the road was mostly a life of sameness. But that sameness came to include what for me, initially anyway, was wasted time in roadside bars and more than a few city taverns. Merri took me in when I was too young to drink and plonked me down across from her, table or booth depending, but even when I became old enough, I would still sit and nurse a Coke and write and nibble on the house special rather than drink whatever it was my mother was having – whiskey mostly, sometimes bourbon, or vodka and orange juice if it was breakfast time.

Out of conversation with me, mother's eyes would bounce around, alighting on the faces and bodies of fellow travelers and wary locals while the few-and-far-between lights in those dim barrooms danced off the red frizz in her greying hair, and ricocheted off the medallions, pins and buttons on her vest, the layers of chains around her neck and the rings that she had screwed onto every finger.

Merri could be quite dazzling, especially compared to me, prim and demure in a white blouse buttoned almost to the neck, a single strand of pearls (the only thing I would let her put around my neck), hair combed prissily, finger nails cleaned, trimmed and buffed, my tablet open to a back-lit page, whose white rectangle more often than not was half filled with random thoughts. My strategy for life, clearly, was to be not like her.

Some men would send drinks over, the bravest of them turning to wink at Merri when they saw them delivered with the hope that she might crook her finger and wiggle an invitation to join us. But others of greater courage would come to our table, particularly if the jukebox were playing a danceable tune and try to pry her out of her seat. Not many succeeded over those years, but some did.

None of them got her where they wanted to go, however, whether that was into deeper conversation or into the fogged-up darkness of their truck or car. Many of them recognized her because they had done time at the roadblocks of a local town and thought that they could cozy up to Trader Merri Weer on the basis of that firefly moment in time. But as long as Merri was thinking about Lilith – which was almost all the time – not a man jack one of them made it past her thanks-and-no-thanks curtness. If a guy didn't hear that, well, I was the ace up her sleeve, because I had to be fed, watered, put to bed or driven to the next place on our never-ending tour.

It got a bit risky at times, though. Some men think a smile and a little pleasantry is flirting, that flirting is an invitation, that an invitation is an opening, that the opening is theirs for the taking. They didn't reckon, if mother was still sensible, on her wildcat ferocity. But if she were drunk and not able to drive them off, I would throw a bucket-of-cold-water on their feral two-step, just by being me.

- I'll take her from here, sir.

- Hell's this?

- Mother is going to throw-up on your boots, sir. Any second. I've got to get her out of here.

- She's OK. She's OK.

- Well, no sir, she is not OK. As you can plainly see.

- We was having fun.

- She's been grieving. In her own way.

- Grieving?

- A great loss, sir, yes.

- Husband?

- In the prime of life.

- Well, golly.

- She would thank you for taking her mind off it if she could.

- I lost a daughter.

Lost a daughter. Lost a son. Lost a wife. Lost a house, a farm, a way of life. Lost hope. Lost self respect. Lost. And in the recollection of losses, and in the presence of a shining daughter holding up a sometimes-lost mother, these men would open the door for me and help me get my mother to her sobering bed, and many would tell me what a good girl I was.

One night in some other place, not too many days after we had left Folsom, we were heading north into Washington in the lee of the mountains, mother buoyant as usual because she was still feeling her lover's kisses on her body. Our work done, we decided to stay in the lot of an abandoned car dealership where our customers had met us that night.

It was quite open but we wanted the van to get fully charged under the aborning sun and that would take all day. Mother said I could stay with the van if I wanted but she was going to TJ's restaurant across the highway for flapjacks and eggs if I wanted to come. It was surrounded by cars and trucks as it usually was. There was still some tidying up to do so I told her I would to it. In fact, I also wanted to pull the van around to the back side of the building - an extra dose of caution.

I took a quick shower, pulled on a T-shirt and jeans, added just a touch of lipstick, but didn't spend much time combing out the wet tangles of my hair, then crossed over the near-empty highway where I found my mother three quarters of her way through her pancakes, a cup of cold coffee at her elbow and calling for a second screwdriver.

- Don't look at me like that.

- I'm not.

- I just want to take the edge off.

- Off what?

- Never mind. You gonna eat?

There were still some folks at the back side of the bar listening to music and dancing. TJ never let a crack of natural light get in that area if he could help it. Well, here's the point of the story: some guy who had been drinking and partying all night came out to the restaurant side to get something at the register. He saw us sitting in our booth, opened the package of gum he had just bought and put a piece in his mouth then fixed his lizard eyes on me. He strode over, looked down and asked me if I wanted to dance. I don't know why but it shocked my mother because no one had paid me much attention before. It had always been her.

- She sure as hell does not want to dance, Merri said.

- Didn't ask you old girl.

He didn't stay around to take the abuse she shot at him, but by the time she was done with him, I was already on my way back to the van. When she climbed in and closed the door behind her, I was laying down on my bed, looking at my tablet, eating an apple from our small refrigerator. She stood in the doorway of my little room.

- I guess your pretty much a woman now, Wicla.

- I could have dealt with him myself.

- You think so? Hah!

- I was kind of flattered.

- I'm not going to let those filthy bastards lay a hand on you.

- He's just a guy, mother.

- And you know what they want? You know?

And I did know what they wanted because I wanted it myself, but not from that man. I wanted it from the guys to whom I had been singing my secret lyrics for almost two years using melodies that I kindled from the sparks of an emerging me. My own touch was not enough to satisfy my need for more, even when my fingers transcribed them into the vice that kept me sane and turned them, ultimately, into woman-famous songs.

*Brave the bonfire of the body's burning blessings.*

# Song 12

Twice a year we made it back to Fort Ketchup, to that convent that wasn't a convent, despite the strictures of Abbess Willia. Mother made sure we stocked things that our black sisters could not get unless they went to Portland – almost an impossibility - and so we all had fun during our day of trading, because the unstated promise in every bottle and package was that those magic potions and lotions, the lipsticks and glosses, the hair piks, combs, brushes and barrettes, the over and undergarments, the flotsam and jetsam of the jeweler's and clothier's trades, would work their magic in life's mating games when and if the ever-hopeful could get those games to commence.

The older women, spinsters all, did a lot of window shopping to see what was on the market, but because they had given up the idea of marriage and family, spent their money thriftily on stuff that would last while they took their fun teasing the young and naïve.

Willia, as businesslike as Merri, would shop privately, but not for herself, only the kitchen, the linen closet and the nursing station where she stashed the one-a-year pills that insured that if a romance blossomed or a tryst was accomplished, it would not result in the discharge of one of her girls for a pregnancy, either wanted or not. When she went off script it was to buy something that her beloved Cladine might cherish.

We also bought all the beautifully wrought shoes and

moccasins that the Fort Ketchup women produced because, apart from the fact that Merri wanted to make good on her debt to them, they sold well – extremely well - wherever we went. Our endorsements were on our own feet, in fact. So, it was that the Fort Ketchup brand spread to corners of the west where their well-made footwear was the sine qua non of the well shod woman.

I remembered the name Erato because she was still at the Fort when I was a tot but had taken off for the city by the time I could form a lasting memory of her from those days. Mother remembered her well and wondered when we had gone to see Titus and his friends in Portland, if that was Erato, she saw walking the hooker's beat, floating in a heroin haze on the street that separated Gaytown from The Pearly, where the Blacks kept themselves safe. That's what Merri called those ghettos. Not my words.

- Did you say hello?

- No.

- You didn't stop?

- No.

- Maybe you could have saved her.

- What from, herself?

- You could have taken her back to the Fort.

- I don't like to interfere.

By then, mother knew she wasn't even going to try to seek her own salvation let alone someone else's. Life would play itself out on its own. A fatalist, always.

Tithy was still there, and a lot of other young women who stay in my mind to this day: Tay, Aster and Neph who worked in the kitchen and took care of the blockade rooms, Epi, Melaina, Daph, and Meira who worked in the fields and barn with other nameless but not faceless Fort women.

I remember Daph and Meira especially because they sang backup to Cladine when, after dinner on a special occasion such as our visit, Cladine pulled out her beat-up old guitar and we all disappeared into her songs, drawn out of the ordinary now as Cladine breathed her tunes through the back of her throat, as she howled and growled in the spaces between notes and thumped the body of her instrument like a drum.

Cladine sat on the small stage set up in the corner of the dining hall, head hanging in quiet reverence for the lyrics that she had just finished singing, allowing the last notes she called out of Old Mud, as she called her instrument, to fly off into the rafters of the building where they would still float if they could. My mother was sitting at the head table beside Wil and like everyone had been taken by Cladine's singing, with Daph and Meira cooing behind her, into some deeper part of her soul. But mother was uncomfortable there so she broke the communal silence with a whoop, then got a round of applause going. Then she leaned forward on her forearms and turned her head to Wil.

- Wicla can sing like a bird, Wil. Like a bird. I'll be driving along lost in my own thoughts, but then some song she's practicing at the back of the van brings me up like a bubble to the surface.

- You always liked to sing to Merri. We used to hear you in that little room where you brought her into this world.

- But I'm no singer. Wicla, well…

- Then let's get her up for fuck's sake.

Wil rose and went over to Cladine who was just getting ready to leave the stage and whispered something to her before returning to sit beside Merri.

- We got a surprise for you tonight, ladies, Cladine announced.

I knew what mother had done.

- Wicla? Said Wil, talking loud across the room to where I sat with some of the younger women. You gonna sing for us?

I shook my head no, but I wanted to do it.

- C'mon now. A girl's gotta earn her goddamn keep around here.

Big smile as she coaxes me out of my chair. Everyone started clapping, including Daph and Meira, who left a big hole on the stage for me to step into when they left it, wondering what kind of tune a white girl like me was going to try on this room full of black women. I loved the applause, loved mother smiling so widely where she sat, head up, looking directly at me as I walked through the other tables.

- What you wanna sing girl? Cladine asked confidentially.

- Ache in the Water? You know that one?

- I do. At least I think I do. So, you start off and I'll catch up.

It was the first time I sang publicly, a bit throaty and high pitched because I was so nervous, but Cladine's playing was impeccable. She got me to the finish line and the chords she played got everyone in that room, mother included, wiping away a few tears. When you feel like you've been drowned in the river of time, that song is going to rip your heart out. She called me over to the stool where she sat holding the guitar by its neck and half whispered some good advice.

- We'd better give them something to raise their spirits, Wicla. You know this one?

And she began playing The Shoes Under My Bed, about a woman caught *in flagrante* by her nearly blind husband. Are those my shoes under your bed? Why yes they are, oh husband dear. Then whose shoes, dear wife, are the ones I'm wearin'? We all like a bit of mischief.

After that, every time we returned to Fort Ketchup, Cladine and I would entertain the women, usually with Daph and Meira calling in the high notes as they swayed behind us. If Merri and I had been spatting that day, or if she was nursing some grievance toward the highway system, or the warehouse managers of Blaine or Bakersfield, or some new guy officiously manning a roadblock, or toward some bitch amongst her customers who didn't take to Merri's brusqueness, or even toward herself for choices made in the dim past, she might skip the meal, or eat it quickly then take-off to the van where she would take her whiskey medicine, cast her thoughts to Lilith and eventually fall into a forgetful sleep.

I'm not sure when, but not long after I first sang at the Fort, mother would make sure the bars and inns we stopped for food or respite were mostly places where live music was on tap. Mother was a master at forming a plan and then letting it unfold so subtly you didn't think that the constant movement of our lives was done to plan, but instead reflected a kind of rootless chaos. Initially, we'd pull into a lot of one of these establishments just as the first set was about to start, but she'd chose a seat in the dining area.

Mother herself was a kind of star by this time, so she and I would be warm-welcomed wherever we went, sometimes treated to complimentary fare or a free drink or two, especially if she pulled in other people who, when they saw our van parked in a lot, would come in to take a look, cadge an autograph or take a 3D of themselves with her, and sometimes me, and then wish out loud that Trader Merri Weer would stop by their town soon.

Once inside the barroom, it wouldn't take me long to cock my ear toward the other end of the house to listen-in so I could parse the tunes and figure out the story of the lyrics. I got to know the names of singers and bands by asking waitresses as they came to take our orders, or from posters and flyers stapled to trees and posts or hung in storefront windows, or by searching on my vice, and though I didn't know it at the time, I was taking mental notation of different voices, male and female, of how different singers styled their phrasings, how the personalities of different frontmen and players were transmuted intact through their instruments, like water changes to steam when it's brought to a boil.

Then one day, a day after my eighteenth birthday, Merri turned right where we used to turn left, and took a table in the back of the bar. Suddenly, that which I had only seen through a doorway was in front of me – well, almost. Even at the distance between us and the stage, it felt like I had walked into the stable where baby Jesus was being born, to witness the mundane reality of human life, most always private and done behind curtains, raised to something public and miraculous.

Up there, on a raised platform, wise men and women would bring their gift of music, bang their glittering drums, cradle their guitars tight to their bodies, raise their voices to hosannas that could, if things were going just right, stir the soul. To tell the truth, even the most inept singer straining at the most forgettable song, produced a kind of miracle, and always does wherever anyone dares to make a go of their little or big talent as the case may be. If you need a new beatitude then let it be this: blessed be those who make our music.

A few nights like that and I began to lose, then lost, the

self-consciousness that had first accompanied me into those dark spaces. Merri drank and looked around, being patient, while I tapped my fingers and feet, sometimes singing with the performers under my breath, transfixed. Sometimes I'd catch her looking at me, with vicarious pleasure because she was getting ready to spring her happy trap.

We were in the center of Auburn, California, a town that was just getting back on its feet after too many desolate years, and went into the Next Next Bar, which had given up its ghost years and years before but had recently been restored and slightly renamed by a laconic guy named Chaplin Dufour, otherwise known as Chappy. He was as genial as they come, but then he could afford to be because he was about six eight, barrel-chested and strong as dirt so no one, even when he was a slightly stooped, bald sixty-year-old with a paunch, ever caused trouble in his place.

More to the point, Chappy knew my mother well, knew what she liked to drink and could say things that would gear her down to a slower pace of consumption and make her feel equally genial. He had also watched me grow from a tadpole, but until this visit, he didn't know I was a near-grown frog with a small talent for croaking.

Chappy was also the entertainment at Next Next, so at some point in the evening it was time to go on. The place was packed as it usually was on a Friday afternoon and everyone, including me, was waiting for him to ring the brass church bell which hung at the end of the bar - his signal that all present were expected to have fun, starting now. That done, he strode through the tables, slapping this and that person on the back, or grabbing someone's shoulder muscles in the vice of his hands to make them wince, and made his ways to the platform where his sidemen tuned their instruments. He kicked off his first set with a rousing rendition of one of his own songs, Sew that Hole in the American Flag, and then worked his way through a series of requests that came at him like a storm of wiffleballs from the audience.

At the end of the first set, he stepped down, said hello to a few people and chatted where a chat was interesting enough to waylay him, then returned to the bar. Mother said excuse me and went over to say hello. But it was more than an hello. Oh shit, I thought, as Chappy looked over Merri's shoulder to where I sat in a pool of amber light.

- Act Two you motherfuckers, yelled Chappy as he marched back the stage for his second set.

He strapped his guitar on and grabbed the mic stand.

- You all know the infamous and beautiful Merri Weer, a trader of some repute in these here parts.

Heads moved and looked back at mother, raising a glass to all.

- That's right Trader Merri Weer - her very self, right here in Next Next where every miserable son of a bitch feels right at home. But what you didn't know is that Merri has an even more beautiful daughter. That'd be her, right back yonder. Good evening Ms Wicla Weer. Maybe you could stand up and say hello.

Heads move again and I'm stuck in the gaze of a couple of hundred people and so I stand and just nod and mouth my hellos, knowing full well what's coming next.

- Now, it turns out that Wicla is one helluva singer. I have that on faith of her mother whose guarantee is considered ironclad if you ever get one out of her, which is rarely. So, I'm hoping this young lady will join me here on this little platform and bless us all with a couple of tunes.

What's a girl to do, right? So, I do what I am bid to do, and oh my god, what a thrill to walk through the smoky ripple of applause to that stage, then to get pulled up the small rise to where giant Chappy is clutching his guitar by the neck with his other monster hand and where we have that short, inaudible-to-all-but-us conversation that is needed to settle on the song that we will sing together.

Chappy is pleased – beyond pleased – to find out that I know a few of his songs, because – he didn't know this – I had figured out what my mother was going to do and I had prepared myself for this very day, this very moment.

Chappy mouths the song's name to the other guys and off we go with Your Dream of Me, a tender ballad that tells a woman she should give up on the man she loves because they'll never see one another again. He's doing life for avenging a wrong that was done to her by some evil bastard in time past. Then we did two more of his songs, Pothole Highway and Remember Hollywood, before I called enough (the audience wanted a lot more).

- Well, damn, said Chappy with unfeigned astonishment as I made my way to my beaming mother where she perched at the end of the bar. That girl can carry a tune.

Later that night, everyone is gone but mother and me. Once Chappy and his wait staff have put the room back in order and the women have split the tips and doffed their aprons and make for the back door, Chappy comes and sits on a stool beside us, with me in the middle.

- Thankyou, young lady. Thankyou for that. I gotta say, you took me by surprise. Everyone.

- Told you she could sing, Merri chimed in.

- You got the gift, Wicla.

- She does. I told you.

- So, what are you going to do with it?

- You think she could parlay her singing into a few dollars.

- More than a damn few, Merri. Hell, I'll pay you to sing here anytime.

- How much? Asks Merri, as I get up.

- I'm tired so, I'm going to say good night to you Chappy. Thanks for asking me to sing. I will never forget it.

Mother are you coming?

She isn't, so I shake Chappy's giant, dry hand and buss him on a stubbled cheek and head for the door, knowing his man's eyes are on me for I am young and, in those days, so very pretty. I could hear the murmur of their conversation as I opened it and walked out toward the van. The last thing I heard Merri say – again – was how much?

We slept a few hours and then headed south where we would make one more stop before we would go to Ojai to see Lawrence and Javier, rest for a few days then hit the road yet one more time. Mother took the wheel because the next stop was Folsom, which was less than a hundred miles away.

The only sound in the van was the sound of tires running fast on the highway. I was thinking about what had just happened in Auburn; mother was thinking about what was up the road and around the corner, neither of us realizing at that moment why memory and expectation always lead in opposite directions, and can, if tethered to one another, pull the human soul apart.

*Oh heart, hear how the holy and the humble howl.*

# Song 13

I took the wheel and drove the pitted Lincoln Highway west out of Folsom at a steady pace, breathing deeply to quiet a heartbeat that would boom too loudly if I didn't. The onboard vice was off so the interior of the van was not filled with its usual chatter or song. The venting windows were closed because the day was cool, so not even the thin whistle of the van pushing against the dry air disturbed the enforced silence inside. Mother lay crumpled on her bed at the back of the van, knees drawn foetally up to her chest, both hands covering her stricken face but with clenched fists.

I skirted Sacramento and finally got to the I5 AutoWay, where I relinquished control of the van to the self-drive systems which we hardly ever used, commanding it to take us to the Buttonwillow turn-off near Bakersfield where I would drive the secondary road to the forester's cabin a little bit north of NewB. I had already given Lawry a heads up and asked him to warn Javier, which he would have done anyway.

While we were on the AutoWay I was able to sit on the edge of the bed by Merri where I could stroke her back and forehead because, despite the considerable anxiety that was stirring in my guts, I knew she needed to be comforted. When she finally fell asleep, I made a pot of tea and made a sandwich, which I ate in glum, and I have to say, almost disgusted silence on the couch behind the driver's seat. A couple of times I thought I heard her whimper, so I went to her, finding her asleep, but on both occasions in the ravel of a hard dream, dreams that she would revisit many times in the years to come.

So, what had happened?

Our visit to FSP was to be a surprise for Lilith, and a surprise it was. It was almost dusk when we pulled into the Bee Zone as usual, evoking a happy flutter from the women there, and then parked in the place where we always did our business. Mother stopped the engine as she rose out of the driver's seat, spun toward the door which she unlatched and pushed open, then jumped down, already in full stride as she made for Lilith's quarters – she would be there by this time – calling back to me in a breathless voice above the jangle of all her ornaments to say she would be back soon. Yeah, after all the work is done, I thought.

I hadn't pulled half our stock out to the side of the van before I saw her coming toward us in a fast, angry and bewildered march. When she got to the small pile of stuff I had already brought out, she grabbed the topmost box and heaved it into the van, then another, and another as I stood amongst a two or three deep semi-circle of women watching mother's red-faced show of unmitigated anger.

- Mother, what...?

- Get in!

- But...

- Get the fuck in the van!

She reached her hands up to the door jambs, pulled herself up then turned to glare at me.

- Now!

As Merri sat herself down in the driver's seat waiting for me to get my sorry ass into the vehicle, one of the women, who'd been standing beside me while we were watching Merri, put her hand on my arm and leaned in.

- The Warden's got a new girlfriend. One of the Bees.

So, a betrayal.
Mother had knocked on Lilith's door. Lilith assumed one of the guards needed her.

- Come!

Mother entered, saw Lilith standing at the chest that served as her liquor cabinet pouring drinks. She did not see, not right away, the other woman, freshly scrubbed, blonde, slim if not skinny, a bit toothy, sitting languorously on the couch across the small room, one arm draped along its back, a pillow behind her. The same pillow upon which my mother had rested her head as Lilith, kneeling on the floor, flicked and tickled my mother's fancy. Pardon my euphemisms.

Now here she was, in the driver's seat, inebriated with emotion, sweating, panting.

- I'll drive mother.

- No.

- Yes.

- Go lie down.

- No.

- Yes.

Short standoff. She relents because tears are welling and she does not want me to see her distraught and vulnerable and looking like a damn fool.

Are Lawry and Jav going to be OK with this, I wondered, as I wound down the friable Maricopa Highway. They had always been good friends to us, always. Years ago, they cleared a patch beside their driveway to make way for Trader Merri Weer's truck, and they ran electric and water to a fat post beside it so, when we came we could connect with a little bit of civilization. We slept in the van, a practice established when I was an infant, when mother regained her senses – sort of - and surrendered the bedroom she used during her first stay there. More than anything, the boundary then established enabled the friendship to endure.

When we were there, most nights we took evening meals with them in the house – they often go out to party in Ojai – with everyone chipping in on kitchen duty before and after. We had a lot of fun goofing off, playing games, dancing to music that I only liked when I was with them – club music made to inspire the body, not the mind. Lawry doesn't drink much, but Javier does and mother's presence always liberated him he would say, pinching Lawry's stick-in-the-mud cheek when Lawry gave him the hairy eyeball for overdoing it. Lawrence and I usually sat talking to one another from either end of the long leather couch while Merri and Javier cut it up on the makeshift dance floor – where the coffee table usually sat - sometimes slopping drinks which made irritated Lawrence run to the kitchen for a rag.

Jav was now head of the Studio's Creative Division, and Lawrence had been promoted to Head of Security not just for the Studios but for the City of Ojai, and the Ojai Park where they made their delightful, art-filled home. They were mostly grey-haired, more than middle-aged men, by the time I pulled into the cabin drive and they had both had a lot of practice dealing with difficult customers as they called them.

Mother wasn't a piece of cake sometimes, but they could handle her. Not that they wanted to. But by then, I was like their daughter too, and so, I have to say, for my sake, they went above and beyond and they knew me well enough to know that if I was coming to them with a very hurt Merri in tow, it was because the hurt was from a quick-deep wound that needed proper tending to. That I, in fact, would be suffering under the weight of a responsibility I should shake, but wouldn't.

No doubt, Lilith Morrigan convinced herself that mother's reaction to discovering her with another woman was histrionic. How could mother be so naïve as to think that Lilith would not entertain dalliances in the six months that usually passed between our visits to FSP? How, especially, when she had an army of women more or less at her disposal, many of whom were heterosexual to their core, but not unwilling to float on

Lilith's large breasts and kiss her dry mouth if extra privileges might ensue? Especially when Lilith had revealed, in her all too brief hours with Merri, a huge, grunting, groaning appetite for sex whose strength and noise lifted Merri off the heavy planet she traveled into a firmament of cosmic release and orgasmic sparkle. It would be too bad for the Bees that Merri would not come again, but she could easily lay that at Merri's misunderstanding feet - and did.

But for my mother, Lilith's nonchalant promiscuity cut deep and severed some necessary cord of sanity. Merri was never the same. Oh, she continued to do our business and pulled her weight, but the jocularity that had leavened her toughness went missing. She bargained tougher, was less forgiving of those who wanted her to take as good as she could give, was not as generous as she used to be when some poor soul needed something to take the sting out of her misery, and she averted her eyes even to the most pleasant of the women who tried to engage with her, as though all women were somehow complicit in Lilith's betrayal.

Merri now walked and worked in a world where both men and women could not be trusted except to grab her in their hands, bend her to their purposes, split her open and have what they wanted from her, with her own stupid, unwise consent, and sometimes, as I found out once we were at Ojai, without.

One morning, Lawrence and I were chatting on the deck behind the cabin looking out into the trees that populated the downslope there. I told him about singing to the women at Fort Ketchup way back when, how Cladine's singing and playing made me feel, how I spent my time when mother was driving scouring the cloud for songs and singing, how the vibrations of song penetrated my outward calm but made me feel caught on the rim of an ecstatic whirlpool. I told him how as a culmination of all of that, just before the last fateful visit to Folsom, I had taken the stage with Chaplin Dufour and I confessed to the fact that I had gone into that bar ready to perform, so that I would not have to play the role of the surprised amateur deserving of polite attention and courteous applause.

-   Well then, you are going to have to sing for Javier and me, aren't you?

-   I'll hum a few bars, how's that?

-   I know a place in Ojai where they love to hear from new talent.

-   I don't know if they will like my type of music.

-   What kind?

-   Not club.

-   I didn't think so. Trust me.

Behind us we could turn our heads and see Javier and Merri working on a salad, clinking quarter filled glasses of a red wine recently obtained by Jav from a local vineyard. Javier sipped, mother gulped, poured herself more.

Later, dinner done, a drunken scene that caught Javier, Lawrence, and even me, by surprise. Merri became sloppy, slurred her speech, got off balance even sitting in a chair. She burbled angry words into the open mouth of her glass. Javier, who had been floating above the table, happily as only he could, came crashing down. Lawrence twisted his napkin and laid it beside his plate as he stiffly pushed his chair back from the table, disgusted at the unfolding scene. He looked at me where I sat at the table, kitty corner, coming to a boil in the heat of a rising anger. I stood and moved toward Merri so I could pick her up under her arms and drag her, kicking and screaming if that's the way it was going to be, back to the van, and out of the presence of the horrified men.

But the animal in my mother would not be cornered. She too rose, then shifted to a knuckles-down stance leaning on the other end of the table, breathing fire.

- I was raped! Raped!

- No mother.

- Merri, c'mon now, said Javier as Lawrence shot a what-the-hell-do-we-do now glance at him.

- Don't you dare say it didn't happen, she said looking at me. Don't you dare you little shit!

- By Lilith, mother? I asked.

- Not by Lilith. No. No. No. No. By those men!

- Where mother? I said inching closer to her.

- Give me that goddamn glass. Give it!

Thinking it might calm her, I handed her the half-empty glass of wine that was shimmying in front of her barely eaten food when she slapped the table with the flats of her hands. She picked up the glass and used both hands to hold its bowl while she guzzled it, some of it drooling down her chin. She wiped her mouth with her sleeve. I stood beside her and took the glass from her. She took her head in her hands then, sobbing.

- Tell us, I said leading her to the sofa.

- I can't. Whimpering.

We sat down. Lawrence quietly sat down on the other side of her, Javier pulled up a hassock in front of her, while I stroked her back.

- After you left that guy, Clem? Those two men in Fort Smith?

- I don't know what that was. Not rape. I just let them do what the fuck they wanted to. I didn't care.

- Who raped you, mother?

She shifted suddenly and sprang to her feet.

- Get your goddamn hands off me.

She rushed the dining table and grabbed the nearly empty wine bottle and tried to pour what was left in her glass.

- Enough Merri, said Lawrence.

She drank all that she poured.

- Enough Merri! he repeated.

Staggering, she made for the kitchen. Javier got around in front of her and blocked the way. She tried to get around him but couldn't. Lawrence was now behind her. Stepping laterally, she got out from between them then backed up, and wagged an accusatory finger in their faces.

- No, no, not again. Not ever again.

Lawrence and Javier looked at one another.

- We're not going to hurt you, said Javier.

Lawrence looked at me.

- Mother stop!

I stood and approached. I just wanted to get her out of there. She did not realize how angry Lawrence was becoming, what damage was being done. Backing up she collided with a chair and knocked it to a tilt. She turned to try to stop it from falling to its side and lost her balance and tumbled with it. She caught her forehead on one of its arms and drew blood from a gash above her left eye. Now on her knees with hands down on the floor, head hanging and dripping blood into the rug upon which she kneeled and shuddered, out of breath, drunk. Then in that moment of silence that comes before a prayer, she drew herself up, sat back on her haunches suddenly alone in a church of pain. A she cried, she cried out of her soul's belly.

- Oh, Lilith. Oh, Lilith. Oh, Lilith.

Once we got her to her feet, I walked her out to the van and put her to bed. That done I went back to the house where Lawrence and Javier were finishing the dishes in the kitchen, saying not a word between them. I gave them each a wordless hug and when I finished, they both came around me and supported me in the circle of their arms, a pitied girl.

Some weeks later, after as much prying, needling and insisting as I needed to wear her down, mother finally told me that many years before things had broken bad in Albuquerque when she was still working Route 66. An episode long forgotten, or so she thought.

She had rolled into the city during the mid-morning quiet, looking for a place to park the van so it could charge-up and she could get some sleep. She saw a deserted car wash with its big roll-up doors open at both ends and drove around to the back of the building. Not a human in sight, not on the highway, not by the other abandoned buildings on the strip, not on the flat, pulverized dirt that extended out behind the car wash to the low, purple mountains in the middle distance.

She made coffee, eggs and toast, ate listening to some version of the news as it fell out of the vice propped on the egg carton in front of her, tidied-up and then went for what she called a lie-down on the couch behind the driver's seat, peeling off a pair of high, Western-tooled boots before swinging her legs up off the floor. A deep, dreamless sleep, from which she was awakened by muted voices just outside the van an hour or two after she had closed her eyes. Voices of men. Two of them.

Bang on the van door. Bang Bang. She freezes. Bang Bang.

- Anyone home?

- She's gotta be there.

One of them tries the handle, and finds the door locked.

- It don't make no sense, Buzzy.

- Nope.

Bang Bang.

Merri stands up, pulls up the bench of the couch and extracts a loaded pistol from underneath.

- What do you boys want? She says finally.

Some inaudible whispering which she cannot even make out with her ear to the inside of the door.

- Sorry ma'am. Sorry to disturb.

- We wuz just hoping you might have some water.

- Water?

- Yes, ma'am.

- Ma'am, are you that Merri lady we hear about?

She can't decide what to do, pauses.

- Yeah, Merri Weer

- Our mammas told us all about you.

- Just water ma'am. It's already a hot day and we have to walk into town. But if you ain't got any...

- Sorry, I don't have enough to make a drink of.

- That's OK, we'll be on our way. Ma'am, thank you.

She heard more inaudible whispering, then footfalls as the men walked away from the van. She likes to help people. Sometimes the fear instinct has to be overridden. She puts the pistol in between two columns of boxes standing near the door and opens it. She leans out and sees them at fifty feet or so, walking west toward town.

- Hey!

They come back.

- I'm Buzzy. This here's my brother Toodle. Toderick. But you know, he answers to Toodle.

Sweaty faces, unshaven, Buzzy balding and thin, Toodle heavy set with a tuft of dark hair on the top of his heads, but with shaven sides. Bizarre creatures, both with equally bad teeth, and clothes that haven't been laundered and pressed for a good long time.

They had been using the back office of the car wash as their doss house for quite awhile and had been asleep when Merri pulled in earlier that morning. Toodle went out for a piss then ran back in and woke Buzzy to tell him about the van parked at the back of the building.

It was a mistake to open that door and give them a drink of water while they craned their necks to see what goodies lay inside, to give them what was left of her bread and cheese even if she would be replacing it later that day. It was a mistake to be so damned friendly because some men – a lot of men – don't know what to make of garden variety amiability.

It was a mistake to tour the car wash with them because as soon as she walked into the old office, she should have known that they were too fucking insane not to know that it's stink and filth and clutter were a place they should never bring any woman they wanted to impress. But by that time – a few hours had elapsed as they all made merry. She should, at the moment she entered that room, have realized they did not take her to that room to impress her. All those brother-whispers behind her back were the audible scrawls of their ultimate plan.

She turned to leave. They grabbed her and each took their time to rape her while the other held her down, punching her face and blackening her eyes when she resisted, turning her over for another round while she lay face down, hardly able to breath in the infested rags that one of them called a bed. With them laughing at the other's alleged incompetence and giving one another instructions on means and methods by which to have their way.

They left her laying there, exhausted, naked below the waste, shirt hiked-up over her breasts, cut and abraded where belt buckles had dug into her arms and legs, head spinning from the clouts they had administered to stifle her unheard noises and the useless twisting of her invaded body.

She got up. Made her way out to the long hall where cars used to be jerked on chains through a series of scrubbers and hoses to be cleaned, and out toward the back. And then she knew how dumb those two bastards were, because she could hear them in the van, rummaging through her goods. She managed to step-up in behind them, left arm dangling because it had been wrenched so badly, and found her gun where she had left it in the boxes stacked by the door. She stood there pointing it at them until they sensed her presence.

- Oh shit! Said Buzzy.

She got them outside then marched them into the desert behind the building, looking around for any sign of a witness while the men begged for the kind of mercy that might, if they could just crack the code of Merri's quest for personal redemption and salvation, save them because nothing else was going to and they knew it. They were going to pay the price.

- OK then, said Toodle. I get it. We got it comin.'

Three hundred or so yards off the highway, Toodle on his knees, all begging done. Bang Bang. Buzzy standing in defiance, looking into the morning sun. He lurched at Merri. Bang, Bang. Dropped dead in his tracks.

*In the busted bastions of belief, we burn.*

# Song 14

The van was just passing through the north gate on the Maricopa when I awoke, with mother at the wheel. She was putting distance between herself and last night's hysterics. She cut me off when I tried to talk about them; cheerfully said she couldn't remember a thing, while she sang to the happy song playing on the vice and promised a fun trip ahead. She kept the song's beat, tapping on the steering wheel, jangling the dozen bracelets hanging from both wrists.

- Maybe this time, she said, we'll stick to 99, then fork off on the old 395 route. You always like that route. Right? Right?

- We're not going to Folsom?

- Of course not. Why would we go there again so soon?

We stopped at Bakersfield as dawn broke, loaded the van, then parked in our usual spot until late afternoon and headed north once again. Only this time I felt tricked and trapped, feelings I could not discuss with Merri, even if I could have articulated them, any more than she would confide her truest feelings in me had she been able to find the means. But in the cell of my room, as far away as I could get from her, I worked with words on my tablet to the no-nonsense hum of the wheels as we drove to Yuba, and watched in some amazement as a small, ridiculous poem appeared before my eyes. I would later put some music around it.

*I'll feed my baby when she cries;*
*I'll let her go when off she flies.*
*The hunger's hers, but the nest is mine.*
*We do what we must under blue, blue skies.*
*I'll let her go when off she flies.*

There were other verses, but you get the drift.

We made three circuits on that trip and another three on the next one, never stopping at Folsom or Fort Ketchup. We avoided Ojai with excuses that I messaged to Lawrence and Javier, who understood of course. But on those circuits I did get to sing at a few more roadhouses and bars, covering all kinds of tunes played by a myriad of bands while my mother sat in the darkness drinking and finger-whistling when I finished a song. From time to time I'd look down on a dance floor in front of me, and there she would be, eyes closed, turning and turning with hands in the air, dancing with some man who'd asked her at just the right time, three or four drinks into the night. But woe betide him if he tried to leverage her momentary joy into something more intimate.

My spirits lifted and so did Merri's because now we both had our reasons for being on the road, reasons rooted in a dark need for adulation, each with our own talents for drawing it out of people who would bestow it upon us if we gave them a way out of the humdrum, pinched routines of their lives. Trader Merri Weer's fame spread farther and wider – we were dipping our toes into the western reaches of Idaho and Nevada - not least because she had a daughter with a talent for singing. What was her name? Wicla? What kind of a name is that? Wicla! But damn that girl can sing.

We were poking along Highway 101, some of the old stretches took us close to the coast, but it swung inland onto miles of new pavement where the old highway had more or less fallen into the ocean along with some of the towns it used to connect. We were doing business in a scrubby little place called Leggett when we got a message from Tithy telling us to come quick, Cladine was dying and Willia was in a state.

My hand shaking and my heart full of dread, I showed Mother Tithy's message as she was trying to conclude a deal. A stout, fierce looking Indian woman with a hairlip was trying to barter a couple of woven baskets she claimed to have made herself for a box of loose and jumbled jewels and trinkets. Merri was wondering what the Indian lady had seen in the box that she herself hadn't but guessed there might be something more valuable in it than two dubious baskets.

- Mother, I said, as I again showed her my vice.

- Sorry, ma'am, my daughter can be a little rude at times.

I let her finish doing the trade but she walked away. I knew she had seen Tithy's words; that she had been stricken by them. I caught up with her as she started to open a couple of cardboard boxes a gaggle of women at the other end of our table had been hoping to take a look at. She wouldn't look at me.

- I'll tell her we're coming.

- It's been a long time since you ladies have seen anything like these, she said, folding back the box lids to reveal the silk panties – all sizes and colors – inside. Silk, not cotton, just in case you forgot what real silk looks like. Your old men would love to get a whiff, eh?

- Mother!

The women pawed through the undies with their rough hands, most of them looking for large sizes. Mother could feel my glare.

- Tell her two or three days. We'll be there in two or three days.

Once the last of our customers had left, I was ready to pounce.

- I told Tithy we'd be there tomorrow.

- No can do, dear, said Merri, while she broke down the empty boxes and tied them in a bundle.

- I told her tomorrow. Cladine is dying.

- Cladine has been dying as long as I've known her. Now, let's get this place tidied up. Sooner done, sooner we can start heading north.

We stopped at Piercy for awhile, then at a place between Benbow and Garberville, moving through the redwood forest, still doing its best to outlast the life of men. I kept pleading with her to skip these visits, but she made one more stop at Phillipsville to see if we could move the last of our stuff, but it was not to be. So, she pulled-up in Rio Dell with just a few more things to flog, a place like all the others where no one gave a shit about Cladine and Willia, notwithstanding that many of them were now shod with Fort Ketchup boots and shoes thanks to my mother's and my proselytizing over the years. She would have stopped in Fortuna too if at Rio Del I hadn't already put myself in the driver's seat and told her I was driving. By that time, mother had gone quiet. Indeed, sitting on the couch behind me with a pillow clutched to her chest, she was silent as lakewater from there all the way to Fort Ketchup.

Cladine was dead by the time we arrived. I was furious, but too sad to let fly at Merri who was at any rate, dealing with her own terrifyingly silent grief. The women would bury Cladine the following day after two days of waking her out in the dining hall. Tithy told me that Wil, whose hair was now shockingly white, had been sitting beside the rough-made casket on a hard-backed chair, regal in her pain, staring straight ahead, taking no food or drink, mute for as long as Cladine had been resting there. Cladine's guitar, fully strung and probably tuned was laying across the top of the casket, no doubt, I thought, to be buried with her.

The other women of the Fort were milling under the over-hangs of the blockade buildings, or in small clumps in the quadrangle. I found Tithy in Wil's office trying to deal with matters that Wil had let slip while she nursed Cladine through

Cladine's final days.

- Wil needs food, Tithy. Something to drink.

- We tried, Wicla.

- Maybe if I try.

- No harm in that. Where's Merri?

- She went to her room. Well, you know, her room from way back when. She's dropped off at last.

- That's what we still call it too. Merri's Room.

- Why don't you get some sleep Tithorea? It will be a tough day tomorrow.

- I gotta do this shit.

- No, you don't. It will wait.

I went in the back way to the kitchen and prepared a sandwich and a cup of tea for Wil, then pushed through the saloon doors into the dining hall.

- Wil. It's me Wicla.

I came around in front of her holding the plate and saucer.

- You should eat something.

She looked up at me.

- I have but one fucking thing left to do in this old world, Wicla.

- We'll give her a fine send off tomorrow, Wil.

- Put that down over there and draw up a chair, girl.

I did, and I saw what I had not seen earlier. Willia's old face was thin and drawn.

- Grab hold of that there guitar, wouldja?

I stood up and took hold of it by its neck and felt the sudden weight of Cladine's thick body come along with it.

- Sit.

I sat and laid the guitar across my knees.

- That is the sum total of Cladine's remaining earthly possessions. Almost the last thing she told me to do was to make sure you got it.

She leaned over and put her hand on the guitar.

- This is your fuckin' guitar now. Old Mud goes with you.

I started to protest.

- Now, don't you say a fuckin' word, girl.

- But I don't know how to play.

- She taught you everything you need to know. Just like
  she taught me what I goddamn well needed to know,
  she whispered.

She used a damp handkerchief to press against her eyes,
trying to dam the tears that were pooling in her eyes.

- Now, I just want to be alone with her, Wicla, and pardon
  me, but...

- I understand.

I stood, still holding the guitar.

- Take that fucking thing with you. You'll need it tomorrow.

I walked quietly out of the dining room feeling a sense of
dread, knowing that Wil had turned back inside herself. All the
Fort women had retired to their quarters and turned off their
lamps. The black square in the window frame of my mother's
room said that she too was asleep. But a light still shone in the
office window where Tithy sat feeling overwhelmed, and I was
mortally awake.

Once I got the van warmed up a bit, I sat down on the couch

and pulled Cladine's guitar to me and I did what I had done so many times in the past even though I had nothing but air to play with. But now, I fingered the frets with my left hand while I strummed these real strings with my right, and I half sang songs I knew from all the times I had sung with Cladine and Chappy and all the other bands along the road, wondering what Willia meant when I said I would need the guitar tomorrow. And I shoved down the idea that I would be expected to play and sing at the funeral, but with the full realization that was exactly what she meant.

So, all night Old Mud and I worked together and through the night, I felt Cladine's presence close at hand, her round, beautiful, smiling face looking on as I struggled saying c'mon girl, c'mon girl, breathe. Easiest thing there is in life. And by morning, Cladine and that guitar had delivered me into a new world.

A commotion outside the van. Vehicles arrived. Voices. Doors opened and closed. Woke me from my hard-going reverie. Old Mud leaned against a stack of boxes like a drunk fallen asleep on his feet against an alleyway garbage bin. The door to the van opened, the van rocked as mother put her weight on the step and bounded in, right to me where I lay, gave me a shake, saw my eyes already open.

- Sit up. Wicla, sit up.

- What's wrong?

- I have to tell you something.

Was that crying I heard inside the stockade? Wailing? Someone in the shoe factory was banging nails with a heavy hammer. More vehicles arrived. I heard the shudder of a bus stopping, and then the trample of more feet and the whisper-talk of more people. I sat up and put the plaid blanket that I had drawn up over me the night before around my shoulders then Merri sat down beside me. She put a hand on the back of my shoulder and held it there for longer than she had ever done before.

-   Willia's dead, Wicla.

Did I hear her say Willia?

-   Cladine. Cladine died, mother.

Is she that out of touch with reality? I wonder.

-   Wil took her own life, dear.

Has she ever called me dear before?

-   Willia took pills. They were the pills she asked me to get and bring next time we came.

I felt mother stiffen as she looked up and out the door off into space. Not my fault she was thinking. I'm pretty sure she was.

-   She downed them all and then went to sleep right on

that chair she was sitting on and God himself couldn't get her to stand up let alone ring the breakfast bell as she always did.

A short pause as Merri realized her own head was hanging. Grief creeps in for some; hits others with a thunderbolt that fries their soul. Mother felt the approaching darkness. I was burning where I sat.

- There was a half glass of water sitting on Cladine's casket, she said. She must have used some when she took the pills.

Through the open door I could see a couple of the Fort women carrying a new-made casket toward the Fort gate.

- They're going to bury them out by Boy Adam and the others. So, c'mon, we have to do our bit. Respect is due here today. God knows it is.

What is all this God talk? I feel inside the smoke of my being rising from a kindled flame.

- I'll be right there, mother.

She saw I needed a moment.

- I'll go join the others. Wear something warm. It's nasty cold and there's a stiff breeze blowing off the water.

When I stepped out of the van there were buses and cars neatly parked outside the palisade on a stretch of grass where on sunnier days the women played soccer and field hockey, but no one was in sight. I carried myself, with Old Mud slung down my side from my shoulder, toward the gate where I could hear nothing but silence within.

The hundred plus women of the Fort, all dressed in long white coats and black Fort Ketchup boots were standing still in three columns facing the porch in front of the dining hall. Tithy stood on the porch, also dressed in a white coat but with a red sash running across her chest from left to right looking out over the assembly. Between the porch and the gathered Fort women, stood a large, black wagon with large, spoked iron wheels, a relic restored under Willia's direction some years earlier to serve as the community's hearse.

Another hundred plus people – mostly women but a couple of dozen men too - stood in the overhangs that fronted the blockade buildings. Some were women who had once stayed at Fort Ketchup but most were strangers to me, probably the husbands, lovers and sons of those who refused to remain cloistered and celibate, but who could not shake the values they had been expected to rise to while in Willia's and Cladine's care. All but one were strangers, that is. Erato stood next to my mother in front of my mother's room and shivered in a tattered, buttonless coat, tears streaming down the runnels of her hardlife face as my mother clutched her arm and from time-to-time wiped Erato's cheeks with the back of her hand.

Tithy turned toward the double doors into the dining hall and nodded. The doors swung in and two of the younger girls held them that way while Cladine's coffin was carried out by six women led by Daph. Once it was laid on the wagon, another six women led by Meira emerged carrying Wil's coffin and laid it beside Cladine. Once done, Meira and Daph led these twelve to the front of the wagon where they picked up the shafts. Tithy walked to the front of them and began walking, with Daph and Meira behind her, then the bearers and the wagon, then the Fort women slow marching behind, almost all crying, many sobbing, then the rest of us sad as any there.

Tithy led us through the orchard, today ringed by dozens of locals who had come to mourn with their neighbors, men with hats doffed, women and children standing still with the stiff wind stirring their kerchiefs and hair, a newborn wailing his deft counterpoint, a few apples that missed their picking swinging on their fragile stems. We came soon enough to the burial ground at its far end where Tithy mounted a small hillock just to the side of a large open grave, widened just that morning to accommodate the dead saints.

Tithy's eyes scanned the crowd and found me. I made my way up between the columns of women, some said sing it, sing it as I passed them by. I walked up the hillock and waited for Tithy to walk down, slowly on the edges of her boots because the slick grass was laden with hoar frost.

I hooked the guitar on its strap and pulled it in front of me looking down at it instead of to those who stood waiting for music to accompany their lamentations. I strummed but could not hear the noise I made. My fingers were too cold. I made a start at the first chords anyway and made it through two of the opening phrases. My fingers were too cold; the guitar would not keep its tuning. The mourners looked at me wondering whether my grief had come between me and the music. Tithy's shoulders slumped because she wanted Cladine and Willia to know she could manage and now she might be sending them imperfectly off into their conjoined eternity. My mother was embarrassed and shrunk a bit where she stood in the outer circle shaking her head a little.

But then, I saw Erato come toward me through the ranks. She joined me where I stood, looking alternatively at me, Tithy and all those below our feet, overcoming in this brave act the ordinary pain of those crucified by life, but also the special pains of remorse and shame that had, until this day, draped her whole existence in the far-off city. And then I knew what must be done. I handed the guitar to her and nodded that I would be alright. She put it around her shoulders so it could hang down her back while I beckoned for Daph and Meira to join us.

With Daph and Meira harmonizing while they held Erato's hands beside me, I sang. I sang Broken Rib, one of the old bluesy-hymns Cladine sang to her girls in the dining hall as a kind of moral tale, but sang, most especially into the deep heart of her most dearly beloved, Willia, who always sat through it as though Cladine's singing was a dessert she would take a pass on, but really, behind that tough old mask, making a meal of all that love.

*A woman's made of better stuff*
*Than the broken rib of man.*
*We are the fruit of mystery,*
*We live where life began.*

*I am not the broken rib of man*
*But have a heartbeat all my own,*

180

*From God's own hand I come*
*To you, so we'll never be alone.*

There are a few more verses, all tied together with a chorus that Cladine somehow roared, but in a whispered voice, that I could not imitate that day, but only do my best to get across. The chorus, oh yes, it was sung-out in the frosted air by the Fort women, everyone.

*I am not the broken rib of man.*
*It's of the tree of life I'm made.*
*And in its wood I will be borne*
*Into eternity, but unafraid.*

# Song 15

It was two years before we returned to Fort Ketchup again. Tithy had gone grey trying to keep it going but was failing. Erato had stayed awhile after the funerals, retreating to mother's room where she at last overcame her heroin addiction. She tried to help Tithy by proposing solutions to easy problems that befuddled her 'sister', but neither Tithy or most of the other women, reduced in numbers to about half just two years earlier, would take advice from a drug-addicted prostitute, which is how, in the bitter competitions that festered within the palisade walls, they wanted to keep Erato in their thoughts. So, Erato returned to Portland, but this time, found meagre employment in a soup kitchen where she captured the heart of a man – a white man named Francis, actually – whom she had helped rescue with hot broth and a wicked sense of humour.

Daph, a few pounds heavier and marching into wicked flashes of menopause, and Meira, a few pounds lighter and happier somehow, were still there, but would not be, they told us, if there was somewhere they could go. They lasted another three years before they were persuaded to join a traveling road show where they shucked off the drear habits of the Fort, physically and mentally, and let free the sexy women they had kept under wraps. Who knew? Once they had tasted the outside world, however, and had their fill of its bitter fruit, they returned to the Fort and its privations. Was that a defeat or a victory? Both.

I was prepared to buy a lot of the shoes they had been stitching together for the last many months, but mother was not because, in truth, they were poorly made. Charity was not among her virtues. As a foolish attempt to make it right with the women, I arrived at the dining hall that night with Old Mud in hand, and after dinner Daph and Meira and I seduced the ladies and had our way with them. Had them on their feet in fact, dancing into the wee hours as the disapproving ghost of Willia glared at them, and Cladine's ghost gave them the wink and nod.

By the end of that two years, Trader Merri Weer's routing through the western states was dictated more by the location of the gigs I was being offered on a regular basis than by a sane map. We go where the money is, my mother said, and as the money I was earning was about the same, and sometimes greater at fewer stops, than the money we could make turning over our inventory, these gigs were driving the van. In fact, we often made it close to Bakersfield or Blaine with our cargo space empty when an invitation to do a show arrived, causing us to U turn or allemande left or right down some misbegotten side road or highway to our destination.

Mother did the negotiating with these barroom impresarios, requiring a twenty percent deposit paid in advance into our account. She would get more money out of them than I would – hell, I would probably have done those early gigs for free - plus the right to pass the hat, plus meals and plenty of drink for her, plus two rooms if it were that kind of place, or a safe parking spot if it wasn't. We cut some slack for Chappy, but we made sure we only got there once every six months or so because mother didn't want us to be taken advantage of on sentimental grounds. Word of our imminent arrival would spread and so we were assured of good trading too, usually at one end of the roadhouse lot, if we had cargo at hand.

Merri was already a legend of sorts, but I was the new, new thing, and together we constituted something of a *duo incrediblia* as one of my thoroughly Americanized Latin lovers said. Well, he had Spanish blood, he bragged, as he peeled-off his much-scuffed and thin-soled boots while sitting on the side of my bed. His people had come to Oregon a couple of hundred years ago to pick olives.

I guess this is the time to confess that I had become a bit of a slut once I got the hang of sex. Promiscuous if not sluttish, let us say. Some rough jewel of a man had deprived me of my virginity three years earlier in a storage shed out behind the Next Next, in Auburn, California, where Chappy had allowed him to put a mattress on the floor until better times came 'round. No, I can't say that he took it from me. I donated it to my own cause, which was the cause of satisfying a rising need that I knew was not going to be satisfied in any other way.

I had watched a good deal of porn on my vice by then, while mother drove the van, watching avidly, sometimes with disgust, as men and women or women and women, in couples or threesomes, or orgiastic trysts, moaned and groaned, until the man or men were shooting lassos of jiz out of their penises and the women were shuddering through the last act, face-up, face-down, or in some twisted sideways position that mimicked the grimaces on their faces, as they case might be.

It didn't take me too long, once I had embarked on my own sexual adventures, to know that the men couldn't fake it but those women almost always did. Porn is always about the ego and the cock, isn't it?

So, I knew the basics, knew what to expect, kind of, but did not know, until much later, that all those early sexual experiences were jacked-up on post-show adrenalin and by the demands of my own ego, which was always thrilled by the adulation of the crowd, but seemed also to need the attention, flattery and desire of just one guy. I would single him out from the stage during a gig or in the warm afterglow of a performance when I went to the bar to get a drink.

I learned that a shot or two of bourbon let me find the exact way to let a man think he was conducting a seduction when, in fact, I had already surrendered. He would have me and I would make him grateful because I had learned from the porn goddesses whose studied efforts stream through America's ether, how to serve the cock. But I would not give more to the body whose weight upon me sweated and panted for release because I had no more to give than the singing I had already given to a room. Oh yes, some men gave me a lot of pleasure, or I took it if they were stinting, but my pleasure always felt like an accident, until some years later when I fell into the arms of Wynkyn DeWorde, of whom, more later. For Wynkyn sex was a grand conversation.

Singing Broken Rib at Wil's and Cal's funeral, I was both in the moment and floating above it, and while I was floating, looking down at Old Mud slung across Erato's back as she harmonized with Daph and Meira, I felt an even deeper need than the need for love – the need to sing out of my own soul, to give that instrument a new life now that Cladine was dead. Make it mine in the memory of her.

And so, it was that on the very night we put Cladine and

Willia in the ground, I began to write my own songs and began learning as I did, how to really play that guitar. As time went by, until I started singing at the Polyphemus club, I hardly ever covered the songs of others unless it was to accompany another singer-songwriter on one of theirs, or unless some song-maker friend of ours had died and their survivors wanted to testify on his or her behalf.

At first, I stole time in between shifts at the wheel or a day's trading and concocted songs out of my own feelings, or by figuring out how a popular song worked and using its mechanics to put a tune together. I would do the same with old songs, particularly out of the old blues stuff, one hundred, two hundred years old stuff, that Cladine loved because they tapped something deep in me, plucked at the base chords.

One day while I was listening to a local station on my vice – I was driving at the time – the DJ introduced some really old stuff from the late 20th Century and very early 21st. Who were these people? I learned later: Bob Dylan, Joni Mitchell, Paul Simon, Leonard Cohen, Emmylou Harris and more. I had to turn off the vice because I did not know what to do with my time on earth if it was not to write songs like they wrote and bring them, like they did, off the pages where they were first scrawled and scribbled into their other existence, out here in the midst of moving life.

Don't get me wrong. When I sang those first songs I wrote they hit home. These were the songs of love and longing that somehow wrenched themselves out of my guts and found their way to expression in lyric and tune. I sang a couple even during that last, infamous concert I did all few years ago in California. More than a few, maybe.

My songs get played on the radio, even the versions I did with Old Mud and my original backing band. Other singers cover them too, In fact, some of them do better at the singing part than I did because, let's be honest, there are people who sing better than I do. Songs like Timberfall, Fish in the Net and You Ripped My Heart Out You Dirty Bastard. Remember that one?

*I am the greater fool*
*I believed in love*
*And I believed in us.*
*I loved inside the golden rule,*
*But you did not give unto me*
*What I had given unto you.*

Everyone was trying to guess who the guy was, but actually I wrote it after Merri had done something outrageous that hurt me to the quick. But betrayals are as common as grass aren't they? Inspiration is what inspiration does.

After listening to the songs of those long-dead singers, I was thrown into a period of self doubt. I felt like a lightweight. Actually, I felt like a fraud. It didn't matter that even in those days in some dingy bar or dilapidated theater or even in some old well-lit concert hall or echoing school gym, I would walk on stage and look out over an already cheering crowd, calling my name. Fans would yell out the names of my songs and wait for me to sing them because my lyrics would say to their boyfriend or girlfriend or wife or husband or partner or whomever it might be, what they themselves could not say even though the person they loved so much might be sitting right beside them.

I would sing about love's arrow, sometimes poison tipped, love's disappointments and love's hopes, about loneliness in love, loneliness without love, the loneliness of separations, about long love, short love, love turned into hate. I got the love thing down and I go it from listening to other people's music, not from listening to my own beating heart.

Merri, even though shrunken and spindly by then, would say she'd be happy to take the wheel so I could do some writing but I would insist on staying in the driver's seat. If Merri saw a small cluster of women waiting up ahead, she would tell me she could handle the trade so I could keep my train of thought if I were working on a song. I would join her anyway because my train of thought had gone off the rails.

She thought I might be sick because I was napping a lot. She thought I must be missing somebody I'd met in some bar back in the direction from which we'd come because I would go for a long walk away from the van by myself and had the forlorn look of someone chewing on love's hunger pains. Then she switched gears and wondered what kind of secret was I keeping. Was I pregnant? No way. I took my annual pill religiously, on my birthday. Did I have some ache or pain that might be presaging a cancer I didn't want to talk about? Don't be silly. And finally

- Did that guy hurt you, back there, that asshole you took to your bed even though I tried to warn you he had a mean look and curled fist. Did he hurt you, Wicla? Never ever trust a man with an attitude like that to treat you right, particularly in the bedroom.

- Dando? You mean, Dando, mother?

- He's got a bit of a reputation for beating on women.

- Oh, mother…. We've known Dando for years. When he takes his pants off he's the sweetest guy there is.

- And hung like a horse, I hear. Are you bruised?

In fact, I was depressed, just not so depressed that I couldn't do a day's work, either at the side of the van while we traded or at some venue where I was doing a three-set gig backed up by local musicians. Even when I sang without the passion I usually felt, as I did during that period, my songs sold the crowd, and it made Merri back-off because once she had run through all the horrible possibilities that might have shut me down, she realized I just needed some time for whatever it was that was stewing in my head to be declared done.

We went south to Bakersfield, finally, where we re-stocked. I had already been in touch with Jav and Lawry and asked if it would be OK to visit, feeling like I was taking a chance in doing so. They each replied immediately to say don't even think about not coming. We had been afraid to land on their doorstep and had stayed away but also incommunicado for more than two years. But they were hurt and truly perplexed that in all those months we hadn't been in touch and feared we had thrown them over because of some unfixed misunderstanding. Yet none of us had reached out to the other until now.

In truth, just the right amount of time had gone by for mother's vomited, thrashing confession of her rape to be absorbed by each of us in our own way, for her to be relieved just a little of the brutal self pity that had knotted-up in her guts, way down deep below the level of self-knowing, for us to take some of it and hold it in our own hearts as a true and just pity for the stoic woman we all loved.

Now, about that visit. We had an amazing amount of fun, which is first and foremost what I remember. We ate, drank, danced, sang, hugged, joked, played, and laughed 'til we ached. Jav and Merri drank a bit too much, far too much, while Lawrence and I made sure that we stayed between the ditches where the trolls and monsters awaited a crash that would deliver Merri to them, or any one of us, really.

While Lawry and I were in the kitchen one evening after dinner, scraping plates and rinsing them for a later washing, he turned to me and threw his dish cloth over his shoulder and engaged me with a look I hadn't seen before. Turns out it was pride, a kind of fatherly pride actually.

- What?

- You think Jav and I don't know Wicla my dear.

- About?

- About your singing. You're famous for godsake! Like your mother.

- Lawry…

- I take that back. She's a legend, true. Everyone knows Trader Merri. Everyone.

I blushed.

- But you, he said, you are ascending into the realm of the angels.

- Don't.

- You are.

- Don't.

- Don't, don't me, little girl. So, question one. You're making money, right?

- A little.

- Where's it going?

- Mother's keeping it. Why?

- I want you to meet some people

- Who?

- People you need to know.

- What's your second question, Lawrence?

- Javier made cherry pie. You want some? Yes, you do! C'mon.

There was a party in Ojai the next night that we were invited to. Javier and Lawrence would escort us and keep us close because they knew our nerves were going to be rattled to the point of wanting to flee out of our own nerve-jangled skin if they didn't. Many important people would be there, but there were two people especially who I was going to meet. Lawrence threw in 'for business', knowing that I might pass on a social occasion where neither I nor my mother could possibly fit, but not if there was business to be done.

Javier told mother to go as Trader Merri. These folks are showbiz mostly and costumes are their stock in trade. But I was to dress-up properly so he had already raided the costume department at the studio where he found a long, sleeveless, scarlet gown, a set of heels that he knew I could manage with a bit of practice and a string of pearls, the real thing. He took me into the spare room where all were laid out on the quilted bed and he told me to strip naked.

- Oh, Wicla, wicked, wicked girl. My god you look so delicious that I could eat you myself.

- You're gay, Javier.

- I almost forgot. And here I am with a little woody just for you.

I blushed again but laughed.

- OK, first thing, hair and makeup.

Off to the bathroom for that because it had mirrors and excoriatingly bright lights where all my blemishes were disconcertingly visible. Eyebrow plucking – who knew what a ticklish pain could feel like. Every pluck exquisite in its own way. Eyes. Cheeks. Hair combing and spritzing. Wow! Look at me, I thought. I had only ever used a bit of lipstick, usually a pink rose color because it always felt unseemly to advertise one's mouth. I would let my singing do that. The blood red that he dabbed on my lips and told me to smack-smack amazed me because it set my full mouth off perfectly against my always pale skin. Well, I thought it did and so did Javier.

To the bedroom for the dressing. No underwear. That surprised me, but Jav said that this gown needed to slink over my butt with no seams from any undergarments no matter how seamless they might claim to be. He helped me pull it down and over my body, then put his hands under my breasts to lift them up into the cups of the dress.

- Ooo la la.

Some shifting and straightening before he stood back, hand on chin, gazing at his creation.

- Heels.

I was going to sit on the edge of the bed to slip them on.

- No! No! No! Be ye wrinkle free Wicla. Sin ye not!

He stood beside me so I could use him as a prop while I slid the black shoes on, then took me to the full-length mirror on the back of the bedroom door and removed the towel which he had put there earlier to prevent any sneak peeks by me, thinking I might have second thoughts about coming out of my cocoon as a startled butterfly. He put the pearls round my neck and clipped them at the back of my neck, now bare because my hair was piled atop my head.

- Voila!

Fuck me, I thought. That girl in the mirror is beautiful, not quite registering that she was me.

So, yes, Merri was gobsmacked and wanted a hug to make sure it was me – but had to be denied for the time being as part of Jav's do-not-touch directives. All Lawry could say was my, my, my, my, as he shook that big grey head of his and slapped his own cheek with the flat of his hand.

- You would, he said teasing Jav about me, feeling a little awkward as I balanced on my new heels.

- I would most sincerely consider it, yes I would, said Javier, excitedly.

Off we went to the home of Harold and Maude Carney, arriving a little late in the cool evening. Fortuitously, Harold and Maude had been vacationing in Europe and so survived the LA quake where mother had worked her way out of adolescence into the first phase of her womanhood, now more than thirty years ago. He was an accountant, short, balding, stocky, but ferocious in his networking habits, and Maude, who had been his receptionist way back then had evolved into a chirpy socialite who made sure the threads of that network were taut and spider-silk strong. Harold was one of the people Lawry wanted me to meet.

The other was an entertainment lawyer cum talent agent, Belle Rophon, who had crawled out of the rubble of Mendocino, husbandless, childless and shaken to her core during the same quake. She had taken one look at the burgeoning refugee camp that was Bakersfield and walked out of town, with her stomach growling, heading south.

She hitched rides as far as Ojai, down the Maricopa, and found it to her liking even though it too was caring for a multitude of lost souls, most of them with white collars and money in the bank. She took a few hours rest, she told me, then walked over to a camp kitchen, found an apron on a hook, then went out to the serving tables where she ladled out soup for long, feet-numbing shifts for days on end. That got her a cot in a tent with three other women and a purchase in what was really the re-founding of the old town.

Merri liked neither of them because their recommendations were meant to pry her loose from me, at least financially speaking. Ultimately, I accepted their recommendations and became their client, and got mother to come around to giving them the respect she begrudged them because they also set her up properly.

Merri would be perfect, Belle said, as the subject of a documentary, and she knew just the people to pitch, and lo and behold, the following year, starting April, a film crew followed us everywhere we went. Belle told me privately that she was able to get it done because Trader Merri Weer was accompanied by a rising star, her daughter, Wicla. It's still online if you want to take a look, capturing the work we did out of the van, our nights in the taverns, bars and roadhouses where I sang, the tedium of the road for which mother's habitual singing was not always the antidote, the always strained, but never to be doubted affection of mother and daughter, my cool grace they said, a cinematic counterpoint to her hot temper. It's called Two Women Day and Night. Simple.

After I had been given proper introductions to a few of the people in the cluster around Harold by the faux fireplace at the end of their big living room, and once Merri was in Lawry and Jav's good, moderating hands over by the bar - where she eventually fell in with movie-makers and other creatives as they called themselves - Maude came to get me. She took me around the various rooms where her guests were mingling, but with the kind of purposefulness I did not suspect at the time.

Once I seemed to have met almost everyone, knowing the always estimating eyes of both men and women were watching as I was taken around, she said there was one more person I might like to meet. He was standing with a couple of men at the other end of a long dining table laden with a nearly demolished buffet of catered food, talking politics. As the other men were bending his ear, he too had watched me as I was making my way on Maude's arm around the adjacent living room, had already caught my eye, but with a studied insouciance. I returned a look that said I didn't see you either.

- Paul. This is Wicla.

- Wicla, Paul Munro.

- Paul is out from New York. In fact, this party is really in honor of him.

Maude knew her man and liked to serve up beautiful young women to him, even though he was married. Thus did she curry favours even if the favours sought would not be delivered well into the future.

Handsome. Yep. Maybe fifteen years older than I. Dark hair, combed back, impeccably dressed. A smooth manner that puts one at ease. Solicitous and graceful. Dark eyes, square face. Just the hint of a shadow on cheeks and chin, but it was getting late after all. Tall, over six feet. Trim, athletic. Smooth, deep voice. Not one of the men I encountered every day. Truly, he was frightening.

- I am one of those nasty Canadians you hear about.

- Oh, I've met a few, already, I said. I like them.

Long story short, Merri and I prolonged our stay at the cabin. Every evening she would take the van to the Studio lot where she did business without me because, I said, I had to go into Ojai to meet with Harold or Belle or both. I did that, but meetings over, papers signed, futures discussed, thanks and air kisses all 'round, I would meet up with Paul who had also extended his stay. To raise even more money, he told his grateful wife. And all night long, we would make love. Make love and talk politics.

His wife was Senator Cora Munro and she was mounting a campaign to become President of the United States. So, ours was a national affair, but it was painfully short and no one knew about it, except the impeccably discreet Maude, perhaps.

Cora Munro was elected, and a couple of years into her term, as we all know all hell broke loose.

*Bemoan the burden of the broke-back beast.*

# Song 16

Mother and I were once again in the northwest reaches of Washington State, a little into Idaho, in fact, when we heard that a monster storm was heading toward the coast, coming out of a Pacific Ocean that was riled-up and ready to pounce again with its hooligan fists.

The question was, should we try to make Blaine to restock or stay away until the storm blew over. It wasn't so much that the rain might fall and the winds might blow, but whether Merri's customers and Wicla's fans might show-up at our appointed stops or stay at home. It was easy enough at that stage to let the venue owners where I was to sing know that we were re-routing. They didn't want to pay me if there weren't enough people in their rooms to cover costs, let alone turn a profit.

My deal with Belle allowed me to complete whatever arrangements I had already made prior to signing with her, but once those were done, every new invitation was to be routed through her. Apart from the appearances I was to make in upstate Washington, the only one that remained was at Chappy's so we pointed the more or less empty van in the direction of Auburn, passing through Kennewick and Bend on the way. Chappy knew what I did not know, that my appearance at Next Next was going to be my last there, so he promoted like crazy and put me on for three exhausting nights running.

- This isn't my farewell gig, Chappy.

I showed him a copy of the poster he'd plastered on every surface for miles around.

- Sure it is. At a place like this? You just don't know it yet.

- What the hell are you talking about?

- You're under professional management now. What do you think is going to happen? You're in the big tent now.

Chappy was nearly blind by now, but he could move fast around his barroom because every detail of it was etched into his brain pan. He'd also crossed into old man land – there was something in his face, its pallor, the eyes sunken deep into his skull, remote and rheumy, the way he held his body, like Merri's now, slightly stooped and rigid across his shoulders. Or maybe it was the way their bodies held them. His voice coming from the bottom of his lungs, scratched-up and raspy as it came out of his thin-lipped mouth, but still uttering the indisputable smalltown wisdom for which he was, in those parts, notorious.

- I'm still the same person I always was.

- No, you ain't.

- I've written a bunch of new songs.

- Look, Wicla, all I'm saying is that you're saying goodbye and farewell to all of this.

Right arm cast in an arc around the ill-lit room.

- But I'm glad as hell you've got some new songs.

- I'm gonna try them out right here tonight.

- And I'm gonna be listening.

The room was packed; mother was thrilled, of course. She sat the whole night at the bar on a stool right next to the register, except when she got up to dance with some young cracker whose buddies had put him up to it. There she was on the toes of her high-boots, turning and turning on the floor right in front of the bandstand, sometimes with people around her in a circle egging her on with rhythmic clapping and foot stomping, with her new boyfriend hoo-hawing and pulling on a bottle of warm beer. Made me laugh.

I sang a few songs that everyone knew, then I confessed I would try out a couple of new ones and hoped they would indulge me because they were the first to hear them. They weren't, in fact. Merri had heard them come together while she drove and I wrestled with Old Mud and fingerpoked my lyrics into my tablet while it jiggled under my fingers as the van bounced along some dirt road she'd found quite by mistake, or along some familiar stretch of potholed highway.

First, I sang a love song to my mother, On the Bridge, about the storm of motherhood and how it crashes into all that came before and ties two lives together. When I finished, everyone was looking over at her, where she sat dabbing at tears she pretended not to have. Then we played something a little more up-beat for the restless folk of the world, Stone in Shoe, and finally a darker tune, Crack Me Open, that, looking back now, failed to do what I wanted it to do, even though I got a standing ovation for it. Bear in mind, Chappy's audience may have been more than a little potted when I got to it.

*In the room of night*
*I learned the politics of love.*
*With me below and you above*
*At the center of my body and my soul*
*You cracked me open*
*Out, flew a dove.*

I wanted to express the gratitude a woman should have when the chemistry of love and sex and a new regret all combine to turn you from ice to steam in one sublime instant of time. When your whole state of being changes. But all I managed to do was re-strum the oldest song of all, to say your love left me in pieces. We've all wiped that tear away.

The thing is, while I was able to craft a song that just about everyone seemed to like, I knew I was not, just not, getting something. I needed to be pushed off a cliff, off the plateau upon which I was living my life. Little did I know or even suspect that I – and my mother – were driving straight toward the precipice.

Someone in a place called Kingman had sent a message asking me to appear at a local venue. I sent it to Belle, as agreed. In Ojai, she told us she'd done the booking.

- Kingman! That's on Route 66. I haven't been there for

years. We're not going back there.

- Now hold on, Merri. The highway has been cleared, it's all open now.

- It's a shit town.

- It's changed, Merri. Believe me it's changed. It's a hive now. Look, Wicla, the invitation came from one of my old clients, Ozzy Mandis. Do you know that name?

- You worked with Ozzy Mandis?

- Back in the day.

- I thought he was dead.

- Not nearly. Retired from the life of stage and screen. A bit of an impresario now. He says he can pull a thousand people and maybe a good deal more than that to a show. He'll put a band together for you, and I guarantee it will be a damned good one.

Mother had been listening to Ozzy's songs for years, as long as she had been on the road. And I knew a lot of them well, especially those from the early days before the hard, clever candy of his youth turned into toffee and he became a latter day, pot-bellied king of Los Vegas.

- When? I asked.

203

- Two weeks today.

Money? Some upfront, more regardless of outcome or fifty percent of the gate which ever was greatest. Belle said she would work it out so Trader Merri Weer's van could park right up near the door of the new arena and do as much business as could be done.

We took off from the cabin, with Lawry and Jav on board. Ozzy had worn the guise of a ladies' man during his career but he was queer and in the queer community a legendary cocksman. Lawry and Jav were big, big fans and were not going to pass up the opportunity to meet him even if the hero's triumphant sword had also gone to soft tack. Fun trip that was – us singing Ozzy songs, one after the other, as mother pounded the steering wheel to keep the beat. Jav and Lawry had packed a lunch which we ate at a way-by under a gibbous moon and a star-splattered sky.

Shock one, for all of us, was the apparition that appeared on the horizon as we approached Kingman. Looming up out of the shimmers of morning heat and illumined by an already hot sun was a high, opalescent dome that spread across the desert floor, perhaps for a half mile, maybe more. The highway started to bend to the north around it but snugging the low circle of the twenty-foot-high wall upon which the dome itself sat. We saw a sign: Welcome to the Kingman Hive and just past it, the opening to a wide ramp that led down below the dome, where selfdrive cars and trucks and were entering and exiting.

- What the fuck? said Merri.

- We heard about this, remember Lawry? said Javier.

- Stop here mother, I said. Just pull over for a minute.

I called Ozzy. He assured us we had come to the right place. Just drive down the ramp, take the first right and park at the loading zone just inside the building. He'd greet us there. He wasn't hard to spot. He stood, in the company of two burly men in coveralls, upon the dock of a long loading bay wearing a purple caftan that had risen from his boot tops almost up to his knees because his arms were so high above his head as he waved at us.

- Color of royalty, said Javier, tidying his hair.

- Which he is, agreed Lawry, damping the sweat from his brow, both excited to be rolling toward Ozzy's augustly dishevelled presence.

Ozzy, now well into his seventies, had a deeply tanned, deeply grooved, long face with bushy white eyebrows ornamenting an over-large head frizzed with wiry, white hair, some of it hanging in loops of white curls down the tops of his forehead and ears. He had red eyes, like a rat. His large head was held aloft like a balloon attached by a stringy neck to an emaciated body that was covered with brown parchment. His body seemed to be nothing but a loose concatenation of knobbly joints, but which also seemed to be jerkily electrified by some well-hidden battery. That battery, of course, was his big heart. He came down the steps of the dock to the side of the van just as Jav stepped down.

- And who is this?

- Javier, Mr. Mandus.

- And you?

- Lawrence, sir. Lawry. You can call him Jav.

- Sir? No. No. No. Call me Ozzy. Now you two gents seem to be one of the great tribe of heathens I call my own. Am I wrong in that? No. Didn't think so. Now, where is the little girl? Where is…? Ah, there you are.

I was standing in the doorway of the van, mother pushing on my rump to go down.

- You young lady have quite taken the world by storm. Yes.

- Not really. I, uh…

- Well, if you haven't you are about to. I promise you that.

Mother started down the stair.

- Ah…Trader Merri Weer. Must be. Come dear lady, join us.

He walked over, offered to take her down, but she refused.

- I can manage, pulling her hands up like a praying mantis.

- Of course you can. But pride goeth before a fall I always say.

Mother shot a sour look at him to which he replied with an ironic look followed by a wink.

- Well, let's go up. These two gentlemen will assist with bags and baggage.

- We don't really have any, I said, so...

- Of course you don't. But you are welcome to stay over. Arrangements have been made, and can be adjusted to accommodate Lawry and Jav – did I get that right? Yes? Instrument?

I fetched Old Mud who now lived in a much-abused blue case with a bent carrying handle.

- I'll lead the way.

Hive towns are common as grass these days and so I won't spend any time at all describing what we saw as we came up from the underworld. But I will say this, the first time you find yourself under a dome of that dimension your brain can't quite figure out what is happening. You are stepping into a completely interior world, but you feel like you are stepping outside into a new world strangely lit, but lit with a kind of profound benevolence, into a new world with different air, clean and plump with oxygen.

- This isn't Kingman, said Merri, looking around the town inside from where we stood in its main square, two hundred feet below the top of the dome.

- It is and it isn't my dear woman, replied Ozzy. Some of the old buildings remain but the city was almost completely rebuilt around them. They are historical artifacts but well-kept and loved as old buildings should be.

Years ago, when he was in his mid sixties and near broke despite the millions and millions he had run through his fingers, Ozzy escaped Vegas which had run out of water and run out of customers with actual money in their pockets. But Ozzy had risen from poverty and knew its touch and feel. He had always predicted he would die impoverished – undoubtedly brought its return on himself by his profligate ways he whispered to Merri – and so he was not about to grieve his fall from grace. Divine justice, he called it.

The saving grace of Kingman, and why it, and not Los Vegas, was now bustling inside a hive is because Kingman had a stream running through it, clogged and cluttered as it might have been when he first arrived. It still burbled and flowed with almost potable water from an underground aquifer.

Ozzy used the last of his own cash to place a bet on an old mill that had been made into a tavern when Kingman was a thriving town back in the 20th century. The tavern remains a featured building in the hive, and that stream, now cleaned-up, still runs right by it and on through the rest of the town, past markets and schools and parks, and homes that are handsome, solid, and here to stay. Ultimately, it runs out an opening in the wall on the far side of the town, into an agricultural belt that grows what the townspeople need in the way of food with some left over for sale at its roadside stand.

- Mr. Samuels himself oversaw the building of this hive. It wasn't the first, but it was among them and it was state of the art at the time, Ozzy said.

We had no clue who he was talking about, but I would find out in good time just who Samuels was.

- Long before he built the dome, he used to come to town from time to time. He'd come into my bar and order a coca cola and sit in the corner pondering. Strange man but look what the hell was in his head. Amazing.

Long pause.

- You're on at 8 PM sharp Wicla. Now, I suppose you all work on reverse hours, but hive towns are back to normal, so 8 it is. There's the hotel so when we're done at the arena make your way back here. Rooms are now booked so-rest up, enjoy. See you later.

Mother and I and Old Mud got to the so-called arena two hours before the show to meet the guys in the band – well, three guys and one woman on fiddle – and to run through the numbers we'd be performing. Merri had already found out that there was no way to bring the van up to the plaza and was thumping around about breach of contract, but she soon got tired of that, because the rest of us were paying no attention at all as we wandered around stupefied at just about everything – and everyone – we encountered.

- You know what I'm not hearing in here guys? I said. Gunfire.

- Maybe they ran out of bullets, said Javier.

- Got some down below in the van, said Merri.

The day went by and because my bandmates for the night knew my tunes, rehearsal was easy. At 8 PM, Ozzy stood on stage and introduced me, his latest discovery, as he called me. I don't mind a little good-humoured bragging if it fires up a crowd.

I have to say, the concert was a stunning success. I didn't carry any of the doubts I had been mulling the last couple of months on to the stage. I couldn't. I needed to cleave to the tried and true just to get through the night. I wasn't playing to a couple of hundred people in some dingy roadhouse in the back of beyond. Behind me, Zimbo on drums, Jack Fate on rhythm guitar, Tedhum Porterhouse on the milkwood keys and Anna Mae Bullock on fiddle delivered me out of my back-of-the-van string-plucking solitude into the symphonic RoFo thunderation I had already heard in my head, which, turns out was my destiny. My destiny as a performer, I mean.

There were three thousand people sitting in the seats of the Kingman amphitheater that night, another seven or eight thousand craning their necks from the surrounding squares or looking down from the windows of surrounding buildings. Nearly every citizen of the town was there, and more than a few from the surrounding area. Those in town had been taxed to the tune of twenty-five cents each when they went grocery shopping to pay for the gig – a new way of doing things – and damned if they weren't going to get their money's worth from Wicla, daughter of Trader Merri Weer, especially if Ozzy Mandus had put his approving stamp right on my forehead.

Ozzy had me under a spotlight more or less the whole time, so I couldn't see too far into the audience, but I could hear them – I could actually hear them singing along to some of my songs - and I knew the band and I were connecting. And so did Ozzy who stood off in the wings nodding at me and clapping and hollering along with everyone else. Javier and Lawrence who were standing on either side of him, stunned to watch their child take control of the stage like I did. If I really hit a song on its nose, Ozzy would put his arms around their shoulders, pull them tight and give them each a big wet kiss. Bonus for them.

Mother was sitting dead center in the first row, and never once stopped grinning at me, the very daughter whom she had brought into her crazy life. She looked like she'd swallowed the proverbial canary whole and that the canary had returned the favour. Just as in the bars where I'd paid my dues, where I would watch her turn in magic circles below my feet, boozed-up and sometimes delirious, she was up on her booth-eels at Kingman too, in the midst of all the people who came down front to dance and sing along. Only in Kingman she was not drunk, nor close to being dangerous as she often became, but spinning in the jingle-jangle of her ecstatic motherhood.

The truth is that both Ozzy and Merri knew the stuff of which stars are made - guts and glory with a measure of talent and panache - and here I was, spotlit on a broad stage below the oculus of the Kingman dome, proof positive of their predictive powers.

- You are a white-winged horse of a different feather, Wicla and you have been captured by Belle. Do what she asks and the world will be your oxster. Beware the close shave!

Chappy was right. Next Next was now behind me. Now, now and now had become the ever-changing present of the next very short years. Starting now.

*Deep and divine is the deceptive and downward drop.*

# Song 17

Vegas. Utterly deserted in the desert night but for a few sightseers like Merri and me. We left the blessed afterglow of Kingman soon after the show, leaving Lawry and Jav in the good hands of Ozzy and a few of Ozzy's local friends, gentlemen of the caftan and pillow room. They rented a selfdrive a couple of days later and returned to Ojai, much the worse for wear but consoled by the uplift. They dropped immediately back into their dedicated monogamy from which a short vacation was due from time-to-time, but with one another, and within the bounds of their expansive love.

I did not want to wake up in a Kingman the morning following the gig. I did not want to walk in the ordinary, even in such an extraordinary place, or to encounter people who, like me, had been transported for a couple of hours by music. When we have had that experience we are never capable of articulating why and how we feel. We can only utter the dumb, tin-sounding platitudes that reside in the back of our constricted throats. I did not want to have my autograph requested, for I did not want to scrawl the name Wicla without adding Weer for fear of offending my mother. That night, Wicla is who I had fully become. Wicla the Singer.

It was in dead, near-dawn Vegas, dragged down by the fatigue that lives on the far, played-out edge of used-up adrenalin, with my mother sleeping at the back of the van, which delivered me to the epiphany that was laying in wait there, like

Merlin in a forest clearing awaiting the long-expected Lancelot. Its energy had been forming up in me for months, but I had denied it's existence like a brave child disbelieves the monsters she has herself conjured in her mind, the monster rustling under the bed, the monster rattling the hangers in the closet, the monster moaning behind the window curtains. What you get for your bravery, should you attach it to holy quest, is not the monstrous, but the magic.

As in Kingman, in Los Vegas, I did not hear gunfire, but unlike Kingman, which was populated by the living, Los Vegas was empty, empty even of its ghosts. Inked black in the violet desert air, looked on by an indifferent wall of purple mountains in the west, the hulking silhouettes of desolate casinos and hotels loomed over the van as I picked my way around the detritus that had accumulated in the avenues that ran through the city. The road I was on forked and where it forked stood the broken statue of the man himself, my new friend, Ozzy Mandus, his torso tilted back, a beringed right hand holding a microphone to his lost mouth, the hand of the other outstretched arm grabbing at the cosmos as if he could pull down a fistful of stars if he wanted to. On his plinth, below his name, the words Emperor of Entertainment, deeply carved in granite, but below the plinth, his chipped and fractured bust, with eyes closed in the dream of some song now unheard.

A stranger might think that Ozzy had died into the firmament of the long-remembered, but we know that Ozzy had just moved on. The empire that the gods of Vegas had created at his feet had gone to rubble, but Ozzy himself lived, still a work in progress, not quite anonymous, but close to. And I take great comfort in that, because I too have lived on after the Wicla the Singer crumbled into dust, became a wife and mother, and finally a murderess whose crime will likely go unreported. So, even in my evil doings I will not be reborn into a new celebrityhood.

A lesson learned then. We must be careful not to assume the death of those who were once so vivid because really, they were just vivid in our imaginations, vivid in the spotlight cast upon them by those who had the power to wave a wand over them, to give them a stage upon which to strut their stuff for an hour.

I had had it mind when we left Kingman to stop in Vegas, to walk its broken streets with Merri, to see if I at least could re-conjure the illuminated gambles of which its living had once been made. But it seemed better to move on through; to get out actually, as fast as I could, before the light of day came full-on with its shadowless intensity, before I would have to see how the dry heat and fervent desert wind was tearing at its molecules and casting them down to the desert floor out of which Vegas sprang almost two centuries ago. How it had been reduced already to a monstrous, self-pitying existence like some strung-out old showgirl lost to the delusions of time's mirror.

A shaft of morning light shot out between two buildings as I headed north, falling on a monument into which were chiseled the almost sixty names of those now long dead fans who had been in Vegas at a concert when a mad man turned automatic fire on them from his hotel window. And then I could hear the gunfire again, the rat-a-tat-tat of the madman's guns, and I could feel the devil-terror of those moments, and then the wailing pain of those who survived somehow. And even though it was so long ago, I felt sad, ineffably sad, as I accelerated away, because those clever people with their magic wands had somehow called the desert heat and the desert wind to carry the horror out to the lone and level sands that stretch far and away, where it was never heard or felt again, until now, by me.

North I drove, under morning sky. Many miles, across the arid land. Merri awake, came forward.

- Oh, those were dreams I wouldn't visit on anyone.

- No?

- No.

- Going to tell me?

- Wish I could but...I, uh...

- Gone now? You have to wake yourself up and commit them to memory.

- I just remember catching myself looking into a mirror... time's mirror.

- Spooky.

- Where are we?

- Not sure.

- We have to get to Bakersfield to load-up.

- OK. Yep.

I turned left, saw the sign pointing directly into Death Valley. So, did mother.

- Yay though I walk through the valley of death….

- The valley of the shadow of death, mother.

- What?

- Shadow of death. There's a big difference.

- If you say so. Coffee?

We stopped on the side of the road at Stovepipe Wells half-way through the valley and stretched our legs for all of ten minutes. The sun was high and dangerous; it was ferociously hot. Hell hot. Merri took the wheel and I slept until we got to Bakersfield where, as mother joked with the men on the dock and issued commands at the same time, I finally turned my vice back on to check my messages. I found a few from Javier and Lawrence gushing with praise mostly, a thank you, thank you from Ozzy, a note from Tithy, blissfully unaware of my Kingman triumph and hoping to see us soon, sooner the better. Titus texted asking if what he heard from his sources in Arizona was true, and there was a score of messages from Belle Rophon that went from being wildly congratulatory to vehemently angry because I had gone missing, purposefully she supposed. There were a dozen booking requests to consider, with more expected, and how irresponsible was I going to continue to be?

What both my mother and Belle would soon discover is that I was going to let them worry about business. I was going to write songs and sing, but not as usual. Doing a few circuits with Trader Merri Weer was a necessary – the necessary – part of that. It was toil and trouble, but how else was I going to stay on ground level, how else re-experience the people or the landscapes that had not yet had the chance to teach me all their lessons because, to tell you the truth, I had blown by them and through them with such blithe indifference. That meant that if Belle were going to book me into venues whose owners were pounding on her door, they had to be in California, Oregon or Washington, and the dates had to be worked-out so mother could build a trade route around them. And that's what we did, at least, it's what we tried to do, because I was putting everything down on the epiphany to which my heart had finally opened in Vegas.

Ground level was the level upon which we rolled, upon which we dickered and sold the goods in the van. The highways and roads we took were on the ground, the highest and lowest bridges that carried our weight spanned the rivers that flowed beneath, but they connected the ground on both ends. The homely concert halls and theaters where I played, vibrated on mother earth. The people we met, traded with, sang to, ate and drank with, fucked and loved, made laugh or made cry, all those we took advantage of or bestowed our generosity on, all lived upon it, and everyone, except those who, in other parts of the country were parked on a shelf or vault in one of the Heaven's Gate malls (also, it turns out, built by Mr. Samuels) was buried in it.

Ground level was not, emphatically not, where Paul Munro lived so even though he came west a few times and wanted to see me, desperately he said, I would not turn myself over to him. I would not relent even though my body burned when I thought his of tender-tough hands on me, which was often. Paul lived in the sky, on planes; he lived in a tower in New York, in an arrogant condo enclave in Washington, in the realm of high ideas if not ideals, in the thin atmosphere of national politics and in the tangle of blue-sky projects of vast human potential or so he said. And it was quite possible that he and his wife would someday soon, if all cards were played exactly right, come to live in the White House where it floated in the rarified air of American myth above the banks of the swollen Potomac.

Maude prevailed on Belle to see if I might come to her home when she was throwing a party in Cora's cause, that is when Paul came to town, but she was expert enough in her role as go-between not to push too hard because she did not want Belle to know that her chirpy tones of solicitation were, in fact, a disguise for Paul's heavy breathing. She knew her man and she knew that he had bedded me and that he wanted more. Once it became clear that Paul would not be allowed to have me again, Maude made another introduction, to a raven-haired beauty, a recent widow named Ada Lovelace, also visiting from the unsubmerged heights of New York.

-   Don't worry about Paul, said Harold, to me when I explained I was cutting things off with Paul. He's just looking for a little affection and attention. Cora's a bit of an iron lady and he's a needy romantic. He'll get it where he can.

In those days and all the days that followed, it is almost impossible for anyone who did not live close to the ground to know how difficult it was to just survive. Disaster followed on calamity, society was riven by a complex of fractious ethnic divides, criminals were born out of parental abuses, mostly of the neglectful kind, everyone fended for themselves, or themselves and their own if they still had family, millions fled the decaying old cities and larger towns leaving those who could not escape to the brutal, hard pavement realities of both day and night, almost everyone lived in armed enclaves, and those who didn't kept loaded guns close by and slept light.

Long before I came along, Merri had lived and worked in this broken world, first enduring the trials and tribulations that came as she moved back and forth on Route 66, then along the spidery network of roads and highways that she and I traveled and were still traveling. She had been viciously raped, probably more than the one time she had blurted out during her howling, drunken kick at God's implacable face. People had beaten her, cheated her, stolen from her and lied to her. But all of it was unremarkable to any who lived in the near-lawless hinterlands of old America, a sign of weakness to bitch and complain or to collapse under the weight of your woes, or to ask others to help with your problems because yours were theirs. And if they weren't, then you were either too far gone to require help, or you were living so far above the ordinary as to deserve their bitter contempt.

Not much had changed once mother left Route 66 and

began the north-south life we lived together. If trouble looked like it was brewing, she'd have a gun quickly at hand to waive off the danger, or she would raise such a ruckus that no one wanted to tangle with her, or she would mollify an offended party with just the right words, or, all else failing, she would vacate the scene. She did her business only with women and stayed away from men as much as possible. Hungry for intimacy and friendship she gave herself over to Lilith Morrigan, but she was not naturally a woman's woman. Lilith's betrayal was not the simple betrayal of a lover, but the continuing betrayal of the human race, the hard soil through which we ploughed our van, convinced there were no greener pastures.

Once I became a featured act in the bars and roadhouses along our way, Merri would drink and dance with men, but she would not flirt with them even when her guard was down, and she became adept at deflecting any and all attempts at seduction leaving some men perplexed and disappointed and other men, lashed by her acid tongue, feeling humiliated in their ineptness. And I think she let herself – may even have made herself - evolve into an uglier creature than she was by rights. You look at the early 3Ds of her and you can see how beautiful she was, open-faced, smiling, full-lipped, lithe and curvaceous at the same time. A feast to be had by any man, but especially a discerning and sexually gifted man like Paul Munro had they met at the right time.

Over time, she thinned out, her mouth crooked down on both sides, she wrapped herself in garments bristling with pins and buttons and placed dark glasses over her eyes which became evasive and almost always cast down to her shuffling boots. Now age, and the toxic effects of too much booze pulled her down into a curling stoop, slowed her legs, weakened her back and arms. No matter as long as I was there to be her muscle and her driver.

Remember this: that world was my ordinary too. Only up until lately, I had not seen it for what it was. I was never beset by dangers that I could not and did not handle. Certainly, I had not been raped or even come close to being raped. Also, I had the legendary Trader Merri Weer to protect me and god knows she did, although I can count on one hand how many times I was aware of it.

My promiscuity was a kind of preventative measure I think – give-in to some man I could at least stomach before another man with darker needs could slap a victim label on my ass. I craved orgasmic pleasure, especially after singing to an adoring audience, so I raised hell when a man left me disappointed, oh yes I did. Sad to say that until Paul the joy of love was never mine because I had absorbed my mother's anxieties and mistrusts and that was too thin a soil for love to bloom in. Besides, we were always on the move, and the contemplation of trying to sustain a relationship where I would be apart from someone for months at a time, was a foolish contemplation. Lilith proved that case beyond the balance of probabilities. After Paul, and after Kingman, I guess I was ready to love myself a little more, and you can't do that and be promiscuous too. At least a woman can't.

When we arrived at the outskirts of Bakersfield after coming through Death Valley, I heard, really heard for the first time, the sound of gunfire. People were being killed or wounded somewhere in the great surround. Sometimes a single shot then nothing more until the same thing happened in another part of the city. Sometimes a small burst and then nothing more. Sometimes the prolonged hyphenated claps from an automatic. Sometimes the noise of a gunfight. Were it possible to hear the slashing and plunging of knives, and the thud of clubs on heads, the pound of fists on faces, the sudden snap of bones, I would have heard those too. Heard those and heard also the cries of the antagonists, the wail of the killed as they fell out of life, the moans of the wounded, the sobs of the survivors who loved them or even hated them in their own, non-lethal way, but who had nothing now but regret and sorrow.

Heard for the first time, because, in the plangent screech and scraping of Anne Marie Bullock's fiddle-playing back in Kingman, my ears had caught the high notes of something out of the ordinary: the forgotten, neglected beauty of the human soul. Gunfire was, and in many places in America, still is, the unheard background music for life on the ground. Its absence in the busy precincts of Kingman, in the ruins of Los Vegas where an ersatz Statue of Liberty lay busted around its plinth, and all throughout the arid expanse of Death Valley, created space for the sounds of silence. I don't know why, but I knew upon hearing the first gunshot in Bakersfield that I could no longer compose songs to the fantasies of love, but only to the blood-red realities of our life, our life in the land of is as my mother called it.

*Grieve ye the ground and ghosts of grim Golgotha.*

# Song 18

Belle was upset by the message I sent, but after some to-ing and fro-ing she understood that until I had at least a dozen new songs I was not going to step foot on a stage.

- How long? she wondered, be.

- I don't know, I replied.

Songs materialize out of thin air, and for those who don't breathe that air it seems a kind of magic. Belle was one of those.

- They may finish the new dome over Ojai before you're done.

- Ojai?

- Yep. They've already started.

- Looks like Maude had her way with Paul Munro, said I.

- What do you mean?

- Paul is connected. Very.

- What about the new Hive in upstate Washington? Have

you heard about that?

- I don't know anything about that, I said.

A lot of projects were underway that were stunning in their size and scope. The Gatesport dome on the coast of the Olympic Peninsula was a brand-new hive being built from the ground up. The Ojai dome, now underway apparently, was like the one in Kingman but would be larger, especially if it encompassed the NewB studios, which was not certain. In western Oregon and Washington mother and I had now seen a half dozen or more structures that the farmers there called litter boxes. Under the flat expanse of the same crystal the domes were made from, herds of cattle fattened on lush grasses and acres of crops yielded their fruits as they had never done before. The double pipeline that would take vast quantities of Pacific salt water to the Yellowstone caldera to be distilled into potable water was nearing completion. That water would flow west and east down the now dried up riverbeds of old, and someday soon would bring new life. The dead were increasingly being interred in Heaven's Gate mausoleums, really just old malls converted into our new necropoli, but rather than being somber and diffident they came complete with food fairs and kiddie rides.

Not that any of it made a difference to anyone I knew. If you happened to live near one of the projects you might catch a glimpse of it, might if you saw it, be awed, amazed or tickled depending on what you saw, but, even if you knew about the other undertakings, you wouldn't begin to understand that one, just one, progenitive power had concocted it all, or comprehend its inexorable and transformative impact. If you thought there was nothing new under the sun, you would have been wrong. As we traveled through the western states, Merri and I were as well-equipped as anyone to bear witness to the changes, but really we didn't put it all together either. Things were too spread out, to disparate in their nature, and we were too damned busy trading and song writing to pay much attention. It was long after mother died, in fact, and only by happenstance, that I could and did. Put it together, I mean.

It took a few months but finally I was able to tell Belle and Harold, and Lawry and Jav too, that we were on our way south to Ojai. Mother needed a good rest and guess what, I had a few tunes in hand, songs I thought a few people might like. Would she please pull together a band, preferably the one I had worked with in front of the Kingman crowd, but if you can't get all of them, I am begging you please do your damnedest to track down the fiddle player, Anne Marie Bullock.

She was an intelligent woman, Belle Rophon was, and while she did find them, all of them, she did not sign them to any deals. They would come to Ojai for two weeks to sweat out the new material first. If the songs were as roadworthy as I thought they were, well then, further investments might be justified. By me, not by her.

Harold prevailed on one of the studio heads to let us use a vacant sound stage to rehearse, which was convenient for everyone especially because all around the periphery of Ojai, people were at work on the dome, which would not encompass the studios after all. Eventually, a sub-dome would rise over it, but not until much later.

Mother was able to set-up shop in the studio lot and did so much business that she had to make a trip to Bakersfield to re-stock. Twice, I think. A sizeable trailer was put at the disposal of Jack, Tedhum and Zimbo, a smaller one for Anne Marie. Mother and I parked at the cabin as always. Lawry and Jav hosted dinner for the band three or four times, and new friends were made all around. Much laughter, good fun, intense debate usually centered on the prospects of a win by Cora Munro, first woman to take a chance at the Presidency for fifty years or so. Me keeping thoughts of Paul, too many of them maudlin, to myself. Tall tales of the road were delivered in a rasping, whiskey-soaked voice by Trader Merri Weer herself, who was on very good behaviour I have to say, and there was, perhaps, a little too much flirting between Jav and young stud Tedhum. But what the hell. Lawry was an expert on protecting his territory and at six four or so, when he pulled up to full height, he could blast Tedhum with a look that could split an oak tree, let alone cool the younger man's ardour.

Once, Belle came out to the Studios to see what we were up to, but on orders from me, Lawry's people shooed her away. Not just her but anyone hoping for a sneak preview. It was enough, I thought, that the worker bees and their mavens at the Studio were able to hear our music as it drifted out the sound stage's doors and windows. I didn't want anyone to judge us based on half done songs, or songs done one way when we first played them, that might be done another once we worked and re-worked them. Belle later told me that her nerves were twisted tight throughout the whole process because some know-it-all guy who worked in accounting at the Studios said it all sounded like shit to him. I told her she should have taken that as a good omen. Cheers, she said, clinking her glass on mine.

Every member of the band, myself included, are taciturn

people and in the work setting, rehearsals and performances, little was said unless it was expressed through one of my lyrics. But Jack, a perfectionist with a ton of courage became the unofficial spokesman for the others, me being, inevitably, the boss lady. When we worked together you could hear Jack say, Oh yeah, good one, but we can't hear your voice. Or, after a whisper from one of the others, can we try it this way? If I wandered away from the group to get water or to go to the WC, more than once I listened to them jam one of my songs because rather than argue with me about some thing I was insisting on they realized I could be won over through my ears.

Toward the end of the second week we should have been ready, but it didn't feel that way to me. My nerves were frayed. I wanted to stay in rehearsal - forever. But Jack, Tedhum, Zimbo and even Anne Marie were having none of that. They were hardened session people, had backed some of the recent greats, together and individually, and they knew when things were working and when they weren't. And in this case, Jack said, they were, while the others nodded.

- I've got an idea, said Jav.

I had followed him to the kitchen while at the dining table mother was telling the others about each of the buttons and pins on her vest, sipping at a large bowl of wine, and slowly losing herself in the sentiments that traveled with each.

- Let's throw open the doors and have a small concert.

- At the Studios?

- Yeah. Those big doors open to the lot, so, we'll bring the stage forward and you can try your stuff out on whoever wants to come. It'll be great.

So, we did. Belle, Harold and Maude and a few others came out from Ojai and joined the ranks of over a thousand Studio employees who stood in the light of dusk in front of our stage. From the moment Anne Marie started-off our first song with a long wailing cry from the heart of her fiddle that invited me to sing its lyrics, they stayed with us. They stayed until we finished ninety or so minutes later with a solemn coda - a trailing, grave-digging drum beat perfectly executed by Zimbo while Jack and Tedhum flooded the audience with the hum of guitar noise and I held a middle note that sounded like a prayer until everyone in the place was gasping for air.

And then, silence. Not a peep. Sound of bird in some high tree in the overlooking mountains, now gone dark. Wind flapping a flag on the main stage building. Slight movement of heads and feet. Then a shout from the back of the crowd.

- Brava! Brava!

Then, applause, applause and whistles.

- Told you, whispered Jack in my ear as he took my guitar.

I looked at my band mates, then swept my arm in their direction and uttered thanks. Anne Marie's big toothy smile while she looked right at me. Slight rat a tat tat from Zimbo on the snare. Tedhum pointing at me with an unbent finger.

- Go on take your bows, said Jack, pushing me forward just a little.

As I was bending to a last bow, mother came up from the side of the stage with Lawry and Jav and brought me flowers. Lots of flowers. And the crowd cheered and clapped again but as I looked over them from behind a cluster of roses I could see Belle striding toward her selfdrive, back stiff, and what must have been, I was sure, a stern look in her face. How could she not have liked that!? Later I received a text message from her: Important meeting, my office, 10 AM.

- Don't worry, said Jack coming up behind me. You can get any agent you want.

I went alone to Belle's office where Belle greeted me warmly with an ebullient smile on her face. Harold was there and came over to plant a kiss on both cheeks. I did not see the man sitting on the couch behind her as she walked me into the room. Thin and rangy, with long legs sticking out in front of him.

- Here she is.

He stood, walked toward me, shifting his hat from his right hand to his left so we could shake. Probably mid forties; high forehead, receding hair line, blue eyes very much alive, wolf like.

- Wicla, this is Wynkyn DeWorde. He's your new manager.

- But, I have you.

- No, I am your agent and lawyer. Wynkyn is your chief operating officer.

- I don't understand.

- Wicla, said Harold, you are about to become a corporation, and probably a big one. So...

- We're already working on your schedule, said Belle.

- Think you can be ready to hit the road next week? asked Wynkyn in a reedy, forest-smart voice.

- Next week? No...no.

- Sure you can.

- I told Belle a long time ago, I go where mother goes.

- We're going to have to reverse that, Wynkyn said almost as an instruction.

- She'll be fine, said Harold. I'll talk to her.

- We can't all go in the van.

- She'll follow the buses, Wynkyn said.

- Wynkyn has called in some favours, Wicla, added Belle. All will be ready.

- So, let's make sure you are, Wynkyn winks. First stop, El Cajun.

- South? To Gran Mexico? We don't go south.

- Merri Trader Weer never made it there, but Wicla, oh yes. She goes south. She goes everywhere, said by Wynkyn, but with the nodding affirmation of Belle and Harold.

They ushered me out of the office with lots of congratulations, kisses, handshakes and all the rest of that palaver. I met up with the other members of the band for lunch and told them what's what, that contracts would be forthcoming, of course, and did my best to answer their questions, but with guesswork only. Belle, Harold and Wynkyn stayed in holy conclave to work on the logistics of our forthcoming tour. The new Popess had been elected by the unanimous vote of a thousand clapping fans making too much of a puff of smoke.

*I hop through the hoops of heaven and hell.*

# Song 19

Trader Merri Weer had never gone to southern California because, in her mind, it had become part of Mexico. Not true, of course, but it was a foreign place compared to what she was used to. She meant it was not as 'white' as the world she preferred. A racist sentiment? No argument there. Did I hold the same views? Maybe. But I had never given it much thought, and I didn't suppose I did. San Diego, Chula Vista, La Jolla and other coastal towns and cities had been as ravaged by rising seas, quakes and tsunamis as those of their northern counterparts, so even in the days of my first tour, it was difficult to find venues in any of them where we could play to a sizeable crowd.

El Cajon, like Bakersfield, had become a refuge, but a refuge that mixed whites, blacks, Latinos and Asians in near equal measure. The bloody conflicts that had broken out thirty years earlier and had erupted sporadically for years afterwards had quieted as that sprawling conurbation broke-up into interlocking ghettos where, inside their kingdoms, strongmen kept the peace with ruthless tactics and played one another off to ensure a balance of power. No one begrudged them their immense wealth because it was taken as the cost of the pax, and if anyone did dare to speak-out it was because they lived in one of the ghettos within a ghetto where their insane voices went unheard in the din of a million other gripes. Anyone who had a chance of gaining political traction or who otherwise challenged the Top Men as they were called, eventually succumbed to the intimidations that were visited upon them. That, or a bullet in the ear.

Wynkyn knew a man who knew a woman who ran the El Cajon arena, which was available when we needed it for our first show. If our first show didn't go well, hardly anyone but those in attendance would care and the calamity would be absorbed in the hubbub of the city and in the dusty fraught air between El Cajon and Ojai. The same would be true of any glory that might be claimed of my inauguration, but at least we would know whether what we were doing was working or not.

As it turns out, it was a great success and led to a demand for a return visit, which we made a year or so later. By that time, my firsthand impressions of El Cajon and the knowledge I gleaned from listening to those who knew something about how things worked down there, found there way into a song I wrote, You Can't Beat the People. Some low level thug took it upon himself to warn us to never come back - because that song roasted the Top Men and became a cha-cha anthem to a growing, grass roots resistance. The higher-ups, however, preferred the money that was set aside to piece them off and ignored the satire.

*The clubs of the mariachi men*
*Make us dance under sun and stars*
*They are the top guys they say they are,*
*Because they always beat the people.*

*The beat, the beat, the beat*
*Of the people on their feet.*
*You can't beat the people*
*Who've been beat and beat and beat.*

Belle and Wynkyn scolded me for taking them on, but they soon found out I had more of a temper than I let on, at least when it came to what songs were going to come out of my mouth.

From El Cajon to the Salton Sea, then to Palm Springs. From there to Riverside, Anaheim and Pasadena. We overnighted in Ojai, where Wynkyn and I debriefed Belle and Harold and those three tinkered with the plan under which things were going so well. Then we headed north with Merri, who had refused to go south, who followed the tour our buses in her van. We did many concerts as we caravanned close to the tight wall of the Canadian border giving Merri time to restock in Blaine before we turned toward home again. On the way we appeared in Bellingham, Redmond, Eugene, Portland, and the near-independent state of Napa, where a billionaire managed to snag our final date out of the hands of another billionaire who had bid for a San Francisco appearance. Mother was so exhausted that when we got to Ojai, I took the wheel of the van and drove it to the cabin where Lawry carried the thin wraith of her into the spare bedroom and, with Javier's soothing help, finally got her to settle into a sleep that lasted two days. Mine, without the benefit of booze, lasted almost as long.

It's a pretty dry recitation, isn't it? But the video archive tells the story of a triumph. It captures the sizzling rapture of our concerts with such 3D veracity that you feel you are almost standing on your chair in the heaving mass of the crowd. Everyone who was there, me and the band included, were carried into the winds of a divine madness, sometimes lifted on the force of my voice, sometimes held there by a lyric, or the guitar work of Jack or Tedhum, sometimes marched into dangerous memory by Zimbo's drumming, sometimes cut and slashed to the nervy quick of sentiment by Anne Marie's fiddle work, sometimes drowned in the roiled waters of hope reborn and sometimes rocketed into a fourth or fifth or sixth dimension when our musicianship suddenly combined to smash through all the defences of human intellect into the raw meat of our damaged animal souls.

Wicla the Singer, if I may call her that, came along at just the right time, when a generation of young people who had not endured the hardships and privations of their parents and grandparents were nonetheless stuck in the grooves of their forebear's lives. Their antennae were up, twitching in the wind of a different future, one in which they did not have to scuttle, bug-like out from under a killing sun or duck when the gunfire got too close or head for cover when the hot currents of the Pacific threw hurricanes at the coast or when the night sky crackled and hurled lightening at the parched and flammable scrubbery that rooted in dry ground everywhere and somehow managed to survive the vicissitudes of these times.

I shared their trepidations and their inchoate yearnings and somehow, after singing out the last of my love songs in Kingman, after bearing witness to the ruins of Vegas, after coming through Death Valley, after traveling for years with a woman who lived every day in stubborn, brave defiance of all the barriers and obstacles that held just about everyone else in check, I found the words and music that could articulate them – told the truth about where we now found ourselves, said, with mothering defiance, there is a different future we can make. Must make.

And who else was doing that, but with the sharp rhetoric of

a political woman who knows what she wants, Cora Munro, campaigning for the Presidency against some guy whose name now escapes me was thumping the same themes. My generation was listening and feeling the stirrings that come with belonging to a movement and not to the static dreariness of the here and now, but the movement had no shape, no direction.

Out of all our vices she spoke, spoke like a piano out of which the concerto of a new America was being composed and played at the same time. From platforms banged-up just for her in the arenas of the old cities, and from rostrums set in the squares of the new hive cities that were springing up all through the eastern states and starting to be built in places like Kingman, from podiums set on the stages of concert halls and theaters throughout the Midwest, she called on us to account for ourselves, to ourselves. She was coming west she said, would come and ask us to rejoin the Union over which she intended to preside, God willing, she said as if God was still in the game.

Rejoin?, I thought to myself, at first baffled by the word. But then yes, I realized the truth of it. We in the west, the very west where my mother and I worked our business, where my band and I were now performing, had let our connection to the country slip away. It was just one more thing we were too busy to hold onto, our hands too full to wave the flag under which our losses and disappointments were unending, when the most of us lived under the banners of our protectors, the men at the barricades around our towns, the strongmen of El Cajon, and even the tough women of Fort Ketchup who ruled the otherwise unruly. I should add Lilith Morrigan and the other wardens of the sprawling, violent prisons into which so many had been - and were being - chucked and forgotten.

And what then did Cora Munro mean when she said, her voice rising, we could not, must not allow a new division to take hold? Outsiders and Insiders alike, she said, capital letters on both words, must make common cause and under her Presidency, would be given good reason to make it. Ponder that, I did - and then some more, and talked about it endlessly with Ann Marie, Jack, Tedhum and Zimbo as we rolled from place to place, and especially with Wynk, whom, one scorching day on the outskirts of Bellingham where we stopped to recharge our vehicles, found his way to my bed. Found his way because I was standing in the doorway of my bedroom beckoning him hither.

If two waves meet at precisely the same moment they merge into one and double its dimensions. Imagine what overwhelming power there is then, when there is a confluence of three or four, as there was at this moment on our tour, how it moves so fast and massively to a far-off shore that one wave of itself could never reach. But the agitated unhappiness of the people, articulated in the music of our band, converging with the dictates of a new politics, and riding on the seesaw rhythms of love and sex, carried us there. Carried us there and drowned us, though we did not know it.

Why Wynk? Because he was so tall and angular, so long of finger and strong of arm, so much a man who listens, who shaves his face, who smells of ancient forests and urban streets, who told the artist in me to be more ruthless with herself, who put the everything I needed around me when I sang, who cupped my chin with a tender hand and raised my head so I could see in his cool green eyes the calm that had escaped me, who kept our focus on all our purposes, who told me when I needed to be told to love my mother more, whose age, when he let me hold him in my arms reduced itself to that of Paris in his youth, who, from our orgasmic heights fell headlong into the dark womb of my blessed womaness and flipped from the great power of his manliness into the utter frankness of a nothing.

That day, from her van, Merri had watched Wynkyn knock on my trailer door. She knew I was tired in my bones and hoped he would not stay long to talk about whatever business he had to discuss, for Wynkyn seemed all business to her, and relentlessly so. But he and I were not talking business but had somehow fallen into conversation about Cora Munro then followed the many tentacles of our discussion into the multifarious immediacy of why we were doing what we were doing.

I told Wynk I had met her husband Paul, but I did not confess to our brief affair. I had been watching Wynk over a few weeks by then and had formed an attraction that I kept to myself, so it was partly for that reason I kept Paul's and my secret from him. I did not want him to smell the musk of another man on me. That and because, hearing and watching Cora campaign, I felt a secret shame for trysting with her husband, a secret disgust toward Paul for not being consumed by her, a great beauty doing great things with her superb mind, her splendid, animated and feral body.

I poured Wynk a glass of wine, we talked, we had another glass or two. Silence came, as it sometimes does in a long conversation. Eyes locked because it was impossible not to. Desire floated its scents into nostrils that could not stop breathing in the warming air. He tried a kiss, was not rebuffed. I rose and seemed abruptly to put an end to things.

- Sorry, he said. Sorry, boss.

I stood, poured us both a little more wine then carried my glass to the back of the bus, turning around in the doorway of my room to face him where he sat.

- Come.

- What?

- I want you. Please come, Wynk, please.

Mother told me later she had come over to the bus and pounded on the door to roust him so he could not bother me any longer with his business shit. And then she heard Ann Marie's fiddle noise coming from the other bus. She looked at Ann Marie sitting by a window stroking her instrument like she was pulling a cock over a zipper, while Jack, seriously jealous of Wynk's conquest, and Zimbo and Tedhum looked out at her with salacious smiles on their faces. Mother spun to look at my bus, which may or may not have been rocking on its wheels, and finally got it. She raised her arms high in the air and jangled her bracelets, did a couple of turns in the dirt, then sauntered gaily back to the van where she toasted my release from whatever it was that had kept me dry in the crotch, as she so wincingly called it, since we had departed Kingman all those months ago.

*Subtle and serious are the sublimations of sex and sin.*

# Song 20

That first tour ended with our appearance in Napa, or the Kingdom of Napa as the code-surfs and digital mechanics who still lived and worked there called it. In the wake of the big quake that knocked San Francisco back on its pins, tens of thousands of its survivors rushed to the valley seeking safety, but they were not well met by those already there. Sometime in the 2020s, an electronic, drone-supervised fence had been constructed around the valley to keep out spies, competitors, speculators, reporters and other assorted riffraff. But as one disaster after another pushed people into the valley and out of where they had once lived, valley people stood in the fence gaps and pushed back. The electronic wall was hardened, patrols sent out to play rough with interlopers and drones, armed with guns, fired maiming pulses at anyone who refused to read the no-trespassing-on-pain-of-death signs.

Even though the population of the valley had declined by huge numbers, those who had ways and means of surviving inside were still intent on keeping it more or less to themselves, just as the good citizens of Ojai were doing with a once-public park that they claimed for their use only and with their new, indestructible, four-gates-only dome.

Napa and the other valley towns, the spaces between filled with a vineyard-eating sprawl in the first years of the new century, was an eerie place. Massive industrial plants lay shuttered, office buildings were vacant or under partial use, the campuses of billion-dollar companies now choked with weeds, and all but one or two buildings in each of them mothballed. But they were ready, their optimistic owners said, to be recommissioned once the economy started buzzing again. And yet, a couple of hundred thousand people, as worried as the rest of us, still lived within the fence, absolutely determined to keep the world, which had once been the oyster they ate every day, from eating them.

It wasn't just the long string of disasters that had reduced the population from its earlier heights, although they did prevent the glorious revolution of artificial intelligence from taking hold as its proponents had predicted. The infertile ground of our broken, bankrupted country had little practical use for things that were smarter than humans or cost too much to do the farming, small business, road building, housework and child-minding that the times required. But putting themselves out of work, the clever boys of the old labs had created AI programming bots that turned on them, didn't say thankyou, and gave them the back of the hand while they handed out pink slips from their robotic hands. The bots worked day and night on programming the code for a new utopia that never dawned, while their human minders carried the metaphorical oil cans that kept them purring.

The valley people got the same show that everyone else got but with a bit more hot sauce added to the stew because the band members, Wynk, and I were feeling pretty pissed at the temerity of the billionaires of a generation ago – including the woman who invited us to perform – to finance what was really an armed expropriation. We wanted to see if our music could rip down the fence, tear open the gates that had kept

Trader Merri Weer out all these years since and re-open the public highway that ran through the valley. Too bad Merri wouldn't be able to set-up shop outside the stadium where we were appearing. She was laying in a foetal position on her cot in the van, in the grip of a boundless delirium, too sick even for soup, while I drove south through the Calistoga gate at the tail end of our indignant convoy.

The concert was actually held at an outdoor amphitheater at Boyes Hot Springs. Wynk had viced a message to our hostess to let her know we would arrive soon, but our progress had come to a near halt because the local roads were choked with vehicles that were converging on the village. It was almost midnight when we pulled in behind the stage a couple of hours later, a full moon high in the sky blessing the event as though we were about to deliver the Sermon on the Mount. She was there to meet us, sitting at a small table while several retainers standing around her waited for instructions that hardly ever came.

What a shock. Mary Paulpetter was black and ninety years old give or take a couple of years, but she had the spunk of someone much younger than my mother who was many years her junior and now laid-up in the van, unconscious and moaning under a blanket of pain from the virulent flu that had invaded every cell of her body.

Wynk and the band stepped down from the bus and Mrs. Paulpetter sprung to her feet.

- Reminds me of the old days, all this excitement, said Mary walking toward Ann Marie with a bony, beringed hand outstretched. Welcome, welcome, welcome.

- This is Ann Marie Bullock, Mrs. Paulpetter, said Wynk, who then introduced himself and Ann Marie's band mates.

- Well, damn it all. It is good to meet you. But where's the star? Where is Wicla the Singer? Everybody's been waitin' for hours. A lot of them are already starting to howl. Can you hear them?

Those little white teeth of hers still had a lot of bite. I had come down out of the van and was walking up behind her.

- Hello, ma'am, I said.

She cranked her head around without moving her feet, and then swung her cane in my direction and pulled her body around with it. Then she lifted her cane and pointed it right at my face.

- So, you're her? Wicla!

- Yes, ma'am.

- Well, goddamn it. It is a pleasure to meet you.

- Likewise, ma'am.

- You gonna sing for us?

- What I'm here for.

- Oh, yes you are. Bought and paid for.

- Ma'am?

I had taken offence at her remark.

- Oh, she said, I didn't mean it that way. You see, I had a bid-war with Jackdor Sai down in Frisco. He thought he had you sewed-up. He's a good friend of Belle Rophon, but I also knew her because she represented some people I knew. What Jackdor didn't really grasp is that Belle speaks only one language. She speaks the language of money honey. So, it was no contest because Mr. Sai is saving his money for a rainy day and I'm looking for ways to spend mine before they put me under.

She hooked a scrawny arm in mine and turned me around as she walked me toward the stairs to the back of the stage. Wynk had already gone up to make sure the set-up was OK and to do a sound check while the crowd roared their approval that something was finally happening. Tedhum and Jack tuned their guitars, Ann Marie waxed her bow and Zimbo stretched while holding his drumsticks.

- It costs money to put on a show like this, Wicla. You know that. So, don't take offence at this old lady. I would have paid any money to see you sing.

- Why?

- Why? Because there ain't been nobody like you since before I can remember. I met my husband at a rock concert back in, oh hell, it would have been 2005 or so. Outside too. Chicago. Long time ago. We got stoned, that's what we used to call it. On weed. What do they call it now? Crumb? It's still around. Hell, I think it's a cash crop in the valley. But anyway we danced, oh we danced. He was pretty damn good for a white man.

She unhooked and did a little jig.

- Little did I know he'd go on to make all the money he did and then become the mighty prick he became, but it don't matter now cause he's dead and I got all the loot and a lot of damned fools who will do my bidding. Here's to the rich and old. Say it loud and say it proud.

Then she brought her wrinkled nose close to mine, looked over the top of her specs, and uttered a confidence.

- But I ain't danced since that day and I sure plan to tonight. That is, if you're as good as they say you are. Now go on. Have a good time, otherwise what the hell's the point?

Well, I didn't exactly sing the kind of music anyone dances too. After singing a couple of tunes I looked down to the front of the audience where Mrs. Paulpetter had plunked her little table and saw the disconsolate look on her face, illuminated by the moonlight but also by the spotlight falling on the stage that made the corona of white hair that framed her face glow blue.

I walked over to Jack and whispered a few words in his ear, then called Wynk out from where he stood behind the side curtains and whispered to him. I pulled the mic around in front of my mouth again to speak to the audience.

- It's been a while since I sang this song, but you know what? We have a very special lady with us tonight. You all know Mrs. Paulpetter, don't you?

The crowd roared because she was well known in the valley and loved for her eccentricities.

- Mrs. P wanted to dance tonight, and so she shall.

Jack started playing The Bones of Love, joined by Tedhum, Ann Marie and Zimbo. And once I began singing, Wynk came out in front of the stage wearing the jacket of a natty black tux he'd pulled out of his closet in the bus, bowed deeply to the old lady and extended his hand. She stood, curtsied, and then took his hand so he could walk her to a patch of open grass right down in front of me where they danced like they were doing the two-step in a grand ballroom. Everyone stood up and as Wynk and Mrs. P danced, they sang to help me through the chorus, tearing-up as they watched an old romance play out before their very eyes.

*We met on a dare in the dark of a night*
*When the passion of youth was our courage.*
*We met under stars on the hill of desire,*

*And we burned in the flames of their fire.*

*We danced to the tune of two beating hearts*
*And spoke nothing but truth from our mouths.*
*We flew through life on the wings of a dove,*
*And never fell from the blue sky above.*

*Oh, we danced in the bones of our love.*
*We danced with our bodies entwined.*
*We danced and we sang to our song.*
*Oh, we danced in the bones of our love.*

When the last note was played, Mrs. Paulpetter put her arms around Wynk's back and held tight for a few moments, her head against his heart, which I knew was still ticking out the tune we sang for her. Then she pulled away, averted her eyes, saw the way off and left, forgetting her cane that she had laid on her table, and forgetting for the moment, I supposed, the arthritic discomforts of the present compared to the nubile memory in which she had just floated. I received a message from her a few days later. I got my money's worth, she said.

I turned to Jack and nodded. He kicked into Out of the Mud and I grabbed Cladine's guitar, electrified now so I could be heard up in the gods, and we tore into it. Oh fuck we tore into it. We just didn't want to dwell in the sentiments of old women. Too painful.

Just a few licks in, the valley people were standing again. Tedhum came forward with the bass guitar and dug down to its growly low notes. Soon the crowd started clapping and stomping out the four-four beat that drives the song. Some I saw on the moonlit slope of the theater pointing at the face of the full moon, shooting at it with their finger. Bang, bang.

*Out of the mud came a walking man*
*Gun in hand, gun in hand.*
*Shot his neighbor and his neighbor's wife.*
*I put no price on my neighbors' life.*
*I can take them out with my gun in hand.*

*Out of the mud came a wild child,*
*Gun in hand, gun in hand.*
*Shot the teacher in the head at school,*
*He hadn't learned the price of life.*
*He didn't care, with his gun in hand.*

*Out of the mud came a woman crazed*
*Gun in hand, gun in hand.*
*Shot her husband, son and then herself*
*The sad-eyed woman of the low, low land,*
*Just wanted out, with her gun in hand.*

Did we bust down the electric fence and the gates around the Kingdom of Napa that night. We made a start, but it took Cora Munro's order to the federalized National Guard to make sure the plug was pulled once and for all.

*Beware the baleful bite of the bootless benediction.*

# Song 21

Mother awoke, not quite painless, but more or less sober. I was in the bathroom preparing for a visit with Belle and Harold, humming quietly as I lined my eyes with mascara and dabbed a bit of rouge on my cheeks and a bit of lipstick on my dry lips. Lawry and Jav had already departed for work and being generous of spirit, had not left the slightest whiff of disgruntlement in the air despite their anguish over Merri's condition. We had all come to accept Merri's inebriated habits because none of our protestations and alarms had done anything but make her climb on the wagon for a few days, crying and momentarily ashamed. I wanted her to go to rehab. She wouldn't. When I pressed, she snarled like a wet cat and bared her claws.

- Nobody in a white coat is coming anywhere near me. You can get that out of your pretty young head right now.

- They don't wear white coats mother.

- Whatever.

- You're getting sick.

- Hell I am. You ever see me not put in a full day's work? Being hungover ain't being sick.

- I'm worried about you.

- Worry away. Where's that going to get you?

- Mother...

- Let's be perfectly honest Wicla. You don't really give a shit. You're doing your own thing now. You and that Wynk. You and the band. You and Belle and Harold and all the rest of them. What's that song you were playing the other day about the star-making machinery. You're right in the middle of it like farmer joe on his tractor. Well, you know what, Trader Merri's still on the road and still doing business, and she'll be there for a while yet. Drunk or sober, I get it done and nobody, not even a big star like you, is going to tell me how to live my goddamn life. You got that!?

Noise. There's always a lot of noise when an addiction is fighting for its life. It grabs hold of mind, body and spirit and it will use any and all means to hold on. Shit flies from the addict's mouth like a vomit to disgust the weak of stomach, and anger does what it can to fend off the weak of heart. So be it. I was my mother's daughter and my retreats were always back to the high ground from which I would develop other tactics to free her from the grip of booze. I would find a way because I was not going to let it kill my mother.

Belle was already putting my next tour together, but we wouldn't depart for a month – time enough to work up some new songs she hoped, and to rehearse them when Jack, Tedhum,

Ann Marie and Zimbo returned from the various places they had gone to get away from me and one another. Wynk was at a hotel in Ojai, writing a book he said, but really only thinking about what he would write once he started. He was also waiting for me to separate myself from Merri a little because she was too dependent on me, he said. Really, he just wanted more of me for himself. Fair enough. I was not going to admit to him that it was I who was dependent on her.

So, we had a month in Ojai and we would not be under all the stresses of road travel. Merri could lower her consumption, maybe even be persuaded to hop on that wagon yet one more time. That would help. What else could I do? Change our living arrangements. Get her away from the familiar and the habitual. Put some distance between her and Javier because, even though he was not a sot, when we were at the cabin he liked to drink with her. Besides which, I had always had the feeling, and never lost it, that Merri and I were imposing on him and Larry. I wanted to put that right, and now that I had money in the bank, I was in position to do something about it.

Saying I'd be right back, I left and drove into Ojai, entering from the west gate into the vast new underground parking and turned the van over to autodrive which used GPS to guide me to the area just below Belle's office. Wynk and I did our business with Belle and Harold then went out into the streets, now empty of all vehicular traffic, but under the buzz and swooping of a few drones making deliveries or ferrying people to wherever they needed to go.

The dome construction was almost finished. Looking up we could see that the ring of the oculus, high up but off center toward the north, was in place, held there by the rib work of the rest of the dome. The crystals that formed the skin of the dome were multiplying rapidly at this point and would put the whole town under cover within a couple of months.

- We need a real estate agent, Wynk.

- Why?

- We're buying a house.

- A house?

- Let's look for an agent.

Wynk thought I meant only for him and me, so no resistance on his part.

- OK. I'm in.

- I'm buying it Wynk. It will be my house.

He stopped in his tracks.

- For us, I said. For us and mother too.

- Your mother?

- You love her. So, shut up, said with a smile as I took his arm and moved closer.

We found an agent, a perky little blond who chattered ad nauseum, and that day we looked at four or five houses. Our first time in a drone taxi too, and the first time either of us had seen anything from on high. It was an incredible thrill, but let's save all of that for the book Wynk or I may – or may not – ever write.

- I like the old Selman place.

- Which one was that?

- White stucco. The bungalow with the pool outside the living room. Remember, the sliding doors were… And it was secluded. Semi secluded.

- Oh, c'mon, Wicla. It's a trash heap.

- It had a guest house…

- For me?

- Uh uh.

- Ah! OK. OK!

It turned out that in the hive towns and in the bigger hive cities, no one could own land outright. You just leased on a long-term basis. Fine by me.

Phase two of my strategy was already underway. Keep us all busy during that month in Ojai, especially Merri, who would evaporate into thin air and cease to exist if she were not doing something. She loved the idea of the guest house; it had the contained feeling she always had in the van, everything close at hand, including guns and hooch, which she had stowed away when we weren't looking.

She also liked the idea of keeping one loving eye on me, even if I were inside at the other end of the pool, while she kept her other, suspicious, somewhat jealous eye on Wynkyn DeWorde. Not that she disliked him. She liked him a lot but her easy, but wrong calculation, was that I had withdrawn some of my love for her to bestow on him. She liked Wynk even more when he swam naked in the sparkle of the pool, doing lengths with his hands cupped and his legs fluttering in the water until he was tired. She liked it even more when he jumped in or pulled himself up on the side because his judiciously large willy flopped around and made her feel more comfortable around men simply because it was not priapically charged to inflict itself on any nearby women, especially her.

And busy we were, me writing songs and then when my bandmates returned, rehearsing. Wynk proved himself a splendid handyman in his own right and put his management skills to superb use as the supervisor of all the tradesmen who made their way to our happy home and were pressed into service on our behalf.

Mother, in turn, supervised Wynk as she sipped cold, alcohol-free drinks from a chaise lounge she had set-up on the little patio outside the guest house, knowing that the bright sun's otherwise deadly rays were being filtered by the Crysalinks of the fast-growing dome. If I were late getting back from the studio, she would even try her hand at making Wynk a meal, usually suggesting he go for a swim to cool-off before eating, while she sliced and diced the veggies and peered through a forest of cactus plants at the sleek, wet body moving through the pool and chuckling at his dangling willy on his way in or out of the water.

I finally got her to see a doctor – she'd never had a check-up in her life – and she made the fuss she usually made when she didn't want to do something but relented a lot sooner than I expected. The appointment was set for a day that I was rehearsing so Wynk said he would go with her. That's the day she had her first – and last – ride in a drone taxi, swearing never again. They walked back to the house.

- How did it go at the doctor's mother?

- Fine.

- Fine?

- He says I'm healthy as horse.

- What else? Did he run some tests?

- Nothing else.

- When will you get the results?

- Goddamit, Wicla, you'll be the first to know.

One hot night, long after midnight, Wynk and I couldn't

sleep. We held each other's hands and talked about the forth-coming tour – he still hadn't heard the new songs – and all the logistics that he would be responsible for handling. He thought he might use industrial drones to cart our equipment from place to place rather than use ground transport.

I didn't care one way or another, but listened to his soft, low voice hoping it might put me to sleep sooner than later. He turned toward me and placed his arm around me and pulled me close so we were spooning. Last thing I wanted on top of the heat of summer was the heat of sex. I wriggled away from him as much as I could. He moved closer. I felt his stiffening penis next to my bum. He cupped my breast in his hand. I turned toward him.

- Not now, Wynk. It's too hot.

- Let's go for a swim, he said suddenly, brightly.

- No, Wynk…it's late.

- So, what? C'mon. Merri's sound asleep.

He shook my shoulders.

- C'mon, he said. You'll feel better.

Both naked we slid into the pool, trying to see if mother might be watching from her sitting room by the windows, but it was black inside her cottage. We paddled around, we splashed one another as quietly as we could. I may have giggled. I did giggle. He put his hand over my mouth.

- Quiet. Let's not wake her up.

He was right in front of me. Face wet, stubble glistening, hair matted. We pulled one another close and kissed. Kissed deeply. Then he moved me against the side of the pool and put a knee between my legs and then, after I raised both arms along the side of the pool and flattened my hands to hold us there, he pulled both my legs up around his back and sunk his aroused penis into the very center of me. And there we fucked, with my ankles crossed up and around his back, my held tilted back, wet hair draped on the flagstone surround, moaning with eyes closed, locked together in aquatic bliss.

I heard a sound. Looked toward the guest house and saw my mother standing in the dark frame of her door, looking at us. I came to climax as Merri's eyes looked into mine and saw me tumbling through time and space, and she was still looking as Wynk shuddered, as he bit my neck when he groaned, and as his body went slack in the water. And I could see that she was very happy for me. Was happy for me, but with a happiness into which was woven the thread of a bitter but dying regret, of never knowing a man while he and she were in the throws of a gentle but furious love. She retreated into the blackness of the cottage.

- Do you think she saw us? Wynk asked, trying to see again into its windows.

- She's dreaming, Wynk. Far away.

Mother was sober. I hadn't seen her take a drink since we moved into our new home. But she was agitated and more than a little withdrawn. I assumed because she knew on the following Thursday our second tour would get underway. I don't know why, but I had convinced myself she wouldn't be following along on this trip, maybe because our schedule was going to take us through Albuquerque – and not just through it.

After Phoenix, Tucson, and El Paso we would be performing there. Buzzy and Toddles bones were probably laying out there in the desert where she left them, bleached an immaculate and purifying white, because nobody would have gone looking for them. A horrible memory to chance stirring-up and a good reason to stay home. Denver, Colorado Springs, Ogden Utah, where a brand-new hive was slated to be built soon, then on to Boise, over to Bend, then south through familiar territory, with stops at Klamath Falls, Redding, San Jose, and guess where for the final stop? - Bakersfield. Two buses only this time – one for the band, one for me and Wynk. All the gear was to be hopped around by drones, as Wynk had envisaged.

The night before we left, we had a big party at our house. Attendance of all required: band, tech crew, agent, accountant, real estate agent, advertising people, Lawry and Jav, spouses, girlfriends, boyfriends and kids - about thirty-five people. We had kept everyone away until then because it was such a hovel when I bought it and we wanted to show it off when it was done. Mostly done.

There were still rooms in the main house unfinished; paint tarps, paint cans, step ladders, our electrician's and cabinet maker's gear and other such paraphernalia sat behind closed doors awaiting the return of the people who knew how use them. But the main rooms were done so those who wandered in from the pool area got a feel for what we were creating. I gave Lawry and Jav a look at some of the unfinished rooms because I knew they could see immediately what we would be doing in them. Or trying to do.

- Is Merri going on the tour with you? Lawry asked when he got me alone.

- No. She's really been at peace here. Really.

- Been a good girl then. She really looks wonderful. Look at her over there.

Merri was chatting with Jack, who hadn't been warned about keeping her away from the bar, and I saw him mouth something like he was going to get another beer. She followed him.

- How do you like dome life? Lawry asked.

- Love it, I said, cranking my head to see if Merri had a glass in her hand.

She did. By midnight, Merri was puking-drunk and once again we had to put her to bed. She was still sleeping next morning when Wynk and I got onto the drone that would take us to the place where we and the band would board the buses to begin our tour.

I felt lighter in spirit – almost physically lighter in fact - as we made our way to Phoenix without mother in tow. An hour or so out of Ojai, Wynk and I pulled over to the side of the road and put our bus on selfdrive, then joined the band in the other bus, which was already on selfdrive. We played Wynk our new songs, all of which he pronounced amazing, and kicked-back and enjoyed the long trip. We had just arrived at the lot behind the arena where would be doing the show, when Tedhum stepped out of the bus. Holy shit! he yelled, then pointed down the road in the direction from which we had just come. We all piled out and stood around him, looking at a white van approaching. It was Trader Merri Weer herself.

*Swim ye not in the salty simulacrum of a sea.*

# Song 22

You may find it odd that the thing I remember most about our second tour is that, for me at least, it occurred against the backdrop of the Presidential election. Before and after gigs, I would grab my vice and check the news feeds to find out if anything had happened to derail Cora Munro's drive to the White House. As we drove from place to place, usually at night after a performance, I was constantly looking for a quiet space where I could escape the antics of my bandmates, or the claims for attention that Wynk or my mother kept plopping into the soup of my distraction.

We moved through the desert landscape past the weird silhouettes of rock formations against a purple sky, heard the castanet dance of lightning on the parched sands, and would have, had we stood on an Indian lookout in the great somewhere, watched our white buses and Trader Merri Weer's van slide slowly past, seen their tiny shapes illumined under the thick milk of stars above. And yet, it was the magic of Mrs. Munro's disruptive politics which grabbed me most.

In Phoenix I debuted our new songs, inserting them carefully into a line-up of those we had performed on our inaugural tour. By the time we got to El Paso, one of the new ones, Inside Out, had found an unexpected purpose on the Munro campaign. Just before we went on, Wynk walked quickly to me with his vice tuned to one of her rallies. After she was introduced to an already cheering crowd, Inside Out was cranked-up in that far off auditorium in the Carolinas and I watched as it pulled the thousands who were there that night up off their seats, and got them all to raise their arms high above their heads to clap and clap and clap as Cora Munro walked in from stage left, striding toward the podium in a scarlet dress like an immaculate conception.

I suppose I felt a shock of pride. Wynk's 'wow!' had given me permission. He raised the vice and pointed the video feed in the direction of Jack, Ann Marie, Tedhum and Zimbo while he nodded his head and broadcast a toothy, approving smile. Wow because we had broken through an east west wall; wow because we had only put the song out there two nights earlier and did not understand how or why something like a song could move at the speed of light. Wow because none of us – especially me – had been touched by politics before, and we were by no means certain we wanted to have its stain laid on us.

After the show, when Wynk and I were alone I was brooding on the sound of Inside Out in the political arena.

- Can they do that?

- Sure. Subject to royalties.

I frowned.

- We could object. That's a time-honored ritual.

- You think we should?

- I thought you were a fan of Cora's. You want her to win,

right?

- I am. I do, yes.

- So?

- There are a lot of people in our audience who hate everything she stands for.

- Life's a bitch.

I hadn't realized until that very moment that I might actually have to suffer for my convictions. And not even that much. The number of people who would stay away from a Wicla show just because one of my songs had become a Democrat could be counted on two hands and a foot. In the meantime, according to Belle's and Harold's ecstatic reports, I would die rich because we were now being listened to from coast to coast.

On we went through the rest of the tour, with Trader Merri doing only so-so business where her legend had not been established. But things picked up for her once we got west of the Rockies. She was long out of stock by the time we got to Bakersfield for our last show, drinking little, but tired. Wynk and I went to the warehouses with her to help her load the van and then took her to dinner where she ordered a whiskey before the food came, but mostly let it sit there undisturbed collecting the golden light from a table lamp. From time to time she would flinch and shift her body.

- You OK, mother?

She would straighten up and look at me, with a gaze that fell on my face, but anywhere other than my eyes.

- Of course I am. Just tired, that's all.

- It's been a long day.

- I'll get some sleep after the show tonight.

- We'll come and check on you, said Wynk.

- I'm coming to the show. Now, Wynk, you just make sure I'm down front and center. I wanna watch my little girl sing.

Merri had not come to any of the performances since we departed on the tour. So, in one way, I guess we shouldn't have been surprised that she would want to see the last one. But we were. She had been much more reclusive than at any time before and she had established patterns and rituals around the day that seemed more and more like an attempt to keep the world – including the strange world of concert touring – at bay. She was traveling with us, but she wasn't either.

None of Bakerfield's venues could accommodate the number of people who wanted to see the show, so Belle and Wynk decided on one of the local parks. It had grassy slopes that formed a natural amphitheater where tens of thousands, every race and creed and all age groups, could make themselves comfortable. No one got in the gates carrying a weapon – I insisted - on the pain of not performing - if gun toting had been allowed. Bakersfield people were unsettled by a demand that they come unarmed to anything, so the fact that they came to the concert in such numbers said something. Guess they like you, said Jack Fate, looking at me over the top of the sunglasses he took to wearing at all times like the ROFO great he was.

He chugged a glass of water before he and the others went out to do the tunes that always warmed up the crowd. That night, he and Ann Marie gave one another a kiss and a hug first, the kind that lovers give. I hadn't even realized they'd hooked up. Jack stepped to the mic and while he introduced me, Ann Marie worked the fiddle, stepping almost to the edge of the apron as she made it rasp and howl – a kind of sound I used to hear in Cladine's voice - as a spotlight caught me in its cone and walked me to center stage to take my place in front of an audience fully roused from its post-dinner dullness.

I searched the front row and found Merri there, holding the arms of a canvass chair that Wynk had set-up just for her, in a row of others who were sitting on the grass. She wore a thin smile, like a queen not sure if even she wanted to be at her own commanded performance. I pointed at her then blew her a kiss. She raised a hand to say stop it, stop it, but in fact, the daughter-to-mother attention thus bestowed truly warmed her heart.

We worked our way through our repertoire and as we did we got into it. Deeply. I mean, me and the band and the band and the crowd and the crowd and the night sky full of stars again, as though we should be surprised after living and dying under them through all the millennia that have passed, that they should still be there. Be there for us humans and all the other feral creatures of this old world.

In the spaces between songs, guess what, just the sound of people yelling out requests, the crying of babies, a few people stifling coughs, the rustle of people tearing open bags of food, but as yet, no gunfire sounding out there from the great, violent sprawl of Bakersfield. Until we all heard a gunshot, and then another.

The unarmed audience fell quiet. All of Bakersfield was inside the park. Who was out there shooting and killing? A ripple of fear washed over the crowd. They looked at me, as I too stood with my ears cocked. They wanted something from me. I looked over at Wynk, who was pulling his chin with a nervous hand. Looked down at my mother. I saw her mouth something. I was not sure what she was saying. I kept looking at her. She turned her head and looked behind her, then at the people stretched out to the left and right of her and mouthed the name of a song again. And then I understood.

- Here's a song that you might have heard these last few days.

I strummed a couple of chords to signal the band and then I played a couple of other chords.

- You know what? If you want to see some change you might want to give Cora Munro a shot. She's got some things to say that we need to hear.

A few boos from the crowd, but not many.

- So, I'm going to sing this song to you on her behalf. This is Jack Fate on rhythm guitar; Tedhum Porterhouse on bass. Over there is Ann Marie Bullock on fiddle and guess who that is on drums? That's right, that's Zimbo. And we're going to sing Inside Out.

And we did. We turned political right then and there. Or at least I did. I got the fact that I owned the stage and the stage owned me, and whatever gift I may have had for penning lyrics and tunes and for singing them out to the people was a healer's gift and that I would be damned to hell if I did not use it to heal. I might inflict a little pain in the doing, but we would come through it.

*We drove the busted roads*
*Beside the rusted, ancient tracks,*
*Crossed a thousand rivers*
*Where all our rubbish flows*
*Down to the dreaded sea*
*Oh, down to the dreaded sea of time.*

*We hear all men and women shout,*
*What spirit turned us inside-out?*
*And all our rootless children cry*
*What spirit turned us inside-out?*
*In the mountains there we saw*
*Burning trees and empty springs.*
*We had a view of desert lands below.*
*We heard the bird that never sings*
*But pecks his message on our bones*
*Pecks his message on our brittle bones.*

*We hear all men and women shout*
*What spirit turned us inside-out?*
*And all our frightened children cry*
*What spirit turned us inside-out?*

*By a wayside on our road we stopped*
*Where a sacred wind still blows.*
*We felt a blessed rain begin to fall*
*That fed the flowers and the grass,*
*That fed the flowers and the leaves of grass.*

*We heard every man and woman shout,*
*We heard our ever-hopeful child cry*
*We are just our little selves, you gods,*
*Outside-in and inside-out.*
*And our spirits shall always be as one*
*At least we must forever try.*

It is a dark lyric, but at its end our music lifts it into a blue and cloudless sky where there is no poison sun to drive us to the shadows. That night, everyone stood to sing the chorus, everyone but Merri, whom I saw bent double in her chair, hugging her knees, hiding her tears from the child me.

*Cry, cry-out for the country crucified.*

# Song 23

Cora Munro, of course, won the election so she and Paul went to live in the White House where, rumour had it, they were not getting along very well. She was busy and Paul, though publicly gracious, was put on a short leash and snarling in private. According to Maude, as relayed to me by Belle, he was seriously disgruntled by his confinement and by a rigorous lack of intimacy with his beautiful, but preoccupied wife. He had First Husband chores to do, and a couple of charities to keep him interested in life beyond the White House fences, but Cora forbade him from working with the sun kings of New York who, until her election, had employed him to do much of the shadowy work that raveled up the deals they wanted and unravelled those they didn't. These same men were his boon companions too, so the loss of their scotch and soda company in well-appointed offices, in the plush clubs of the city and at their bespoke lodges on the shores of pristine lakes, made him sad. A sadness, alas that sounded to Cora like ungrateful anger and annoying irritation because that is, in fact, how it came out of him. It's hard to turn one's body over to a man whose resentments add an annoying heft to his middle age weight.

I cared not a whit about Paul, to tell the truth. I wanted to know if Cora were going to do what she said she would when she stumped for the Presidency. All I had to do was sing songs, but she had to mobilize a buggered government to re-establish America as a somewhat civilized country in which everyone could pursue their happiness – whatever that meant. What I had gathered from listening to her without really understanding what she was saying in the first instance, was that a new threat to the Union was rapidly evolving. But remember, she had a perspective rooted in her experience in the eastern states, where entirely new cities – hive cities – and a very large number of hive towns were springing up. They were quickly being connected by hyperloop and hydroloop systems that wove them together in a matrix that was almost impervious to the dictates of the national government.

It was a hard case to make because – as I had seen for myself in Kingman and Ojai – the world inside the hive towns, and, I guessed, the hive cities, was a helluva lot more agreeable than life on the outside. Mrs. Munro was no troglodyte. She didn't want to restore what *was* - as though our sun was going to suddenly become benevolent again. She wanted to bring as many people on the outside into hives as quickly as possible. She wanted to throw the weight of her government behind that effort and dome all the big old cities across America – cities like Chicago, Boston, Atlanta, Dallas, Seattle and all the others – so the millions and millions of people who lived in their rotting precincts could renovate their lives. But she ran into a high, hard wall.

Clement Samuels, who had discovered the crystal out of which the domes were grown would allow the doming of smaller towns, but he would not allow the doming of the old cities, which he said, would merely fester inside and make things much worse for the poor souls within. The new hive cities, like Clinton, Reagan, BushBush, Obamaport, CashCarter, Roddenberry, and the others now under construction, including

Gatesport on the Pacific coast, were either built close by the old or on some promising chunk of real estate at a distance, but they were built from the ground up.

It looked to Cora like Samuels was creating a new divide in the country – the deepest yet – and she was not going to have it. Hence the use of my song at her rallies and at many of her post-election speeches. In fact, she dubbed me Queen of the Outsiders for exemplifying the hard life of those who were stuck out there (her words, not mine) and for giving expression to the tough, angry, painful, urgent feelings that such a life, she concluded, would inevitably produce.

God I hated that designation, but I let it be because, well, she was my Robin Hood, and I had jumped into her quiver and was ready to be shot at whatever targets she pointed her long, manicured finger at. The President also sent me a private note of thanks for supporting her and for allowing her to use Inside-Out royalty-free, with an open invitation to visit her at the White House. I wish she hadn't, because, ultimately, I made a desperate plan to go there to see if I might be the one to pull her out of the sea-deep depression into which, at the beginning of her second term, she had fallen – or probably, I thought, been pushed.

Cora Munro went after Samuels relentlessly. She was a lawyer and used lawyerly strategies. Crysalinks was a natural material – couldn't be patented she said. But all the processes he discovered to grow them into structural elements, like the litter boxes now in use across the country and in the hive domes were. So were some of the techniques used to build those structures. Maybe so, but the crystal itself is public domain she declared. Samuels had the crystal moved to some inaccessible location, known now, but undiscoverable back then.

Crysalinks was vital to the national security, she argued. Samuels' lawyers argued back. The dispute stayed in the courts for a long time and may still be zigging and zagging its way through them even now.

He lied to the investigators she decried as she held up a sheaf of papers that presumably proved it. Not really, it turned out. The papers were of dubious provenance.

Wait, wait, she said, backtracking a little to procedural gotchas. He contemptuously removed the crystal after being told to hand it over. She got him there. They mulched him in damages and threw him into a prison – a very tough one. And there he died, died at the hands of other prisoners who, for reasons I only discovered recently, were egged-on by policemen planted in the prison population on orders from on-high. Why did Cora ever think she would be the beneficiary of that man's cruel death?

Oh, dear. I sound so cool and dispassionate as I sit here and talk. It feels like so much more time has passed than actually has between then and now. Probably because the two years that followed after we completed our second tour started with great promise, but came to a shattering, time-compressing conclusion. Really, it is difficult to bring it all back to mind. But continue I must.

Not much to say about our third tour except that mother peeled-off about halfway through and returned to Ojai where she awaited our return and tried to shake the body flu, as she called it, that had seized her just after a restocking visit to Blaine. I told her in no uncertain terms to just get on the Autodrive and let it take her south as far as possible. She startled me by saying she had no idea of driving herself and would let the buggy take her home.

After she left to go home, one of our gigs was in Gatesport – about as far northwest as you can get on the US mainland. By the time we got there it already had a sizeable population – maybe a half million or so. The folks who now lived there had made there way out of Seattle and Portland and most of the other small cities and towns of the Pacific Northwest. The sudden depopulation of those places accelerated their long decline. It spun many of those places with such violent speed, in fact, they went into a final death spiral. The voices of those who remained went as unheard as sailors lost to sudden storms far out at sea. Except by me, that is. I wrote a couple of songs in which I tried to capture the murmur of their fatalistic despair. Town Idiot was one of those songs, Shattered Windows the other.

In Gatesport, following the pattern established in the eastern hives, the new arrivals took hold of truly incredible homes under long term leases. Their vehicles got parked, maybe forever, in the vast underground below the city. Those who had them, put their guns in the Hive's armoury to await the unforeseeable day when the city might come under attack and they enrolled their kids in the hive's schools. Virtually all who wanted or needed to work found employment inside, or just outside at the separately domed hydroloop port or in one or other of the new integrated industrial or agricultural plants. Lawyers, accountants, doctors and anyone else professing this or that hung their shingles, tradespeople plied whatever trade they practiced, storekeepers set-up shop. And everyone switched to old time, some of the old folks even cocking an ear to an imagined rooster who crowed their memories awake at the crack of dawn.

The instant I came up the escalator and stepped up out onto the vast expanse of Gatesport's public square I finally got what Cora Munro had warned us about. The Insiders now lived in a manufactured heaven, the Outsiders in the same old hell. Why would anyone be surprised that one would look out and down on the other, while that other looked in at their counterparts with bitter resentment and at their government as their ultimate betrayer?

We did our concert there and it went over as well as anywhere we performed on that tour, but I didn't enjoy it. The Outsider's Queen felt hypocritical in her bones. I think Ann Marie and Tedhum felt as I, but I am not sure about Jack and Zimbo. Wynk, who admittedly was too tired from all the work he was doing to care much about the mixed disposition of the band, let alone my precious feelings, told me to get over it. Our audience, who paid in the same was as the good people of Kingman had three years earlier were numberless. They were wild for us, I think, because, although they were now under the protection of the dome, they had not yet shucked-off the feelings and outlooks of those places they had recently fled and had in the course of time absorbed our music into the Outsider blood that still flowed through their veins. That would change as time went on.

At the end of the tour, long before we got to the gate at the north end of the Maricopa Road on our way to Ojai, I was overtaken by sentiment and nostalgia, and it turns out, something deeper. You're just homesick, said Wynk. Yes, I was. You miss your mother. I did. Really missed her. But I missed the woman she was when I was still in my teens, the Merri who was at the wheel of my whole existence. My bold, brave mother who jingled and jangled, laughed, swore, barked at the moon, ploughed through time and space, road the back roads into the lives of other women and delivered to them a wagonload of courage along with the stuff that made life a bit easier or more tolerable in the places where they lived, penned in by barricades, hemmed in by men who had found manly purpose in the dangerous world we all lived in.

But it wasn't just Merri whom I missed. Vivid images of Lawrence and Javier staked-out a large chunk of my mind too. I had seen them quite a lot, mostly at parties at our house in Ojai. But I had not visited the cabin in a long time. I hadn't gone to the Studios for a couple of years, even when mother went over to do business with all her friends as they changed shifts. I always begged-off because I thought I deserved time off after a tour or was too busy prepping for the next. I texted Lawry a short message: can you give a poor girl and her momma a meal? His response came seconds later: Friday evening?

Even mother put on a little lipstick for the occasion. We drove over in the van and parked it in 'our spot.' They had both been waiting, standing behind the front window, excited. The dining table behind them was set with their best china, best table service, their crystal wine glasses, and a perfectly composed array of flowers spread gloriously around two burning candles.

They came out of the cabin and each took one of our hands and helped us down from the van.

- You could have droned over, said Lawrence.

- We could have, I agreed.

- But you were absolutely right to bring that banged up old rig to see us, said Javier. Old times. I think you really should let me have your sign painted on it Merri before I retire.

- Give us a kiss, said my mother. And you old fool, you're too damn young to retire. So, shut up.

Lawry took my arm and escorted me into the cabin. Javier followed, Merri's arm through his as they bumped one another's hips and giggled.

- You didn't want to bring Wynkyn? asked Javier.

- Wynk would know to stay away on a night like this, Lawrence, said Jav. He's a smart man. Knows his women.

- Drinks?

- Small one, said mother, surprising Javier.

And so the night began. We settled into one another's good spirits and stayed within them the whole time, each taking stolen moments to look long and deep at the others, to reckon out the real changes from the momentary. We picked up the threads of conversations left unfinished and of unimportant disputes left unresolved, and we started a few new ones to give us something to grab on to next time we met. I gave an account of a singer's life on the road, much contradicted or scorned by my mother, while she claimed to be as hard driving as ever when we all knew she wasn't. Lawry and Jav confessed they had been secretly married and had us pledge silence because no one knew but them and now us.

- What's the point of that? asked Merri. What the hell is the point of a secret marriage? she asked, as if some cosmic rule had been violated.

- He asked me and I couldn't think of a reason to say no, said Jav, holding up a finger with a gold band on it.

- We're still in love, said Lawry.

- 'Til death do us part, said Jav.

- But...

- Mother, I piped in. Sock in mouth please.

- OK, then, she said. Here's to both you old fags, and she clinked an empty glass on each of theirs and mine and refused the offer of a refill.

Mother took a corner on the sofa as Lawry and Jav and I cleared the table and carted the dishes to the kitchen.

- Ow! We heard her yelp.

I ran out.

- Mother? What?

She had tears in her eyes and had brought her arms around her chest.

- Nothing, she said. Nothing. I banged my elbow on the table here. Goddamn it! She patted her right elbow with a bony hand.

- You're sure?

- Well, damn it Wicla. Of course, I'm sure.

In the kitchen, I perched next to the counter behind Jav and Lawry where they stood, backs turned to me, as they cleared the dishes and counters and put our scant leftovers in containers. Lawry saw my reflection on the window in front of him and turned to face me.

- You aren't going to believe this, Wicla, but its true.

- What?

Jav turned around too.

- The night I proposed to him, I went down on one knee.

- Of course, I said, big smile on my face. You're a romantic.

- Jav had the vice on.

- As always.

- Playing our favourite song.

- Our new favourite song.

- Oh yeah?

- I thought, now's the time, said Lawry. That's when I went to my knee. Right Jav?

Lawrence dropped to his knee and took Javier's hand and started singing. It was one of mine, one of the old love songs I hardly ever sang after Kingman.

*The thing about you is*
*The thing that I can never be -*
*Is alone without you.*
*I would never last a minute*
*Without you in eternity.*

As he sang the first verse, mother walked into the doorway of the kitchen and looked on, and then, after Lawry rose, while he and Jav sang the rest of the verses together, to themselves and with a flourish to us, Mother Merri came to me where I was leaning against the range and stood me up. Then she put her arms around my back and squeezed her body close to mine.

\- I would never last a minute, she said. Not one minute.

*Trust the tangled testimony of time itself.*

# Song 24

Fourth tour. We did a repeat of our first tour's schedule but with a couple of changes, including a stop at Auburn, where I wanted to repay my debt to Chaplin Dufour, and at Fort Ketchup where I wanted to record a video for a new song with Daph and Meira singing backup. I had already heard their voices in my head, and there was no way I wasn't going to weave the plangent threads of their sound into the recording.

Daph and Meira were still living at the Fort under Tithy's rule, and were, Tithy said, eager to add their voices to whatever I might concoct. But of course, there would be a fee, something for the two women, but also something for the use of the Fort itself, and a little to cover Tithy's own significant commit-ment of time, and well, they could also cater our meals while on site - for a price- and take care of cleaning out the buses, laundering clothes, and performing such personal services as might be wanted by our tired, dishevelled crew and band, such as massages, manicures and barbering. I had no doubt that if someone wanted a bit more from the women of the fort, it could be bought and paid for.

In light of these revenue neutral visits, as Belle called them, Belle cut our budget, which imposed more work on Wynk and the diminished road crew and put our security at risk because there would be fewer men between the stage and our audience, or between our vehicles and the predators, both spontaneous and organized, who always bedevilled our passage through the still dangerous countryside. The whole operation, which required the use of trucks to carry our equipment instead of the drones that Belle had redlined, felt inexplicably and unnecessarily threadbare, and made everyone who was going on the tour resent the cheapness of the venture. They knew damn well we were the biggest earning band in the country - on the road, online and everywhere else – and that money was flowing like the rivers of legend.

Everyone – especially Wynk – had climbed on board our transport burdened by their resentment toward Belle, sure, but also toward me because it seemed to them that I had put up no fight at all. Having traveled all those years with my mother – talk about threadbare – I was quite accustomed to all sorts of privations and even though this tour was skint by comparison to the last, it wasn't all that bad. Besides, as Wynk well knew, and the others would learn soon enough through the on-tour grapevine, I had used my star power to get Belle to agree to our visit to Chappy's and the Fort and I had no fight left in me. But not wanting a Spartan rebellion on my hands, I made a deal: I would, I declared at a meeting of the disgruntled, make up for it. At tour's end, I would share a good swack of the profits with everyone, high to low. They were mollified, not lip-smackingly so, but at least head-noddingly satisfied with the bargain.

Initially, mother was not going to come on tour with us. Trader Merri Weer had had her day she said. She was so emaciated and wan, frail to a degree that made me worry. She was not quite sixty but she looked years older. I put it down to years of hard living on the road and too much whiskey over too long a time even though she was hardly drinking at all by the time this tour was ready to go. And then there were the pills. She kept a bottle in the pocket of her vest, where they rattled quietly as she pottered about the house and garden, or in her pants pocket on those days when it was too warm to wear a vest, where they bulged just a little against her thin leg.

Both Wynk and I made a note of how often she was pouring two or three of them into her hand then pushing them down with a large swig of water, almost always with a pained look on her face. Merri was trying to hide her pill-taking from us, but it was so habitual now that she forgot herself. We were both worried that she had been prescribed something that had wormed its way into her addictive brain and had become her poison instead of her medicine. We tried to find out what she was taking but she always took measures to get in the way of our meddling as she called it, rearing-up like a fanged snake if we got too close, hissing as only Merri could.

- When you two become doctors, you let me know. I will have all kinds of time for your opinion on that very day. In the meantime, please do keep them to yourselves.

A few days before we were to depart Merri found the full tour schedule among a bunch of papers Wynk left in the living room. I had given her an abridged copy of our itinerary in which I omitted the stop at Chappy's and the Fort because I could predict what would happen if she knew about them.

- You weren't gonna tell me about this? She asked.

She waived the schedule in my face and pulled at the back of my shoulder so I would turn and face her. There was no way she was going to stay home on her fat ass – really it was road runner skinny and coyote bony by then – while we went gallivanting all over the countryside having a damn good time and forgetting about her all alone back in Ojai dripping teaspoons of water on the cactus garden.

- You wouldn't even know these people if it weren't for me. Or are you forgetting that?

- There's no room on the buses, Merri, said Wynk at dinner one night.

- What's your point?

- You just can't come along for the ride. Sorry, but Belle...

- When did I ever just come along for the ride you son of a bitch? I'll be right behind you with my van. In fact, Wynkyn DeWorde, I might even lead the parade.

I heard them laughing in the kitchen later, and there may even have been something of a water and suds fight by the sink. Those always ended with Wynk running from the kitchen as Merri snapped at his butt with a coiled dish rag and cursed his Dutch ancestors as though they were her own. That night was no different. The sound of them playing with one another always made me grin like a monkey and once I got to that point, a decision I didn't like having been forced on me by my undeniable mother, I wasn't going to pout let alone raise the roof to lay down some law that would have been disobeyed anyway.

Off we went. Going south the skies were clear and blue as always with little change expected. We paid little attention to the rest of the weather report which included a tedious discussion of disturbances in the cold, deep waters of the Bering Sea and unsettling currents of warm water and prickly air in the mid-Pacific that were moving north and looking, as one caster put it, for a fight, a brouhaha.

There were larger crowds - by far - at every venue, mostly young people for whom our music was not just a break with the past but a step into some kind of future where theirs – and our - idealism would be made manifest. They were joined by large contingents of people in their thirties and forties and a good number of people who had slid into middle age – or even old age – too. You could feel change in the air. It had a lambent quality before and after our shows, but when we were performing, my singing, the band's playing, the electric hopes of everyone in those huge audiences sparked into a dancing, multi-colored brilliance that enveloped all of us, somehow melded us. One writer covering the tour dubbed it the aurora musicalis, that otherworldly thing that actually can be of this world.

Merri did follow - or lead - as the case might be as we made our way. Sometimes I would join her in the van just to keep her company or I would take the wheel myself when I knew she was too tired to drive safely, or at all. She did a bit of business wherever we stopped, but not like in the old days. More and more of the stuff she sold to women was now readily available at local stores, but a lot of women wanted to see her again or meet her for the first time – her legend was still powerful – and she was Wicla the Singer's mother after all – a legend she had begat and raised. A lot of women bought things just because they wanted to say they had done business with Trader Merri Weer, or because, having come, they didn't want to disappoint her. Mother was no fool. She knew what was happening – was almost glad that it was.

- The tough days are behind us Wicla.

- We're doing greet, ma.

- Not for us you, dummy. For them. Hell, imagine not being able to buy a good bra or panties, or get some napkins.

- Or birth control pills.

- Damn right.

- That's one of the reasons I decided to come on this tour.

- Meaning what?

- Meaning we have to adjust and to adjust we have to know what's what. We have to change up the inventory now. Get some stuff they can't get anywhere else.

- Like?

- Like the shoes we can get at the Fort. Like we used to

before you got so wrapped-up in this music business and had no time for our friends.

Case in point. We had planned to go see Lawry and Jav before we left, but the day of departure came on fast, and it didn't happen. Even now, I want to give myself a kick for that. A painful, gluteal smashing, in fact.

With El Cajon behind us once again, we headed east and north, did our gigs, then crossed back into California where we had shows in Anaheim and Pasadena. We had one more performance to do in Fresno before the long-awaited night at Chappy's but Merri decided to skip it so she could get to Auburn before we did. I didn't want to let her out of my sight, so I made the mistake of telling her she couldn't.

- I can't go?

- No.

- Who the hell do you think you are?

- It's not safe for you to be...

- Who the hell do you think you are? She raised the volume more than a little.

- Wynk? I yelled across the stage in Pasadena.

He didn't want to get into the middle of it but put down the ring of tape he was holding and walked over slowly, like a cat making his way on a rug littered with broken glass.

- Wynk, tell mother…

- You stay out of this Wynk, barked Merri.

Arrested in his tracks, he put his hands up and backed away.

- Now, get out of my way.

She pushed past me, muttering imprecations.

Merri got to Auburn and to Next Next and started working on Chappy right away. He told me later when we got some time after the show that he had been shocked to see mother whittled down as much as she was, but he quickly added, just physically, of course.

- Hell, she walked in that door over there, saw me fiddling with some lectric cords up by the stage, fixed her eyes on me like a latter-day Medusa and started in without so much as a how do you do. Hell, we hadn't laid eyes on one another for over two years. Two years is it? Damn.

Was everything ready? Was there going to be a crowd? Had he done all the advertising necessary? Was the electrical system in good working-order? Lights? Did he oil the hinges on the front door to stop the squeaking that she couldn't help but notice as when she walked in? Did he hold back enough parking space for the tour buses and trucks? Could they get the gear in the back door because they sure as hell weren't going to be using his shitty old amps and speakers? Were our rooms ready? That was always the deal and nothing had changed except maybe a little passing of time. Did he know Wicla had a man now and that the old bed would not do, no sirree? King and a spring. Let's get it done, chop-chop. Did he spring for a few flowers in the room, you cheap bastard? Wicla is gonna put this dump on the map. No, I won't have a drink and settle down. Well, maybe a short one, but I've tapered off a bit.

- It's gonna be a good night, Merri. All is ready. I promise you.

Chappy, like my mother, was getting on in years. But like her, he was still vigorous of mind and spirit. A bit more stooped than he was last time we were there, paler if that is possible, balder up top, pouchier, sadder eyes than I remembered, but eyes that still surveyed his domain, constantly looking for anything and everything that might hinder the flow of his trade, or cause the loud voices of a dispute to ratchet up into a furniture-breaking melee. He didn't abide gambling, prostitution or drug dealing in his establishment and discussions about politics and religion were seriously frowned upon unless he said, the politician complained about or the God being blasphemed was sitting at the table do defend himself. Or herself, he said, winking at any women within earshot of his dictates. His barmen knew to pour generous shots and serve cold, cold beer; the waitresses were efficient and friendly and ill-advised to flirt beyond the point of good fun; the cooks were told to put a lot of love into their food, and anyone who graced the Next Next stage better deliver some hunger-inducing, thirst-making good fun because eat, drink and make merry was the order of the day. Every day.

- You do realize I'm doing your daughter a favour?

- Say again. She's Wicla for god's sake. Maybe you haven't heard, but she's a star, Chaplin Dufour. A bona fide star. This place is going to be packed-out.

- With her or without her.

- What?

- I can fill this place any night I want.

- What's your problem, Chappy?

- No problem. But she sings them protest songs.

- So?

- So, people around here want their spirits lifted out from under the heavy boot on their necks, not be reminded of the fact.

- Oh, she'll get them going. Don't you worry about that, you cranky old bastard. God you're getting old.

- Refill?

- Soda. With a twist.

Chappy also noted her pill-taking and said I might want to keep an eye on it. Doctor's orders I said.

Our night at Chappy's was one of the best nights of my life. Ann Marie, Jack, Tedhum and Zimbo had all come up through the rough bars and small clubs of Arizona, Utah and New Mexico, but after playing behind me to tens of thousands in arenas, stadiums and concert halls we had become used to the big separation between us and our audiences. You can try to make those feel like intimate experiences. It's a mind game that might work on any given night, but you can never achieve true intimacy. It's better to be big and powerful on those stages, better to place your faith in the grand gesture, the flamboyant riff, the theatrical use of the body and your instrument, better to strut the stage, to think of the faces in front of you as a veritable sea. You conjure magic while you are performing and when you do you assert the ultimate power that gods must assert lest the crowd surge forth and you be drowned in their angry disappointment.

In a place like Chappy's you can smell the leather on some guy, get a whiff of a woman's perfume; catch the sound of laughter, coughs, sneezes, burps, farts, chairs shifting, bottles tipping over on tables, waitresses whispering as they deliver plates of food whose odors waft up to the stage and make you hungry, the scrapes and pings of cutlery on plates.

You can hear snippets of arguments starting, gaining speed or coming to their end, bits and pieces of jokes, the seeds of rumours as they are floated to new ears in the semi-dark, sly seductions, slier rejections, heavy breathing, light sighs and all the other noises of people at their leisure. And it is these noises you try to silence with your own noise, noise called music, for just a few minutes with each song, until you draw forth the applause that makes you and every member of your little band whole.

I wanted to win Chaplin Dufour over and knew that if I did that, the crowd in the bar would be won over too. We played quite a few of the old songs that were more or less hatched in Chappy's bar, or places like it. As we made our way through that first set, I could see him standing way back at the end of the bar in deep shadow just behind Merri who was perched on the stool she had claimed for herself a few years earlier.

Chappy's face softened; he uncrossed the arms he had held up to his chest, looked over the ranks of his blissful customers and knew that whatever we might throw at them next, they would be ready for it. More than ready. I could see him lean in toward my mother and whisper something in her ear, the kind of thing that old people say about young people who surprise and please them, issue of their loins or close to it. Merri didn't take her eye off me but did raise her hand to where he sat and held it there while they listened to the dying chorus of Bed of Roses, the song we were singing.

*You chanced their thorns for me*
*In that ancient garden where they grow*
*And gathered flowers in your hands,*
*To make a bed of roses.*

We came back to do our second set, which we kicked-off with songs, not of protest as Chappy convinced they were, but out of our book of revelations whose songs painted the realities of Outsider life including the primal beauty that lay behind and beneath the surface dangers and the dispiriting clutter. We sang of the courage that allowed us all to endure what we had endured for so long now but could also be roused to force the changes that we all fervently wished for ourselves and our descendants.

I saw Chappy moving through the tables and picking up empty glasses and bottles that he ported back to the bar. In mid song I snuck a look back to Merri's stool where a huge, big-bellied man wearing a black shirt and a big hat was now sitting like a bull on a fence post tapping his feet in time to our music. Mother had gone up to her room, got into bed and curled into a foetal position, listening to the hollow thump-thump of our bass beat as it came up through the floorboards until it carried her off to sleep, a bottle of pills clutched in her fist.

She told me some time later on our fateful trip east, that on her way to Auburn she had done something she wished she hadn't done. She had pulled off the highway at Folsom and made here way to the prison. She might not have done it, she said, but as she drove down the highway past the town, she had been listening to one of my songs and told me I really need to be more careful with what I write because they affected people in ways I might not appreciate.

She stopped at the gate and told the guard she was there to see Warden Morrigan. When asked to state her business she couldn't, because she wasn't about to tell him that she just wanted to kill the bitch. He wouldn't lift the gate to let her pass, so she said she'd drive right through the goddamned thing if he didn't tell the Warden that Merri Trader Weer was here on business, and I mean business, she said. He called up to Lilith's office while Merri fumed.

- She's in a meeting, he told her. But she said you could come back tomorrow.

By this time two self-driving squad cars under the control of someone in a guard tower above had arrived. One came from inside and stopped on the other side of the gate arm in front of her, and another came from behind the south wall and pulled up just short of the side of mother's van. She backed out and drove down the prison road to the highway with the two selfdrives following, but halfway down she took a left on the dirt road she knew would take her to the fence that surrounded the woman's camp.

When Merri got to the place where she had stopped to toss diapers a few years back, she got out and called to the women inside the chain link fence. She went in and out of the van and pulled boxes and boxes of whatever she was carrying and began to toss it up and over, all the while yelling at the women to come for free stuff, free stuff! Soon, the place was in an uproar, women from across the camp were stampeding to get to where Merri was tossing things over, where women jammed against the fence line were fighting tooth and nail for whatever they could get their hands on, even ripping it out of the arms of someone who made first or second or third claim to it. Lilith Morrigan now had a full-scale riot on her hands and had no means of quelling it. She had to let all that female violence play itself out, which was long after Merri had decamped for Auburn, trailing a cloud of Folsom dust in her wake.

You said it yourself, Merri told me, trying to explain herself, justice is a woman.

*Justice is a woman with a balance and a sword.*
*Be fair, oh women everywhere, take my word,*
*When it's a case of life and death never be afraid*
*To weigh the good and bad or swing the bloody blade.*

When I went up to check on Merri after we finished the show that night at Chappy's, I saw the yellow pill bottle clutched in her fingers. I pried it loose and walked into the hallway to read the prescription label. It was a powerful opioid, to be taken as necessary. In the mind of a woman like my mother, the word 'necessary' had a fatal connotation for it could be a sometimes thing, it's true, but her pain was becoming an always thing.

I put the bottle down on the side table by her bed and left the room, pulling the door closed gently behind me. Worried? What do you think?

*Place your peace in the pseudo-Psalmist's palm.*

# Song 25

As we worked our way north we cocked our collective ears more and more to the weather reports coming in from the coast. We still had a lot of time before we got to Seattle, even more time before the show in Portland and the two-day vid shoot at the Fort that would follow. It was getting nasty and the casters were predicting that gale force winds would be putting ashore around the same time we would be in the area.

- It's no problem for us, Wynk said. All of the venues are safe enough. But...

- But?

- If it gets too blowy people might stay at home.

- Not if they've already bought their tickets.

- We'll see.

- We just need two good days at Fort Ketchup.

- Yep. It might be a bit gloomy, weather wise, but we can light the place up and make it look like sunny days are here again.

- Whatever.

Wynk was one of those people who are invariably cheerful in the morning, a talker about everything and anything, usually at a volume that irritated everyone in the vicinity of his voice, or the pots and pans he rattled on the stove top, or the cupboard doors he opened and closed as he ferreted for a bowl, his cereal, the sugar and all the other things of which his holy breakfast was contrived. Did I say everyone? I mean me.

I would be bent over my first cup of coffee breathing in its rising steam, letting the smell of caffeine pry open my brain cells while Wynk streamed his thoughts about last night's show and made mental notes about all that had gone wrong – he was a perfectionist - so that they could be righted for the next show. His perfectionism was the butt of many a joke – and the source of many a resentment - on the band bus and among the tech crews, but they knew, and I knew, that it was Wynk's attention to detail that had enabled our show to evolve out of the curious debacles that characterized our first tour, into the tight and powerful show it had become. Tight but loose was Wynk's war cry because the thrust of all he did and demanded was to give me and my bandmates a platform upon which we could be as spontaneous as we were inspired to be on any given night.

But that morning, Wynk was speaking about the weather – the weather for gods sake - through nearly closed lips, leaning back in his chair, breathing heavy, speaking impatiently in a low tone. I could feel his steady gaze on me as I stirred milk into my coffee while he waited for me to raise my head and look at him. He was angry. A couple of weeks before, Wynk was working in one of the equipment trucks where Ann Marie and one of the roadies were enjoying a few minutes of post coital intimacy behind a stack of amps. She wondered aloud, knowing Wynk was nearby and listening, if her new boyfriend had also seen Jack and me locking lips. No way! Said the roadie. Really? Ann Marie wasn't sure if it was true but doubt once sewn grows rapidly as she well knew.

- Rumour has it that you and Jack are fond of one another.

- He's a good guy. Yeah. We're all fond of him.

Fond was a peculiar word to use, I thought.

- As in fucking close, said Wynk.

Counterattack.

- You know Jack and Ann Marie were a thing for a long time.

- I guess.

- You know Jack put an end to it.

- He'd had his fill. Too needy, our Ann Marie.

- Yeah. More than. She was pretty upset about being dumped like that.

- As she would be.

- Scorned woman. Furious. And hurt.

- So, you think she's spreading rumours?

- What do you think?

It sounded like a denial. But Wynk's no fool. He just went on guard and stayed there.

That morning he decided the moment for a confrontation had arrived. I didn't get a vote. Wynk didn't have any more information about me and Jack than he had two weeks earlier. But he figured the distance I had put between myself and Jack was a sign of attraction, otherwise why would I do that. Worse, worse by far, was the fact that when Wynk snuggled close in our bed I would shift out of the way. When he moved closer to my back and pulled near to spoon with me, the heat of my anxiety was an awkward warning to not come closer. When he cupped my breasts with a warm hand or caressed my tummy before moving his hand down between my thighs or pressed his hardened cock against my naked buttocks, I shook him off, sometimes with a nasty growl, pleading fatigue.

Some nights I would leave our bus and just disappear. I'd find my way to whatever bus the party was happening on and spend time I use to give to Wynk with the band and crew, or I'd climb on board Merri's van and go to sleep on my old bed, explaining the next day that Merri needed me, or I that I was especially worried about her, or that I had simply fallen asleep. Fatigue again.

The truth was, Jack and I had found our way to one another's arms. God knows he'd been trying to bed me for a long time, ever since we first met in Kingman really. But I had given up my days as a loose woman and I never allowed Jack near me even though he was darkly handsome and moved like a randy cat. Once we got the band together, I was his boss, so I had a new reason for rejecting his overtures as promising as they were of hot sex and a few laughs. Once he hooked up with Ann Marie, I was not going to chance losing her fiddle playing by getting between her and her man, and besides I had taken on Wynk by then. Being faithful to him was easy because all my energies were being channelled into becoming - and being - Wicla the Singer, Songwriter, Performer, Queen of the Outsiders and devoted daughter to Trader Merri Weer.

Wynkyn De Worde was a kind and careful lover to be sure, and he loved me, really loved me. In fact, I see now that he more or less engineered the world around me - to let me be me - while he blended into its background, wrenches in hand, barking at those who were also hired to serve me to serve me better, at peace with his self-abnegation, and proud of the woman I was and was becoming. The nights we spent in one another's arms, talking, kissing, fucking and sleeping were numberless, but I guess I could not let them be without end.

Jack Fate had no desire to father me. He played me like he played his guitar. Anyone who watched him during our concerts would see him range-up through my tender ballads, eyes closed as he found the chords that made them that way, up through the romping tunes that we used to rouse the happy spirits of our Outsider audiences and that required him to bend over his guitar and ride it like a jockey urging on a race horse, and then, knowing where I was going next, he would play a lick to fire-up the ROFO anthems I'd penned and lift them off the song sheet so they could soar.

They were the ones that made him rise up on the toes of his boots with his lithe back arched like a bow, his guitar held out higher than his taut chest, as he pushed himself and his instrument – and me and a million fans – to our triumphant climax and then past that moment, further into the song's dying obligato as we all came shuddering and exhilarated back to earth, guided by Jack's playing of the grace notes, which calmed the final twitches that continued to shake our bodies so we could give ourselves to the shared and sacred silence that made us one.

I don't even know how Jack and I found the times and places where we came together. But we had fucked a few times before Wynk decided to confront me. All he wanted was the truth and by then I was ready for the truth. I couldn't let Wynk make love to me, could not betray him by letting him enter my body, now electrified by lust for another man. I could not betray Jack, even though Jack wouldn't have cared one way or another, and I couldn't betray myself by allowing my deception to transform itself into an unforgiveable hypocrisy.

It was painful. Horribly painful.

- I'll stay with the tour until we're back in Ojai.

- A lot longer than that, Wynk, I said, reaching across and taking his hand.

I hadn't thought about the band's future without him. He

pulled his hand away from mine and stood up.

- I'll trade places with Jack, Wynk said. I'll take his room and he can stay here.

- I don't want that.

- Too bad.

- That's not what I meant. I don't want Jack in here. Trade places with Ann Marie. Or better still, you keep this bus. I'll ride with Merri.

- Ann Marie would be OK with coming in here, away from the boys.

- I'll ride with Merri. Actually, I'd like that. You keep this bus.

- OK. Long pause. One more thing, Wicla.

- Yes?

- I'm just an employee now.

He retreated into his stoically embittered self, and from what I have heard over the years he never came out again.

We did our shows in Yakima and Spokane under skies that became increasingly black and so low you could almost reach up and grab the spokes of lightening that cracked beneath them. The casters were still predicting tough, gale-force winds and drenching rains as we headed west toward Seattle. The tour vehicles were put into selfdrive mode because they could adjust to the sudden buffets of gusty winds faster than a person could, but the selfdrive on Merri's van was an old one. It was better that it be driven even if we fell behind the convoy. As mother was too weak to hold the road, I was at the wheel the whole time.

To tell you the truth, even at night it was glorious coming through those mountains. From time to time the winter rains would come to an abrupt end and above the silhouetted peaks all around, the clouds would part, allowing a gibbous moon to pour down its light on a world that seemed to be floating on rainwater.

Even under a sky filled from horizon to horizon with battens of ominous, flashing clouds, the dance of light, there, or there, or over here, thrilled me, as it exposed the jagged peaks or slanting sides of rockhard mountains, or in a second of time illuminated great oceans of new-growth trees that sucked at the heavens for as much water as the heavens could throw at them.

Merri, asleep at the back of the van, clutching or not clutching her bottle of pills as the case might be, left me alone in my beautiful struggles at the wheel, and those other struggles I always had when I was alone, with images and words and melodies that formed-up in me as new songs. Songs I might sing one day if they would just unlock their secret tribulations and come with their same secrecy to resolutions that sounded old as dirt.

Sometimes I think I merely pilfered lyrics from my mother's dreams, grabbing at her legacy now, in case she packed it away in some secret place and left me bereft. As I drove that night, I got something, a hymn maybe, but just a little, a first verse, if that.

*Down the road we traveled on*
*I prayed to the coming of the dawn*
*Because the night had left me shaking*
*In a dark of my own making*
*And my dreams were telling truths again*
*As I journeyed in the land of is.*

I would work on that lyric and a melody that began attaching itself almost immediately for weeks to come – a melody I'm sure that I made out of wind and rain and sudden flashes of light.

Coming at last out of the mountains along the Old Cascade Highway we drove straight into the storm from which we had been protected in the deep valley from which we had just emerged. A series of gusts bashed the side of the van and woke Merri, who came forward. I had slowed to a crawl by then because even at full speed the wipers were not clearing the windscreen.

- We can't drive in this Wicla. Pull over.

- We can make it.

- Make it where?

- We've got a concert tonight.

- There won't be any concert, sweetie. Have you heard from Wynk?

- I haven't checked.

- Oh, for gods sake. Give me your vice.

She found it in the console beside the driver's seat. I had been so preoccupied with my thoughts and with driving I hadn't bothered looking at it.

- Jeezus.

- What?

- This is the leading edge of a hurricane. He says get off the road and find a place to shelter.

- We're a long way from the coast, mother.

Merri was thinking about the night she got caught on the bridge over old Astoria when she had crashed and almost killed herself and her unborn child, me. Her fear always ramified into anger.

- Wynk says the concert's been cancelled, so you have no goddamn reason not to get this buggy off the highway and tucked in somewhere where we can ride this out. Now, c'mon.

Through the vapours on the windscreen I saw the gauzy shape of an overpass ahead.

- There, I said, and pulled the van to a stop, snugged as far to the right under the abutments as I could get.

- I'll make some coffee and toast.

While Merri made breakfast, I checked the vice for more news about the storm. Over the last two days, the offshore gales that had gestated way out to sea had been wound into force five hurricane, appropriately called Hecate, which was now hurtling toward the northwest conjuring violent spells. It would make landfall at the mouth of the Columbia. I jumped out of my seat and rushed back to the galley.

- Mother.

- Almost ready.

- Look.

I held the screen of the vice up to her face. She had heard the urgency in my voice. She slid her readers down from her forehead and looked.

- Oh, shit.

We were in the outer spirals of that storm, out of harms way, but Fort Ketchup would soon be in its very eye and no amount of song or prayer could save it.

*A grieving Gaia never groks the gagging gag.*

# Song 26

We shut the systems down inside the van. We'd been drawing on our batteries since we left Spokane and there had been no sunlight at all to recharge the vehicle. No matter, over the years we had gone into hibernation mode on more than a few occasions and had learned to organize ourselves around cold food and drink, sleeping a lot or doing things under portable lights that could illuminate a book or a board game or the skeins of wool and needles that my mother had recently taken-up because she found they loosened her stiff fingers while she knitted stuff that no one really had a use for.

It took two days for the hurricane to tear itself apart on the ragged tops of the coastal mountains but by then the damage it had done to everything in its path was beyond calculation. Even parked under the overpass we were not immune from its ravages because pieces of rooves, sides of buildings, the loose chattels of everyone in the area, unless too heavy for even that storm to pick up, had been sent sailing on its winds far from their original resting places or had been sent skittering down hard surfaces like roads and highways until they had become lodged in a ditch or up against some resolute fence line. A lot of stuff banged on the back and sides of the van and threatened to smash our windows but didn't. Thankfully, we had parked with the windscreen facing downstream, so it remained intact too.

Until the sun finally showed itself on the third morning, we were fixed in place. But when it did, Merri got the van going and rolled it out to a shadowless place just beyond the overpass where, while we ate a small morning meal, we gave the van batteries and our vices an hour to recharge. Several messages from Wynk were waiting, the gists of which were Where the hell are you? Are you OK? Seattle cancelled. Portland cancelled. Not sure about rest of tour. Everyone freaked out. Call in if you're still alive.

I called. The band and crew were fine. They had sheltered in behind the arena where we were to have played. But he said, Seattle is a wreck and he understood Portland to have been torn-up so badly it would take months to put it back together again. He thought we should get in touch with Belle and have her cancel all our appearances in southern Oregon and California and get everyone back to Ojai to regroup. I agreed and said Merri and I would get underway ourselves once the van was fully charged, but in fact, Merri and I had no intention of returning, not yet.

- I wonder if Titus is ok. He wasn't doing so well last time we saw him.

- And Erato, said mother. But she's tough. She'll be ok.

- I'll send them a message.

- We can't go to Portland yet.

- I know.

- Tell them we will come as soon as we can.

It took a long, hard day to drive to Fort Ketchup. Bridges were washed-out, forcing detours. The roads were cluttered with debris that we couldn't always drive around. Sometimes we had to lift stuff out of our way, sometimes push it to the verges with the van. There was hardly any south going traffic, but there was a steady stream of cars and trucks heading north loaded down with household goods and glum children who had given up their useless crying miles and miles before. There were also a lot of people, entire families, walking on the shoulders, carrying everything they could on their backs. They were heading to Gatesport, giving up on their lives on the Outside now that the houses and lives they'd made of straw and stick had been blown apart.

When we stopped to clear our way, it would take no time at all for people to gather around the van. Some recognized Trader Merri Weer, many recognized me. Did we have water, food? We did, but said no, lying to their devastated faces, more often than not drawing vehement curses because our prevarications were the transparent lies of the rich and privileged, the high and mighty. What we couldn't say is that we were happy to give it all away and would – every last drop, every morsel of food – but not there, not at that place. We were hoarding it for the women at Fort Ketchup, and we still had a distance to go. We were ready to resort to our pistols if anyone tried to stop us or take anything from us.

Merri and I arrived at the Fort late in the afternoon just as a first snow was falling but could not take the van up the last two hundred yards to the just-out-of-sight gate because the road was covered with blow down and other bric-a-brac. The stuff would be easy to move but it could wait. We walked in, but I had to help mother, which slowed our pace.

At the hundred yard mark the wreckage that used to be the Fort came into focus. The palisades were mostly blown flat or left at such an angle that anything on legs could run up and over. The gates were ripped off their hinges, the roofs of the blockhouses nowhere to be seen – they were probably beached somewhere at the mouth of the Columbia, or still bobbing in the roiled eddies of the salt chuck after having flown into the Lewis and Clark River just a little to the east. The cook house and dining hall was the only thing standing that was not off kilter, but virtually all its windows were smashed, and the overhang above the main door looked as though it might fall under the weight of just one more snowflake.

There was no sign of life, but there was no sign of death either, so when we stepped through to the quadrangle, upon which a white mat of snow was recording our tentative foot-steps, we took some comfort in the fact that the women may have evacuated before the storm hit in force. As it turned out, all but a handful did. Tithy was not about to relinquish her hold, or her rule, over Fort Ketchup so she stayed in the misbe-gotten belief that she could ride it out. Daph and Meira, always a bit foolish, and far too loyal, said they would stay too. A couple of others, the two youngest, whose names I now forget, could not bring themselves to abandon their friends.

Merri heard a cough coming from the dining hall. That is where we found Daph and Meira, shivering under the weight of blankets that should have kept them warm, but could not, under those circumstances, mitigate the fear, anxiety and hunger which had overcome them. Meira saw us first but did not move a muscle. Daph was leaning against her with her eyes closed, forehead taut, mouth set in a downward grimace, trying, I supposed, to find some rest that simply would not come. She must have felt some subtle change in Meira's body because she opened her eyes, straightened up, and with the same look of stunned belief as Meira had on her face, cast her eyes in our direction.

The snow cover and dense air outside had muffled our sounds, and when we entered the dining hall, we had entered like the wind must have entered just a couple of days earlier, by throwing open the doors which banged against the walls inside and brought a wake-the-dead screech from their rusting hinges.

- My god, Daph, Meira! I said.

- Wicla? Merri?

- Oh, girls what are you doing here? For god's sake, said Merri.

Merri went to her knees in front of them and stroked their faces.

- Your so thin.

I stayed on my feet and looked around the dining hall.

- Are you the only ones here, Daph?

- Yes, now.

Daph pointed toward the doorway into the kitchen.

- There are more women in there?

- Dead, said Meira. They're dead.

- Who's dead? I asked.

Merri stood up and came to me, taking my elbow with her hand.

- Don't be afraid darling.

We opened the door to the kitchen and pushed through, with Merri leading the way. We could see no one else in the dim light of the dying day hardly making its way in through the kitchen's small windows. The doors to the pantry and cold room were shut. Mother opened the pantry and stood looking into its darkness. She walked in, feeling her way along the shelves on either side. No one, she said when she came out.

We both looked at the nickel-plated handle on the heavy cold room door. Daph and Meira came in from the dining hall. Meira pointed at the cold room, Daph put her hands around her face, sobbing.

- In there.

I felt for my pocketed vice and once in hand, turned on its flashlight. Merri opened the door so I could hold the light up and illuminate the cooler's interior. Three bodies lay inside stretched on the floor, their feet toward us, one of them the unmistakably heavy body of Tithorea Oakwood. The smell of the dead women, of meat going bad, of vegetables and fruit starting to turn, of sour milk and cream, flooded out and engulfed us.

- We didn't know where else to put them.

- You did right Meira. You did right.

Daph clung to Meira. Merri and I walked in. I froze in place.

- That's enough, Wicla. They're beyond caring now.

She tugged at my coat and pulled me out.

All of them had broken limbs splayed out at odd angles to their torsos. One of the women looked like she had a broken neck as well. Tithy's face was smashed by a huge splinter of jagged wood that still protruded from the side of her bloody face just by her right eye. Her left eye was open. Cleodora's and Melaina's eye lids had been pulled down.

Daph and Meira told us that during the whole week before Hecate hit, even as the winds increased, even as the Fort was being pelted by an almost horizontal rain, even as the casters were begging everyone along the coast to get to safety, Tithy refused to countenance an evacuation. But even two days before the full force of the storm hit, things became so wild, so horrifically frightening that a few of the older women called a meeting to say they were getting out. Going to Portland. Erato had contacted them, told them to come, before it was too late. But

Tithy wouldn't go. She belittled our fear. It's just a storm, just a storm. She remembered how Willia and Cladine and all the women of those days rode out a hurricane – the one that had brought my mother to Fort Ketchup thirty-five years earlier - and all was fine. Just fine. Fort women are not cowards. Not cowards, she cried, as everyone but she and her four acolytes boarded the bus for Portland.

Just hours later, when the storm was attacking the Fort's roof shingles and already blowing hard things through the glass in the Fort's windows, Tithy led them from the game room where she initially thought they could pass the time in relative safety to the cookhouse, declaring they would be safer there. When the hurricane began howling and roaring all about them, vastly more violent than Tithy had dared to believe was possible, they took refuge under the kitchen's counters and tables. Under the table where cooks used to roll-out dough for pies and pastries, Tithy came to a fatal realization. If she were to save these women and herself, they too would have to abandon the Fort. She would call for help. But she had to get to her office at the far end of the quadrangle to make the call.

- Stay where you are, she ordered. I'm calling the State Police.

She ran out the kitchen door, across the dining hall, and unlocked the doors to the quadrangle, then pushed hard against the almost irresistible force of the wind and rain, propelling her body into the maelstrom on her tough, short legs.

Thirty minutes passed. Daph and Meira and the other women in the kitchen thought Tithy had got trapped in her office. They rose in the din and went as a group into the dining hall where sharp curls of cold wind were funnelling in from the doors Tithy had left open and tearing at the framed pictures on the wall, stripping the notice board clean of its stapled papers, and lifting even the heaviest of tables off their stout legs until they were ready to topple. Closer to the door itself, out in the center of the quadrangle, Tithy's round body lay in a heap, her coat and dress rippled and flapped like torn sails on a fat man's yacht.

They wanted to help her. Daph and Meira held back, overcome by fear. The other two looked at one another and elected themselves. Out into that storm they went, hoping to rouse Tithy into consciousness, to bring her back so they all could take refuge once again. Daph and Meira watched. One of the women went down on her knee by Tithy, then looked up in horror at the other woman. The wind screamed, the crack of a tree breaking off at mid trunk penetrated its shrieks, a ripping sound rose into the air close by, and then a piece of roof from just above the room where Merri gave birth to me, spun like a discuss down into the quadrangle where it smashed the head of the women standing and fell heavily on the back of the other, breaking it.

Daph and Meira pushed the doors to the dining hall shut against the killer storm then flew back to the kitchen and held on to one another under the butchers' table, waiting for the building to blow apart and the entire mad, revolving black sky to fall down on them. But they didn't die. Hours went by. The worst of the hurricane blew past at last and headed for Portland where it would joust with humanity's steel and cement constructions, fastened there upon a long-inhabited ground.

It would do its damage, it would kill a few more people, but the tenacious city held on.

In the morning light of the third day, the two women went out to the quadrangle. They shifted the roof fragment from the three bodies, and one by one they dragged them inside and lay them where Merri and I found them in the cooler. And then they waited for the help they felt sure would come. What else were they to do? What else could they do?

We took them back to the van and gave them a meal. We gave them our beds and let them sleep and took a little rest for ourselves on the couch behind the driver's seat. Next morning, while Merri cooked them a breakfast, I excused myself, I went to the drive shed behind the Fort, and in its wreckage, I found the tractor with its backhoe still attached, still in running condition. I drove it out through an opening in the side of the building, then into the orchard where the apple trees remained vibrating in their resolute and leafless rows. Close by the place where we had buried Wil and Cladine, where the other women of the Fort who had died over the years were interred, near the grave of Boy Adam, I dug out a new grave large enough for Tithy and the hero-women who tried to save her.

Merri, Daph, Meira and I stood over the bodies now laying with arms crossed across their chests, faces washed, wounds closed, and we sang our praises and our pity in low voices under the wet, cold glower of the grey heavens. I had built another verse to my song and made a church with my mother and my sisters.

*In winter's fruitless orchard*
*We sing of losses and of love*

*Under the immortal sky above.*
*We hold to one another hard,*
*And cleave to memories we trust*
*Ever awake in the land of is.*

# Song 27

Not much snow had fallen on the Northwest in the last one hundred years. Up in the mountains, yes, there were years of abundance when peaks like nearby Mount Hood were capped in white, but not down in the valleys where most people lived. That year, maybe because Hecate had blown away the ambient warmth that had long settled on the area, perhaps because its ferocious pinwheels had ground open a hole to the cold upper atmosphere where water sucked out of the Pacific would crystalize instantly under the sun's distant stare and fall earthward before it could evaporate, snow piled-up fast and high.

The snow immobilized us for days after we arrived at Fort Ketchup forcing we four women to share the cramped space of the van almost around the clock. The shock of seeing the Fort ripped apart, of seeing it empty of life, of seeing the dead go to their graves had worn off and was replaced by a wearying humdrum. The sudden vigour that mother showed in the face of the catastrophe had ebbed away even before we buried Tithy and the others and so she spent almost all day and night curled up in her bed. Now and again, we would hear a pained whimper coming from her small room and the rattle of her pill bottle, now almost empty, as she opened it. I knew we had to get to Portland soon, to a doctor who would see she got more.

It had taken me a lot of trial and error to use the tractor and backhoe to dig the grave for our friends – I made quite mess of it, in fact. There was nothing neat and square in that final resting place, but at least it was six feet deep, more or less. I had almost tipped the machine and myself into the hole when I confused its forward and reverse gears, but as I worked I wrestled it to a mutual understanding. I put it to work again clearing the road from the Fort back to where Merri and I had stopped on the day we arrived, then pulled the van closer to the gate.

Daph and Meira really did not want to bestir themselves from their enforced languor and seemed, when they stepped down from the van, a little frightened of the monochromatic winter landscape with its glinting, weird light and the undulating shapes of drifts and snow hillocks that buried the detritus and debris the hurricane had scattered everywhere. But soon they were glad they were out in the cold fresh air, unworried about the effects of the shrunken winter sun, bright as it was. That sun was again pushing its power into the skin of the van and filling it full of the energy we would need to get away. So, knowing we were in the act of freeing ourselves, with me on the tractor and the girls pulling the fallen branches to the side of the road, we opened a track down to the main road, where I was able to dig out the heap of ice and dirty snow that a plough had thrown up across the drive.

When we returned to the van for lunch, Merri was gone. Leaving Daph and Meira to heat soup and make toast, I went looking for her. Standing at the gate to the fort I could see small footprints leading into the quadrangle where she had stopped and made a few small circles as she had looked around, probably bewildered, no doubt with the bone-deep sorrow that Daph, Meira and I all felt too. We would be leaving this place after lunch never to return.

Out of the circle of tracks at the center of the quadrangle I could see a spoke of footprints leading to the blockhouse, to the doorway of the room where mother had given birth to me. I walked that way too but stopped short because I did not want to interrupt my mother's reverie. I watched her with her arms folded across her belly, head down, rocking on the edge of the bed that Hecate's winds, after ripping the roof from the block-house, had set askew to the log wall. The storm had replaced the room's low wood ceiling with the arc of an open blue sky, across which tufts of white cloud were marching eastward, fixing my mother, and me too, for that matter, as mere specks in the endless white landscape in which we were struggling, again, to survive.

I confess now that I had been indifferent – no, that's not the right word – I had been purposefully disbelieving of my mother's pain. At her knee, I learned to be tough and resilient, to endure difficult things without complaint, to rise above even the most trying inconveniences, to go around immoveable obstacles, to smash through those that were frangible and fria-ble, to meet threat with counter-threat, to raise my voice higher than the loud voices that were hurled against me, to deal with mean people meanly, to keep danger at a distance, to keep my pains private unless I could mediate them through song and make them less about me than about all of us.

Merri had taken to whiskey many years ago after Lilith's betrayal. I had called her on it and been told where to stuff my concern, to mind my own business. So, I did. She had become alcoholic, but I was able in those days to do all that needed doing when she was incapacitated. I could drive the van, stand in for her on trading days, take inventory, pick stock at the warehouses in Blaine and Bakersfield, and, small and thin as she was, I could get her to bed when she got so besotted, she could not manage. I cleaned her vomit and even, from time to time, got her out of wet undies into clean ones. If she stumbled or fell I would pick her up and put her right and if she banged her head or cut herself, I would salve her wounds. It was my lot in life and it was my duty to meet her challenges without complaint, and mostly without anger, though, yes, I did let fly more than once.

I was not going to flee from her as she had fled her mother or the memory of her mother. I could not leave the road as she had left Chicago. I was an unsettled child from the start and I was not going to settle in some place or other just to avoid pains I knew I could endure. Maybe my early self hid itself in music, but as I got into my late teens and twenties, music was where I found myself, and I knew full well that life with Trader Merri Weer, with Mother Merri, was the always bursting font out of which the burble and froth of our life together resolved itself into lyric and melody.

It was clear that mother had switched from whiskey to pain pills. I was foolishly glad when it happened because now her incapacitations were quiet. They didn't improve her level of functioning, but they did not worsen it either. She was no longer sloppy and pathetically boisterous when she came to one of my shows; she was sedated and usually parked in some deep shadow to give me all of the light. She didn't slur as she delivered herself of opinions that could be - and usually were – offensive to just about everyone in earshot. Instead, she reached for some thought or other that was turning in her mind and got it only part way out in a slow, trailing mumble that no one heard.

Merri had aged beyond her years during her whiskey days so her continual reduction now was, I convinced myself, just a more or less natural evolution. I had some vague understanding, of course, there would come a day when she would go to bed and not get up again, but I put that day a long way into the future. I could carry her the entire, abstract distance. Love her all the way to the end by doing for her what increasingly she could not do for herself. I did not see – because I did not want to see – that she was dying, that the pills prescribed to her by her Ojai doctor were for real, acute, physical pain, and that she would allow me to construe her use of them as an addiction, so I would let her be. Let her be and keep my focus on my ascendance in the tower of song.

She knew me better than I ever suspected. So, as I watched her in the blockhouse room where she now rocked herself, not knowing she was being watched, sobbing while holding on to her guts, it all came clear to me. My love was no love at all if it only served my purposes. And the shame – the palpable shame – I was feeling in that moment came from knowing the inner workings of my own complicated, easy-to-deny duplicity.

I stepped out of view of the door a few paces so she would not know that I had been watching and called out.

- Mother? Mother?

I stepped back into view.

- Ah, there you are. You OK?

I stood in the doorway.

- Time for lunch. You hungry?

- I think I am.

- Good.

I walked toward her and took her hand and helped her to her feet.

- We'll be leaving for Portland right after.

- Portland?

- For a few days. We have to get you some more of your pills. I know you're running out. Maybe Titus has a doctor.

- His partner is a doctor.

- Is he?

- I stay in touch. You might try that sometime.

The roads to Portland were driveable but slow going. I stayed in the driver's seat listening to the other women playing cards back in mother's little room. I put the van into selfdrive mode and let it take is to the city while I talked with Wynkyn on my vice. I had messaged him – and Lawrence, a few days earlier to let them know where we were, that we were safe, but I had ignored Wynk since then.

- Did I get you at a bad time, Wynk?

- No, we're just hanging out by the pool.

- We who?

- Me. Zimbo. Jack. Tedhum made a quick trip back to Kingman. When we need him, he'll come back.

- Where's Ann Marie?

- She's here too, yeah.

- OK, well I'm off to Portland. We'll be stuck there a few days.

- Good. Good. Well…we're waiting to hear from Belle about some of the re-bookings.

- I'll call her.

- Look, Wicla, I know it's been shit up there but if you're going to be talking to Belle, you need to tell her to process our money.

- What do you mean?

- She won't pay any of us. We're all short.

- What do you mean? Why?

- She says we didn't complete the tour. No one gets paid until its over.

- What? That's crazy.

- Remember what I said, Wicla. I'm an employee now. Me and the rest of the band and crew. So, I'm not going to carry this. Everyone is in a total uproar here because they haven't been paid. That tour is over.

- I'll talk to her.

Long pause.

- Wynk? You still there?

- Yeah.

Shorter pause.

- Wicla, I need to tell you something.

- Okay.

- Ann Marie and I...

- It's okay Wynk. But she's young enough to be your daughter.

- You were young enough to be my daughter too Wicla.

- Yeah but she's not me.

- Well, I'm just telling you so you don't hear it from someone else.

- No grapevine here, Wynk.

- Jack's been talking about you.

- Gotta go.

- We'll see you when we see you.

I called Belle. It took four calls to get through to her and she only picked up the last one because she calculated she really had no choice. I told her she needed to pay Wynk, the band and the tech crew. She reiterated the rule about not paying until a tour was completed and that she was working on rebooking the shows we missed and those were really just part of the original tour. I instructed her to have Harold do an accounting right away then pay them what was owed up until Hecate interrupted the tour. She changed the subject.

- We've heard from a big-time promoter in Denver. Colorado. They are guaranteeing a four-show sell-out.

Huge money, Wicla.

- That's a long way to go.

- If you drive, but no one's going to drive. Fly in, fly out. Or hyperloop. The new hyperloop will be ready by then.

- I don't know. No. Mother won't fly anywhere.

- Don't say that. I've already got the deposit. Fifty percent against anticipated gross. Merri can stay at the house for a few days. No need for her to make the trip.

- Have you told Wynk?

- Didn't want to talk to him before I talked to you.

- OK. I'm in.

- Great!

- Pay them.

- OK. If you say so.

- I do say so.

The bitch set me up. Set us all up. But I didn't know it at the time.

We reached Portland late in the day, just as the city was

waking from its daytime slumber. Even in the dim light of dusk, we could see it was a broke-down city, a complete and utter wreck from the ravages of Hecate, and still, although city officials had made an effort to clean up the worst of the clutter that fouled the city's streets, it remained dishevelled and disconsolate.

Power remained down throughout most of Portland's ghettos rendering life even more dangerous for those who went out alone. So, unless you were desperate or unwisely brave, you waited until a neighbor or friend would join you – more than one if you could manage it. You would carry a lantern, or keep your vice in flashlight mode, you would whistle, scuff your feet as you walked down the center of the road, pretend to be in conversation, keep a hand in your pocket where you could finger the nozzle of the spray you carried in case you had to sting the wild eyes of those beasts of prey who wanted your money, or your jewellery, or who, in their own crying desperation might steal your life.

With mother standing by me now, hand on my shoulder as I drove, we threaded our way through the streets into The Pearly where Erato was awaiting our arrival at the Mission where she and her husband, Francis – know locally as The Saint – tended to the worst-off of the dispossessed. Back in the early part of the century, The Mission had been a popular restaurant. It had been abandoned in such a hurry that all its accoutrements and fixtures had been left in place. It's kitchen, though full of now very old equipment was still fully functional and the upstairs rooms, once the chichi offices of lawyers, accountants, psychologists and interior designers had been converted easily to dorm rooms.

One floor was set aside for women, another for men, and no couples were allowed unless they agreed to be separated. If a man or woman were caught on the wrong floor, they would be put out on the street without ceremony, although many were welcomed back if contrite and if on the pain of banishment forever, they agreed to house rules.

We had dinner at the chef's table in the main dining hall in the company of fifty or so street people who could count on a hot meal at least once a day, free of charge. Their cutlery clattered on the heavy white plates they had brought from the food line, they slurped their water and coffee, scraped chairs and benches on the plank floor, some sneezed or coughed, a few horked-back a mouthful of phlegm to the great disgust of their seat mates, but hardly anyone talked.

The atmosphere was respectful in its way, but a weird smell made of equal parts entitlement and gratitude wafted above the tables and comingled with the odour of scruffy clothes and unwashed bodies. The sound of talk really only came from our table in the back of the room by the kitchen. On one side, Daph and Meira sat with Francis, high of brow, winkling eyes, long of nose, gaunt of face, a hard, two-day stubble prickling his jowls and chin right up to a mischievous mouth, above which sat a rogue's moustache that had remained untrimmed for some time so that some of its hairs bent into Francis' mouth, where his dentures chewed his dinner and snipped the ends of his words when he spoke.

Just as we sat down, a column of women came through a doorway leading to the stairs that led to the upper floors. The already seated men stopped in mid forkful to watch them enter. A few of them cat-called the women or whistled. Once the women were seated, Francis gave us a bit more of the history of the place including the story of how it came to be that he and Erato were now in charge.

- I am an old whore, said Erato, and I ain't the least bit prudish, but the doings of man and woman in a place like this will make hell out of heaven in no time flat. Oh, we learned our lessons early on, didn't we Fran?

- Hell, yes. The people who used to run this place...

- Now, you just keep quiet...

- They didn't have no rules like that. Erato and I were houseguests here and we were up and down stairs all time of day and night...

- Fran!

- Going at it...causing all manner of disturbance to those who didn't want to hear us banging away. And what with her being a hooker and all...

- Francis, you stop right now.

- All I'm saying is that a lot of the men thought she was fair game, so they started searching her out.

Erato was now standing arms akimbo leaning over her side of the table and glaring at her husband. Everyone in the dining hall stopped eating to see what Erato would do next. They all knew she had a hot temper. Francis leaned forward and looked Merri in the eye.

- Well, look at her. A beautiful woman like that. They all wanted to fuck her. That's when she cornered me and told me I would be marrying her and taking her off the market. Or words to that effect.

Merri was laughing and slapping the table so hard she started choking. As I clapped her back I have to admit I started too. Daph and Meira finally, after days and days of terror, fear, grief, the remorse of survivors, and the stuck boredom we all found ourselves in, got into the fun too, and allowed themselves to giggle into their hands. I hadn't noticed before, strangely, how they mirrored one another's behavior. Back up singers to the end.

- Now sister Erato, said Meira, don't you go getting mean with Mr. Fran.

- Sounds like you knew a good man when you saw one, sister, Daph added.

- Oh, she made it worth my while ladies. An offer I couldn't refuse. She told me she'd make an honest man out of me.

- And there you are, a Saint to those who don't know you, and an old devil to the one who does, said Erato, as she picked up a few dirty dishes to clear away.

I too grabbed some dishes then followed Erato to the kitchen where we hugged again and fell into easy conversation while others came and went, bringing in yet more dishes, as the kitchen workers made short, but noisy work of the cleaning up. The door to the dining hall swept open and closed and when it was open I could hear mother, Francis, Daph and Meira, laughing and enjoying themselves.

Erato was a doyen now, a doyen and a chatelaine who had acquired an exquisite dignity and graciousness as she moved into her forties. She was just a few years older than I, but more mature by far, far abler than I to bear the heavier, and I thought, more important burdens of her life, a life chosen, not stumbled into. She kept her hair straight and combed out, but a few grey hairs managed to work their way up and through her tresses anyway. She wore just a bit of makeup – a touch of rouge on her high cheek bones, a layer of pale lipstick on her full lips, some eyeliner, but just enough to make her eyes seem larger and rounder and more awake than they really were. The creeping disgust of her life worked on her body too, rounding the once square shoulders that she used to waggle at the johns when she first worked the streets and had to lure men from other girls.

I had been in touch before we left Fort Ketchup and asked her to take Daph and Meira for awhile. She agreed immediately, of course. I told her that as soon as my people had rebooked our interrupted tour, I would take them with me so they could sing backup, so they could earn enough money to get their lives in motion, wherever they might want to settle down.

- There is some talk of a big concert in Denver.

- Denver? Why you want to go all that way?

- Girl has to earn a living.

- That's true. Wicla, I have heard your singing on the vice. I gotta say, you are quite something else. You have a following. You know that?

- Who would have thought?

- Me. That's who. You were always something special. You are a woman with something to say, and you are saying it. I love you for it.

I was a bit embarrassed by her words.

- So, Daph and Meira would go on tour with you?

- I sure hope so.

- So, not just charity to two lost girls?

- To tell you the truth Era, I always hear them behind me when I'm singing. They might as well be there in the flesh and earning their keep.

- All right then.

Dawn was coming on fast – too late to intrude on Titus – but, even though Fran and Erato would have given us a bed,

Merri and I made excuses to leave, telling Daph and Meira as we hugged them goodbye and digested the words of thanks and love they bestowed on us with tears welling in their eyes, that we would be back for them soon, once the tour was reset.

We didn't move the van from the place where we had parked it on the street. We felt secure enough to stay the day there, but, I have to say, it was a safety reinforced by the guns we kept close at hand. Just in case.

Well, we did see Titus, that very night, at his home where, for the first time, we met his partner, Dr. Arre Cina, an internist who had decided to ride it out in Portland rather than decamp to Gatesport or one of the eastern hives where he could easily have hung a shingle and made a lot of money. Arre and Titus were, like Lawrence and Javier, deeply in love and even though life in Portland was dismal and difficult. It was the place where their love had taken root and the thought of digging it up to transport it elsewhere aroused anxieties in both men.

Titus had cut his once long hair short. It was fully grey now and sat like a well-kept lawn of stiff winter grass on his large head. Arre liked to run his hand over it. It's like a cat's tongue, he said, which brought my mother out of her chair to feel it for herself. My god you're right, Arre, she shrieked, pulling her hand away. Titus was a bit more jowly, though he tried to cover it up by pushing his chin forward when he talked. Years of laughter at life's idiocies and at secret insights into life's absurdities had etched themselves on the side of his face in the form of crows feet, but whatever merriment he displayed there was belied by the deep furrows that now lined his brow and the knit of flesh at the top of his broad nose. He had put on weight on his belly, legs and rump, and moved slower than in the club days of old where he was a notoriously good dancer, but it didn't seem to bother Arre much.

Arre was tall – taller by inches than Titus - and lean, angular in all parts of his body. His long wavy hair had not gone grey yet, even though he was about the same age as Titus, and his grooming was meticulous. It was subtle, but I thought I saw signs that he was using a little make-up to help ward off the advancing years. His blue eyes were bluer than they had a right to be. Arre had the arrogance of a good doctor, if I can call it that. He spoke about uncertainties with certainty, ambiguities as though they were fully self-revealing, but you could take him to task – pop the balloons he floated, skewer the assumptions upon which his great hopes for the future – his and Titus's - seem to be built.

It didn't take me long to ask Arre, when we chanced to intersect as I was going to the loo and he was off to the kitchen, if he would give my mother a check-up. A thorough one. She was in pain, I told him, and a long-time user of an opioid she was in danger of running out of and a sudden withdrawal would be catastrophic on the order of Hurricane Hecate. It didn't take him long to say he would.

- She's quite ill.

- Yes, I said.

- What's wrong with her?

- I don't know. She won't say. I'm worried that it might be cancer.

- She's pretty spry for someone with cancer.

- She's just happy tonight.

- I'm sure it's something a little less…. Well, no use guessing. Look, bring her to my clinic tomorrow, just before closing. I can spend some time with her. You think she'll let me do the necessaries?

- Have you ever wrestled with a wild cat?

- Every day.

- Titus is a pussy cat.

- You got me there. I'll do my best to make her feel comfortable.

Merri went. She submitted to the examination – being in the hands of a gay doctor roused none of the ancient fears she always had around normal men - as she called them. Whiskey had helped to mitigate those fears, even to dispel them on occasion, say in the bars where I used to sing; her pills did not. Knowing that Arre would find what she already knew after visiting her Ojai doctor had infested her body, Merri swore Arre to silence, called upon him to keep the confidences to which all patients were entitled. She really only wanted an update, a progress report because she was quite convinced that all her fraught heart was doing these days was marking time. Well, that's true for all of us, isn't it?

But Arre did not make any definitive diagnosis and he did not want to share his dark suspicions with her, let alone anyone else. Tests were done. Results would take two or three days to be completed, but in the meantime, he gave her a scrip for a different opioid. A more powerful one.

Three days later we returned. When mother came out of his consulting room, with Arre trailing behind her, she looked ashen but worked hard to sound cheery as she slid her winter coat over her vest.

- You feeling OK, mother.

- Never better. Those new pills work a miracle. Everyone should have them.

- How is she, Arre?

She shot a hard look at him.

- Let's get out of here, Wicla. He's a busy man.

When mother turned toward the door, I looked at Arre. He mouthed 'talk later' but was smiling at her again when she turned to face us.

- C'mon. Time's a wastin.'

So, I did talk to Arre later. Mother was napping so I went back to the clinic and waited while Arre met with other patients on appointment. When he could, he called me into his consulting room.

- It is cancer, Wicla. Sarcoma type in the intestines.

- Treatable?

- For a time. To tell you the truth, she can't do much more than use her pain medicine.

- Terminal?

- Yes.

- How long?

- Months.

- A year?

- No.

I walked out of the clinic into Portland's frigid winter, stunned and panicked. I walked a long time, dangerously alone but under the protection of a gloom so deep and fraught that any beast of the wild and all the beasts of the city's shadows, would flee for fear of falling over its spiralling precipices into its engulfing and bottomless darkness.

Little did I know that more bad news would come so quickly and that I would be the one to tumble into the abyss where ultimately it manifested a murderous intent.

*The muckers of magic and myth magnify mortality.*

# Song 28

Wynk's call came a day later, a call that came from the dark side of the moon, cold and distant.

- You're not coming back are you?

- Hello to you too.

- Yeah, well....

- If you mean, am I coming back and then turning around to come right back to Portland for the rebooking, no. What's the point of that? Merri's not feeling well and I'd rather just let her catch her breath here for a few more days.

- Belle hasn't paid us. She's not taking my calls.

I could feel anger welling up in my throat. Toward Belle.

- I asked her to.

- She hasn't.

- I was very firm with her.

- You've almost got a full-scale mutiny on your hands, Wicla.

- Well, just keep everyone calm.

- You don't get it. Everyone's taking their lead from me.

Wynkyn DeWorde was a mercenary. Belle herself had told me right after he left on the day she introduced us.

- I'll call her right now.

- I'll wait by the phone.

- At my house.

- Yeah, well deduct the rent from my pay check.

Belle did pick up, but not on the first, second, third or fourth tries. Not on any of her numbers. I messaged her. She did not reply. I called Wynk to tell him. He more or less ordered me to call Harold Carney. I did.

- Wicla! Hi. Long time. You back home?

- I'm stuck in Portland.

- OK. What can I do for you?

- Have you heard from Belle Rophon in the last couple

of days?

- Saw her last week. Said she was going out of town.

- Where'd she go?

- Not sure. Sounded like a business trip. Europe.

- She hasn't paid Wynk, the band or the techs.

- Can they wait 'til she gets back?

- I want you to pay them out of my personal account. I'll square with Belle later.

- OK.

- Like right now, Harold.

I called Wynk to let him know what I had done. A miserable thanks for that, but it was a premature thanks nonetheless. Harold called me back within minutes.

- There is no money in your account Wicla.

- I never take any out. A little. But…

- It's all gone.

- I'm not sure I…

- It was emptied last Tuesday.

- Harold...

- And there is no money in the band account.

- You were a co-signor.

- The account authorizations were changed.

- Belle?

- Belle. She left last Tuesday. We've been fucked over, Wicla.

- We?

All my savings. All the money from the tour less whatever was expended up until the day we cancelled. The big deposit from the Denver show. All the money that was sitting in the account to underwrite future 'projects' as Belle had called them. Millions.

Before I called Wynk, I called Lawrence at work.

- Come home, Wicla, he said. Just come home. We'll figure it out.

Oh, did I want to do that, but in that moment I was paralyzed by a drenching anger that was washing away my original denial. I wanted to inundate Lawrence with my rage to rouse his warrior spirit. I wanted a big, fierce Black man with veined muscles and barking guns and hot, red eyes to go looking for Belle; to kill her noisily and eternally wherever he found her, to drop her on the marble floors of the hideaway hotel lobby, through which she would be walking so nonchalantly on her new-bought heels, to blast her from her swim-suited toe perch on the diving board's edge so she would fall disembowelled and bleeding into the blue piranha water below. I wanted the violent radiation of her fall to reach every shore of the known world.

But then, in the very moment when I was jumping off the edge of incredulity, a rising current of calm wafted me up to where the largeness of Belle's crime occupied just a tiny space in the landscape of the future that was rolling beneath me.

- Merri has cancer, Lawry. In her guts. Tell Jav.

I disconnected. I did not pick up when he called back. I did not reply to his messages. I was slumped against a wall along the street that separated The Pearly from Gaytown, collapsed into the painful, invisible grooves of the hooker's beat. And there I stayed until Erato leaned down then pulled me up by my arm so she could walk me back to the Mission. There she fed me soup like I was a child, stroked my hair as she said there, there, and waited until I came around. Merri had told her some months before about her cancer but pledged her to secrecy. Erato now saw that I knew. Francis walked into the kitchen.

- Get out you damned fool. Don't you know when to let women be?

He spun on his feet and left.

- I'm going to bring Merri here for a night or two, Erato. Is that OK?

- You got something to do? Why doesn't that surprise me? You just bring her right over and we'll look after her, Francis and me.

I told Merri we had to get on the road again, which she was happy about, but that I had to get the van tended too – axle problems – so we'd be staying at the Mission for as long as it took to get things fixed. Once she was safely in Erato's and Francis' care, I drove off and parked where mother wouldn't see me. I called Wynk and asked him to gather the other members of the band around so they could all listen to what I had to say. Tedhum hadn't returned yet, but the rest of them trooped into view while Wynk connected Tedhum remotely.

Do I remember that conversation? Just the shocked silence at first, then the shouts of the expletives I shouted when my emotions overcame me – first disbelief, then anger. I suppose I could have made promises to pay them somehow, someday. I could have begged them to stay with me so we could earn money from a few last gigs. That would have made the most sense. But I didn't. I didn't want to because the blade of Belle's guillotine had already fallen through my submissive neck. I had accepted that she had cut the head off Wicla the Singer, Queen of the Outsiders. I was looking for a new head already to go on my zombie body.

That night I had dinner with Titus and Arre at their

apartment on the far side of Gaytown. I had hardly set foot inside their door when I began grilling Arre about mother's cancer, about the certainty of her diagnosis, because I needed absolute certainty, about the kind of care that would prolong Merri's life. She should not lose a minute of whatever time we could give her by providing the exceptional care to which she was entitled by dint of her legendary status, by virtue of her being my mother, by having a doctor as a new, good friend. Did Arre know of treatments he wasn't telling me about? Were there trials for new drugs, new surgeries? Were there snake oil cures or shamanistic practices that his doctoring scruples prevented him from telling me?

- Wicla, Arre isn't keeping anything from you.

- Are you, Arre?

- Don't ask him that Wicla. He'd tell you if there was some hope.

- OK, look, said Arre, there is an oncology clinic in CashCarter. They have been working on some new techniques for sarcoma type cancers...

- Why didn't you say?

- They haven't got out of animal trials... I know the guy who's running the show. I met him when I went to Clinton last year for a medical conference.

- OK. OK. This is good, I said.

- But, given current practice, Merri's case is hopeless.

I slammed the table with my fists and made everything on it jump.

- That's a good thing, said Arre.

Titus put his fat hand over mine to calm me.

- It's good because they might agree to use your mother as a guinea pig.

- Right. Right. I get that.

- It's a long way away.

- CashCarter. Where is that?

- In Tennessee, said Titus. It's one of the new hive cities. Near Old Nashville.

- You've been? I asked.

- No, said Titus, but I have been keeping up with what's going on back there.

- I'm not sure if they have an airport yet, but you can fly to Nashville and get a selfdrive.

- No. We can't do that. Mother won't fly. Can you get them to see her, Arre?

- Maybe I can get them to consider her. I can try. But they may reject her if she's too weak, or if the cancers too advanced. And Wicla, there are going to be costs. Heavy ones.

- You let me worry about that.

During the next few days, while Arre made enquiries and made the case to his colleagues in CashCarter to at least examine Merri, I began plotting the journey east. But Titus brought me up short.

- You're crazy. It's winter, he said. You won't be able to drive up and over the mountains – not until spring.

Spring was still three months off. We might, he said, catch a break if the weather lifted earlier, but no one could tell yet. I told him I thought I should go south then get on to Route 66 and head east. I have a better idea, he said, showing me a route he had laid out on his vice.

- Stick to Indian lands all the way to the Mississippi. You'll be safer and if you need help you'll get it.

- You know people?

- My Indian brothers and sisters.

- What do you mean?

- I'm a full-blooded Indian.

- No.

- Nez Perce.

- Titus isn't an Indian name.

- My Indian name is Sakhonteic. White Eagle.

- No.

- Yep.

- Who gave you the name Titus?

- The boys. The club boys. Well, sort of. They called me Tightass. One Halloween I went to the Pumpkin Ball as Titus Androgynass, emperor's crown, scepter, slave boy at my beck and call. You should have been there.

- Oh, stop it.

- The whole Tightass thing was old news anyway, but the name stuck as Titus as things will, you know.

Arre convinced me that I could wait two, maybe three months. The team in CashCarter wouldn't be ready much before then anyway. He was lying. He knew Merri wouldn't make it there, or if she did, that they would take one look at her and make their excuses. But he couldn't bring himself to tell me because I was not ready to accept the reality of her death.

I told mother that we would be doing the concert in Denver. But I had already asked Harold to cancel the show. There was an ongoing hullabaloo about that, threats of a lawsuit that the promoters did, in fact, file sometime later. Five years or so later my husband's lawyers negotiated a settlement that put an end to it, but the damage to my reputation had been done by then.

Despite some ritual grumbling on Merri's part, she accepted the fact we would stay in Portland until February then drive to Denver, there being no point in going all the way south in weather she knew, from listening to the casters, was still fouling the highway system. Ploughed and shovelled snow was piled-up in hard, unthawing heaps at the intersections around the Mission, not shrinking but growing larger with each fresh snowfall. If rain fell, it was a cold rain in the sunless shade of the city quickly formed an icy carapace on these piles, making them impervious to temperatures that might occasionally rise above freezing. The Pearly, just a small part of it in fact, was her whole world at the moment, and as far as she was concerned, everyone else's world too.

Merri was happy at the Mission, very. Francis would tell risible tales that made her rock on her chair and slap a knee. Erato would gently and patiently tend to her few needs and brush her hair. If it were one of those days when mother said she felt doomed to Mission life, like one of Erato's regulars, Erato would dab a little ruby lipstick on Merri's lips. Sometimes, mother would resent the charity being extended to her so she would pitch in to help with a meal, or after a meal. She would sit on a stool by the dishwasher and scrape leavings into slop buckets before putting the dishes and glasses into the large trays that would be rolled into the washer. Daph and Meira were put to work too, ladling out food on the food line, sweeping and washing-up and they too made life easier for mother, but like Erato, they were careful not to make mother feel like she was shirking, lest she bite their hands off at the wrists.

As the days went by Merri made friends with other women at the Mission. They loved hearing her stories, so over time, she gave them a handwrought mental map of the west that was both huge and small, unknowable but familiar, beautiful and brutal, mean and charitable, full of characters who couldn't be trusted and people who would saw off their own leg if it would make you feel better. The air out there, beyond the edge of the city, Merri would say, was filled with storm clouds, unending rain and deadly lightening. It carried the sounds of guns fired in anger and the screams of the dying, but it was also redolent of jasmine and sage and honeysuckle and you could, if you were patient and of good heart - for all animals, including us, know the difference between good and evil - call a sparrow right out of the sky to alight on the back of one hand so it could peck at the birdseed you would always have in your other.

In her secret parlay with the other Mission women, Merri made sport with the men there, too, with Merri laying bets that one had always been a decent sort, but that another was a terrible brute, or was not so long ago, before life had beat the hell out of him. That one was arrogant and so, she reckoned, was still going to get a few more lickings before he learned what's what. That guy was grandiose; that guy had no feelings for anyone but his sorry self, that guy had lost so much it had left him a kind of nothing, a sad sorry nothing that nothing could restore. There were men who some said were down on their luck, but she said they were further down than that, for luck was high above them bobbing on the choppy surface of their reality and they didn't have enough air in their lungs to rise toward it.

There were thieves and conmen, men who had cheated on their women and cheated at cards, because cheats were cheats. There were ladies' men who had got by too easy and were now bitter that their charm had no currency at all in the hard life of the streets. There were lazy men, irresponsible men, there were sad men who had fathered children and abandoned them to the never-never. There were men of the cloth who had lost their way, there were prayerful men whose outlandish prayers could not be answered. There were men whose brains were broken and could not be fixed. There were men who had succumbed to alcohol or drugs, but not the drugs that her doctor had prescribed for her, she said, giving her bottle a shake, but illegal drugs, drugs administered by the devil himself right to the center of the man's brain by a long, red-hot needle.

Somehow, at the Mission, watching, listening, sitting invisibly close to all these men in the dining hall or in the reading room, she came to love them. She was so thin, so brittle, so cadaverous in her own appearance she was not in the least way attractive to any of them. They were not interested in her stories because, wonderful as they were, they could never compete with the myth each man had made of his own past. She could not, therefore, catch the slightest scent of the lust that still resided, and sometimes burned, in all but the oldest of the men. She knew the smiling one-eyed serpent still lurked in the apple tree where it waited for any of the daughters of Eve who might still take a bite. But for Merri, mankind had become defanged and, at last, loveable.

The moment I resolved to go east, my anger toward Belle dissipated. I told Titus and Arre about Belle's defalcation, but only because her theft of all my money meant that I had to scrape a few dollars together. They were happy to lend me what I needed, but that's not what I wanted. I was happy to sing for my supper and mother's too. They knew some of the club owners and I wanted them to make the introductions. They laughed.

- You're kidding Wicla? Titus said.

- No. I'm not kidding. I have to earn some money.

- That's easy.

- I don't know any one in Portland.

- Everyone in Portland knows you, said Arre, looking at Titus like I was crazy.

- You're Wicla the Singer for godsake, Titus said. Give your head a shake.

- You could play some small rooms and put a few dollars together, Arre said. Could be done. Right, Titus?

They both leaned back in their chairs and looked at me like I was missing something. Something obvious.

- Or you could put on a big show, Arre said.

- Win the lottery, Titus added, leaning in toward me eyes, locked on mine, waiting for me to understand.

And then I did. Belle had burned the Portland concert promoter too, had taken his deposit and run off with the loot. He might be mad as hell, but he'd love to make his money back and then some. Don't let anyone tell you differently, said Arre, forgiveness can be bought.

Ziggy Firenze was not happy to hear my voice.

- Not interested in apologies, he stammered.

I offered them anyway. This was a negotiation and even though I would turn and walk away from any man spitting angry words at me under any and all circumstances, I stayed on the vice.

- You owe me money. An angry bellow.

- I would like to pay you back. Calmly said.

- Good. How about today? Slightly less angry.

- How about next month? Nonchalantly, as though I were languorously pulling of a pair of long white gloves, finger by finger.

- What's wrong with now?

- Can't do it now.

- What's going to change in a month?

- We need to meet.

Ziggy had an office in Ratville, an area that bordered the old banks of the Willamette and was contiguous along its western border with both The Perly and Gaytown. I walked over, trundled up the steep, dark staircase to the second floor and opened the door into a fiercely disordered hovel illuminated only by the diffused, grey light of the oncoming dawn. The Willamette moved slowly in its narrow stream out in the middle of its ancient channel, muddy and glistening from all the recent train.

I assumed Ziggy was in another room and that he would have heard the door close as it banged shut behind me, pushed firmly shut by a pneumatic spring fixed to the door and its frame at their tops. I thought he would appear through the only other door in the office, set in a dirty, purple frame on the wall to my right. But Ziggy was already there, leaning back in a swivel chair with his feet crossed at the ankles on the only remaining space at the front of his large, cluttered desk. The scuffs on the forward tips of his soles were looked out at me like two round, ghost eyes which made his feet look like just another of the toys, trinkets and memorabilia that were clutter-scattered on every surface in the room.

He snorted. I looked around but still could not find him. He cleared his throat. I turned in the direction of the noise and found him. The back of his chair was being supported at a dangerous angle by the stuffed bookshelves behind. His bald head, now tilting in my direction as he looked me up and down, looked like it was a cheap bust perched precariously on the shelves, between two massive, never-opened volumes of the OED. His arms hung straight down from his shoulders, his hands not quite reaching the floor, so he had the posture of a stuffed costume from some madhouse, not a live creature.

- Mr. Firenze?

- Ziggy.

- I didn't see you.

He sat up quickly, put his hands on the desk to pull himself forward, then stood and walked out from behind his desk and stopped right in front of me, as if to say, 'see me now?'

- So, you want to make an arrangement?

Said like a loan shark to a delinquent debtor.

Ziggy was a tiny man, very short, I mean, but thick on every part of his body. Not fat, a tall, well-muscled man who had been compressed into a shorter frame by some laughing god. Napoleonic, not just in stature, but in the decisive, visionary manner of his generaling, which I saw firsthand once we came to terms.

Just as Merri accepted the obstacles, disappointments and frustrations that came her way, Ziggy did too. Problems and crises are endemic to the life of an impresario in a world where people part slowly with their money, and almost never for art (as he called the noise of music). He met all life's challenges with a single, move-on declaration: Così è la vita! That's life. He'd stomp his tiny feet and his eyebrows, Velcro-like black bars that sat on either side of the bridge of his enormously wide brow would rise to the middle of his forehead. At the same time, in strange accompaniment to what the rest of his body was doing, he'd throw his arms in the air, disgusted by whatever had tried to flatten him, but dealt with once again. After our work together in Portland I would never see him again.

Once Ziggy removed a stack of old industry magazines from a chair near his desk, I took a seat and we got right down to it. He dictated his terms. He would book the arena, find back-up musicians, get us a place to rehearse, advertise the show and sell the tickets, ten comps for me. He would take seventy five percent; I would get the rest.

- No.

- No? Goddamit, Wicla, you have nothing! You stole my deposit. You disappeared from sight. You want me to do all the work. Goddamit! That's the deal.

- No can do, Ziggy, sorry.

I got out and walked to the door and pulled it open. Silence behind me. I walked out, the door banged behind me. I started feeling my way down the staircase in the dark. The door opened.

- What do you want?

- Sixty percent.

- Sixty! Are you crazy?

- So I'm told.

I continued down the staircase.

- OK. OK. Goddammit!

- I'll be back to sign the contract tomorrow.

The landing door closed at the top of the stairs. I could still hear the primal scream, door closed or not. He hadn't reckoned on the stubbornness and guile of a woman raised by the legend Trader Merri Weer.

A month to the day after our meeting, we put on a grand show and even the cynical, seen-it-all, penguin-suited Ziggy Firenze, standing in the wings beside my mother in her wheelchair thought so.

*Impious indeed are our invisible imperfections.*

# Song 29

But for the tour my husband arranged later, the Portland concert was the last concert I would ever give to an Outsider audience. Oh yes, as we crossed the Indian lands east of Portland and up and over the mountains, and as we wended our way down the roads that followed the Missouri River, almost all the way to the Mississippi, I played to our hosts, sometimes with musicians recruited from the tribes, but more often than not it was just Old Mud and me.

We got underway in the middle of February. An early spring had surprised us all, and from Portland east to the steep slopes of the mountains, Titus assured me, I would not find a cup full of snow. The land was greening again as grasses sprouted and trees came into early leaf, flowers poked-up on the verges of the roads where they watched us drive by and balmy winds shook the tiny blossoms of meadow flowers on the awakening farms. In a few weeks, under a hotter sun, most of the color would be gone, leaving stubbled fields or stony landscapes of muted browns, yellow ochres and dark, burnt sienna.

Titus and Arre came to the Mission to say goodbye to us. The day before I had taken Merri to Arre's office for a check-up and he told her that he thought she should stay where she was until she felt better. No, she said, I've been sitting on my ass for too long, so I think I'll go on a drive with Wicla. Big concert in Denver. Wouldn't want to miss it. She knew that Arre's declaration that she would get better was the prognosis of a lying doctor, but she was prepared to love him anyway. As she told me later, even though he was a man and even though he was lying to her, she had to consider the hospitality, courtesy and generosity he and Titus had extended, and the fact that he was gay and therefore only half as bad as other men.

Erato, Francis, Daph and Meira all knew that I was taking Merri back east to CashCarter, that the Denver concert was a pretence. They didn't tell me until the morning of our departure that Merri knew it too. What my mother did know, Erato told me when she got me alone, is that for whatever reason, she knew I needed to go back East, that something was calling me there, that something was stirring my brain, maybe some evil spirit, and that my asking her to come along was my way of saying I was afraid of it and I needed my mother to face it. Those are the kinds of things that make you chuckle when you hear them because they seem old-woman silly, but later, the words come back as a haunting suspicion – a certainty even – that old women have the antennae of a super race.

Daph and Meira got me alone too, to thank me for the money I had put in their new accounts.

- You earned it you two. You sang beautifully the other night. I wish I could take you with me... I would have, had that concert in Denver come off, but...

- We'll be OK, Wicla, said Meira.

- You just go take care of your momma, said Daphne.

- Mr. Firenze says he can put us to work. Says he knows

other bands who need backin' up.

- Nobody like you, Wicla, but at least we'll get a chance to shine.

And they did. I kept in touch with Erato and she gave me periodic updates about her girls as she called them. Ziggy's business picked-up as times improved and he- and then Daph and Meira with their husbands - moved into the new hive city that was built right over Fort Ketchup and the surrounding area a few years after mother and I left Portland.

Those women were constantly on the road with the bands that followed in my footsteps and they especially loved it when the got to sing back-up if the bands they travelled with covered a song I wrote all those years ago. Over time they would see Wynk, Zimbo, Ann Marie, Jack and Tedhum, all of whom found new work, sometimes together in various combinations, sometimes on their own, with bands that found audiences in the Outsider west.

Francis pushed Merri's chair to the side of the van then Titus lifted her up and carried her into it and laid her on the couch behind the driver's seat. Arre went up too to make sure she was comfortable, had her pills, and made her re-pledge to do all that he told her she must to keep herself well. I think it was something along the lines of eat, drink and be Merri. She let them both kiss her forehead and though she made a bit of a show pushing them away, I know she would have drawn them into a tight embrace if she had known how to hug a man, and if she had had the strength.

We all hugged and kissed, made the stupid jokes that sad

people make when they have to part company and feel the loss already, and off we went. They all expected I would return one day - without Merri of course – but one day. I never did, though I may soon. Those people form a circle around me as they always have. They are the only humans left who can help me mend my very broken heart.

And what were we off too? After seeing Kingman and Gatesport and the litter boxes that Merri and I saw when we rambled the back country, where cows now grazed and crops grew so astoundingly, after seeing the Heavens Gate burial mall near Ojai, I thought I had some idea. But Arre said no, no.

In their singularities they are but portents, he said. They are like what the increasingly astonished Indians must have seen, standing in the shadows of their forest kingdoms, when they watched the digging of the newcomer's first gardens, or as they watched the first fence lines go up around the white man's metastasizing colonies, or what they must have seen – and felt - a short time later when they watched the settler's dwelling homes rise behind those fences, built out of axed-down trees and dug-up rocks transformed into walls and chimneys. But the Indians could not go to Europe in their dugouts to see what was coming, what would change their world and change them utterly.

The night before, at dinner, Arre talked more than he ever had to me.

- When you go back east you will see, he said, the real future of the west, of the whole country really. So, whatever you think you see in your mind's eye now, whatever dreams your mind projects on to the back of your eyes, it is the merest glimpse of what you will find back there.

- Trust the road, Titus, now Sakhonteic, said. It goes where you go.

- You are on a journey of discovery, Arre said, eyes locked on mine.

Arre tried to describe this brave new world where people live once again to the tick-tock of old time because the deadly rays of the sun are filtered by the domes and diffused to lesser intensity in its plazas and streets and softened the hive's daytime shadows. People live and work in its warming light, sleep during the hours of night. And, he said, leaning-in to make sure I understood, they live in peace without guns and the worrisome rancour that makes them go bang.

A dozen gigantic hives had already been built while at least a hundred smaller towns had been domed by now, with more new cities being built and more small towns being domed each passing year, all of them connected by a network of incredibly fast hyperloops and coastal hydroloops that make you feel they exist in an imaginatively scattered oneness.

- You will be as dumbstruck as any half-naked Indian would have been if he had been transported to the heart of Paris in the 17th century and asked to dance a minuet.

The old cities, like New York, Boston, Atlanta, Philadelphia, Baltimore, Charlotte, Nashville and others were almost empty of people and crumbling where they stood. All had been displaced by hives built on empty lands nearby. Clinton, near New York, was the new seat of financial and cultural power, while Washington, despite the billions spent to keep it as it was, was struggling to remain above water behind a snaking fence of dike works.

The politicians of the Capitol were struggling, more than they had at any time in the past one hundred years, to be relevant and purposeful in the face of the trillion-dollar oligarchies who nested now in the moneyhum of Clinton. Cora Munro, was one of those politicians, of course, tilting on her high heeled shoes with the lance of her not-to-be-underestimated determination leveled at the oligarchs who built the hives.

I would learn for myself, when I finally arrived there, that CashCarter had driven a nail into old Nashville's coffin – had driven all the nails, in fact – but the pluckers of strings and the blowers of horns and the bangers of drums now conjured their music on the inside of the new city. And if their new music was not the earthbound stuff of legendary Tennessee, it's stainless steel notes and uncracked voices still managed to tell stories of human survival, for in those first years, the people who moved from the Outside were people who had escaped as much trial and tribulation as any cowboy or farm mother who lived two centuries before had endured.

CashCarter, for whatever reason, had also become a leading medical center, offering its services to the body as well as its musicians tended to the soul. I had decided to go there because the white-coated doctors and vigilant, efficient nurses who practiced there were imbued, Arre had intimated, with the magic powers that would, I felt certain, bring my mother back into the fullness of her life.

Obamaport, east of Atlanta, was now the quintessence of egalitarian hyperactivity as it did the busywork required to route American trade to and from Europe and Africa. Old Miami was up to its arm pits in sea water, and would soon, it was said, slip forever below the waves. A new floating hive would take the submerged city's lost name and, when completed, rise and fall imperceptibly on the waters above its drowned suburbs and the barely visible sandbars of the Keys.

All of those cities, along with Reagan city in Illinois, BushBush and Roddenberry in Texas, and all the rest of the dozen hive cities and domed towns then extant, were thriving and flourishing, but the outside world through which mother and I eventually made our way east was being reduced rapidly to a kind of burnt wasteland, and the people who lived there had been given a Hobson's choice. Move inside as space permits or die poor on the ground they walked on.

Mrs. Munro was no fool. She could not restore a world gone by, but she would, if she could force the government to move, put these new technologies in the public domain and move a damn sight faster to give all Americans, including the millions and millions who were sheltering miserably in the fetid, fractious and dangerous old cities, protection from the killing sun. I thought she had a case that would smash the opposition of the oligarchs, but I was Wicla the Singer. What did I know?

*In flickerfire is forged the fate of fretful man.*

# Song 30

We travelled out of Portland as dusk fell and arrived three hours later at the first of the Indian barricades, at a place called Rock Fort on the south shore of the Columbia. For at least two decades the Chinook tribe had stood their ground here, under the looming shape of Mount Hood, which squatted wide and high in the middle distance. They guarded the entrance way to the lands that they and the other tribes of the Indian confederacy now controlled, not just with the firearms the men at the gate carried, but with artillery seized from abandoned armouries of the National Guard in the 2030s. Those pieces now sat in the mouths of caves the tribe had carved into the slopes overlooking the roads in and out of their camp.

No one could go further except by special dispensation, granted to Merri and me, of the Nez Perce, issued to us upon the request of Sakhonteic, otherwise known as Richard Yorke in most of the white man's world, otherwise known as Titus in Gaytown. You will need no papers, Titus had assured me. They will know you, he said.

And true enough the Chinook men did know us because they felt quite sure we fit the description given to them by the Nez Perce: Two women crazy enough to cross the not-quite-end-of-winter mountains in an old white van. We pulled up to the gates, one baby-faced youth looked at me through the driver side window and waved at someone else, and the gate went up. As I pulled through, I watched baby-face in the side mirror as he picked up a vice and uttered just a few words – to someone upstream, I guessed.

We made it to the outskirts of the town of Kennewick by dawn and there, despite mother's sudden display of impatience with the pace of travel, I had to stop. I was too tired to drive further.

Titus told me that once we entered the Indian lands no one would bother us. I took him at his word and found a place to park the van so it would get fully charged in the day's sunshine.

- What god forsaken place is this, Wicla? Where have you brought me?

- We're near Kennewick, mother.

- We've been here before.

- Some time ago, yes.

- We did good business.

- Yeah, but there's no business to be done now.

- Thanks to you. We could have gone to Blaine and loaded up.

- We didn't have time.

- Oh, no, Wicla the singer never has any time. Well, there's no point in staying here, is there?

She was standing by the driver's seat waiting for me to get up.

- I'll drive, she said.

- Not a chance, said I, looking at her in a way that made her walk to her room in the back of the van, grumbling.

How could arms as thin and muscle-less as hers hold the steering wheel on the wild bends of the roads we were on, let alone if she lost control? That's assuming she could see the road. They couldn't.

- Mother, I called out.

- Not here, she said, petulantly.

- You could help make a meal.

- I'm not hungry.

- I am.

I heard the rattle of her pill bottle.

- Help yourself. You know where the grub is.

She swigged water out of a canteen to wash the pills down. And then she mumbled under her breath just loud enough for me to hear.

- You want to do everything yourself. Fine. Well, your old momma ain't gonna raise a finger. Denver my ass.

I made soup from a can, then set two bowls and a stack of buttered toast on the small table near the galley. A few minutes later she emerged from her room and shuffled to the galley.

- Maybe I'll have some, Merri said, sitting down kitty corner to me.

- There's more once you get that down.

- You have it. Girl works as hard as you do needs her vitamins.

It was her way of apologizing.

We spent all day sleeping. I was awakened by a message from Titus relaying what he had learned from his cousin at the reserve. He warned us not to travel to the Nez Perce village at night. Snow falling. Roads treacherous. Pitch black. Travel at daylight. And indeed, when I looked out the van windows I saw that a light snow was falling. I checked my vice to see how long we would be stuck where we were, but the weather report for the area said that temperatures were rising, we might get some rain, the roads would be clear in the lower reaches of the mountains the following morning. So, we had to stay all day and then one more night.

Long into the afternoon, we drove into Kennewick – the town was outside the Indian lands - and talked our way past the white man barricades there. One of the old timers on duty remembered Trader Merri Weer and let us through for old time's sake. Like just about every Outsider town, this one was full of middle age and older people marking time, still going about their business, which wasn't much. They ambled past a lot of vacant stores and offices as they went from a grocer who was still hanging on, to a lumber store for a washer or a few nails, to a restaurant for a cup of cheap java and a homemade piece of pie. The daily routine. I parked the van as close to the restaurant as I could so mother didn't have to walk too far, and even then she was grousing because the air was cold and the sidewalks slippery.

I left her in the coffee shop after I'd eaten bacon and eggs and went for a stroll, nodding my head at the very few people who came toward me. I felt their suspicious, who-the-hell-are-you looks on my back as we passed one another. Everyone knew a stranger when they saw one, and it was a peculiar person, indeed, who didn't think you were there to steal their money or rob them of their last earthly possessions when they turned their eye from you.

The visit to Kennewick was like a visit to the dozen or so other towns – maybe more – that Merri and I visited on our way to CashCarter. So, I am telling you about this one to spare you the pleasureless and confused reminiscences I still carry of all the others, as I try to place them on the map. The truth is that whatever used to make one town different from another had been buried under the weight of their current dilapidated sameness: the muddy red brick and tarnished concrete of the larger buildings, the khaki color lumber under the curls of paint, usually white, flaking off the walls and window frames of the wood buildings, the unkempt black of loosening roof shingles, the array of grey-shaded, potholed streets, the drab clothes of their aging inhabitants, their white hair, the pallor of their skin, the thin red blood of their shrinking dreams, the blues and yellows of their sadness and resentments, the far away greens that shone only in memories of younger days.

I had been spared the pains of longing I surely would have felt had mother settled down in one of these places to raise me. Back in the restaurant I sat down in front of her and asked our over-solicitous waitress for another cup of coffee. I took Merri's hand. She looked up at me.

- Thankyou mother.

- For what?

- For taking me with you.

- Whaddya mean?

- Wherever life took you. You took me too.

- Didn't have much choice.

- Sure you did. You could have settled down.

- No, I couldn't.

- Well, I'm glad you took me with you. I love you for it.

- Now, don't you go getting all sentimental.

I pulled my hand away. Maybe I was a bit misty eyed. Whatever it was she saw, she put her hand on my face and held it there until we were looking at one another – really looking I mean.

- I love you too.

That night, while Merri slept, I cuddled up with Old Mud and tried to work on my new lyric. Usually, with the melody in hand, I could get a verse down pretty fast, but this one was a torment. It took me awhile, but I did get another verse. And then I slept the sleep of the empty mind.

Next morning, we followed the Snake River out of Kennewick, once again in Indian country, sipping coffee. Mother sitting in the passenger seat, shrivelled but eyes bright as we crossed the wide, long, unexpected prairie, past the tilted, faded signs that mark the ruins of towns and villages once lived in, on through Eureka, Lamar, Prescott, Dayton and others, into the foothills upon whose rises the rusted hulks of old windmills poked into a blue and cloudless sky.

Just past the wreck of Tucannon, we headed east again, immersed in the brown, rolling scrubland whose tight vales were dense with trees in holy communion with freshets of runoff percolating at their feet, past Dodge and Pomeroy then Pataha, further to Silcott where the coils of the Snake finally reappeared next to our road again. We let the road and river take us to the manned barrier at Clarkston-Lewiston, now the main town of the Nez Perce Indians. There the river snaps in two, called the Clearwater as it continues east, but still the Snake where it branches south.

All rifles were shouldered, all side arms holstered. Broad smiles on all their faces. A man's hand went up and asked us to stop. He and another came to the driver side window.

- We have been waiting for you, Miss Wicla.

- We couldn't take the chance of driving at night. So, we are very sorry to make you wait.

- No worries. We all slept like babies last night. Our friends told us of your prudence. We knew you would arrive today.

- Mother, said the second man looking at Merri, are you well?

- Not too damn good, but better than dead.

- The council waits to greet you, Miss Wicla.

The Nez Perce council convened in a high ceiling room within the confines of a Romanesque pile of sandstone that had served decades past as the white man's civic theater where one could still hear, if one listened closely, the brave, amateur speeches of Shakespeare's villains, the ribald music of Old Broadway revivals, the hanker of people in those days to mine again the gold of past glory for present burnishing.

As we entered into the council chamber a hundred people – maybe more – rose as one and applauded us, mother in the wheelchair I had stowed secretly in Portland, and into which she had been gently seated by our escorts at my request. They graciously ignored the curses she bestowed on them and me for declaring her an invalid. They took us to the front of the room where the councilmen and women stood, joining in the applause. The head man nodded his head at someone at the side of the room. Three drumbeats sounded on a deerskin drum, a signal to all to sit. All but the head man, who came around to greet us. He bent over and extended his hand to Merri who looked at me, then at his rheumy-eyed and leathery face, all smiles, and she put her hand in his.

- Welcome Trader Merri Weer.

- You know me?

- The Great Mother. Your name has been on our ears for many years. Why have you not come before? Our women are women too.

- Well, I uh…You're a bit out of the way.

- We are at the center of all things, Mother.

He came to me.

- Wicla the Singer.

He took my extended hand, squeezed a handshake with his right, large and strong, enveloped his and mine with his left and clasped them in a warm, loose grip as he looked into my eyes, searching.

- We dance to your songs. The voice of the Great Spirit comes through you.

- No. No. I'm just a…

- You have been a good friend of our brother.

- Titus?

- Sakhonteic. I am Kiyiyah, the eldest brother. Call me Ed. There is Peopeo. Call him George, he said, pointing to another man at the council table. Dick is the youngest. We are all sons of the same father, children of the same mother.

It was impossible for me to think of Titus as Dick, giant Titus with his long, delicate fingers and small feet, Titus who kissed Arre and held him close so Arre's brittle fears could settle, Titus who danced in the strobe-lit rooms of the GayTown clubs, who satirized the androgynous pretentions of the those who lived their lives in the middle with his outrageous send-ups, who every day amused his colleagues with sly jokes and infectious humour, who cut to the nub of things with the knife of wit, who gave so completely whatever I wanted or needed from him, who wrote sarcastic lyrics to my tunes to keep me level.

I could not think of Titus as Richard or Dick, but I could think of him as Sakhonteic, warrior spirit. He came to mind, vividly as Ed held my hand. I heard Titus' voice. Fuck you, world, I will stay in Portland and I will die here dancing and laughing with all the other fuck-you people whom I love. Save me, he would say, from the inauthentic and the shamsters, for they shall inherit the kingdom of shit. Pass the wine.

Double doors opened from the council room to another room where a long buffet table was set with an immense amount of food. Two drumbeats called everyone to their feet again as Chief Ed led the way to the tables with me behind him and mother, pushed by one of our escorts, rolling along beside me. Then the room flooded with everyone else who had been in the chamber, while serious women and girls came and went from a kitchen, doing, alas, what women and girls everywhere do, serve and tidy and clean in the buzz and chuckle of all the fun.

We met and talked with many of the Nez Perce that evening, learning a little about their lives, about the renaissance of their culture and the culture of the other tribes around them, how the Outsider world was their world really and always had been, how its brokenness would be fixed as the white man retreated to his new cities, how weather and time would wear the white man's doings into a dust, into a dirt where the Indian's sacred plants would take root once again.

Ed and George came to me and interrupted a conversation I was having with an intense, beautiful Nez Perce girl about songs and song writing.

- Kaya is singing tomorrow night, Wicla.

- Wow. Good for you, Kaya.

- We hope you will sing too, Kaya said

- Uh. Mother and I should… We are running behind already.

- You think you will lose another day?

- Yeah, I…we…

- You will not lose a day because George will guide you through the Bitterroots to Lolo. You will save a day, Ed said while George nodded. He will take you on secret paths.

- Show her the stage, Kaya, said George.

Kaya and I stood at the center of the empty stage looking out at the auditorium where hundreds of people would hear us sing the following night. She told me as we talked that her Uncle Dick had said I would sing. Not a bet on a possibility, a sure thing. George read me right. He knew the evening had filled me up, that some well-fed part of my soul wanted to sing.

- He knew I couldn't refuse.

- Don't you want to sing, Wicla?

I stood on the stage, thought of Jack, Ann Marie, Tedhum and Zimbo making music behind me, thought of Wynk standing in the off-right shadows fidgety with the desire my songs raised in him, thought of my mother on the toes of her boots with vest jangling down in front of the stage, arms in the air, turning circles. I heard the gathered voices in the audience singing the choruses of my songs.

Then I realized, Trader Merri Weer had died at Fort Ketchup as she sat rocking on the edge of her bed under a hurricane-opened sky. She come back as Mother Merri, still living, but riddled with cancer. When Chief Ed welcomed her at the council meeting as Trader Merri Weer he was welcoming her from the spirit realm in which that version of her old self now resided. Chief Ed, I could tell, was a traveler in that world and he could see her in the flesh of her once robust, determined, and powerful presence.

And I? I had been grievously wounded at Fort Ketchup too. I had tumbled down into a bed of woe, had arisen into a time of constant care for her, had tuned myself out, or so I thought. I had done the Portland concert as a duty, done by rote, for money, for the long trip east in hope of our salvation and maybe my redemption.

- Yeah. I want to sing, I told Kaya.

We stayed in the van that night right on the street outside the theater. I got mother in bed and then got in mine, exhausted. Knew then that Titus had put me on the spot. Wanted me to be Wicla the Singer, not nurse Wicla. Grabbed my pad, looked at the scrawl I had put down the night before. Read it. Hoped I could do better, started another verse, and then fell into the same sleep again, empty of agitated thought. I was on my way somewhere.

*Walking the city streets alone,*
*City from which the angry birds have flown,*
*Where cry the women of the night,*
*And men howl in the window light,*
*Their shadows cast on the land of is.*

The van stayed in the sunlight all day long that next day. Sometimes I went walkabout by myself, keeping to the shadows as always, bumping into Nez Perce. Some greeted me with a reverence I could not possibly deserve, while the shy among them stepped aside to let me pass with eyes averted. At one point a group of adolescents trailed behind me singing verses from Out of the Mud, whose horrid gunplay excited them and made them, I suppose, think I had been writing about righteous rebellion, not the sad carnage I really had in mind. In short, they were, at that age, misunderstanding fans.

At noon I went back to the van where I found Merri standing by the galley sink wiping vomit from her chin, while assuring me it was only dribbled soup. Her face was wracked with pain. I found her pills on the little stand by her bed and took them to the galley. She swallowed two, wanted more. I got her into her coat, down the step to the street and eased her into the wheelchair, then rolled her along Lewiston's main avenue to one of its busy restaurants where we had a lunch of homegrown food. Mother's face slowly relaxed, but she said not a word as she ate the little lunch she could get down.

The Nez Perce breathed the deep, cold air of the Outside, drank the icy mountain waters of the rivers running through, planted corn and potatoes in the nearby fields, raised cattle, horses and pigs for milk and meat, and then, full of the energy all that had given them, brought a bristling kind of optimism and purpose to the town that made it unique among all the towns and villages Merri and I had ever visited, and filled it with the new life that comes from making love. Making love a lot. There were children everywhere.

That night I was on stage with Kaya facing a standing room only crowd of expectant faces. She would sing first then give the spotlight to me and then, grand finale, we would sing one of my songs together. That afternoon I had wondered, slightly irritated, why I should have to share the night with a girl amateur, pretty as she was. But you know, she was a niece to all the Yorke men, a dark haired, smoky-eyed daughter of the tribe, so I would wear a mask of graciousness, not knowing if or how I could hide my condescension.

Brother George was the taciturn and humble MC of the night. His voice hardly carried to the back of the theater when he introduced Kaya. She walked on stage to the stool set before her mic and strummed her guitar. Well-played, I thought. Then she began singing, something she herself had composed, an aria in which she caught the sounds of tribal drums, of hooting warriors, of arrows flying, of hard running in the forests, of night falling, of wolves howling at the moon, and at the end, of silent dawn. I wished I had brought Merri to listen and watch instead of telling her that she must stay in the van and rest, for this girl would have injected her with a pain killer that might well have lasted until we reached CashCarter.

The crowd jumped to its feet at song's end and applauded her until she knew she could settle them down with her next tune, an elegy, dignified and soulful. A fast tune next, toe-tapper, hand clapper, whistle maker. Love song following, maybe sung to some sweetheart out there in the dark. Hymn next, sung to wind and water, and to the old, old sun. Songs only, no talk between. Stood to take her final applause, standing straight in the spotlight, corona of faint blue light around her head and face, took a deep bow to honor her people, deep enough to put her forehead into the black pool of tribal memory where, I suspect, she saw something swimming that would appear some day soon in a new lyric and song.

Did her singing arouse my competitive instincts? No. She had pierced my heart too, and left my desire to win, desire to please, dying, right there on the backstage floorboards. I could feel the soul of my own people and my own soul too, white, black, and Asian, stirring in me.

I went out on stage where Kaya and I embraced, and I whispered to her, below the hearing of the happy uproar in the auditorium, the only words that came to me. I love you. Thankyou. Thankyou. Then, once she had made it to the shadows, standing to the mic in my street clothes, looking hag-like compared to Kaya, I sang five of the songs I had written to the Outsiders. I must have found in the profundity of the moment, ways and means I could not now articulate, of joining the Outsider's circle with the circle of the Indian nations, for the people in front of me that night bestowed their blessings on me just as they had Kaya.

We sang a last song together, a song of mine, and it became, as our guitars talked to one another, one of those seemingly simple, easy performances that belie the cosmic complexities of which they are composed. Among other things, I realized later, it contained the rage that would consume me later.

The chords of that night hung in the dusk when next day,

Merri and I restarted our journey. George and Peopeo led in a battered truck, going east out of Lewiston through the deepest part of the Nez Perce lands, first cleaving close to the Clearwater River, still foothill land on its south side, but the hillocks and rises becoming higher and higher, longer and more rounded, rising and rising slowly. Just past Ahahka the road turned south, still following the narrowing river, to Kooskia where we veered east again along its middle fork where at last the slopes of the not so far off Bitterroots came into view in the background.

At the flattened outpost of a place called Lowell, we took the road north, leaving the Clearwater to go south to its head-waters, while we grab the road running parallel to a different river, the Lochsa, that had carved its way through the tight-ening, ever-higher hills. As we went further, the river was safe running in its bed, fast with spring run-off. But the men who built the road here had to dynamite the forbidding granite that lay below the roots of the pine and fir forests clinging to the overburden to make room for the roadbed. We climbed slowly but steadily on its carved-out surfaces.

At Mocus Point, we spied the peaks of the Bitterroots again, dull and blue, wreathed in wet clouds, and then, passing through some indefinable boundary we were in them, where snow had fallen and was holding to the ground on either side of the still bare highway and the narrowing stream of the over-hung river. We are come at last to Lolo Pass where the landscape suddenly flattens, and where, two centuries earlier, pioneers made meadows among the trees, ranching and doing all they must, in the company of their cows, to survive the constant changes in the weather of the mountains.

George signaled then pulled his truck to the side of the road. He and Peopeo got out and stood in the road. They watched as I slowed down and then stop the van behind them. We have driven almost six hours. Now we had arrived at the Great Divide.

- On this side, George says, the rivers flow west. On that side, all go east. This foot is in Nez Perce country. Idaho. This foot is in Montana. Shoshone territory.

I turned and saw Merri through the windscreen of the van looking to the east. I could see she did not believe it was the promised land.

- Our brothers will treat you well, Wicla the Singer. They know what you are doing for the Great Mother.

- I don't know what to say, George…Peopeo.

- You will sing again, Peopeo. That is enough.

- I will tell Sakhonteic we have brought you to this place.

I reached to George for a hug. He took my arms at the elbows before they closed around him then stepped me back one step and looked me in my eyes.

- You do not want to see the tears of an old Indian. They will fill the Laksha until it bursts its banks and floods the world. Go in peace.

He waved at Merri, looked at her with a hand over his heart. She waved back then he and Peopeo got back in their truck, did a U turn and started the long drive back downhill.

Mother and I now stood at the turning point. The west we knew was behind us. The unknown was dropping a light snow on our very heads, obscuring our vision of the road ahead. It would keep us on the knife-edge of the continent for another two days.

*Cringes the cat of catastrophe in our crazed cacophony.*

# Song 31

I stood before the mirror in the dressing room of Polyphemus, the club in CashCarter where I became a lounge singer, putting on my coal eyes through which, as I sang, I would scan the mostly indifferent men and women passing time in the wee hours. It was a few months after mother died. It was the night I would meet the man I would marry and one day murder. A door knock as usual. Five minutes Ms Weer. Five minutes.

As I put on my mascara, rouge and lipstick I worried a little about the lines creasing my forehead and the slight loosening of the skin on my neck, and the brightening red tone of the skin that plunged down between my breasts, held aloft by an obligating bra. As I brushed my dark hair to buoy it up and give it shape, I counted the silver strands running through, calculated the loss of lustre of all the rest. Slight downturn at the corner of my mouth too, but then, a dentist in the city had given me a perfect smile, a brilliant white that I framed with ruby red. I would be singing in the bar shortly, where I would trick my fans to make them think that under the mystical lights of that small stage I was a darkroom beauty, just out of reach of all and any. Just me at forty and Old Mud, ageless.

I looked into the mirror, looked and looked as I leaned on the sink my face close. Saw that my eyes were keeping the facts of all that had happened from Lolo Pass to here a mystery, saw pain there as though it were not mine but belonged to some person I once knew. Looked for clues.

Ours had been a long downhill trip that took days and days. It started high up in the Bitterroots, where overnight a blizzard came blowing from the west and threw a winter tantrum as though it were a child of Hecate. Just a few miles east, it closed the pass. We retreated after a couple of hours to where we had started, then struggled south to the pass at Lemhi, letting the selfdrive find its way on the snow-buried road.

The hours passed slowly. At Lehmi, we parked on the side of the empty highway again and during that day waited for nightfall while the van sucked at the far-off sun for the energy it would need to take us forward. I napped when I could. Mother stayed in bed, sipped at the soup I lifted to her mouth, ate a corner of the toasted bread I offered. Said thank you then fell back again and slipped under the covers I pulled up over her shoulders. I patted her shoulders gently then leaned over to kiss her head, almost always turned away. Heard soft moaning that wrenched my gut.

Around Noon, sitting in the passenger seat nursing a cup of coffee, feet on the dash, looking into the black and white world on the other side of the windscreen, my wandering mind came back to me, found me sitting lonely and afraid. A deep longing to be at the cabin near Ojai came over me, to see, hear and smell Lawrence and Javier and to be in their untroubled home. I had not talked to them since just before the concert in Portland when I begged them to come, but they couldn't. I spoke into my vice and told it to dial Lawrence. The dial tone sputtered, but Lawrence answered.

- Wicla? Wicla?

- Lawrence it's Wicla.

- What? What? I can't...

- I'm at Lemhi Pass.

- Where? What? Wicla.

Up here, at the height of the divide, the signal falters and breaks all our words into frustrating nonsense. All the fractured syllables of his words fly into the air between him and me, freeze in the upper atmosphere where satellites spin under a blanket of stars, but come down like flint-tipped arrows to my stationary heart.

- I will call you later.

- Later? OK. OK. Love to Mer....

Lemhi let us through at dusk, and down we went. Hold on tight, I called back to my mother in her bed. The road made a black path through a white wilderness illuminated by the scorching light that flung out from the front of the van. All night, down and down, out of the mountains around dangerous curves and dubious switchbacks until we came to a Shoshone barricade in the cleft of the mountains. just as dawn cracked at the horizon far to the east.

A truck and another vehicle sat idle behind the barricade. A tall man and a tough-looking pregnant woman were there to greet us, stepping out of their beat-up car, out of its warmth into the cold morning air, every breath instantly vaporizing before their faces, now turned our way. Two other men step out of the truck.

The tall man, Cameahwait, narrow-hipped and broad shouldered welcomed us to the Shoshone Nation. He was grateful, he said, that his brothers on the other side of the mountains had sent us there. He introduced the round-faced woman whose face was encircled by the fur of the hood she wore, his sister, Saca, whose soft voice belies the tense female strength of her body, which is evident even through the thick blue coat she wears and under the weight of her late-stage pregnancy. The other men are introduced but I can't remember their names now. We shake hands with our gloves on.

- Where is the Great Mother, Trader Merri Weer? Is she with us still? Cameahwait asked.

- She is sleeping, I answer. She is very ill.

- We have heard, said Saca.

- She has a cancer.

They looked at one another and nod their heads. Cameahwait doffed his cap, took off a glove and ran his hand through his still mat-black hair.

- We will ask our medicine man to read her eyes, he says. He will say whether the white man's ways can work.

390

Saca elbowed him, but I knew already he was not insensitive, but a seeker of truth, even when it might bear pain. And Saca too, as if that trait had been bred in their family's bones.

They asked me to follow them, and so, my lungs now full of cold, clean air, the tension of the last miles broken, my shoulders dropped at last, I took the wheel and drove behind them, out of the mountains then across the dry brown hills on their east flank until we come to their ranch at a spot on a frigid, ochre prairie my GPS called Grant. The other men remained at the barricade.

Once I had tended to Merri, I went to the house. I knocked on the kitchen door, but I could not be heard above the sound of the wall vice inside. I opened and walked through the kitchen toward the source of the noise and there saw Cameahwait standing a few feet from the large screen, Saca sitting on a couch close by, both watching as though shocked and immobilized by the sight of an oncoming tsunami. The President and her husband had been kidnapped.

The troubled couple had taken a few days off at a castle owned by a friend in Scotland, the anchor said, to repair their marriage. As Merri and I slept and napped at Lemhi Pass, men had come from behind the fireplace in their room and spirited them away. The kidnappers had videotaped two men wearing balaclavas and dressed in black as they shook the First Couple awake in the green light of the video cam, guns to their heads, shushing them on pain of death.

Cora Munro and Paul, both naked, were brought to their feet on either side of the bed shivering in fear, silent. They instinctively grabbed blankets and covered themselves as they were marched to the opening behind the fireplace then roughly forced into it and then jostled down a greenlit passageway on their bare feet, down to a freezing cave only open to the North Atlantic at low tide. Hours had passed since their absence had been discovered by the Secret Service men stationed down the hallway outside their room. The owner of the castle was being questioned in Clinton where he resided, as were the servants who worked there.

The month that followed is a month not just of The Show as the video feed of their captivity is dubbed, but of our government's frantic search for Cora and Paul Munro. It is a fraught muddle, a siren-sounding, gun-booming, jet-screaming muddle where above the noise of human machines, human voices break through in shouts and sometimes whispers, when the crying of the frightened is heard one moment, the warnings and threats of the bellicose the next, when assurances fall on deaf ears, when the yawns of the always-awake cannot be stifled, when the sour belly grumbles because it goes unfed, when the relieving groans of a quick fuck fall quickly to more distracted speculation, when the constant stream of The Show pulls 'ah, see', 'did you see that?' and 'I told you so' from the billions of mouths, from the mouths of the know-it-alls, who, just like Merri and I, are transfixed by what we see coming out of the bungalow where the Firsts are penned in middle class boredom and secretly videoed for the entertainment of the world.

And then there was our noise, my mother's and mine, as I listened to the vice for more news of Cora and Paul Munro, wheels of the van whirring on the roads we drove, when I knew that one more pill would not silence her painful whimpers, when I clattered our galley pans to fix a bite of lunch or dinner for both of us, when I sang to her softly as I combed her all-grey hair, when I heard the tiny slurps she made sipping from a glass of water or a spoon full of soup.

When I tell her the little I know about why the President was kidnapped and who might have done it, she said as if confirming some ancient truth, it's money. Money or revenge. Or both, she said with a coughed-up chuckle, pleased with her simple wisdom. I gave her the time she needed when we stopped along the way to tend to her needs, but when we stopped, I always switched on the vice above the windscreen to watch the stream because no one could turn away from what was going on in that bungalow, not really.

I had a thousand conversations and confrontations with strangers we met along the way to Cash Carter. But no matter who or where or why those conversations took place, when it came down to it, they all came around to what was happening with the President and the First Husband. In their twentieth century bungalow, the Munros were, it seemed, being held behind invisible bars in a time of peace and plenty in the country's now long past.

The Show made us look at that past, so, yes, we were all wrapped up in the enigma, mystery and riddle of the kidnapping, the who, what and why, but we were also put to the larger, more insidious question of what had happened to us all.

The nostalgic domesticity of The Show, that tidy, front-porched bungalow situated in a cul de sac in its green suburb was a painful reminder of our destroyed country, but, looking now I can see that we were programmed with a vague desire for the clean, the bright, the peaceful world of the new Inside world of the hives. So, who really cared about my dying mother, sometime legend? No one but me and a handful of people who lived way over there in the Outside, on the other side of the Great Divide.

A couple of hundred Shoshone came to Cameahwait's ranch the night after we arrive, to meet me and Merri. And I knew I had to sing for them because it was the currency they expected me to repay their hospitality with. Even though the temperature was dropping, I was to sing outdoors from a makeshift stage he put against the barn at some distance from the house. A few men had come during the day to help build a stone-ringed bonfire and to drag in big pieces of timber they had scavenged off the hills we had driven out of the day before.

Saca carried a torch to the side of the firepit just before their tribemates started arriving and lit the kindling, which burst up out of the guts of the wood pile and touched off a fire that was leaping thirty feet into the air and casting its light two hundred feet in every direction. Those who came the earliest sidled up to the fire, but later arrivals were two, three and four deep.

But the outdoor show was not to be. My fingers were cold-cramped, Old Mud wouldn't tune, my voice was too dry. I couldn't make enough noise to get the Shoshone to turn to the stage. Oh no, they were perfectly happy to stay where they were. Cam would not be denied, however. His house was big enough to move the party inside so he cat whistled to get everyone's attention and moved them into the house. Several of the youths hustled the heavy tubs of iced beer that had been nestled at just the right distance from the firepit into the kitchen, and the women raided the refrigerator and laid-out a buffet with what they found. A huge coffee table was moved to a corner to make room for the growing crowd, but also to serve as my stage, and from there I did my level best to make myself heard.

The next day, I did what Saca advised. The fastest way to get to where you want to go, she said, pointing at a map, is to go north to Grand Falls and follow the Missouri River as it flows east. At Grand Falls the Missouri stepped down to the burnt plains below as it ran the five cataracts there. Outside the town of Grand Falls, I sang for the Blackfeet. Further along to the east I sang to the Mandans on a stage set -up especially for me somewhere on the expanse of the Berthold lands, recovered just a couple of decades ago from the skullduggery of local authorities.

I sang to the Lakota Sioux at their reserve near Sioux City, under duress really, subtle as it was, because they didn't buy the excuses I made to not sing, and I sang lastly to the Osage where I could see, off to the side of old Kansas City, the shape of a new hive rising. Its official name was CharlieParker, but because flocks of birds were perching in their millions on it rising dome the locals had already started to call it BirdTown.

And that was that. Out of the Indian lands we drove, out of the protection of their federation toward the uncertainties, and maybe the dangers, that lay on the far bank of the shrivelled Mississippi. Admittedly, I felt some resentment toward the Indians for making me perform – well, making is too strong a word.

I sang and I did not stint because I understood as I got to know them, the deeper purposes of mutual respect that underpinned the workable peace that existed among the tribes. That respect – or its lack – colored every relationship within the tribes themselves. So, whatever I felt, it was not their fault but mine. I was tired. I was worried about Merri almost to the point of sickness myself, and if I could have shirked just one duty, ignored just one obligation, I would have.

It all sounds civilized enough, doesn't it? I did not stint, as I said. But I ended up singing to myself even though my so-called audiences were standing right in front of me. Every last one of them was heads down into their vice watching whatever the hell Cora and Paul were up to, or they were tuned into a news channel listening for clues as to there whereabouts, or to Vice President Ovans or some other government spokesperson making excuses why the combined intelligence operations and military forces of the United States couldn't find the Firsts.

The hoots and hollers and other exclamations that rose up out of the crowd were not for me, but for some thing Cora or Paul had said or done, or for some prevarication coming out of the mouths in Washington, and on more than one occasion, for the video streamed operations of special forces soldiers dropping unexpectedly from the sky onto the roofs of suspects in some far-off desert city on the other side of the world where, so far, they had always come up empty. There were scenes of combat jets screaming through the skies, and navy's churning the waters of every sea you could name, laden down with sailors snapping salutes and preparing the big guns for that moment of retaliation that every red-blooded American wanted to kick-off with fireworks.

But, that 1960s bungalow the President and Paul were living in was nowhere to be found and hardly anyone you talked to was unable to get it of their heads that where they were was not a real place, but some craftily engineered set that preyed on your imagination, that made you feel, if you were an Outsider, the unhappiness that you almost always kept to yourself.

The Indian Lands were pock-marked with the old, now fenced-in towns where non-Indian people still held sway. That was the result of the so called New Indian Wars back in the 30s, when the two 'nations' slugged and shot it out. Now, coteries of white men – with few exceptions - stood with guns not necessarily at the ready, but close at hand.

Things had settled down and there was none of the devastating, enervating raiding and counterraiding that had gone back in those days. But men with a purpose are better than men without one, except – ask any woman - when their purpose always seems to involve protecting the weaker sex. That meant keeping the women inside the fences, mostly at home, mostly doing all the things that brave men run from, like cooking, cleaning and raising the little ones. Food on the table, sex on demand. Manly appetites? Oh, yeah. So, yeah, in the noises that I heard wherever we went were the base notes of men wanting something there and then, and the throatscreeched complaints of women bitching.

Mother had usually dealt with the men at these places when she traveled as Trader Merri Weer, and she just accepted it for what it was, but I hated driving through them and avoided them wherever possible. But it wasn't possible at Butte, just north of Cameahwait's place, or Grand Falls and a helluva lot of the other still-living towns along the Missouri. Fortunately, the men at the gates also had their heads down in their vices, probably doing exactly the same thing as their women and everybody else was doing – as I was doing as I drove.

I new Paul, knew his voice, soft but urgent when he asked me to turn over my naked body so he could take me from behind, loud and commanding when he was speaking on some stump on behalf of his wife, clear and articulate when he was pursuing some task that required tact and persuasiveness. Every watcher now heard those voices, for whoever captured them, did not scruple to edit the love scenes from the bungalow or anything else for that matter. Even after Cora and Paul realized they were being taped, they carried on as normal, although I now understand they were also putting on an act in furtherance of their escape. Well, he was.

And we heard Cora's voice too, her political voice at least, familiar to me and everyone else because we had watched her on the public scene. Now we heard her sharp tongue as she cut into Paul's fleshy insouciance. We heard her humming melodies as she did the housework in the bungalow, the lion's share that is. We heard her breathing hard on the treadmill her captors had installed in the house. We heard her remonstrate with her always-out-of-sight neighbors. We heard her mind at work as she talked politics with Paul, for ever the optimist, she was planning a second term campaign, and planning not to lose.

Both their voices were in my head, and the voices of everyone I met on this journey, all the noises that streamed off all the channels on all the vices within earshot, and the comingled voices of all my friends coming clear and strong out of the west to which I knew I would never return. Wynk's solicitous voice. Jack's voice as he plucked me like a guitar. And I heard my own voice doing whatever the hell I was doing at any given time, singing maybe, trying to work out the lyric of the song I had been working on, reacting in anger or astonishment at the stuff I was hearing on my vice.

I heard myself say the precise things I would say to my father should he ever dare show up on my doorstep, heard also the things I would say to Cora and Paul if I could battle my way to their door and save them, without ever letting Cora know that her man had had me too, this way and that and every other way.

And I heard the voice of mother Merri, coming to me out of her bed at the back of the van, not just her voice now, always in pain, but her voice from the past too, when I was a little girl, or a teen or a young woman, telling me to grow up, telling me to be strong, ordering me to be brave and bold, to be ruthless with myself, but no one else. I heard her say, nice song kiddo. What hat did you pull that rabbit out of? Her two-fingered whistle coming out of the tumultuous audience to whom I played, backed-up by my band. Her tow tap, hand clap, circle dance on the plank floors in front of the stage in the clubs where I played early on. The jingle jangle of the vest she wore now hanging on a hook just inside the door of her little room. The howl that came from her drunken mouth when the memory of her rape in Albuquerque could not be kept quiet for one more second. Her weeping at Lilith's betrayal into a soaked hanky, eyes averted as if ashamed of a weakness that might kill her.

Still, I look in the mirror, looping back again to those nights at Lolo and Lemhi, snowbound at the heights where the country folds east and west. I am bored. No signal for the vice. All the books I have on board – not many – all have been read by me more than once. I paced. Looked in on mother, laying flat, but with her head turned to the outside wall, gently breathing, free of pain I hoped. Cups and dishes cluttered the sink. I washed them and then toweled them dry before putting them away, quietly. A couple of pots to scour. Slight banging against the sides of the soapy sink. Putting the last one away, I dropped it on the thin carpet covering the metal floor. It boomed on its bottom, then did a ringing circle dance on its rim before it banged against the cupboard below the sink and came to rest, calling mother back from her dreams into the disoriented present.

I sat beside her on the edge of the small bed. She curved her body and rested her head on my lap. I stroked her head and pulled gently at the strands of her thin grey hair. She mumbles something. I say, what? Then she told me a story from her days traveling and trading on Route 66. She met a guy in a bar in one of the small towns she passed through, which one she can't remember. He was, he admitted, a heavy drinker, a gambler too, but that night he's trying to stay content with ginger ale, trying to make a turn in his life. He was sad beyond sad, Merri said. He was distraught. The parents of his niece had died and her mother's will named him guardian. He loved her deeply and she loved him, but the executor of the will was pressing hard to have her taken out of his care. He could not right the past and a sober future seemed uncertain.

- I told him he deserved to lose her, Merri said. Why mince words. Face-up to it, was my message.

- You don't understand, he said.

- I understand you're a drunk and a gambler. What more is there to understand?

- I'm not drunk enough to tell you.

- Tell me anyway.

- She's my daughter.

Merri stopped talking. I waited.

- What happened, mother?

She stirred, then sat up as much as she could.

- I stood up next to him and slapped him hard across the face.

- What?

- I did. I walloped him. So, you fucked your brother's wife? I said. He nodded to me while rubbing his cheek because I had set it on fire. I saw his eyes welling. I jabbed my finger hard into his breastbone and called him a despicable excuse for a human being. He nodded, but when I stopped yelling at him, all eyes in the bar now on us, he told me his brother was a cruel man who beat his wife. I loved her, Merri, I really did, and she loved me to, and one thing led to another.

- And that's how she got pregnant? I said.

- Well, duh, said Merri.

- What did you say to him mother?

- I clubbed him again. I clubbed him again and said, if I

ever have a child I will do everything and anything to keep her safe, to give her a roof and food and clothes, and all the love she needs. And I will kick her ass when she needs it so when she's old enough she will stand on her own two feet and think twice about getting involved with men like you. I promise you that. Nothing, nothing would stop me from being a proper mother to my baby. You get me, buddy?

Mother was looking with her eyes wide open, looking back I knew, into the darkness of that old bar, long before. Then she leaned back to her pillows once again.

- When you get knocked a good one on your head, don't count the stars.

And then she closed her eyes and within seconds she was asleep again.

Twice more as we made our way east she told me stories of traveling Route 66, episodes that stick in my mind even today, so many years later. My mother always sang a little, mostly to herself while driving along. I learned my first songs from her. What she told me for the first time is that sometimes she took on a disguise, another identity she called Kitty. Sometimes, when low on money, Kitty would sing for her supper in some roadhouse where it was ok if you could barely carry a tune. Out in Southern California, one night after singing she fell in with a couple of guys and off they went to some jazz club where they met up with one of their friends, the trumpeter in the band, and his gorgeous wife.

-   She was hoity toity from New York. You could tell she
    was snooty most of the time but not that night. When
    her husband went to go play, she and I got to talking, and
    all the while she was pouring bourbon doubles down her
    gullet, two or three to my one. So then, while the other
    guys are smoking fags and tapping their toes to the tunes
    coming from the bandstand, she leans into me and says,
    look here Kitty, and opens her handbag to show me a
    pistol, a small thing but loaded with bullets that would
    kill you anyway. It didn't bother me and it didn't surprise
    me because everyone carried then, just as they do now.
    But she says to me, he's trying to kill me so push comes
    to shove I'm gonna....

-   Who was trying to kill her, mother?

-   Her husband, the trumpet player. Yeah, that's what she
    says.

-   What did you say?

-   I said, what the hell are you doing with a man who wants
    to kill you?

Merri stopped her story right there, then scrunched up,
turned away from me and pulled the blanket up over her head.

-   Mother, did her husband really want to kill her?

-   Wouldn't you? Needy woman like that.

- What the hell is the point of the story.

- You need a point?

Long pause as I shook my head, visions of mother as Kitty under some blue light, singing, vision of a platinum blond babe from New York packing a gun to kill a jazz man, vision of a couple of road warriors keeping my mother company and a vision of her being raped again. But she pulled me out of all those thoughts when she turned her head around to me again.

- It wasn't him who was gonna do the killing. Turned out she was going to kill him, in self defence, of course, so she could get out of a marriage her society mother back in New York disapproved of and find her way back into her mother's will.

- So, what's the lesson?

- Jazz is the devil's music.

- Mother!

- The point is, don't get hooked up in a kill or be killed relationship with some guy who tickles your fancy.

There must have been many more tales she could have told me, but she only told one more. Well two, if you count what she told me about Clem.

The van was in selfdrive taking us to Sioux City, in Indian

404

land still. I was feeling disgruntled because I knew I would have to sing again. The edge of the desert that had bloomed in the Southwest was now moving over the already-dry world of the Sioux's. The desert wind was pulverizing its precarious, rock-heaped landscape into dust and sand. That enervating wind picked-up and blew at man and beast in its constant effort to drive us out, to grind down everything that was human. But it also ravaged any natural thing that might dare to shoot a green leaf or a flower into its expanding bleakness.

I was fingering my way through messages on my vice, reading them but feeling unready to answer because I did not want to tell anyone the misgivings I was having about taking this trip. How's your journey of discovery going? asks Javier. Where are you now? From Wynk. Have the tribes been good to you? Titus wanted to know, and really had a right to know.

I sat hours in the driver's seat, sometimes bent over the steering wheel as I tapped my fingers on the dash, sometimes, drifting into more doubt, with my back against the side window and my feet on the passenger chair. I made an effort to toy with the lyric to my song, did not know if the glow of the red rock formations through which we were travelling was the kind of glow that I should use to illuminate the elusive themes still hiding in my invented tune.

There was a stirring in the back of the van. I stood and saw Merri in a threadbare nightshirt standing in the doorway of my room holding herself steady against the jam. She inched forward to the galley, grabbing on to nooks and crannies to stay on her feet. Toothpick legs, scrawny arms, two shriveled breasts hanging behind the unbuttoned garment. I raced back, took her arm, let her walk to the small seat jammed in between the stove and sink where she sat down, exhausted. She was hungry. She could have just called me. I was tired of being tired, so I was peevish.

I boiled water to make hard eggs. She can have that and toast again, a little jam, I decided. A thimble full of apple juice out of a jug given to us by Chief Ed, whom I imagined as I poured it, will soon be leaving the tribal offices to do his evening walk-about in Lewiston, gathering as many facts and rumours as he could because he knows they are the sound - and sometimes the fury - of the Nez Perce drums to which he is obliged, and accustomed to, to listen.

- I met a bank robber once. Old man who never got caught, Merri said, as I put the eggs in the water now boiling.

- Uh huh.

- He'd hatched a lame scheme.

- Uh huh.

- You listening to me?

I looked at her to assure her I was.

- Some young town girl had got herself into some trouble by fleecing gamblers at a crooked card game she had set up. At nineteen she was already shark smart, but she got caught.

- So, the old guy was going to pay off her debt and have one last fling with her.

- You have a filthy mind, Wicla.

- What then? I asked, popping bread into the toaster.

- He'd robbed that bank oh maybe twenty years ago. Twenty years ago from then, not now.

- I got that.

- There was still a price on his head. Big reward to anyone that turned him in.

- So, she decided to turn him in.

- Just listen. She didn't know his story. He told her that he wanted her to turn him in so she could get the reward and go straight. Hell, he was in his 80s or 90s. A comfy bed, three squares and some doctoring in a jail would be ok with him.

I gave her a plate with a peeled egg and a piece of toast. Set the apple juice on the counter near her with a couple of her yellow pills and waited for the rest of the story. She ate and drank in silence until I couldn't stand it anymore.

- So, did she turn him in?

- Course not.

- Why not?

- I have no idea.

- Why did you tell me the story?

- You got me.

She tried to stand but she couldn't quite make it. So, I helped her up and then into her room where I got her tucked in. I thought the story was over but just as I turned to walk out the door, she piped up again.

- There's always an empty cage looking for a bird.

- What the hell does that mean, mother?

- Like you don't know.

Exasperating woman, my mother.

- Anything else mother?

- Yeah.

- What?

- No bird can learn how not to fly.

She turned to the wall again. She struggled to find comfort under her covers but couldn't.

- I need another pill, Wicla.

- You just had two.

- Who's counting? Sharp groan.

You don't say no to pain. Not real pain.

Drive on, drive on. Sing, sing again. Dark of night. Down a road near Omaha, lights of the old city twinkled on the near horizon. Further on, not far, a huge construction site, earth moving equipment, truckloads of dirt are carted off. Men in hard hats scurried around the foundations and deep excavations of a new city, to be called Buffett after some long dead moneyman. High cranes held giant lights above the scene and eliminated the shadows of the illuminated works below, last minute bustle before the sun came up. Further on, what looked to be a safe place to park the van where I could sleep before singing to the Osage Indians that night.

Once parked, I stretched, then stepped out of the van into the pellucid morning, then stretched again, took deep breaths to fill my lungs. Walked into the field by the dirt road and felt the stubblecrunch under my feet. Will rain come this spring? The Indian farmers whose land this is have all but given up, I know. The corn might rise as high as a man's knees, but then wither when the season changes to unforgiving summer. Returned to the van, walked softly to mother's room. Her eyes were open, waiting for me.

- Where are we?

- Near Omaha.

- Omaha.

It wasn't a question.

- Have you been here before mother?

- Near enough.

- When?

- I don't know when.

A long reflective pause followed.

- Have you made coffee?

- I will.

She had propped herself up on pillows against the wall by the time I went back carrying a quarter cup of the strong brew she liked, an oat cookie on a cracked plate too. A bony hand on a stick arm took the cup. Two hands to get into her mouth. Loud slurp.

- When Clem came here, I took off.

- What? Clem who?

It was then that Merri told me about the night a man named Clem came to the van needing help. A long story, told as I watched her face looking straight ahead as if at a movie screen where it all played out. And whatever flickered in her memory there, flickered in her eyes too and I knew that the emotions on her face as she talked, sometimes so softly as to be unheard, were the emotions of the young woman she was then, a dancer under stars, a naked girl washing with cold water pumped by her own strong arms out of a long-forgotten well, hair shining, legs on springs, cunt all tucked and tight, belly taught, breasts high, nipples erect, a singularity that met, that weird night, when she was dressed and made all new again, with another singularity of the opposite sex, body broken, in want of care.

She told me of their few days together; did not mention love or loving, not a word about the fucking they may have done or not done, but I heard her groan, and I did not know whether it was the pain of then or now, a terrible pain or the pain of a singular pleasure. And what was I to make of the tears that flowed from closed eyes, now bulging under their lids out of her cadaverous face, if it was not a horrible regret?

- He was a good, kind man, Wicla. Like Wynk. Gentle souls.

Long silence once she'd told her story. I stood, went to the galley. Leaned over the stove on both hands, knuckles white. Dabbed my own tears. Took a deep breath again, but this time to stifle the shudder in my own soul. I returned to her room but leaned against the door jam while I waited for her to open her eyes and turn to me.

- Is he my father, mother?

- I don't know.

- You don't know?

- I made it so I'd never know.

- You made it so I would never know.

- I was not thinking about you. I did not want to think.

- Why? Why, mother?

- I'm sorry, Wicla.

I did not sleep that day. That night I sang to the few Osage who had bothered to come to the show, but they were as far gone in to their vices as all the rest of my audiences had been, watching Cora and Paul, even though they were only in their bungalow bedroom sleeping, backs to one another, not because of some spat, but because that was their habit after years of marriage. I wondered, even as I absentmindedly sang my songs, why Cora and Paul had never had children. Maybe if they had they would still be facing one another.

Next day, we sat out the daylight hours again on the side road near the Buffet hive. Just before dusk I began driving to the place where the Missouri flows into the Mississippi on the far northern outskirts of fetid and falling St. Louis, arriving there at the tail end of the afternoon. Across the river, sat Kentucky, where we would jump from whatever had gone before into whatever was coming next. Little did I know.

I should have stopped then. I was tired from lack of sleep, and the long drive out of Nebraska and Missouri had left me exhausted, but I was full of a strange energy too. I was excited to have made it finally to this place - an excitement I would be embarrassed by had someone else seen me as joyous as I was. Now, CashCarter was within striking distance, and Merri was still alive after four weeks on the road, even though we had been turned and tossed by the ups and downs of travel as we wended our way through the hard country now behind us. After all the confusion that had come into my thoughts, I was feeling for the first time, in a long time it seemed, some clarity.

We took the Chain of Rocks bridge across the river, a ribbon with wide margins of dried mud on either side, where I pulled over. Without going back to see if mother was OK, I programmed the GPS so it would take us to our destination without me at the wheel. I went back to check on Merri, whose appearance frightened me because her back was arched, her head pressed by the thin, tight cords of her neck deep into her pillow, a kind of rictus on her face.

She was alive, not asleep but unconscious, breathing so shallow as to be almost imperceptible. I shook her, but she did not wake. I got a cold wet cloth and wiped her forehead and cheeks, swabbed the lids of her eyes. I took her pulse: it was slow, too slow. I listened to her heart with my head on her chest, heard at last the drum beat there, sounding as though it were coming out of a hidden valley far away.

I sat with her as the van took us along whatever Tennessee highways it was steering, taking us to those white-coated men and women who would know far better than I how to talk her back from the precipice. But finally, she stirred. Her body relaxed. Her head rolled side to side. She drew up her knees. Some fraught moments later, she opened her eyes, surprised to see me, surprised to be in the tired reality of the van's interior, a van she once drove as a woman she used to know: Trader Merri Weer. I could hear Paul yelling at Cora through the vice I had left turned on at the front of the van. It was a comforting anger, at that moment it was, noise from a world outside this small existence into which mother and I had been crammed these last weeks. A sign of life.

I gave her water. She would not take any food. She wanted pills. After swallowing them, she fell back again and went to sleep even though, I knew, the medicine only dulled the pain, and did not end it. But now that she was asleep again, I could go to my own bed. I did and to my sorrow and to my shame I slept longer than I had slept ever before.

When I woke at last, I sensed immediately that something was wrong. I sprang out of my bed and went to Merri's room. She was awake, wide awake, humming.

- Good morning, dear.

- Good morning mother.

- Sleep well?

- Yeah, I guess I did.

- You've been down a long time.

- How long?

- Quite awhile.

- I'll get you some coffee and toast.

- That would be lovely.

Before going to the galley, I went forward to the front of the van and looked out the windscreen. Talking to Arre about CashCarter, I had expected hills, forests but we were driving in a flat land of endless dirt. I sat in the driver's seat washed over by a creeping anxiety, angry with myself because the GPS showed us traveling Route 22 approaching Tupelo. Tupelo? Where is that? Yes, Tennessee. But we had followed the Mississippi roads instead of cutting across to the hive, and now we were almost four hundred miles south of St. Louis and two hundred or so from CashCarter. The GPS has only done what I had told it to. I was so tired when I had programmed it, I got it wrong.

I had blown at least two day's travel. But at least Merri was awake and alert. I took the wheel and cut east to the Natchez Trace and drove as fast as I could for thirty minutes or so until I heard mother shouting from the back. I pulled over and ran back to her.

- You gonna get me that coffee or what?

It was almost dawn; the van was running out of power. I would have to stop and let it recharge. I made breakfast, took an egg and toast to mother who was still sitting up against her pillows, but with chin down, nodding off. I woke her and she ate a little before sliding down and falling off into sleep again. From the galley I could hear her snore, like an old dog asleep on an ancient carpet running after dreamrabbits but never gaining ground.

The Firsts kept me entertained for a few idle hours. I couldn't sleep because I had over-rested on the trip south. Bored of Cora and Paul's peevish antics, I switched off my vice and grabbed Old Mud. We sat on the couch behind the driver's seat, pad and pen at hand, and we worked once again on my stubborn lyric. Time passed. The van's batteries drank their fill of the sun's power. I picked scrunched balls of paper off the floor and threw their frustrated musings into the garbage bag. But when I sat down again I saw amid the scratchings on the pad beside me, a few words that fit my tune.

*Into the mountains now I go,*
*Through passes once blocked by snow.*
*There the hands of an ancient tribe*
*On rocky faces now inscribe*
*Prayers for us in the land of is.*

*Down to the desert floor I fall*
*There listen for the raven's call*
*To shapes carved by time's long flood.*
*In the holy dirt of baking mud,*
*We leave footprints in the land of is.*

Just after dusk, we can get underway again. CashCarter is not even a half day's drive away. I will not trust the selfdrive now, so I turned on my vice once again and sat in the driver's seat. The Show had become an undeniable habit for me, as well as everyone else in the known world. I couldn't resist it. I had become a Watcher, as the addicted audience members were called by the talking heads.

I admired Cora. But I suspected Paul of not being as there in that bungalow as she was, although he was. He was there. It is Cora Munro, however, who still bristled at the outrage that constituted their kidnapping. She was furious with Vice President Ovans and her government because they had proven to be so feckless in their search for her - for her and Paul, of course, although you wonder why, for her, he has become such an afterthought.

She thought aloud through every plot that could explain how she landed in her predicament, used the logic of law and the logic of politics to drill through the variations - to see if she could find the dark room where the plotters were hiding, who they may be, once unmasked. She kept telling Paul, it had to be Benevolus, but Paul declares, looking up from the book he's reading, no, no it isn't. It could not be him.

Benevolus? Who is he? Oh, yes, their friend who owns the castle from which they were taken. Why wouldn't he be a suspect? Too damned obvious, for crissake, says Paul. He's the richest man in the world. What's in it for him? And I thought, like Cora must have thought, why Paul, what's in it for him is the pleasure of carrying out a crime that only he has the money to pay for. Is it a lark, I wondered? No. Can't be that.

My stomach rumbled. I was hungry. But we had run out of food. The GPS said the village of Summertown was up ahead, not far. Maybe there I would find groceries. Maybe a restaurant for take-out too. That would be a nice change, I thought.

We got there. It was a side-of-the-road village, nearly abandoned it seems, though in the dark it was hard to tell really. There was a roadhouse on the northern end of the place - called Grinder's Tavern. It had a huge sign on its roof to blink its worthy name to all the hard- working truckers who used the road and who might want a little homemade food, a beer to wash it down with. For the wickedly tired, there were rooms upstairs whose beds were made with clean linen, even if they were a tad worn and faded. There was food there to take-out too. I was hungry and I thought, maybe mother would eat a bit of stew if they have one, or soup. She always likes soup. I wanted to take her to that clinic in CashCarter in fighting spirit.

I pulled into the lot, found a place to park just to the side of a couple of large trucks on their way to or from somewhere else, empty or full as the case might be. Mother was awake, so I told her I would be just a few minutes. She seemed to understand. Told me to take my time. She'll just rest she said.

The truth? I was tired of her sleeping. Tired of feeling alone, really. I wanted her back on her feet. I had become angry at her for giving-in to the cancer, but, I can't say I was aware of any of these feelings, not until later. Much later. But she knew it. She had picked-up the signals that I had been broadcasting from the back of my head as I drove. Heard it in my voice as I delivered meals and medicine with terse instructions to eat or drink as the case might be. I had taken refuge inside The Show by then. I had stopped singing, didn't even hum. Something had changed, and not just for me.

During the last day or two, since telling me about Clem - how she had run away from him, from a chance at love - she acquired the look and sound of someone who had come to a new determination. At the very time I had become terse and abrupt, she had become very sweet to me, grateful for the care I had given her. She conveyed it by squeezing my hand or stroking my face with the back of hers. She took time to look at me, as though she were replacing an old image – maybe from the time when I was very young – with a new image of me at forty. She smiled at me too, tenderly if you can imagine it, and if I said something about something that might have been a bit tendentious in circles outside our van, she did not undercut by a jab a few seconds later, which was her usual way.

It shouldn't have been a strange turn of events, all things considered, but it was, and it filled me with optimism – wrongly I soon found out - because I thought, ah, the woman who I am taking to the doctors in CashCarter is a woman with fight in her soul. The doctors there would thank me for that, for not wasting their time by dragging in a woman whose fast-coming death was a foregone conclusion.

A woman came to the register near the door when I walked in and took my take-out order. I could hear a song coming from the bar just around the corner. I took a few steps into the place and looked into the dark bar and saw a man at the other end of the room sitting under a small spotlight playing a guitar. A half dozen people, all men alone, except for one couple sitting right below the large vice hanging on the wall. Everyone, but one guy at the bar nursing a shot, sat in the dimness listening in a desultory way to the musician, but most were also keeping an eye on the screen of a huge vice watching the goings on of The Show and the surrounding foofaraw. The volume was set to nil but you could follow the story if you could read the subtitles and chyrons.

We were all waiting for something in Cora and Paul's story to change, and we half expected it would be a public execution, because the government was bleating and repeating how it would not negotiate with terrorists. The singer didn't appear to care what he was doing any more than I did when I was doing the Indian shows. He was getting paid to pluck and sing regardless.

The waitress brought me a carry bag with my order hot and ready-to-eat steaming on the inside. I paid at the register. But instead of going back to the van right away, I walked into the back of the barroom again and watched the man at the bar. About my age. Lean. Good looking from what I could see. A bit unkempt, but a road weary dishevelment. He looked about as tired as I was a couple of days earlier. He must have sensed me looking at him because he turned his head and looked my way.

Our eyes locked. He picked up the small shot glass and pointed it in my direction, tilted it up a little and mouthed 'drink?' I shook my head, mouthed no thanks, and turned on my heels and walked back to the van, thinking, oh yeah, wouldn't that be nice. A drink with a stranger, a bit of talk with someone new, with someone my own age, some other road warrior all alone in this old world. Flirt and be flirted with.

Merri had fallen back to sleep. Her pill bottle was tipped over on the table beside her bed. I had counted them before I went to the roadhouse – there had been three of them only.

So, when I found it empty, I didn't think she had overdosed. I just wondered if three would get her through the night. I tried to wake her, but I knew she would be asleep for hours.

I took a container of beef stew out of the bag and set it on the kitchen counter and opened its top. Took a spoon from the drawer and dipped it in. Good stuff. A few more spoonfuls. Filled me up. I looked at Old Mud hanging on the wall by the door. Not tonight, Gus, I said. I turned on the vice. Cora and Paul were sleeping, but hers was a fitful sleep. I let their silence fill the van. I paced. Fuck it, I said out loud. I turned off the vice and went back into the roadhouse.

So, what followed is.... I don't know what is. We drank, we took a couple of turns on the dance floor, drank some more, talked nonsense, made fun of the First Couple, laughed a lot. He drove one of the rigs outside, taking stuff from the farms and factories around CashCarter out to the hinterlands where the Outsiders bought all he could deliver. Then he would load up with product raised or grown in the litter boxes close by the smaller hive towns and bring his cargo back to the city. He was on his way home. Wife and kids – he just wanted to be straight about that, come what may.

- Come what may? I asked. Whatever do you mean?

- You know exactly what I mean, lady.

Yeah, I did. He got a room upstairs. Just like I used to do twenty years earlier when I was doing gigs around Oregon, Washington and California. I wouldn't exactly call it making love. Oh no, it was rodeo time, a time where the beast with two backs was bucking and fucking and charging into the grasp and grip of a body never had before. My mouth on him, his on me, me riding him, him me, me on my back tilting my hips up as he thrust into me, me on my knees saying do as you will while he did as he wanted to elicit the pain I needed to feel, and the keening, disembodied pleasure that came yelping after.

We spooned and rocked on our sides then shifted again, so I could dominate. I became so very full of him as I straddled his narrow hips, watching him watching me and neither of us giving a shit if he came again while I went off into the starry, starry night of my empty head to orbit around my sacred, last orgasm until its gravity pulled me down and down where I crashed at last and my body and brain filled finally with a brilliant black, shattering light.

And why do I tell you this now, make such an exposition of this night of sex? Because, because. Because, I am so sorry for not just giving one last supper to my mother, one more night of companionship before I delivered her to CashCarter and to whatever salvation she might there find. Because my mother had found strength enough to get out of her bed where she earlier, in full possession of her faculties, lucid for the first time since we left home, set about to make good the plan she'd made, probably when she decided to tell me about Clem.

She had just pretended to be asleep when I last looked in on her. She made it all the way to the front of the van where she pulled a gun out from its hiding place under the couch and she took it back to bed and made herself as comfortable as she could. At the very moment when I was hollering at my laughing, happy, pagan god, beating his chest with closed fists and demanding more of him, demanding that he give me the cathartic release that I so badly needed because I had become so single-minded numb and stupid in the care of my mother, she shot herself to death. And, I was too far gone in his ecstatic, priapic answer to even hear the gunshot.

Another knock on the dressing room door. A loud voice comes through.

- Running late, Wicla. C'mon. Let's go!

I pull myself away from the mirror. Take Old Mud off the bed where he lays, and I think he has been my only constant lover.

*Songbirds do not sing their sympathies to sullen slaves.*

# Song 32

Another twenty years has passed. A little more, in fact, twenty-two. Out here in the garden, under the private dome that Peter built for us on the north arc of the Clinton hive, I am looking over the high cliffs above the Hudson down to the narrowed river where covered boats make there way under the still deadly sun. I want to fall over the cliff here and go tumbling back into the Outsider's world that stretches out on the other bank, still home to an angry and resolute few.

I may be an empress here, but out there, when I was a girl, I was a queen, and that was good enough. Peter is dead; our children have gone back to the schools that will finish them off at last and let them graduate into their destinies in what some people call the Kingdom of Bubbles. The big house over there at the top of the garden, home to me and my keepers, is empty.

Old America is dead too, replaced by something else. Almost everyone in the country now resides in a hive city or a domed town. The old cities have been left to rot where they stand, although an uncountable number of people still call them home and live out their lives in the furtive shadows of their days and the doom of almost lightless nights. Those cities are being picked apart, for brick and lumber, for iron, steel and copper, and for a myriad of other manmade things. These are the bits and pieces of a rapidly dying world, things that rouse nostalgia in those now ensconced in the new cities who scarce remember what life used to be like, or that pique the curiosity of those who were born on the Inside and have never been out.

So, why does the story already told lead ineluctably to the moment I plunged the knife into Peter's devil heart?

Merri left a note. It was clenched in her left hand along with the three pills she had not swallowed. After even one hour, the pain of the cancer that had almost eaten her would have come roaring back, so by the time she made it to the front of the van to get the gun, by the time she had written the note and resettled herself in the bed, she would have felt the agony of her awful choice: eat the pills or pull the trigger.

The note said only this:

*Love is a forever freedom.*

It was something she said often after she had discovered it inside a fortune cookie, maybe when I was five or six. I got tired of hearing it, but it had lodged itself like a splinter in my own heart, and I was guilty of saying it to men I met along the way to justify leaving them. To all those men I took back to my roadhouse rooms and refused to see again. To Jack, who thrilled me in the throws of passion, but who was a toy bought and sold. To Wynk, when I rationalized my affair with Jack and justified my moving on: love is a forever freedom. Grant that to me, ye Wynkyn, sir. It is a phrase that cuts two ways, severs ties, but, in the case of Mother Merri and me, bound us in the eternity of time and the infinity of space.

She'd let me go now that we had crossed the divide, now that we had crossed the river, now that the old world was behind us and the new world in front. Trader Merri Weer had died at Fort Ketchup under the blue skies that sparkled above the roofless room where I was born. Mother Merri died somewhere on the long road in between, cancerous, in pain, having carried, as far as she could, the buttons and brooches, pins and necklaces that her people had asked her to take on her journeys. She had carried me that far too, and now did what she had to do, to shake me off because I had shackled her to my needs and dragged her bones too far for her or my own good.

The gunshot and bloody mess she left would, she knew, disillusion me of the idea that white man's medicine could make her the mother she never was, might, in fact, let me see the woman she really was. A life chewing pills that made her sleep away her days and nights, or a bullet to the brain? No choice at all. Pull the trigger. Sizzle under the X-ray lamp or travel the open moonlit road? No choice at all. Pull the trigger. Eat the bitter salad of the drugs they'd give her, or drink with friends at every stop along the way and laugh. Keep my daughter from the songs that only she can sing? I can't do that, so pull the trigger. Mother daughter. We give to one another, as we always have, love and its promise of forever freedom.

Get out of the van and never come back. That's why she shot herself in her bed and did not step down to the ground and find some shadow behind the roadhouse in which end her life. She knew I could never set foot in it again. God, she knew how to make a point, how to read me. Police were called and came. Death by suicide. Sorry, ma'am, for your loss. They'll tow the van to the police yard where you can pick it up later.

The nameless man with whom I had shared the room at Grinder's, told me how sorry he was, but he had to go. Wife and children waiting. His big truck pulls out to the highway, disappears over the hill just up the road from where I stand in the roadhouse lot. Dawn breaks and dilutes the strobing lights from the cruisers still idling around the…the what? The crime?

The shame? The horror? The completely understandable end to an unendurable life? Officers compare notes, drink coffee, start passing the time of day because for them Merri's last act is over. The man who drives the coroner's wagon said we should take her to Heaven's Gate at CashCarter. Policemen nod their permission.

Mother was wrapped in a zippered bag in the back of the wagon. I rode up front with another nameless man. Bob maybe. Bob's always been my name for nameless men. Where are Lawrence, Javier, Titus and Arre, where was Wynk when I need them? Where are Ed, George and Cameahwait? Where, for that matter, is Saca, who might be able to guide me through this treacherous grief, better than any man, especially with a baby in her belly? Another mother giving birth to forever love. Where were Meira and Daph, for who better than they to sing behind my lamentation? Where were Erato and Francis who would know how to organize the chaos of loss into a sensible grief?

During the next couple of days, whenever I felt sure I could make myself sound in need of any help at all, I called each of them. I told them mother had died of natural causes before I got her to the clinic city. They knew how sick she was, so there was no disbelief, no incredulity. To tell you the truth, I felt even more guilt than I had before talking with them because to a man and woman they knew I had been on a fool's mission, that mother could have stayed in Portland and died with dignity. But they all knew too, that in the instant of her death, not only had I been forgiven, but I had at last become wise even if that wisdom took years to surface.

The high domes of the CashCarter hive seemed to vibrate in

the morning light. I saw it while we are still twenty miles away and cannot believe how big it was when at last we approached from its southern side. It is bigger than Gatesport, maybe twice, three times as big. Heaven's Gate was built so that some of it is outside and some inside the hive. Bob took us to the outside doors, buzzed the intercom and drove in as the door was rising. He had already viced ahead to say we would be there. He said, we'll leave your mother here. She'll be OK, I promise you. But you need rest. There is a hotel inside the hive, a room has been reserved for you. You can talk to the HG people tomorrow.

Next day, the nice man at Heaven's Gate covered all the options.

- Everyone gets a Lifebook, he said. We put it in the vault with them, but the family can take it home if they wished. We don't advise that. It can get lost, or family members, you know, the start arguing over who gets to keep it. But your choice.

He explained what a Lifebook is. A sample of Merri's DNA would be kept in it, a beautiful vile, crystal if I like, or platinum, gold or silver. It is set in a small book like container – he showed me a range of examples – and set into a vault so that it is integrated into the Heaven's Gate computer network. He didn't call it a computer network but that's what it was. The Life Web. Yes, that's it. That network would keep track of familial relationships – because the DNA of all the people interred was captured and the LifeWeb made all the connections. If a cousin died and his survivors did the smart thing and got a Lifebook for him, well, notifications would be sent out to all his or her relations. So many people were being reconnected it was hard to believe. And, he said, wasn't that great!

- OK, I said. Gold vial. Ironwood box.

- Good choices. Excellent. Now…one more thing.

He said it was less expensive in the long run to take advantage of the family deal.

- There is only me, I said.

- Even so. Dollar saved is a dollar urned. Big guffaw.

I bought the two for one deal. I paid for a double sized vault, so when the time came I could be put in the vault with mother, and I set up my own LifeBook and had it activated. They plucked a couple of strands of my hair to source my DNA. When mother was interred in her vault I did indeed get a notification. The whole sad, fucking episode made me laugh. Made me cry too. I did not want or need to be notified of my mother's death. Had got the message already.

The banks were all tied into LifeWeb too. Mother's bank contacted me once they had received the notification of her interment and verified her certificate of death. I was sole heiress to her fortune, and a fortune it was too, a small one. All those years of scrimping and saving and doing without, meant that almost all the money she made, less the cost of goods sold, as the accountants say, went into her bank and stayed there. I felt guilty for spending any of it, but I did. I used it to take a lease on a good-sized home in the center of CashCarter and to furnish it, thinking that all the weight of the stuff I now had would be an anchor, not the albatross, Merri always thought it would be.

CashCarter is where Merri was laid to rest, and why, because that is where she was, I lived for the next three years. That is when Peter walked into my life. He had received the notification that I was plugged into LifeWeb once Merri was interred along with our Lifebooks. So, why did it take three years for him to show himself, when he knew where I was and what I was doing all that time? His spies had kept watch I later learned, taking their measure, I supposed.

At first, I stayed behind closed doors, gorging on The Show while I fattened my once lean body with snacks and with large glasses of wine that I only sometimes sipped. I did not exercise, so I grew slack on the sofa before the large screen of the vice in my living room, sleeping there most nights, but only when Cora and Paul Munro parked in the bays of dark night and fell to sleeping too. The vice remained on all day and through those hours of unawake. It was their voices, or their movement in the bungalow that pulled me out of whatever dream might have entangled me in its provocations.

After three weeks of captivity in that small home in the CGI suburb in which they were somewhere stuck, the tension between the Firsts became palpable. We Watchers were well aware of the fact that they had gone to Castle Forbes in Scotland to try to bridge the fissures and fractures that had developed in their marriage. Bets had been laid on both sides of the guesswork as to what might happen when, like most people, Insiders and Outsiders alike, Cora's and Paul's lives had to be lived, around the clock, within the confines of a tiny world, stripped of money, power and privilege. Would their marriage survive when they could not avoid one another, or make excuses to postpone the inevitable confrontations that might have been avoided or postponed in the vast, complex, distracting, populated spaces to which they had been accustomed and from which they were so violently removed?

One day, Paul finally snapped. Cora had retreated into silence. She moved around the house looking for places to be away from him. Is she done with him? Is she depressed? Many thought so. Many thought not. She's thinking, they shouted into the online world. Leave her alone. That good mind of hers will work its way through the maze, find the way to the exit door. Paul can't help. Not a thinker. But our contending voices were not heard in the bungalow where Cora and Paul, if they had deigned to do so, would have pulled themselves together, argued back. They would have pretended they were of like mind, were working together, and together they would outsmart those who had taken them from their marriage bed. Just as they always worked together to create their astounding, magical lives.

Tired of being ignored by the President, frustrated, angry Paul went into a rage and tossed the place. Cora cowered against a wall, down on her haunches. A policeman came – policeman? – and subdued him. Paul was taken away, red-faced, sweating. Silence in the bungalow. But Cora cried, cried and then shook it off like women do. Cried as she put things back together, tidied up, found the way through the noise of house-work back to the kind of purposeful doing that always helps us recompose ourselves, as we promise ourselves never again, never again. Back to control.

I had known this man intimately, had him when he was sweet and charming and funny and I had let him strip me naked and move my body around so that he could bestow whatever pleasures he wished on me, or could surprise me, so he could take what he wanted too, with my full and happy consent. But though I had never seen him become petulant, demanding or so full of stammering, incoherent temper, I was not surprised. I had spent too many years traveling the Outsider world where men were forever doing their worst, and only sometimes their best.

And yet, I was surprised when someone came to take him away. We had become so accustomed to seeing Paul and Cora alone in the little house that was their cell that we had forgotten that they were kept there by some as yet unknown force that would, once discovered for what it was, come with human faces. The man who came for Paul was one of those faces, strong, quick, decisive, unopposable. He even had a name, Haines, which did not fit his middle eastern mien. Haines for public consumption, for the Watchers and for all the men and women of the government who, for the last few weeks had been scouring the world looking for their Commander in Chief and her husband.

Twenty-four hours later, Paul was brought back to the bungalow. He did not look contrite, not really, but he was calm. Something had changed. Something. Cora picked it up; adjusted herself, decided not to confront him. She knew him better than anyone, so I think now, looking back, she must have thought that whatever young-man courage he may have surrendered as he had aged, he had somehow found courage again. By the end of that week, they would be back home again, and it was not Cora's thinking that got them there, it was, she would brag later, Paul's derring-do. It was, but it was attached to acts much larger in scope than Cora Munro would ever know or want to know.

*In the whirl of wide-eyed wonder, unwinds the watch.*

# Song 33

It was Cora and Paul's startling and heroic reappearance that got me off the couch. Hers more than his. Surrounded by tens of thousands of joyous Londoners she pumped her fists into the falling rain of that Outsider night and walked the inner circle of yellow-jacketed, arm-linked cops to demonstrate that she was defiantly alive. Paul followed in her steps and shook hundreds of outstretched hands as they reached in to touch the glow of a charisma that had been compounded into other-worldliness after thirty days of streamed captivity. Cora, I knew instinctively, was declaring her Presidency again, signalling to those in Washington who were already moving into the place some hoped she would not return to, that they would face a reckoning, maybe even on the morrow. And to her captives to, a loud fuck you, and we'll see what happens next, for she would, those pumping fists were saying, loose the dogs of war on them soon enough.

Once The Show was over, I turned off the vice so I would not have to hear the blathering analysis of the talking heads who over the last days had been so wrong about so much. I went to my bed, stripped off the clothes that I had been wearing for days on end, and slept naked in cool sheets, for the first time truly alone. Next morning, I rose, showered, and left my rooms to go wander CashCarter's streets and avenues where they wended below the hive's shimmering buildings, high and low. I stood for long moments in its wide, sunlit piazzas and took deep breaths.

I felt like I had grown new wings in the confines of the cocoon where I had wrapped myself almost from the day of my arrival there. I listened to the buzz and whir of drones coming and going under the high dome, to the quiet hum of pedestrian walks carrying people at double speed to wherever in the city they wanted to go, to the falling of water in the city's fountains, to children playing in the city's parks, to the rattle of oars on boats passing beneath a wide bridge that straddled the banks of the Cumberland River whose waters flowed translucently through their old riverbeds through the city. High, high above the streets, high above the tallest buildings, my eyes found an oculus open to the north, where a large oval of blue sky hung above, into which I could fly with my new wings if I wanted to.

I went back to the center of the city where, a little more than a day ago, I had joined the huge crowds that had gathered before the gigantic public tron that overlooked the main square. Together we watched Paul and Cora escape the bungalow and fight there way back to the world that had lost them. Like everyone else, during the last week, the last four days especially, I had seen a change come over the Firsts.

We were all uncertain about whether their sudden lack of fraught contention and crossed-purposes was just an exhausted lull in their cohabitation – a truce - or portended a change of heart that would see them through whatever trials would come next. They no longer moved through the small rooms in the house to avoid the discomforts of being in the same room together, but seemed, when they moved at all, to be doing so with purposes no one every saw or heard them agree to but were clearly agreed by both. But theirs was a long marriage and long married people sing their song in voices that other people cannot hear.

As I sat on my sofa and watched – sat on the edge of the seat, in fact, because I could sense – we all could sense – something was about to happen. Both had been given tablets to use. Did Paul or Cora find a way to connect with the outside world? Were men on white chargers on their way to rescue them?

The twenty ninth day of their confinement passed. We watched them sleep through the night. Some of us fell off into our own fretful sleep. Suddenly, on the morning of the thirtieth day all hell broke loose. Haines dropped by. Cora offered coffee. Haines sat at the island in the kitchen. Paul was there too. Small talk. Cora came in behind Haines, smashed him on the head with a fry pan. He fell. Paul took Haines's gun. Cora ran out of the room. Gunshot. Haines was dead.

Outside my window I heard the streets filling. I looked out through the closed curtains and saw thousands of people running toward the main square. Others looking down at the street, like me, saw their fellow citizens herding, and like me, most left their rooms and fell in with the fast-moving stream of people. Safety in numbers.

As we approached the main square we heard gunshots. Coming into the square, up on the tron, we all saw Paul now, working his way through a dark, man-made cavern, gun in hand. He went back to the bungalow, and we see for the first time that the bungalow is not a house at all, but a ramshackle construction with wires and ducts wrapping around it, a false front where we have seen, on many previous days, its faux porch and balustrade, its faux front door with faux door-knocker, the faux front window that always seemed to us to look out on a sunny street in a middle America of a hundred years past.

Paul saw a masked man in a black jump suit on a catwalk twenty feet above. Paul aimed and shot, one, two. The man falls. And then, a fast jump to Cora with a panicked look, body tense, fists clenched standing against a column of bricks to the side of the high, dark cavern. There is another column of bricks a couple of feet to her side with a black space between them. Another man in black dress came out from this space and with a black-gloved hand grabbed Cora and pulled her in to his labyrinth.

Paul made his way in the near dark to rescue her. Close-up on his heroic face, panting, pistol held up near his cheek with both hands on its grip, eyes wide open, brave. We heard Cora struggling, her captor told her in a menacing whisper to shut up. Paul screwed up his resolve, you can see it on his face. He jumped between the two columns with gun extended at the end of his arms, in two hands. Bang, bang. A groan. The sound of a crumpling body. The last of the bad guys dispatched, Cora saved.

We have all watched the footage a thousand times. Paul took Cora by the hand, led her out of the cavernous room where the fake bungalow stood, down tunnels, into other rooms, up metal staircases that clanged under their fast-moving feet, up the rungs of a ladder embedded into a cement wall, into a tight, damp chamber, up another metal ladder, and then…freedom.

Paul pushed the manhole cover at the top of the chamber, put his shoulders to it and pushed hard until it gave way, until other hands from above grabbed it and slid it with a rumble to the side. These other hands then pulled Paul and Cora up into Leicester Square, into the cold, fresh, sodden London air, where thousands upon thousands of astonished people, just like those of us in the main square of CashCarter and ten thousand other places around the world, were watching the final act of The Show play-out on the giant tron above their upturned and transfixed faces.

And, so, who was I to stay in the foetal curl into which the death of my mother had bent me, as though my spirit were plasticine in the hands of grief? If any of us had been taken from our bed by hard men pressing guns into our temples, then marched into a bitter and frigid darkness down four flights of steep and stony stairs, down to the choppy North Sea to be borne away to our probable murder, we might not rise again into anything like the sanity – the so-called sanity - of our previous life. But in the bungalow, President Cora Munro and Paul Munro provide living proof that we can rise above almost anything, and not just rise above it, but take it in stride, go on to do great things, gain what looks like wisdom, looks like grace.

During the days that followed the First's escape, I visited all the clubs and bars in CashCarter, not with the hope of getting back to the gigging life - I was not ready for that yet – but to find a job as a waitress or bartender. In the dim light, the deepening lines on my face would be softened, I could keep a distance between me and the patrons, make a chatting acquaintanceship with colleagues, get happy with a smaller life on the Inside than I had when I travelled through the coastal states out west. Over the following two years I worked in a couple of places that I liked well-enough, but they were missing something that I wasn't even aware of missing until I went back to the Polyphemus on one of my off nights. I had been there before more than a year earlier to see if they had a job opening, but there were no openings.

Polyphemus had live entertainment. They had a small stage where local singers and bands played to a devoted crowd of regulars. The night I walked in a group called the Seegers was finishing a song that could have been written by the devil himself, with fast picking on the rhythm and bass, screeching fiddle work that was chasing after demons the song itself conjured and drumming that came down through the noise like heavy rain and a smash of thunder. By the time I got there the dancing fools in front of the band were coming to the point of sweaty, drunken exhaustion as the front man, a guy I got to know well, was calling out a pig hollering yodel that stretched all the way to Nebraska and only ended when he ran out of breath and the drummer put paid to the noise with a bang bang on the rim of his snare and let those on the dance floor shuffle in a happy glow back to their tables and chairs.

But Stevy Judkins was not finished. He waited for the lights to come down, waited for the drummer to roll softly on the drum skins, waited for the first chords of the song he was about to sing rise up behind him while he put the mic into which he had been yodelling back on its stand, then, with his blue eyes on some blond woman sitting with her boyfriend at a table down front, he stepped to it and began to steal her away.

I saw a stool along the bar just by the register and quietly took a seat to watch Stevy do his magic. You will not be surprised to learn that as he sang I was taken back in time, back to my own early days when I was just Wicla, not Wicla the Singer, when I was just beginning to learn about the power of music, about how to move my body to seduce the imagined lover to whom

I sang. And I also thought, as I sat there by myself, that I had taken my mother's seat, saw myself up there on the stage as she must have seen me, in that far off light, half hidden by the attentive heads of my audience, bobbing when I picked up the pace, solemn quiet when I roamed a ballad, sometimes blocked by a waitress serving drinks, but not for long.

- He's good ain't he?

A man was tapping the register screen behind me.

- He's great, I said.

- He plays here quite a lot. You a fan? I don't think I've seen you here before.

- We've met.

- Really? How so?

- I came looking for a job a few months ago.

He came around in front of me and took a good look.

- Let's say I remember.

- Even if you don't?

- I'd feel less of a cad.

- You're mister Oolyss.

- Call me Homer.

- I remember.

- Sure you do.

- I remember for sure. You didn't have much experience.

- That was then.

- So, you've been working?

- At Hindenburg's.

- I've got a spot open now.

- Well, I'm still working there, Homer.

- They don't have music.

Long story short, I gave notice at Hindenburg's and signed-up at Polyphemus. Homer worked us all hard, but the tips were great and I got to know some of the singers and musicians who came through. Stevy and his band were on a circuit of hive cities and domed towns, which brought them back to the club every six weeks or so. But he lived in CashCarter, so from time to time he would hyperloop back to the city and do his laundry and take a breather.

We got to talking one night after a show, and one thing led to another and within two or three months of me working there, we got close. He was a bit younger than I, but not much. Even though he was close on forty, Stevy was fit and slim, with long legs and a butt as hard as the pool balls we used to shoot on the table in the back room that visiting bands used before and after gigs. He had a bit of a kink in his long, dark hair, a roman nose and a full mouth on a round open face.

Like most people his ancestry was a mixed bag. Black, white, some native, maybe even, wink wink, a touch of Chinese, which would account for his avid love of Peking Duck and soups both hot and sour, noodles crispy, green tea hot and plentiful and lazy susans full of dishes steaming and popping on oven-heated plates. His moods went through all the phases of the moon, but as long as I knew him, he never cycled through any kind of meanness. He was sarcastic about his fellow humans generally, but when it came to politics and politicians – he was an avid reader of the news – he was cynical, to a fault, I often thought. He was also a good man in bed and good was good enough for me by then. If I didn't love him, I loved being with him, because all the chatter that passed between us was charged with a lot of laughter, a total absence of guile, no promises asked for, and none expected to be given.

As they will, things about each of us started coming out. There was not much in his small closet, but in mine, he found the hat that I was trying to keep hidden. Or was I? He kept at me until I had no choice but to wear it. It's a strange kind of name, he said one day when we were laying on the bed in my house. He was on his side facing me, I was looking at the ceiling, now avoiding eye contact.

- What is?

- Wicla.

- It comes from Willia and Cladine. They were two old black women who helped bring me into this world.

- Interesting, but not what I was getting at.

- You're Wicla.

- Yeah.

- Wicla Weer. Wicla the Singer, he said sitting up, but still staring at me.

I remained silent while he stared at me. I finally turned and looked at him.

- Did I ever tell you about Ozzy Mandis? I asked.

- You knew Ozzy Mandis?

- He owns a pub in Kingman, Arizona.

- He's still alive?

- Probably. I haven't seen him for a few years, but I doubt he is any more willing to give up the ghost now than he was then.

- Bullshit.

- God's honest truth.

It took a little while for me to explain why and how it came to be that I was waitressing in CashCarter and to extract a promise that he would not tell anyone who I had been. Who I had been, I said emphatically, not who I am now.

That night at Polyphemus while I was taking orders and delivering drinks and food around the bar, Stevy stepped to the mic and said he was going to sing a song for those who had just come from the Outside and to all of those whose people may have come Inside not long ago, which was everyone. As soon as the band started playing I realized he was going to sing The Human Touch. I'd written it five years ago. Everyone knew it. He didn't say a word about me being there – didn't draw any attention to me at all. But still, I felt like he had betrayed me and left me naked as if in a dream of shame, all eyes on me. That's why I cut him out of my life, right then. Right then, without any possibility of parole. Life sentence.

Homer didn't know what the hell had happened. I dropped the last drinks on my tray on the nearest table and strode back to the bar where I slapped the tray on the counter and tossed my apron in the bin under the register. I marched out of the bar, brushing past Homer where he stood at the door trying to block my way so he could ask me who had upset me so much. But Stevy did not see any of it. He was lost in the music and lyrics of my song, as lost as I ever was when I sang it. I heard him as I stepped from the darkness of the bar into the light of the lobby where I ran for the door and pushed out, heading back to my foetal self.

*Live your hard life without shedding tears,*
*But sister, when it all becomes too much,*
*Be ready to surrender all your fears*
*In exchange for the human touch.*

I don't know why I never listen to my own advice. Looking back now, I see Stevy had no need of my forgiveness. He was singing that song to me because he loved me – loved me far more deeply than I knew - and out of love he wanted to tell me that I was hurting myself by not laying claim to the gift that had been given to me. His was the human touch; mine was the shell on a life I thought had been too hard. The betrayal was mine.

After making every effort to get through to me Stevy finally gave up. He told Homer that he was leaving CashCarter and would not becoming back to Polyphemus. By then Homer knew something had gone down between Stevy and me, but Stevy kept my confidence until, at the end of his latest run, he was about to leave. Thinking Stevy had committed some outrage against me, Homer cornered him in the back room and wouldn't let him go until Stevy fessed up.

By that time, bearing up under a sorrow that was riddled with anger because of my unrelenting obduracy he told Homer that the bitch Wicla was none other than Wicla the Singer, and why was it, he added that Wicla the Singer was hiding out at Polyphemus slinging drinks for minimum wage and tips? It makes you wonder, doesn't, what the hell she did out west, said Stevy, as he pushed past a bewildered Homer, and descended even further into undeserved obscurity. He was a fine, fine singer and a good man.

That very night, Homer came to my home and wouldn't go away until I let him come up. We are going to talk, he said, when I finally answered the intercom.

Homer was one of those older men I met in my life who were smarter and wiser than I ever gave them credit for. By the time he finished barking at me for walking out on him and scolding me for treating Stevy as I had, I was in tears. Then he turned it all around. He got me to confess that my desire to sing had not deserted me, but that I had captured it, put it in shackles and thrown it into a dungeon where, despite my stupid cruelty, it was still marking time to its own inextinguishable inner voice.

And so it was that I became the house singer at the Polyphemus Club in CashCarter.

*An obscure ode obliterates an obsolete obsession.*

# Song 34

Homer wasn't allowed to advertise the fact that I was singing at Polyphemus. That was part of the deal. I wouldn't hide behind some *nom de musique*, so he had to rely on word of mouth to do its magic. It didn't take long. I sang Thursday, Friday and Saturday night from eight to one in the morning or so. The place was packed every night for as long as I was there, which was only a year or so, to Homer's great dismay, with many patrons arriving two and sometimes three hours early to make sure they were in the house by the time Old Mud and I took the stage.

Homer gave me a dressing room and he paid full freight for a backup band of very talented musicians who usually did studio work in the city and a couple of backup singers who rollicked their black church every Sunday. They weren't Meira and Daphne, but they channelled the spirt of my two old friends and gave me the same chills I used to get when I first sang with my friends at Fort Ketchup.

It had been quite awhile since I gave a concert, and a lot longer since I sang in a bar, but with Old Mud in hand, a tight band behind me and an audience feeling lucky to have made it into the room in front of me, it didn't take me long to find my way. I didn't sing my Outsider songs, however. There were a lot of requests for them shouted out from the near darkness of the bar room, but the voices I heard were the voices of Insiders who were disconnected from the experiences those songs tried to capture. I felt I would be dishonoring the songs – dishonoring my mother and everyone I ever really loved - had I struck even one chord of those tunes.

Homer, who had grown up hard on the Outside and whose mind and character had been formed out there long before he washed up at CashCarter, never stopped urging me to sing them, and expressed a considerable amount of irritation that I wouldn't. But I wouldn't. Instead, I sang my earliest songs, the ones I had sung at Kingman, and songs that I had learned from Cladine at the Fort. I don't think I can even take credit for how I handled the songs she taught me. Old Mud had a memory and an ornery disposition, and it always felt to me as though, when we came to one of those tunes, he wrested control of himself in my hands and made me his ventriloquist's dummy.

The audience – save and except Homer and a few other old timers - did not miss the Outsider songs. My early songs became popular all over again, so yes, they liked them well enough. But what they really liked was the blues stuff that Old Mud riffed at them. I guessed that songs like that, and some of the old rockers and country tunes we tried our hands at, even though not heard much in the past few decades, were threaded into the DNA of those born and raised in Tennessee, another helical strand made of notes that vibrated well below the level of their knowing, and, come to think of it, their understanding. Life was easy in CashCarter compared to anything the black folks sang about fifty, a hundred, two hundred years ago, so easy as to make it almost impossible to think of those days as anything different than a medieval fairy tale.

Sing to their hearts, girl, said Cladine. Well, I would do that, but I would not sing as me because I was no more connected to those songs than anyone sitting out in front of me. That's the truth. But what I could do and did do, was sing Cladine. Old Mud dragged me into that woman's long-buried body and together we brought her momentarily back to life. We'd sit on a chair just as she used to and I'd bend over Gus and make my hands look like they were picking and strumming whatever strings he was working. And then Cladine's voice would start coming out of my mouth, guttural, deep, dark, full of pain one moment, finding the way out of life's maze the next, coming into the light of the divine when it shone its truth through the cracks her wailing made in the space-time continuum. And that truth penetrated the sanitizing crystals of dome life, sent shivers into the spines of those who heard the old girl, and put the feel of real dirt under their feet.

When I wasn't working I did the usual humdrum things. Sometimes I'd hyperloop to another city for the day and spend my time gawking at the manifold ways in which hive cities developed, each one unique. I guess I should have been lonely, but I wasn't. I remember thinking, I may never have a man again, but that's OK. Hell, why trouble another one with my inexplicable prickliness, my propensity to cut and run?

Sometimes – quite a lot actually – I made my way to Heaven's Gate in CashCarter to pay a visit to my mother. I would sit on the bench just below the vault in which her DNA was still floating in a tiny portion of a salty sea, alive in some weird sort of way, and so what was left of her was better than ashes, better than bones in a graveyard far away. My DNA was in there too, laying in a vial beside hers. Two peas in a pod. The tiny lights of our Lifebooks flickered as though in conversation, and that pleased me, even though I thought mother was probably listening more to the bits and bites coming at her from the web in which we were now permanently planted than to the living me as I sat before her and rambled on about nothing important.

I carried my vice wherever I went, mostly to keep up with any news I could get on what President Munro was doing. She had run for a second term and won, almost by acclamation such was her popularity after rising out of the cavern under London's Leicester Square. And Paul Munro had become her Vice President, something that had never happened in American history.

The mighty panjandrums of Washington, many scholars and a lot of pundits thought that a husband running for VP was a constitutional outrage, but particularly so because Paul was Canadian-born and next in line for the highest office should something amiss happen to his wife. But if anything, Paul was more popular than Cora. His bravery in the face of overwhelming danger on the day he sprung them from captivity made him the real hero of the story, so the wise words of the opposition went unheard amid the hosannas that were cried out in almost every other quarter when he stood beside her on the podium.

During her campaign and at her inauguration, Cora Munro had made it clear that she was going to do whatever was necessary to address the plight of the remaining Outsiders. During her first term she had tried to wrest control of hive technology but had failed. Now it meant taking on Hive Corp., which was the exclusive licensee of the technology. The company was rapidly building new hive cities and doming salvageable towns right across the country and connecting them with hyperloops and hydroloops. They were also propagating new hives in Europe, Africa and Asia, but in a way that looked to a lot of people like they were forcing them down people's throats.

That was another problem for Cora Munro because Hive Corp.'s aggressiveness caused an endless amount of grief for America's foreign policy. Hive Corp. had also built a floating city way out in the mid Atlantic, calling it an operations center for criss-crossing hydroloops, but many thought it was being used for nefarious purposes too, like money-laundering, gunrunning, and a host of other crimes that lay far outside the jurisdiction of national courts.

In the west where I came from, and in the Midwest and southwest, an Outsider resistance movement was growing. It is not surprising that it was called an armed movement because just about everyone out there was armed to the teeth and always had been. Rhetorical pleading and case-making was getting the leaders of the resistance nowhere, so some of the extremists organized themselves into a shadowy insurgency called the Outsider Army that began sabotaging Hive Corp. infrastructure in Idaho, Montana and Oregon. Down in Texas the Outsiders that may or may not have been connected to the OA marched on the new Roddenberry hive, only to be repulsed by the Hive's militia, which was under the command of professional mercenaries hired by Hive Corp. Temperatures were rising by the day.

I didn't understand the fine points of President Munro's case, but when I listened to a speech she made in which she said that America was being killed by the growing cancer of the hive communities, I was as stunned and disbelieving as almost everyone else who heard it. She said that America was now confronted with an existential crisis and it was time for Americans to wake up. She said that we on the Inside should look around and ask ourselves where, if anywhere, in their cities and towns the American flag was flying.

Well it wasn't, except in a few shops where old flags or memorabilia was sold, but no one was shocked by that because the environment within the hives was always kept uncluttered. No one was allowed to hang anything out any window or to erect signs larger than the back of a park bench and only then above a shop or office building. But hell, we the people lived in whatever State we were in and every State was within the USA, so what was her problem? Everyone in the hive cities was living well, still loved our country. More than ever, because we finally lived in peace, white, black, brown, yellow, men and women, gay, straight and all the rest, on pain of being tossed back outside for breaches of that peace.

In short, only the Outsiders applauded the speech. Two days later, an Outsider group in Montana dynamited the foundations of a new dome near Helena and two night watchmen were killed as they ate their supper. Cora implored people not to believe the threat of the Outsiders was bigger than it was, that they should be listened to. But that was it for her. Her enemies moved quickly to put her in the Outsider's camp, and some even made it look like she was a witting member of the OA.

What about the Vice President? If you listened closely to what he was saying, Paul Munro was not disagreeing with them; he was not standing up for her except in the way he praised her with faint damning. Word got out that he may, in fact, have told some buddies in old New York that his wife had gone cuckoo, a charge he quickly and strongly denied to the forest of mics thrown up in his face the following morning. But what about that strange smile on his face, I wondered, as he fielded the questions put to him? A charming way to deflect a difference of opinion with the President, his wife, that was being blown way out of proportion? Sure. That was it.

It was that controversy that marked the beginning of her deterioration from being America's Boadicea to America's cringing, blank-faced, dyspeptic victim, another woman for whom crying, when she did not get what she wanted, was the ultimate default mode. If you think I didn't sneer at her along with most of my fellow citizens, you would be wrong. If you think, now, I am not ashamed of feeling that way, and also for feeling outraged and angry with her for giving tacit support to the Outsiders, to the Outsider Army, you would also be wrong. I am. Deeply.

Actually, outraged and angry doesn't even begin to describe the chaos of emotions into which I was thrown so violently just two months later when tragedy struck at the roots of my being. Looking back from this vantage point, my recollection of the emotions I felt then has been blunted by the certain knowledge I now possess.

The ineluctable fact is that the worst violence of which humans are capable comes out of the cold, calm duty the righteous assume is theirs. But back then, I knew – knew like I knew nothing else – that she, people like her, and the terrorists for whom they were apologists, were guilty, guilty, guilty, and deserved to die, despicably.

As far as I was concerned, Cora Munro, our President, might well have been there when those terrorists took their guns and torches to that cabin in the woods near Ojai and shot dozens of bullets into the prone, suddenly awakened, terror-stricken bodies of Lawrence and Javier, then set their home and the surrounding forest alight. She had fanned the flames that consumed the dead flesh of my two fathers and to the green wood of the trees around their home. Lawrence and Javier, carried away in the fucked-up flames of a dying cause.

By the time Wynk tracked me down – no easy feat – to tell me Jav and Lawry were gone it was too late for me to go back to Ojai to celebrate their lives or to mourn their deaths in the company of the thousands who filled the main square of Ojai. It was Ozzy Mandis, their fast friend from Kingman, backed by my old band, who came to sing for them, not me. So, I sang for them at Polyphemus the night I learned what had happened, again calling up the spirit of Cladine, the spirit of a blues so deep it made a black hole in the otherwise twinkling cosmos of that little room. Next day I went to Heaven's Gate to tell mother what had happened, and the two of us cried.

Now, in retrospect, how I could fault Cora Munro for showing sadness, defeat and powerlessness in the way women do? I attribute my inability to see her retreat from life to the way the cataracts of our own feelings make all of us, men and women alike, blind to the agonies and joys of others. Everything begins orbiting around our little selves.

I came to see things, experience things and know things that not only made me empathize with Cora right down to the marrow of my bones, but to find the ways and means to avenge her losses. Yes, hers and my own too, so many of which can be laid at the feet of a few, betraying others.

That process began with thinking deeply about a question Stevy had asked me one night while we lay in bed after making love. He was thinking aloud about the night Paul and Cora had escaped from their confinement.

- Why the cameras?

- What are you talking about?

- The cameras. The cameras that followed Paul and Cora out of the underground.

- What do you mean?

- Somebody placed them there to capture the action.

- So?

- Nothing. Forget it. I've got a paranoid mind.


*Beatitudes be the blessings the unblessed cannot buy.*

# Song 35

Just after my forty-second birthday, sitting on the stage at the club, talking nonsense to the audience while I tweaked Old Mud's tuning, I caught sight of a thin, wispy haired, elegantly dressed man sitting at a table by himself, just off to one side, in the second row. He had his legs crossed, so the sole of his right foot was turned my way. Hardly a scuff. I may not have noticed him but for that and but for the fact that he was looking at me with an intensity that might have alarmed a woman not as used to smitten fans as I was by then.

A highball of tonic water sat half empty beside him, a twist of lime still hanging on its rim. He nursed that one drink right to the end of my set and hardly moved, except to wave off his waitress when she asked if he wanted anything else or to cross and uncross his legs. After I took my bow at the end of the night, I walked as I usually do into the backroom, but before I exited I looked over my shoulder and saw he was already gone.

He came the next night and the night after that, sitting in the same place, drinking the same drink. And just as he had the first night, he disappeared before I stepped out of the bar and before the applause of Polyphemus' patrons finally tapered into silence. But that last night, he was waiting outside the door to the club when I emerged with a large handbag slung over my shoulder, wearing heels and still vibrating as I always did after my show. He carried three red roses in his hand and held them up with the expectation I would take them from him.

He seemed harmless enough.

- You're the mystery man.

- Not as mysterious as all that.

He was taller than I thought he might be. Green eyes, open and steady. In the light of the concourse I could see a bit of salt in the thin, blond hair that just managed to cover a receding hairline. Pale complexion. And what was that accent? Not from Tennessee.

- You enjoyed the show?

- I have to say I did. Quite a lot more than I thought I might, actually.

- New York?

- Clinton.

- But, from New York originally.

- Brooklyn.

- For me?

He held out the roses again and I took them.

- Thank you.

- It's corny isn't it? A man at the stage door with a bouquet.

- What's your name?

- Peter. Peter Benevolus.

- Attorney?

- Banker, and ardent fan of Wicla the Singer.

- Well again, Peter. Thank you.

Now I saw it. The awkwardness. Eyes somewhat averted and fearful even when he tried to maintain eye contact. He had practiced overcoming his…what? Shyness? He was one of those men who had cultivated the persona of a confident man. Who was his model, I wondered? What movie star? I couldn't quite place him in that moment.

- Well, thank you again, Peter, I said, and walked away in the direction of my home.

I made it fifteen or twenty paces before he called out.

- Ms Weer!

He caught up to me.

- Wait.

I turned to face him and watched him as he came closer. A purposeful stride into the purposes of his visit. Purposes plural.

- I want to tell you about your father.

Four months later we married in a private ceremony in CashCarter. One month after that I moved to his old home in Clinton. A year after that I gave birth to Bened and Scola.

Marrying me, by the way, had not been one of his original purposes, so assume for the moment there was a romantic angle to our very strange and always fraught marriage. The romance, the attraction, did not last long, just long enough. For a woman who had been raised by the spinster Merri Weer and a woman who had decided opinions about relationships with men being an iffy thing at best, I don't quite understand why I had adopted such an intransigent principle: if I ever do get married, I had told myself on more than one occasion (and told others too, as they snorted in disbelief) I would stay married forever. I would hang in there and fight out whatever might come to ail the marriage. Sooner or later I would die, or he would, but by god we would remain married until that fateful day.

He wanted, that night we first met to tell me about my father. And so, over the next few hours, well into an exhausted morning, starting first on neutral ground at a café close to Polyphemus, he did. To shake our legs, we went from there to the main bridge over the Cumberland where we talked more and then, while I bade him stop so I could let my mind catch up to all the information he had shoved into it, we walked in silence to the city's main piazza where the giant tron that had not so long ago boomed with the noise of Cora and Paul

Munro's escape from the underworld, loomed blankly over its early morning emptiness. Trusting now in Peter's mission, and tired beyond the possibility of sleep, we went to my home, where Peter answered all the questions I could think to ask.

One of those questions was why did it take you almost three years to come here? Peter had received a Lifebook notification that the daughter of Clement Samuels had just joined the LifeWeb at the very moment Merri's and my own Book had been activated in the little vault where she now lay. Had I not taken that two for one deal, I would have remained, in Peter's mind, a non-entity, a non-existent being.

- I don't know, he said. Fear.

- Fear?

- Of unintended consequences.

What that meant would make sense later. But I had another question.

- Why now?

- It was weighing on me.

The guilt of not telling me, I supposed. But one more question came to mind.

- I was supposed to be notified if other relations were plugged into LifeWeb. Why...?

- I had turned Clement's off.

- There must have been a reason.

- His descendants in Brooklyn – cousins, aunts, uncles. An army of them. Seconds and thirds. He had cut them out of his life a long time ago so we didn't want to hear from them.

- We?

- Well, I didn't.

So, my father was Clem. Merri's Clem, the one from whom she fled because the possibility of a love that might go wrong was so powerful a fear in her. He was not a clod-hopper farmer who do si do'd into her life. For Merri, he was not just a side-of-the-road fling with a down-on-his-luck fellow traveler. Clement Samuel's sperm had already wriggled its way into my mother's belly and made little me by the time she tried to drown it with the whisky-stained ejaculate of two strangers. I was conceived, that is, by the time the throb and pain of her hangover worked its magic by crowding out the ineffable sadness she felt when she flew right out of Clems's life.

Clement Samuels had criss-crossed America in a battered Tesla Bat with an improbable and extraordinary belief that in so doing he, the beak-nosed, rake thin, weakling son of Brooklyn Jews, whose whole world up until the moment he set out on his journey, was the few blocks around his parent's deli, would find a way out for all of us. I had no idea that he had founded Heaven's Gate, although I was well-informed enough to know that it was he – not Clem of my mother's memory – but Clement Samuels, the dangerous recluse of modern legend, who had discovered the crystal that was now used to grow the hive cities and towns in which most of us lived just a few years later. That and so much more.

I stood up from the chair in which I had been sitting so long with my legs tucked underneath. I walked to my window and opened the curtains and looked out into CashCarter's now bustling Noon time streets and felt an even greater astonishment than I had in Kingman, or at GatesPort when I first went there, or at Ojai even though I watched it rise, or this place where I now lived and worked, when I first entered it. How did all of this get built by my murdered father? How did he transform his dented, scraped and dirty car into this new world? And why was he so forgotten now and not the martyred saviour he most surely was?

- I need to sleep.

- Of course, Peter said. I'll show myself out.

I walked to the door with him.

- Will I see you again? I asked.

- I hope so. I left my card on the table by the sofa. Anytime.

- Where is he?

- Would you like to visit his final resting place?

- I think so. Yes. Yes, I would.

- I can take you there when you're ready.

I slept more soundly than I had for years. A circle had been closed. No, that wasn't it. A constellation had formed in the dark corner of the firmament in which I had lived my life these last few months. Mother, father, and I, but soon to be lit-up with stars that could not at that moment be seen, a husband and the twins.

A few days later, a story came through the news about President Munro which I now watched with avid intent. She was coming out of a meeting in old New York with Paul Munro, sunglasses on, three steps behind. They were being escorted to their limo which was surrounded by a crowd of Outsider protestors, many of them carrying placards condemning her to hell. The Secret Service men around the Firsts were hard-pressed to keep the crowd at bay but did. They could not, however, protect them from the protestor's shouts and imprecations.

Something had changed. She was no longer in their favour. She had betrayed them. She had come to New York to sign an agreement with Hive Corp. that would enable the company to **build** more hives on public land, a great deal of it in the Indian lands through which Merri and I had traveled, but huge chunks of other land in almost every State too. And she finally agreed with Hive Corp.'s position that the old cities would not be domed.

Mrs. Munro kept her head down and moved as quickly as she could to get into the limo. She looked tired and drawn, feeble almost. But Paul, pink fleshed, puffed up in almost insolent good health, removed his sunglasses and stopped and spoke in a big and pushy voice. He looked into the cameras and spoke, unblinking and sure of himself, to the country, not just to the media people and Outsiders in front of him.

- Let me make this clear. There will be room for everyone inside the hives. That's the point of this deal. All the obstacles that have slowed progress up until now have been removed. No one should have to live on the Outside and if we have our way, now one will. My wife, The President, has committed her government to this deal so things can move quickly, and needless to say, I am one hundred percent behind her.

While Paul was laying down the law, I was trying to steal another glimpse of Cora Munro through the tinted windows of the car. My anger, my hate, toward her was like balled lightening inside my chest because of what the OA had done to Lawrence and Javier, but now it was unfurling itself into bolts that I would have flung at her hanging-in-shame head if I could, because Peter had confirmed what I had heard in the media when I really wasn't paying attention.

She had, Peter said, relentlessly pursued my father so she could expropriate what was rightly his. Peter knew from his own father that a deal exactly like she had just signed could have been done years earlier had Cora Munro not been so stubbornly convinced of her own arguments. Instead, she had

Clement Samuels arrested and consigned to one of her prisons where he was crucified by men who believed - on her say so - that he, the Brooklyn Jew, was just as bad as she had declared him to be. Clearly Peter was as contemptuous of Cora Munro as I was.

I messaged Peter a week later and told him I hoped he had not forgotten that he would take me to see my Clement Samuels where he now lay. He returned the message within seconds. He asked me to come to Clinton and we would go from there, so, of course, I thought, my father was resting in a vault in Heaven's Gate there along with dozens of other luminaries who called the place home now that they were dead.

Peter met me at the Hyperloop Station in Clinton, but instead of bundling me into a taxi drone, he took my overnight bag in one hand and my arm in another then walked me to the Hydroloop platform in the adjoining concourse. He carried himself upright, backbone stretched to full length, and walked with long strides that were hard to keep up to with, his chin jutting out like a rooster's. He was emotionless except when he turned toward me, not smiling as he walked or as he turned his head, but smiling only after he had turned my way, as though his smile were an afterthought.

I realized later, once I had guessed, and he confirmed, that he had Asperger's that such expressions were forethoughts. He made deliberate, usually pre-planned decisions to engage in the mimicry of normal social behaviour when he had concluded it was appropriate or necessary to do so, as though he were lip-syncing a little behind the beat. I also learned later that he didn't often deem an occasion an appropriate or necessary one for him to bother with the niceties. Most of the time his face remained blank, a cypher that was, he knew, intimidating to others.

- Where are we going, Peter?

- London.

- London?

- Then to Castle Forbes.

- Why?

- To visit Mr. Samuels. And my father. They are both there.

- I have to sing tomorrow night.

- Of course.

I was not at all prepared for what I saw at Castle Forbes.

*A fervent fish flies the falls to find his way.*

# Song 36

We arrived at the Castle by copter around midnight. Mrs. Glastonbury, who with her husband Jack looked after the place, was surprisingly awake for an old woman who was obliged to be on duty even at the extreme fag end of the day. She was excited to see Master Peter, who, despite the journey looked as unrumpled and as alert as when he met me in Clinton. I was fading. But then I remembered that I was living on old time in CashCarter, while everyone on the Outside, including those who lived in medieval castles, had long ago adjusted to new time. Night was day here and Mrs. Glastonbury's day was just beginning.

- Will you be having a meal then? I have things at the ready.

- Are you hungry, Wicla? Peter asked.

- A little. Sure.

- Let's eat in the kitchen, Gillian, if it's not too much trouble.

- No trouble at all young Peter. Right this way miss.

Young Peter he would always be to her because he was the

skinny, hyperactive son of Peter senior, the brilliant architect of much of the new world in which we were all now living. Gillian and Jock Glastonbury had helped raised Peter *fils* here at the Castle.

In his younger days, the Glastonbury's had been given authority to paddle young Peter's bottom whenever he broke one of a million rules that Peter senior made-up on the go, usually when his son wanted his attention and couldn't have it. My Peter – I will call him that – was prone to temper tantrums when anyone dared to deny whatever it was he wanted. Many valuable objects were shattered on the plastered walls and stone floors within the Castle and the less formidable walls and floors in the Benevolus family homes of New York, Paris, Rome, Moscow, Cape Town, Rio and elsewhere.

The Glastonbury's, atavistic Presbyterians that they were, had no compunction when it came to the laying on of hands. But by his late teens, she confided to me when he was out of earshot, Peter had acquired the self-control necessary to restrain his fierce impulse and thereafter the Glastonbury's had only to bestow a cross, Gallic scowl should he look like he was about to veer off into temporary insanity. I would come to find out that my Peter's volcanic temper was as close to his calm-seeming surface as the saltshaker on the kitchen table at the castle was to anyone lucky enough to sup there.

I ate just a little, then Peter and Mrs. Glastonbury escorted me up a back staircase to the main level, then up another staircase, whose oak steps creaked under foot, to the corridor where my bedroom for my first night at Castle Forbes was located. A fire was crackling in the hearth behind a wrought iron screen. Its flickering light warmed the room. A high, deep bed beckoned, and it was there, once they left and closed the door behind them, that I fell into a deep and luxurious sleep. The indefatigable Gillian knocked on my door at about Noon and entered bearing a cup of coffee and a light breakfast on a silver tray. Once she had settled me with the tray where I was propped up on a half dozen pillows against the massive bedstead, she tidied the room and then threw open the curtains to the grey sky beyond.

- Master Peter is in the library when you are ready for the grand tour.

- Has he been up long?

- Up? The man never sleeps dear.

- He's waiting for me?

- Aye. And I wouldn't keep him waiting too long. He's an impatient man. Word to the wise.

Well, I had to sing that night, so I did not get the full tour. The library was off the main reception room which was off the grand foyer. A half circle staircase led from the foyer to the second floor – an alternative route to the bedrooms – and I assumed to yet another set of stairs that would give access to the parapets, ramparts and corner towers of the castle.

On that trip, I confessed to Peter a burning desire to see the room from which Cora and Paul had been taken, but he put me off by reminding me that if I did not board the waiting copter for the trip back to London, I would miss the Hydroloop to Obamaport and fail to show up at Polyphemus. Bad form that.

- Is my father buried outside?

- Well, sort of. It used to be outside. Are you ready?

We went through the main reception room to an arched doorway and then into a long corridor where we came to a long glass wall that looked in on an inner courtyard in which I saw a large rectangular pool filled with a luminous, almost fluorescent blue and rippleless water, a colour I had never seen anywhere in my life 'til then. I have never seen since either, except at Castle Forbes. Two ancient pillars stood silently to one side pointing up at the Crysalinks canopy that surmounted the courtyard. At the far end, I could see a rostrum with a dais, a strange thing because it seemed improbable that any orator would address the silences I knew the room contained.

Peter leaned into an eye scanner and the glass doors to the courtyard slid silently open, allowing me to enter, but with Peter's hand slightly pushing at the small of my back, because at that moment I was so uncertain about my right to step into the sacred place it was.

The pearly, diffused light descending into the room from above, the rough granite stone of the surrounding walls, and the worn, pitted sandstone pillars that had been carved by a desert people many centuries ago, bestowed a serenity on the room that almost brought me to tears I was so awed by it.

In the years after, up until the day I killed Peter, I went there often to be with father and mother – for Peter allowed me to lay Merri there in the crypt below the rostrum after we were married and I had left CashCarter to live with him. The twins still come every year on the anniversary of their father's death to see him and their not so long dead ancestors, all of them together blinking and flicking their curious, binary messages into the near dark as they reach out for one another. It remains to be seen whether I will ever be taken from my mother's Lifebook and put in my own, or whether, instead, Bened and Scola will toss my memory into the cold Atlantic where it crashes against the cliffs below the castle. I hope they agree whatever they decide, because I would not want our children to be pitted against another. I never use to pray, but I pray now for their understanding, first of me, then of one another.

During the few months that passed after I first went to Castle Forbes, Peter and I shuttled back and forth between Clinton and CashCarter. For me, it was like shuttling between the ordinary world I lived in and the vastly more extraordinary world that was his.

I learned as I read about him on my vice that Peter Benevolus was probably the richest man in the world, and I suppose, if I had gold digger's blood running in my veins, I might marry him just to be the dolly on his arm. But I was into my forties and while attractive enough in my own way, I guess, I was no man's idea of a great beauty, not even a fading one. His attraction to me was not the attraction of a man who wanted physical perfection in a woman. Hardly.

Peter was not the man I ever thought I would be married to. He was not my type, not physically, and until I got to know him better, not emotionally, not intellectually either. Emotionally, he was, well, not unreachable, but perplexing, full of the need

471

for love I discovered, but not needy, not demanding. He was a fully self-sufficient being. Intellectually, he was far beyond me. I'm a dunce, but he was and remains the smartest human being I ever encountered. I can still hear my mother's voice in the back of my head. Your gonna marry that guy? Gimme a break. You need a real man.

In the end, he sold me, but in the end, I wanted to be sold. I knew there was something more for me in life than singing at Polyphemus until Homer died, or I did, or my repertoire became so dated and played-out that my doddering fans might pass the hat so I could be buried at the back of the orchard at Fort Ketchup with that old black woman I always bragged was my second mother. Now that Fort Ketchup – at least the land it sat on – was buried in the foundations of the new hive city near Portland – even that wasn't an option, as much as I thought it might be a sweet comeuppance for Cladine and me.

- I get to meet a lot of interesting people, said Peter. People who do interesting things.

- I guess you would. All doors are open aren't they?

- They are.

- You're a power player.

- Look, Wicla, power does only two things. First, it amplifies a person's shortcomings, every last one of them.

We were in Outsider Paris. He pointed at the tip of the

Eiffel Tower on the other side of the Seine from where we were standing and said we might go there next.

-   You want to take a ride on the river?

-   Sure. But what's the second thing?

-   You can mostly get away with it.

-   It what?

-   Whatever stuff your shortcomings lead you to do.

-   What about your good qualities?

-   Well, the good we do is oft interred with our bones.

-   Like what.

-   Like why don't you marry me and find out?

He led me down some steps to the walkway by the Seine and then across a bridge spanning its muddy margins to a small landing where we boarded a tourist boat. It was night of course. It was too dangerous to see Paris in the light of day. That was his proposal of marriage. I didn't answer that night. He advanced his cause again the following day when we were flying south. I told him I was thinking about it.

In Italy, I was a different creature. By then, the French had coiffed, shod and dressed me in a manner befitting a rich man's wife. Peter was too pleased by his creation. Well, I have concluded that only retroactively, but still. We stayed with Peter's friend, Ada (nee Lovelace), and her always nattily attired, stiff-backed, formidably moustached Italian husband. The Duke was the most recent progeny of an old family to have de facto possession of the family's grand villa in southern Tuscany.

Apparently there were other siblings in Florence, Rome and New York who were vituperatively steamed about their brother's good fortune, but then, they did not want to crack their polished nails or dirty their soft hands in the sandy soil in which the vines that underwrote their amiable lifestyles grew so splendidly. The Duke was a hands-on farmer.

Ada Lovelace, a strikingly beautiful, raven-haired woman also in her forties, could have claimed the title of Duchess D'Orcia but had not, because she was so resolutely filled with Yankee blood. She was eager to see who Peter had dragged (her word) into his life because she assumed that he had had to lasso me, so maladroit was he when it came to women.

She wasn't expecting me, but when the men left us so the Duke could smoke a cheroot and they both could enjoy a prandial on the wide terrace overlooking the vineyards below, we ladies were left on our own. Should I be ashamed to admit that we were girl-giggling in short order, mostly at the expense of the men?

Peter made an effort to be patient with me, but on the third day he said, 'Time for a decision'. Just like that. Deal or no deal. That's the charm of an Aspergerian mind. It's clear. We were walking in their vineyards at dusk, at the end of every row, a rosebush with blossoms redolent of Italian sensuality, but really rather more like caged canaries in the working mines of these sunlit lands. They were there to provide an early warning of ruinous mildew should it descend so that evasive action could be taken by such as the Duke.

Love is forever freedom, right? I turned toward him, took each of his hands in mine, looked deeply in his eyes and gave him an answer.

- On one condition, I said, half joking.

- What?

- I want to meet Cora Munro.

He looked at me and tried to discern whether the half joke was a complete joke or no joke at all. I decided in that moment to make him take it seriously because as soon as the words were out of my mouth, I realized it was what I wanted and that he could make it happen.

- That's my condition.

He dropped his hands from mine then with his right stroked his bony rooster's chin.

- But you hate her.

- I want to forgive her.

- What? Why?

- My mother always told me that if I truly wanted to be forever free in life I had to forgive anyone and everyone who did me wrong.

- I don't think that's a good idea. I mean, it's a good idea. So, do it. Right here. Say you forgive her. Forgive her.

- Do you want me to marry you Peter?

He turned and started back toward the villa.

- Peter! I called after him.

He yelled over his shoulder at me.

- Yes!

He meant, yes, he did want to marry me and yes he would introduce me to President Munro. Someday. Details to be worked out. Later that night he said perhaps she could be persuaded by her husband, Paul, who was Peter's very good friend and mentor, to attend our wedding. It didn't work out that way – we tied the knot privately in CashCarter. But at the time that was one way he thought a meeting might be arranged. I was not about to tell him that a long time ago, Paul had been my lover.

Men like Peter envy men like Paul, wish they could inhabit their bodies and their way with women, their way with other men for that matter, and they maintain a secret desire to extract a hot and horrible revenge on them even as they enjoy their easy going and helpful friendship.

Actually, forgiveness was not my intention. Spitting in the woman's face while the richest man in the world had my back was what I saw in my mind's eye. And as far as Peter was concerned, even if he had not agreed to my condition I would have married him. We were both old enough to know that the plant that overwhelms you with its summer roses is a thorn bush in that and all other seasons.

Before we got in their drone for the fast trip to the hydroloop station near Rome, Ada hugged and kissed me while Peter bid the Duke addio. When she did the same with Peter I heard her whisper in his ear, while winking at me, do not misuse this good woman, Peter. You'll have me to answer to.

No opportunity every presented itself for us to meet again. Ada and the Duke became fast enemies of Peter's when a little to the north of their estate, a great swath of territory was acquired by Hive Corp. There, the company, with Peter's bank doing the financing, built the first of the hive cities that so disconsolated Italy's old money. It's plastic-looking bubble offended their earth-bound sense of style.

Our European sojourn over, we returned to Clinton where, next day, Peter's people proved to his apparent satisfaction that the construction of our private dome overlooking the Hudson, and the large house he was having built for us within, was proceeding on time and on budget.

- I suppose you will return to CashCarter right away.

- Not if you don't want me to.

- It's fine by me. You should go.

- I'm happy to stay. I could give notice.

- I'm going to be extremely busy, Wicla. You'll be bored.

- You want me to go?

- Of course not.

- Are you saying you don't want to marry me now that you've tried me out?

- What? Why are you saying that? I love you.

When he said he would be extremely busy, that I would be bored if I was just left to watch him, almost twenty-four hours a day, seven days a week, dealing with the ten thousand matters that were pressing on his mind, that's exactly what he meant. I returned home, but it never occurred to me to ask the obvious question: why would he be any less busy once we were married?

The answer to that, became apparent immediately after we married two months later at a chapel in the Heaven's Gate at CashCarter, with Homer and one of the Polyphemus' waitresses as witnesses, is that he wouldn't. He left the next morning for Africa and Asia hoping that I would be at Clinton upon his return a month later so we he could show me the Xanadu he had erected above the sacred river there.

We did spend the night of our wedding together and had the kind of sex that we had already had in Europe. Let's put it this way. It was endurable. Peter discovered that the joys of skin-to-skin, heart-to-heart orgasms were quite different than the lonely ones his virginal self had enjoyed so single-handedly heretofore. He liked them. I left CashCarter four weeks to the day later for Clinton and I am still here.

*Echoes the everything of everyone at every time that ever was.*

# Song 37

The Outsider insurgency became problematic to say the least. Their political leaders focused on the destruction of the country they alleged was Hive Corp's secret plan. In our media, their argument was diluted to a thin soup of complaint about the changes that we were all witnessing, but which were sitting well with the vast majority of Americans now living on the Inside.

No one paid much attention to the Outsider politicos because they seemed unremittingly pathetic as they sat in their dilapidated committee rooms pounding fists on folding tables under lights that made their pale skin seem sallow and their eyes appear to be shadowed in deep wells of doubt about their frustrated cause.

The Outsider Army, on the other hand, was doing its talking with bullets and bombs. They were embarrassing their co-religionists by discrediting any and all attempts at suasion, but worse, for the powers that be, they had brought further development in the Midwest and west to a virtual standstill.

Word had it they might sabotage the Yellowstone distillation plant, and if they did that, all bets were off because if they did, all the cold, salty Pacific water that was now being calmly processed into potable water, would be spewed into the caldera at the rate of a few million gallons a minute and would cause an eruption of biblical, end-of-the-world proportions.

Cora Munro was hiding from protagonist and antagonist

alike, although Paul, looking more and more like the de facto President he really was – according to Peter – was doing everything he could from whatever pulpit he could find, and through every government agency at his command, to marginalize and delegitimize the OA in the minds of the few million Outsiders who were trapped in the no-man's land of the stand-off.

Cora's withdrawal to the cush upper floor of the White House was interpreted as tacit support of the Outsiders, and while the loyal opposition tried to smear Paul with that same brush, his constant challenge to the recalcitrant Outsiders meant they couldn't make it stick. In the meantime, the government, and, I learned later, Hive Corp. had dispatched squads of assassins to track down OA's field commanders so they could cut-off their trigger fingers and slit their throats.

And that's where I came in.

- There is a woman out west who is singing your songs.

Peter was home for a rare night of togetherness. We sat at the long table in our dining room, me at its head, him sitting kitty corner. He wasn't going to usurp the place I took when I ate alone, which was almost always.

- Kaya?

- Yes, an Indian girl. You know her?

- Nez Perce. I sang with her one night when mother and I were driving East.

- She's stirring up trouble. With your songs, and her own, I'm told.

- What kind of trouble?

He didn't have to tell me. I am on record where the power of song is concerned. It's big medicine. Kaya would be giving heart to the Outsiders, blowing oxygen with her voice into their collapsing hearts.

- We need you to go west.

- Me?

- Wicla the Singer.

- I don't think that's a good idea.

We had only been living together – even though most nights and days I was alone – for three months or so. I realized, even though softly spoken, he was giving instructions to me, that he was not asking that I go west to sing but telling me. I resisted and that's when he raised his voice. It echoed in the large, empty dining room and out into the salon, and its high-pitched whine shocked me as much as the words that were spitting out of his purple face.

I don't know how to explain myself. I fought back. I did. I left the table and marched into the salon full of indignant rage. I saw Merri's ghost in the corner, hidden in the folds of the curtains by the large window, cheering me on. I yelled out something like you will never talk to me like that again. I promised I would never do anything I damn well didn't want to do. But he followed me around the room. He loomed furiously but he said no more for the moment. He let me have my counterblast. And then he waited for my good reason not to do what was right for the Outsiders; to account for my hypocrisy.

I saw the look in his eye. I saw that the only possible way for me to remain uninvolved in the Insider/Outsider war was to pull out my woman's card. I told him I was afraid, afraid to go back out there. Mother stood looking at me with arm's akimbo, violently shaking her head in disgust. She flew out through the glass, screaming as she rocketed skyward out over the lawns and looped the tall cedars nudging the low side of the dome.

It was the worst possible tactic to use with Peter. There was no end to the number of things that he said he could and would do to protect me from whatever might hurt or frighten me while I was doing what was right for the country. He loved my weakness. Just loved it. He loved it so much it turned him on.

We were in our bedroom later. I was sitting in my room at my dressing table brushing my hair, eyes red and face just starting to uncrumple now that the fight had gone out of me, when Peter came in carrying two sniffers of brandy. He put one on the vanity and carried the other to the small chair by the fireplace where he sat and watched me, sipping slowly as I tried to prolong the work I was doing to get to a recognizable normal.

-   I think we should make love.

I didn't answer.

- We shouldn't go to bed angry.

I turned to look at him.

- I said I'd do it. I'll go.

- I know.

- I'm tired.

- I know. But…

What the hell, I thought. I'm not going to fight him on this.

- OK, I said.

I stood, walked to the bed, pulled down the sheets and covers, let my nightgown fall and slipped in. He turned off the lights, undressed in the dark, then folded his cloths and placed them on the chair before walking on the noiseless carpet to the bed. I was laying flat on the sheets – arms above my head and legs spread. He fucked me like a little boy, greedy for the candy of my unflinching body. His face was buried in the sheet down beside my ear when he came and I could tell it was an exquisite orgasm, the kind you think you are stealing, when in fact, it's a gift.

Nine months later, Bened and Scola were born.

Peter's people made all the arrangements for my appearances out west. He claimed that they were made only after I had agreed to go, but a tour, even a small one, is a complex thing, so to put it all together and have it begin just a couple of months later, and to have a video documentary team ready to ride along, sent another shiver of wonder up my jellied spine. That Merri was on board from beginning to end, hovering over me the whole time we were on the road was completely unsurprising.

I was set to do four shows, all of them in Outside locations, all of them with Kaya and her band, no longer managed by Wynk who had retired to the new floating hive at Miami with Ann Marie. Kaya was put under contract as the opening act, but we sang the finale and encores together.

How had he co-opted her? She hadn't been. She thought I was joining her in her cause – had no idea that the enemy of that cause was behind the tour. It didn't occur to me that I was part and parcel of her deception. I was just going because I had submitted to my husband's demand. Stupid, eh?

The two months of grace time I had before the tour started was a busy time. Singing love songs and the blues songs to a small audience at Polyphemus was one thing. I could get on my hind legs and carry a tune to the back of the room in my hands had any semi-deaf person been stuck back there, but singing my Outsider songs to thousands in an outdoor arena was something I had not done for a long time, not since I had sung to the Osage nation near KC.

I didn't need a husband to tell me my self-respect was on the line, so I got a band together – performers and studio musicians I knew in CashCarter – and within three weeks, we were rehearsing in Clinton, first at our home by the Hudson, then in a large space rented to test our mettle. We also used the time take our stage set-up from design to portable reality.

But something was missing but I couldn't put my finger on it until another month went by.

My periods had been spotty for the last year, so I hadn't worried too much when I missed one. When I missed the second one I thought, great, I'm going into early menopause. Well, not great, but I had never been one to deny mother nature her will and her way. Nor any other woman for that matter. But every day I was waking up tired to nausea and cramps, and when that started happening I shifted my thinking from the hypothesis of menopause to the reality of a pregnancy that would, if I were not careful, create a problem I did not want.

By the time my doctor confirmed I was pregnant, the horrible fear I had about going on tour had become a try-to-stop-me enthusiasm that every member of the band and road crew felt too. We'd come together and we were as good as my original band and maybe better. But there was something missing.

While I was trying to figure that out, I decided to keep the news of my pregnancy from Peter, and from everybody else. So, every morning when I left the privacy of my bathroom, I made sure I was not looking like I'd just thrown up. Everyone I encountered, Peter if he were in residence (as he liked to deem his time at the mansion), our household staff, the band and all the hands around the set, got Wicla the Singer all aglow and happy as could be. I could carry the act for a few hours because by Noon, I was authentically that way anyway.

If Peter found out that I was carrying his child, I had no doubt he would cancel the tour and order me to bed until I delivered his son and heir. Yeah, he would have not permitted the possible birth of a daughter to enter his atavistic mind. He would have accepted her, but he'd want to keep trying for a boy child until he got one. You can't deny father nature either.

One morning I was so wretched I didn't think I could even get out of bed. But my guts were coming into my mouth, so I ran to the bathroom as quickly as I could and hung my head over the toilet until everything from my throat down to the heels of my feet were cast into the witches' cauldron over which I bubbled and frothed.

I stayed on my knees until nothing was left of me except the shell of a woman who was wondering whether she should wander out to the cliffs and jump rather than take step one on the impending tour. I splashed cold water into my eyes then stood white-faced and vacant in front of the mirror – the mirror again – and stared right into the back of my skull, which I soon realized was filling up with noise. With music. With wailing guitars. Drums. With the sound of a fiddle. A fiddle. The missing something. The sound upon which I could hitch my voice and ride it up to wherever the fuck it wanted to take me. To take all of us.

- Ann Marie, it's Wicla.

- Wow, Wicla! Wow.

- It's been a long time.

- So…

- I am going back on a short tour. Out west.

- Well, that's wonderful Wicla. But why are you…

- I want you to come.

- OK.

- OK?

- Yeah. I want to. I really want to.

- Don't you have to check it with Wynk?

- No.

- Where is he? Are you guys still together?

- He's over there in the recliner snoozing.

By the next day she was in the rehearsal hall standing on the stage and backing me up like she had never left, like no time at all had gone by between the time we last gigged together and now. Parenthetically, I should mention by the end of the tour, she had fucked every guy in the band and decided to move out of Miami and back west with the drummer, not to the Outside, but back to small town Kingman where we first met. But that's another story.

Four concerts, all Outside, were scheduled: Ketchum, Idaho, Fort Spokane, Washington, Visalia, California and Marana just north of Tucson in Arizona. Peter spent as much money as it took to promote them into the successes they were going to be - huge, over-capacity crowds at every one.

A few Insiders dared to step outside their hives and find a

way to the venues, but the vast majority of those who came were staunch and defiant Outsiders. These were the hard cases that Hive Corp. was so worried about. Among them were the Outsider politicos, a number of whom were brought up on stage to kiss my cheek and wave at the crowds and Outsider activists including, we had no doubt, members of the Outsider Army who were blending with the wildly happy crowds and behaving themselves. Behaving themselves, that is, until after the third concert.

Kaya needed no introduction. She was already famous on the Outsider circuits, the genuine article, beautiful, young, brilliant and totally committed to the Outsider's cause. As her career got underway she had started by singing a few of her songs and many of mine, but now it was a rare occasion when she added anything to her own repertoire. She might do one or two of someone else's, and only did mine once in awhile, changing them so that not much of the way I had sung them was left. I was a forgotten soul already, obviously, and that after just three years or so after leaving a land where I had once been the Queen of the Outsiders.

Before the tour got underway, a lot of people in the Outsider communities wondered why Kaya wasn't the lead act and had been relegated to opening act status. Actually, a lot of them thought Wicla the Singer had died or had gone off to snooze away the last part of her life, like Wynkyn DeWorde. The legendary Trader Merri Weer only came to the lips of people with long memories but judging from what I saw when I heard her laughing at the folly of all this, she didn't mind a bit.

Peter's publicity machine had put Wicla the Singer back into the minds of everyone in the west, front and center. People couldn't turn on their vices without a video of me and my band at some gig popping-up, or of me singing solo as I looked into the starry night to some long gone lover who had broken my heart, or of me on a stage at one of my concerts speechifying about the plight of the Outsiders, or of me in a studio somewhere in a broke-down town joshing it up with a DJ like we'd gone to high school together, or me at dusk down at ground level with my mother selling brassieres and cold creams to momentarily happy women in some misbegotten place on the other side of nowhere. I was made into a romantic figure with a power to pluck the hearts of forlorn Outsiders.

By the time Peter's machine got through with the advance work, Kaya was looking like an ungrateful daughter who had never given me the respect I was due, that she had stolen the drum that I had beaten to a fare-thee-well before she was crawling. She was made to look like she was banging on it now, without credit to the great woman who had paved her way in the Outsider wilderness. I never wanted that and could not have anticipated the consequences of a promotional campaign I frankly didn't know was underway.

Kaya was an incredible woman, a better singer, and a better songwriter than I ever was and she was hurt by the not-so-subtle intimations that were propagated by my husband, or at least by people who were doing his bidding. So, in my unmotherly, inarticulate way, once I realized why Kaya had become so chilly and aloof around me I spent a good deal of my time on that tour trying to cajole her out of her growing resentment toward me with the kind of assurances that insecure stars are deaf to and wouldn't believe anyway even if they weren't.

It had not occurred to me either that the tour was made to

look like it was unsponsored. Peter had told me that I must not mention to anyone, anywhere that he was involved, or that the costs of mounting the tour were being underwritten by his Bank or that there was any connection whatsoever with Hive Corp. Being unsponsored it was made to seem that I had spontaneously decided to come back west to show solidarity with Outsiders. No one ever challenged my motives because I was kept away from media people and them from me. No time, said the tour managers. Let the singing sing for itself.

The crew and our gear were moved by truck and bus from place to place, but Kaya's band and my band, and Kaya and I were ferried about in copters and drones, which, in retrospect made it feel that we were lifted off one stage and put down on another, that each of the shows, until the last, was really one show. The people who came to them were made deliriously happy and deeply inspired by all that they saw and heard, which is why the shows are talked about even to this day by those who were there.

Kaya's sets were impeccable. I stood in the wings watching her every night. She had the warrior spirit of her father and uncles, the innate showmanship of warrior Titus, the grounded-ness of her tribe, and a female grace that passes understanding.

And what did I give these audiences? I don't think it's my place to say, but just to say something I will say this: if I gave them anything I gave them the Mother Spirit. I was able to do that because Merri was with me the whole time, flitting about in the lights above my head, and down in the pit below my feet where she danced her jig as in days long gone.

And I gave them the Mother Spirit because I was carrying my own child, not showing yet, but fully aware of its nascent being, as I stood at the mic singing to the thousands there, and as I walked across the stage left and right egging on the band to kick it up, kick it up, kick it up. I knew that my child was in me and listening to everything I was singing and saying and listening also to the sound of hope and relief that rose in the nighttime air and rumbled to the good feelings of the crowds whenever they applauded, which was often. Had I known I was carrying twins, I would have mothered those Outsiders twice as much.

The third concert ended to rapturous applause, but then, when the concert goers realized after our third encore that more from Kaya and I was not forthcoming, all that ramped-up energy devolved like firelight into a wistful, crowd-wide sense of pleasure and satisfaction that was carried to the Outsider enclaves and farms – still collapsing under the weight of change - by everyone who was there. We could do no more that night, although we would have, had we not exhausted ourselves.

I returned to the stage once the concert grounds were emptied of people, and in the coming light of dawn, peered across the open space, and up into the waning moonlight and not as I had for the last several years, into the rarefied air of a hive. Later that morning, still coming down from the concert, I vowed to finish the song I had started just as Merri and I had left Portland on our way east, more than three years earlier.

We would not be flying to Marana until much later in the day. For reasons unknown to me, everyone including the singers and the band, would use ground transport to make the cross- mountain trip, starting in two days time. In the meantime, we circled our wagons and made camp right where we were. So, I found my notebook and Old Mud and got the last verses down, down to the point where I knew sleep would come at last.

> *The Spirit Mother comes to me,*
> *Says never let your future be*
> *Just the product and the sum*
> *Of freedom and forever love,*
> *But all that was in the land of is.*

> *All that was in the land of is*
> *Was never hers and never his,*
> *But always was and will always be*
> *A god within who holds a key*
> *To an inside world where we are free.*

I would sing the song in Marana, I thought as I put the old boy to bed. But couldn't and didn't and will never. I was ambushed.

> *Atone for all the ailments of your arid algorithms.*

# Song 38

That night just after our dusk time meal, Kaya and I walked around the camp, stopping here and there to exchange pleasantries with those who had come out to enjoy the warmth that was rising out of the ground into the fast-cooling air. By the end of the hour, we would all head back to our trailers to take shelter from the frigid night. As we were walking, Ann Marie came running up behind, panting. She was holding out her vice which she handed to me when she caught up.

- You better look at this, Wicla.

- What is it?

- Just look.

She restarted the video that was playing across the screen. Kaya stood behind me and looked on. Someone had put a short doc of me together. It was only three minutes long but it was devastating. When it was over, Kaya stepped back from me.

- You bitch. You ugly fucking bitch.

Ann Marie grabbed my arm and pulled me away before Kaya could launch her claws at my face. She led me quickly back to my trailer, but as we made our way through the camp, crew and techies, many members of the band and others were opening the doors to their vehicles and stared down at me as I went by, some of them cat calling, one or two spitting at my heels. Get in, said Marie as she opened the door to my trailer. Once we were both in she pulled it closed behind her and bolted it.

- Did you know about this?

- The video? No.

- Where did it come from?

- I don't know. I don't know.

A small crowd gathered outside. We could hear angry voices. Angry comments. Someone banged on the door. We didn't answer. He banged louder.

- Go away, shouted Ann Marie.

- She needs to explain herself someone called out.

I pushed by Ann Marie and shook off her hand when she grabbed my coat. Then I opened the door and stood on the lintel looking down into the furious faces of my colleagues.

- It's not me! I said.

Everyone went silent for the moment.

- It sure as hell is you, said one of the crewmen.

I gathered my thoughts.

- I mean it is me, but it is not me. I don't feel that way…
  that doesn't represent my feelings.

- Fuck you, Wicla, came a voice from the back of the
  group.

- It speaks for itself, said one of the local women hired on
  to help with the cooking.

- Look… Somebody has put a lot of shit together. It's
  edited.

I stepped down from the vehicle and was quickly encircled,
but Ann Marie was behind me standing on the step and ready
to yank me in if things got out of hand.

- I don't know what's going on, but I will find out. Just,
  give me until dawn. This is bullshit.

It had become very cold. Our breaths were commingling
above our heads. It was cold enough they were willing to give
me the chance I had asked for.

- I will come to the cook tent at five o'clock, I promised.
  I'll have some answers.

They drifted off but I could hear their angry, frustrated grumbles and feel their sneers and head shakes even though their faces were turned away.

- It's OK, Ann Marie…

- You want to talk about it?

- No. I need to make a few calls. You go back to your trailer. I'll message you if I need anything.

I called Peter but could not get through. His vice was turned off. I reached his assistant at the Bank. She said he was at an all-day meeting in Berlin and had left strict orders that he was not to be interrupted even by me in an emergency.

- Tell him I'm pregnant.

- What?

- You heard me.

Fuck him. And fuck me because I had no where else to turn to. The video was moving like a wildfire around the Internet. Insiders were applauding. Outsiders were in a fury. Peter would learn soon enough, not that I was in some sort of trouble he could do nothing about, but that I was carrying his child, perhaps his son and heir, and things would start happening.

Dawn came. I did not want to face my friends and colleagues again. I had been up all night, re-playing the video over and over. It was me. I was saying things I remembered saying, in places I remembered being, to people who were listening to every word because, well, I was a celebrity of sorts. Wicla the Singer.

A light knock on the door. It was Ann Marie.

- Are you coming?

- No.

- You said you would talk to them.

- I can't.

- It will be worse if you don't.

I opened the door.

- C'mon. You can get through this.

The dining hall in the cook's tent was full. Ann Marie took me around back and we entered through the kitchen. Then Ann Marie nudged me through the door into the dining hall and over to a long table where a single chair was placed on one side facing into the now silent room. Ann Marie went to join the others. Before I sat down I looked around the room, taking a moment to look first into the faces of those who I knew best at the back of the room, then to those who were closer. That's when I saw, sitting on folding chairs down in front, three people I had never seen before. I stayed on my feet.

- I said last night that it wasn't me on that video. But of course, it was.

One of the strangers down front spoke up.

- I don't think there is any question it's you Ms Weer.

- And you are?

- Kent Broca. Bakersfield Online.

The media that had been kept far and away was now here.

- In the video, we see you living your new life on the Inside. CashCarter if I'm not mistaken.

- Yes.

- In one shot you're wearing a little black dress and singing love ballads to a pretty well-heeled crowd.

- Your point?

- Not quite the Outside life is it?

The woman next to him raised her hand.

- Yes.

- Babs Wawa. I'm with Hive Networks.

- One of the enemy then?

- Ms Weer, there are other shots with you coming out of a wedding chapel in CashCarter.

- I saw that.

- Can you tell us who your new husband is?

- He's not that new any more.

- That's Peter Benevolus is it not. So, you are now Mrs. Benevolus.

- I kept my name.

- He runs a private bank.

- Yes.

- He is reputed to be the richest man in the world.

The third man in the front row raised his hand then stood.

- Your husband's bank is sponsoring this tour?

- No.

- Yes. I think it is. They confirmed that earlier today.

- OK.

- His bank is the principal financing arm of Hive Corp.

- I guess so. I mean, it could be true.

- This tour was supposed to be in support of Outsiders.

- Well…I am.

- You are?

There was a shot of me talking to a reporter in Clinton when I was there a few months ago. He had accosted me on the promenade near the main square after laying in wait. He had lived in Portland some years ago and knew I was Wicla the Singer.

He had asked me how I like living in the biggest, richest hive of all. I said I loved it. When he asked me if I had any plans to return west and find a place on the Outside, I threw back my head and laughed then said Are you kidding? He asked me if it was true that Peter Benevolus had built a private dome on the edge of Clinton just for me. I showed a bit of embarrassment at the time, but admitted yes, but not just for me. For him too and who knows, maybe a family at some point. So, you wouldn't raise your kids on the Outside? Absolutely not. Would you? I asked him with a look of sarcastic incredulity on my beautifully made-up face, as I tossed my beautifully coiffed mane over my shoulder.

There were other clips contained in the vid too, and all of

them showing my disdain for the Outside world. The last shot was a few seconds of tape taken by someone at a party I had attended months earlier. A drunk man had trapped me in a corner.

- You used to sing for them Outsiders didn't you?

- Yes, I guess I did. Long time ago.

- Wicla the Singer right? I have you on my vice. Yeah. I still listen to it. Man, you can sing.

- Thanks. Isn't that your wife over there?

- She can wait.

- So, what do you think of them now?

- Who?

- The Outsiders. I mean their so-called army just killed your gay friends, right? Shot them in their beds and torched the place. It was on the news.

- Yes.

- So, what do you think of them now?

- I hate them. They should be tracked down and killed on the spot.

- That a girl.

- Excuse me.

I can be seen strong arming him and walking away, furious, but crying too. Halfway across the room I stopped and turned around.

- I hate them! I shouted.

And that was the last clip on the three-minute video. The female reporter was on her feet again.

- So, why did you come out here on tour? Why are you making believe you love these people?

The Bakersfield guy stayed in his seat but asked the last two questions. The ones that went to motive.

- Did you need the money that badly, Ms Weer? Do you and your husband not have enough?

I looked up into the metal cross beams that held the roof of the cook's tent up. Merri was standing up there holding on to the center pole looking down at me. She drew her finger across her lips, tightly closed, eyes daggering mine to make sure I understood. Say nothing more.

There was no more to be said anyway. Everyone filed out of the tent, including the press people and Ann Marie, who, despite everything wanted to sooth people's feelings toward me. Only Kaya remained. She spoke from the other end of the room.

- I won't be singing with you in Marana. Or anywhere. You got that?

I nodded. She left.

Motive? As in motive for the crime of singing? I went out there to sing because I was asked – told – to do it. No. That's not why I went on that tour. I could have dug my heels and refused. Wicla the wildcat could have pounced on her husband for treating her so despicably. I could have kept my legs closed and told him to treat me better if he wanted some more of what he wanted so badly. And, I would have, too, had I not harbored a secret desire to see the landscapes of the Outside world again, however devastated.

I knew that beneath the horrible clutter of manmade things strewn across the open country there lay a raw beauty, that in its choked and dwindled waterways clear water was still making its way seaward, that despite the sound of gunfire breaking, one could rise into birdsong. I knew that despite the threats of the threatened being yelled through their flimsy doors and breakable windows, the good in people was good enough. I wanted to go down some of those roads that Merri pioneered and that once I was born, Merri and I traveled together. But this time I wanted to go with the living memory of her riding alongside me, not with the near cadaver that put itself out of its own misery back in Tennessee.

I'm not the only one to be caught out saying things out of fear or rage or despondence or out of a momentary happiness and the kind of relief it - or its even happier cousin, joy - brings. Yes, one day, I compared my life of ease inside CashCarter with what I, what my mother especially, endured on the outside and, yes, I swore never to go out there again. It had burned me. Yes, I liked to wear that little black dress and diamond studs and high heels and sing to those people in the dim light of Polyphemus, a different creature than the girl who wore boots and denim while singing to her own kind, first in roadhouses and bars, then on valley stages in places like Napa.

I married a man because I found a way to love him, not because I wanted his money. I didn't and don't. I could not stop myself from hating those who so brutally killed my first fathers in that cabin to which my mother I had returned time and time again for sanity's sake. The Outside Army could never rationalize those murders to me or any other decent human, inside or out. How as a mother, could I want to raise my children on the outside and subject them to its manifold dangers and privations, especially now when it was losing so much ground to progress, or what I was convinced at that time, was progress?

I was guilty of a complex, inarticulate nostalgia, of self-pity in one of its many guises. Guilty of conflicted emotion and thought. Guilty of not thinking at all, when it came to thinking that going on that tour was all about singing, not about a visit back to my lost life and the lost lands I had criss-crossed with Trader Merri Weer, my mother, not about wanting to hear and feel the adulation of those crowds wash over me again and rinse me of the pain that the outside world had inflicted on me and everyone I knew. Guilty, guilty, guilty!

It took a long time before I came to realize that someone had read me exactly right, had made me bait, could make me wriggle on his hook to draw the big fish that lurked in the shadows of our troubled waters.

*A song will sing its singer into a sacred sanity.*

# Song 39

I was eight months pregnant when Peter told me that we had been invited to the White House to have lunch with the President and Paul Munro. While I was carrying the twins – by this time we knew we would soon welcome a boy and girl into our world – I had lain the portable grudge I had once so conscientiously maintained against that woman against the garden wall, or some other place around the house that I couldn't quite remember. It came back to me instantly as soon as Peter's words fell out of his smiling, hope-to-please-you mouth. He too had forgotten my bitter feelings, and had forgotten his own dislikes too, because now that she was a spent force, she no longer animated his grievances against her or her government. His mentor, Paul, was now firmly in charge, paving the road to heaven with golden bricks. Peter needed to see Paul and it was Paul who issued the invitation.

Peter thought the whole thing a happy occasion. It was the first time he had been back to the White House since the Firsts had been kidnapped from Castle Forbes. Cora Munro had blamed Peter, even though the policemen she had assigned the task of proving Peter had been the brains and money behind the operation, could never make her charges stick. Her unreasonable doubt about his character never mounted to a conviction and so for him, at least, this meant that even for her he stood acquitted.

It wasn't true. It was just how his mind worked. Whoever

had snatched them out of their bed had never been found, let alone brought to justice, so in the absence of another villain, Cora Munro never let go of her belief in Peter's ultimate guilt. I thought she was as deluded in that as she was in her belief that Clement Samuels defence of his right to the magic crystal of which the new world was made was traitorously criminal. So, my husband and my father stood together, locked in side-by-side pillories, on the hard ground of her puritanic mind.

I said I wouldn't go to the lunch. He could go if he wished. But I really only wanted to be persuaded so I could claim that I had overcome my scrupulous resentments toward Cora Munro. People admire those who have a talent for forgiveness.

We arrived at the appointed hour and were ushered into the private reception room on the second floor of the White House by Ms Soldipence, Cora's sleek private secretary. Paul entered shortly after and came to me first for kisses on both cheeks (how prim, I thought, considering the way we once sweated in one another's embrace) and then to Peter, with hand outstretched for the ritual handshake. But Paul used his grip on Peter's hand to pull him in for a quick embrace and a slap on the shoulder. Peter endured it well, which was a measure of his affection for Paul, because no other person would have been allowed to get so close. Well, me, when he wanted sex.

A bit of small talk to pass the time until Cora Munro entered the room, so silently as to have been unnoticed until she came to a halt almost beside us where we stood looking out the window into the Rose Garden. I was shocked to see how emaciated and pale she looked. And then she addressed us with a thin and reedy voice.

- Peter. It has been a long time.

Shake of hands.

- And you, Mrs. Benevolus. I know you, of course. Your songs carried me to my first victory.

- She goes by her maiden name, Madame President, said Paul.

- Oh. I'm not sure I ever knew it. You were always called Wicla the Singer. In those days you were.

- It's Weer, ma'am, I said. But please just call me Wicla.

- You're still singing?

- Wicla just returned from a successful tour in the west, Cora, said Paul.

- I wouldn't call it a success, Ma'am, I, we…

- They had a bit of trouble. Their caravan was attacked by the OA.

- Oh yes. I heard. They have been put down though, is that right?

- That's right, dear, said Paul.

- I doubt if they will trouble us again, added Peter.

- Trouble us? Cora said. Hmm...

Cora was 70 years old now. The same age as her husband. She wore a red, sleeveless dress. Single strand of pearls around her neck. Two small pearl earrings. Black high heels. Gold bracelet that would have dropped off her thin wrist had she let her hand drop to her side, which she didn't. Her dark hair, now streaked with silver, was cut to fall just so on her thin shoulders. Her face was gaunt, so her large black eyes sat beside her thin, delicate nose in their sunken sockets, bulbous behind heavy lids when she closed them, which she did when others were talking.

When she talked to you, her eyes opened and sparkled with a fleeting liveliness, but if she forgot what she wanted to say, or suddenly decided that what she had to say was unimportant, or might be boring, they dimmed, and she turned inward. Paul would pick up the conversation almost immediately and re-direct it to some engaging topic or other.

In Cora, I saw intimations of my mother in those days after she had learned from her Ojai doctor that she had cancer but had not yet told anyone. My feelings softened toward Cora Munro, but I kept my shoulders squared, because I did not want to lose sight of my mission. I would confront her about my father's death in prison; about the things she did to provoke the Outsider Army to murder Lawrence and Javier; about the promises she made to the Outsider communities but had not kept. But how to inject that into the news-of-the-day conversation that the men were having between themselves? I couldn't bring myself to do it.

After dessert, Paul suggested that Cora give me a short tour of their quarters, at least the historical rooms. Cora fired a look of displeasure at him because he knew she would rather have just said her goodbyes and retreat to her bedroom. But she would not allow herself to be so graceless as to refuse, so off we went while Peter and Paul went into the reception room for brandy and jokes. Jokes on all of us.

We walked into rooms and down corridors and as we went Cora pointed out various paintings and other *objet d'art*, showed me various bedrooms named for Presidents who had lived there during the previous three hundred years or so, including Lincoln's Bedroom. He had not slept there, but it had been his office, she said, clearly bored of traipsing around with the wife of an enemy, She treated herself like a past-her-prime, forgotten minor celebrity. But there we were in Lincoln's Bedroom. Honest Abe, I thought. If not now, when?

\- Madame President... I, uh...

She stepped into the room toward me and stopped as though the voice of someone new had elevated her, even by a fraction. She looked with her baleful eyes into mine.

\- I have something to say.

I hesitated. She challenged, but with an open spirit.

\- Say it.

I took one step toward her and I took the dare to look as

directly at her as she was at me.

- Clement Samuels was my father.

Pause.

- Was he? Well, you know, I am sorry about what happened.

- Sorry?

- Of course. I didn't want him to die in prison.

- With respect, Ma'am, you hounded him and had him locked up.

- Your father didn't defend himself. He pled guilty.

- That's not true.

- It is, Wicla. No one expected that. We thought we might find a way to sit down with him and…

Cora walked to an oil painting on the wall near the bed. The picture of a family. Then she turned to face me again. Her eyes had welled-up.

- It should just never have happened. I could have done things differently. I should have.

- What?

- I think your father was a good man, Ms Weer. Now I do. Not then, of course. It's one of those things that I did that were based on miscalculations. All mine. I am profoundly sorry. Perhaps one day you will forgive me.

I was speechless. She walked back to where I was standing, now with tears flooding my own eyes.

- What happened out west, Ms Weer? A few months ago?

- It's a long story.

- Paul and Peter won't miss us, and even if they do they won't find us.

She walked to the door and closed it, then bid me sit on the chair by the night table, then sat herself on the edge of Lincoln's bed.

- It's all connected you know, she said.

- What is, Ma'am?

- You went by caravan from Visalia to Marana in Arizona. Right?

She was the President, so she had access to any information she wanted to have. She had studied the tour itinerary.

- Yes. I am surprised you know.

- Don't be. Your caravan was attacked by the Outsider Army at a little place called Chiriaco Summit. What you probably didn't know is that one of the OA's principal hideouts was in the old national park just to the north, Joshua Tree.

- I didn't know that.

- No, you wouldn't have. But there was no way you were going to pass by that park without running into trouble.

- What? Why?

- Because you were meant to run into trouble.

- I don't understand.

- I think you were set-up. You were made a target. Think about it.

- But the attack. It wasn't really an attack. I mean we heard gunfire off in the distance, but they never got near the caravan.

- Of course not. The OA was ambushed.

- They were ambushed.

- They were led into a trap. Someone inside their ranks was actually undercover for the government. Someone inside your crew, maybe a band member, was undercover for the OA. They were played.

- I was used? Are you saying that I was purposefully...?

- Made to look like a hypocrite, a traitor to the Outsider cause.

She leaned over and whispered. Her eyes were wide open. A bit of spit on the corners of her mouth.

- The OA wanted to make an example of you. The government's inside man egged them on. He was close to the leadership by then. Whoever was working for the OA in your camp was giving them info about when you would be where, which trailer was yours, info about the security arrangements around you, which was almost nothing.

- I have never heard anything about this.

- You heard that some of the leaders of the OA were killed. That was on the news.

- Yes, but...

She leaned in further and lowered her voice even more.

- You didn't hear the whole story because you weren't meant to hear it. The OA did come out of hiding and were going to strike at Chiriaco. But they got clobbered by a team of Specials. About fifty men and women – all the leadership included – were killed. Some of them in the short battle, yes. But I think most of them were executed on the spot. She pointed her finger at her head like a gun.

- Bang, bang. No more OA.

- I'm glad, I said.

But I wasn't glad at all. It was a massacre. I couldn't believe what I was hearing.

- You said it was all connected? To my father. He has been dead a long time, Ma'am.

- Oh, yes. Door nail dead. Peter's father mourned him. They were close. Paul gave the eulogy. But with Clement Samuels gone, the way was open to Peter Benevolus Senior to take Crysalinks and use it as for a much bigger and different purpose than your father ever imagined but would have put a stop to had he lived. I'm convinced of that now. Peter Junior is following in his father's footsteps.

- What purpose? What are we talking about?

There was a knock on the door. It opened. Paul walked in with Peter in tow.

- Shit! Said Cora under her breath.

- Ah, here you are, you two, said Paul.

- I've slept here before, Wicla. It isn't a comfortable mattress, but so what? You can't sleep in here knowing that Mr. Lincoln is snoring right beside you.

- He never slept here, Peter, said Cora.

- Well…maybe not.

- What are you two gabbing about? asked Paul.

- History, said Cora. Past, present and future.

- You couldn't have a better teacher, said Paul.

- I came to get you dear; we have to get going. I have a meeting in Clinton to get to.

Dear. That rang hollow.

The two men walked ahead. Cora and I walked behind a few paces. She stopped me and wanted to say something to me but Paul, now at the top of the grand staircase, called out and waved us to him. He was moving things along. He realized his wife was confiding in me. Peter saw it too.

- Wicla. Time's wasting dear. Let's leave these busy people to their duties.

517

I started to walk away from her, but she caught my sleeve and turned me to face her so they could not see her face.

- I will be the last President Wicla, she said. America has been killed.

By this time, Peter was beside me.

- Thanks for the lunch, Madame President. It has been a privilege to come back here again.

- Well, I loved meeting your wife, Peter. Treat her and the baby well.

- Babies, I said.

- Sorry, I haven't even remembered that since we ate dessert. Twins, of course. Well, thank you for sharing your experience with me, Wicla. Looking back, I wish I had popped a couple.

Cora made it sound as though we had been talking girl talk, which, when Cora patted my tummy, the boys seemed to take that for granted.

In the limo on the way to the Hyperloop station in Washington I sat silently with my head against the window.

- So, did you say what you wanted to say to her?

- I tried to.

- She stopped you?

- Yes. But not how you think.

- How?

- She asked for my forgiveness.

- Really? And are you ready to do that?

- I don't know yet.

- Me either, he said. Your father was the greatest man that ever walked on planet earth and she…. Well, she got her comeuppance. Maybe we can let it go now.

I had just seen my mother lurking within the frame of Cora Munro's body. Saw her there behind Cora's eyes, saw her in her gaunt face, her long thin arms, the stooped shoulders, all the spindled leftovers of a once strong, vibrant life. Merri was trying to get me to see deeper. See what?

Peter turned to look out the other window as we passed the Supreme Court building. I'm all for justice, he said. But my thoughts were elsewhere. Who had set me up?

*Murky mirrors magnify the manifestation of our manipulations.*

# Song 40

A month later, the twins were born, but at our home in Clinton, not at the hospital. Peter converted a large room off the kitchen into a sterilized birthing suite and assembled a large medical team of specialists to attend the birth, more for the babies' sake than mine, I assure you. During the birth, which lasted almost twenty hours from the time I went into labor until Scola, and then Bened, were pulled out into the crowded, overheated room, Peter stood by completely absorbed by the process, arms crossed, sometimes rocking on his heels. Absorbed but unemotional. He did not touch me or say a word to me the whole time.

Once the babies were born, Peter waited while the gynecologist checked them, counting fingers and toes and such. He seemed please when he pronounced them hale and hearty, well-formed and splendid in every way, but Peter did not look like he was quite ready to accept the doctor's opinion. Peter had always been a studiously untrusting man, an unremitting skeptic.

When the chuckling, happy head nurse came to present Bened, Peter took him but held him out from his body, not quite sure what to do. He looked at Bened's face searchingly hoping to find clues to the boy's personality, but the baby's squint eyes, flat, flared nose and toothless mouth yielded nothing to Peter's augury. He managed only to bestow a faint, half smile on his son, doubtful that he would grow into the heir he wanted him to be. But that was it for the benedictions. He handed Bened back to the nurse then walked out of the room. No welcome to the world for Scola, no thanks to me, no kiss even on my forehead.

The nurse brought the babies to me and laid them in the crooks of my arms.

- He's just scared, she said.

- Fuck him, I replied.

- Yeah, fuck him, she said with a wink.

- Never again, I said.

- I wouldn't, she said, fluffing my pillows.

I was almost forty-three at the time and very unsure whether my mothering instincts were strong enough to do all that I wanted to do - and should do - to raise Bened and Scola. I did well enough, I suppose, but more time will have to go by before the final verdict is in. Even before I did what I did, they both treated me with a sarcastic disdain. Batty old mother that I was. Batty and aggravated most of the time, a woman who seemed to have more affection for the orchids she cultivated in the green house than for them or their heroic father; a woman who lavished more attention and time on her watercolors than on their long list of teenage grievances toward a world that had denied them nothing. They worried a little about my tippling, but they were never around when I descended into the drunken madness that the servants had to endure (and duly report to the master of the house).

Scola shows signs of forgiveness; Bened, for now at least, wonders why Themis has not come to swing her sword at my neck. The reason for that will be explained to him – to both of them - in due course. They will learn that the running of empires requires emperors and empresses to apply the recondite lessons of Machiavelli, not the simple admonishments of the Ten Commandments. By the time they were in their late teens, I could see that the business their father had left behind had grown to such a size - and had become so complex - that it would have to be divided in some way.

It turns out that giving birth to twins, a genetic accident in our case, had a certain, magical rightness to it. Peter had wanted a son and heir – a little boy made in his own image – but by the time of his death he knew that Scola was as smart, tough and aggressive as her brother, probably more so. He could figure her into his future-making in the same way he had always done with Bened. It meant of course that he imposed his demands on Scola as much as his son, that he had to come between Scola and me as much as between me and Bened. The soft, sweet, compassionate, always forgiving ways I had bestowed upon them when they were toddlers became problematic – for Peter, that is - as they started their schooling.

Peter wasn't around often at any time, but when he was, he was a pounder of tables and a scolder of the first rank. He wanted, demanded and got a kind of perfection from them that manifested itself in their elementary education as fast-learned times tables, multilingual alphabets that could be recited top to bottom and bottom to top, answers to profound scientific questions (why is the sky blue, why is the sea salty etc), and answers to historical, geographic, and literary questions so varied they even dizzied me.

They had to have good table manners, dress well, and learn how to comport themselves in the company of the august souls to whom they were often introduced. He left detailed instructions in his last will and testament concerning their on-going education in the event of his early demise, never really suspecting that he would die as young as he did, but as a matter of care and caution. So now, as I said earlier, Bened and Scola are off to their respective colleges for the finishing-off. Then they will join the family business that they inherited, and someday will superintend, looking down their haughty noses.

When I was laying in the birthing bed, sweating through the wrenching pain of the contractions that were forcing the reluctant twins into the overlapping worlds in which their parents lived, I thought of my own birth at Fort Ketchup. The specialists who were called to attend my mother were specialists in surviving hard times, brave women who took solace in the company of other women, who ordered their day around the getting and preserving of life's necessities, who salved their wounds with kindness, who coaxed the lost back from the wilderness by giving them a community in which to grieve their losses and misfortunes, who used music and song to plumb the depths of their humanity and express their joy.

I gripped the bedsheets with my fisted hands and endured the pain – Peter said no anaesthetic for me because the drugs might dull the children – and I worked it out so that when these two children dropped into the doctor's waiting hands, I would be born again too, that I would drop once again into

Cladine's hands, and be wakened by the fast, sharp slap she would give my infant body to make sure that I was alive and could make the noise of life. I would sing again someday. Write new songs again.

Anyway, life went on. We had a kind of family. I am grateful for that. I am. I kept up with the news and knew that Peter had a big hand in many of the very big things, the momentous things that were going on. He was a kind of genius, really, and despite the fact that he didn't treat me well, he didn't treat me badly either. Despite the fact that he was tough on his children, he loved them, and they sniffed his love as they sniffed back their tears. I had a weird pride in what he was doing, an admiration bordering on envy for his way of doing things. He was confident. He had certitude. He knew how to command. His mind was capable of mastering both big ideas and complex detail.

When he was at home, which was rarely, we would all have dinner in the dining room. He would involve the children in discussions of world affairs even when they were very young. I was not really invited to participate, it being assumed I had no interest, which was not true. He would tell them about how the new world was being architected and engineered, how hives and hyperlinked transportation networks had saved human-kind from extinction and were delivering it into a new era that would last a thousand years – longer if, when they grew up, they were to use their God-given talents to keep pushing its frontiers forward.

I remember the evening he leaned forward over his plate and told the kids that their grandfathers had built the foun-dations upon which all of us were now living our lives on the

Inside and not out there – he lifted his hand and pointed to an abstract 'out there' while he held their rapt gazes, out there on the dirt, out there under the poisoning sun. He reminded them of it frequently.

I used to joke to the kids that their father ran the world and Peter, when the children looked at him with their eyes bugged out, would say your mother is just being silly. Silly as I always was, a trader in trivia, is what he meant. But it turned out it was true. He *was* running the world and I just didn't know it. I mean, I knew he was a big player, but I had no idea that he was the biggest, or that there was a biggest, really. There are eight billion people on the planet and more than a few now in outer space, so who would ever think that the mortal at the head of your own table, the elegantly severe man who pushes peas onto his fork with his thumb, is the grandest poohbah of all?

Let us cut now, to use a filmmaker's word, to the next scene.

In the house, there is a small room, my study, that I call my own. It is only accessible from my bedroom. No husband, no kids allowed. Old Mud leans back a little in a guitar holder in a corner near the window looking out over the lawns toward the Hudson. He has not been plucked upon for a good many years. There is a plush sofa where I can stretch out, a reading chair with lamp beside it, a worktable upon which one of my vices sits.

I usually just use my hand held to keep in touch with people or to check the news, but from time to time I check things online to take advantage of a larger screen. A wall to ceiling shelf has a few books I have scrounged out of antique stores – I like the feel of books in my hand - but it also holds all the note-books I've used over the years to jot down lyrics and musical notations as well as observations I've made about this and that.

One day when the kids were about four, but off somewhere with their nannies, I could tell from the light outside the parlor windows that it was raining under a dense, overcast sky above the hive. I was tired, but I didn't want to go back to bed, so I went to my study thinking I might just lay down on the sofa and nap. I tried, but I was as restless as I was bored. At some point, I switched on the table vice and started rummaging around the online world, touching down here and there, not really focused on anything in particular. I heard a small chime and a window opened on the computer in front of the news story I was reading. Hello was typed into the text area but I saw no identification. I thought it might be a friend, so I typed hello back and who is this?

That initial hello-hello exchange was the beginning of a very long conversation that took place over the next few days, which was surprising because the first few messages were the most chilling I had ever had in my life. Who ever it was made threats to kill my husband, me and the two children.

- Your husband will pay for what he is doing to my country.

- Your country? What country?

- You should know shouldn't you? How can you not know?

- I don't know.

- Croatia, for godsake, you privileged bitch.

\- I don't know anything about it. I am just his wife.

\- Tell your husband we can get to you.

I stopped typing. A long minute went by. Then I typed again.

\- Why?

A few seconds passed.

\- Tell him.

\- No.

\- Then you will all die.

\- I don't think so.

I knew how impenetrable our lives were. More time passed.

\- Tell me what he has done.

He sent me a link to an online site, then he or she disconnected. I clicked the link. Hive Corp. was building a dome over a place called Dubrovnik in Croatia, the first of many planned for that country. A deal had been reached with the Croatian government. But the scheme was massively unpopular. There had been some violence. A resistance movement had formed; many resisters had been killed, many others thrown in jail and others had fled to the nearby mountains and were waging a guerilla war against their own government and against Hive Corp. It was a familiar story to me, another Outsider rebellion.

The person who contacted me was a young resistance fighter. He decided to answer all my questions, believing, as he hid in his lonely mountain redoubt, that the sympathy I expressed to him and his people was genuine. It was. But I think he must have convinced himself that that I could prevail upon my husband to abandon Croatia.

- My husband's bank might be financing the project....

- It is.

- Hive Corp. would just find other financing.

- Why would they?

- What do you mean? I asked.

- Your husband *is* Hive Corp.

- No, he just finances some of their projects.

- That is a lie.

- No. It's true, I said.

- It is not true. He controls all of Hive Corp.

I heard a loud knock at my bedroom door. I heard Peter's

voice.

- My husband is coming. Bye.

Peter opened the door and called my name. Then he rushed across the bedroom and entered my study just as I was turning off the vice.

- You have been chatting with a man.

- Yes. I guess he's a man.

- It's a man named Root. Reedl Root. Do you know who he is? Why are you talking to him?

He booted up my vice.

- Do you know who he is? he asked, his voice rising.

- How did you know?

- Know what? Said angrily.

- That I was chatting.

- It doesn't matter how I know. I know.

Peter searched for the messenger app, found it and then poked around. The record of the conversation that I had with Reedl Root was gone.

- He deleted the thread. Never mind, my people can get it back.

- What's going on, Peter?

- He's an evil man, Wicla.

- Reedl said you control Hive Corp.

- He's a liar. How long have you been talking to him?

- Three days off and on. Why?

- What did he tell you?

- He said that Hive Corp. had bribed the Croatian government and was taking over the country.

- That's preposterous.

- Do you run Hive Corp., Peter?

- I'm a financier. Root is a dangerous man.

He lifted the table vice off the table and was about to carry it away.

- Stop! Don't you dare.

He saw a hard look on my face that he had never seen before

530

and decided he could cut-off Root's access to me by other means.

- Just stay out of the business. Are we clear on that?

- Whatever you say.

He walked out my rooms and disappeared for a week. Longer.

I heard from Reedl Root only once again about three years later. But throughout that period, I tried to get as much information as I could about the bloody goings on in Croatia – or what was Croatia before it was forcibly merged with neighboring countries into the Adriatic States. Things got much worse for the resistance – now called the insurgency - and I always wondered if Reedl had been killed along with the other three hundred thousand or so who perished. But he surfaced again a couple of years ago when he led an attack on a military installation on the moon where he was killed trying to loosen Hive Corp's grip on his now lost country by turning his oppressor's weapons on themselves. But before he departed for his fated, lunar death he sent me a document that sent planet Earth into a new orbit.

Shortly after Root was killed, Peter had his day of reckoning too.

*The riptide rips beneath the reach of ridicule.*

# Song 41

Yes, it was three years later. It is a long time in the life of children, but for the rest of us time is horribly contracted. It goes by too quickly, most of it filled with the humdrum of daily life no matter how rich you are, but in three years there will be moments that are so poignant, joyful or upsetting they can never be erased from memory, events that will propel you back in time to revisit and re-edit your past, then whiplash you back through a present moment as they gather force and shoot you into the starscape of the unseen future, full of hope or dread as the case may be.

I know how dark my story has become. But the point of the telling is to get at what happened and why, not to make a slide show of all the happy times I spent with the kids, with friends, traveling the world, sometimes just Peter and me, sometimes with the children. We saw much of the Outside world, planning our itineraries on a New Time basis for mountain climbs by torchlight, beach holidays under Crysalinks canopies, nighttime cruising along forgotten coastlines, treks across the stubbornly remaining ice at both poles to gawk at glaciers cracking and falling into emerald colored water. There was not a part of the world Peter did not have access to, although he kept us away from all the conflict zones and hot spots where people were killing or being killed in the name of their some-times-indecipherable causes.

We went to some of the great cities of the old world too,

London, Rome, Paris, Tokyo, Sydney, Vancouver (at last), Bangkok, Beijing and many more where the architecture of the past, their mounting ruins and the intractable violence and despair that was enfolded into their streets and avenues fired the imagination - and sometimes the terror - of the children especially. Our bulletproof limos and the retinues of security people who always travelled with us kept us safe.

We also traveled to many of the Hive cities, usually when Peter had to visit on business. While he attended to that, the children and I enjoyed cataloguing the idiosyncrasies of each place. I marvelled how some of the earliest built cities continued to transform and grow as new domes were aggregated on to the old. The network of hives multiplied, not just at home, but abroad, to accommodate the millions who were eager to forsake their lives Outside.

After the argument in my study when Reedl Root had contacted me, I rarely questioned Peter again about his business dealings. Whether he was involved in Hive Corp. or not or was, as he said, just a financier, did not matter in those days. Despite our strange, arm's length marriage, his humorless personality and the rages that would overcome him from time to time, I was proud of him. He no longer imposed on me for sex, which was fine by me, and whether he had a mistress or two parked away somewhere was of no moment. In truth, I could not imagine that he had any desire for any woman.

Lest you think I was completely blind to what was going on in the world - the insalubrious things let's call them - let me assure you I was as sensitive as I ever was. During those three years, as before and as after, things in the Outside world were tumbling out of their rightful places, like gargoyles falling off the corners of ancient cathedrals, or monuments collapsing on their plinths. But no surprise there, however sad it is to think of what might have been or could have been had we not fouled the human nest. These old buildings and testaments were mostly unattended and like any man-made thing, could not expect to remain in place ad infinitum. Ask the Phoenicians, Carthaginians, Greeks and Romans whether their lamentations were an antidote to the exhaustion of their empires.

The bits and pieces of the collapsing world would pile up and in the fullness of time would become buried by the dirt and dust carried in the immemorial wind. I remembered the time I drove through old Las Vegas while Merri slept in the back of the van. I remembered Ozzy Mandis's statute laying broken on the desert floor beneath the shattered casinos where he used to sing. And maybe it was that memory that made me realize that it was not just mankind's physical world – the Outside world – that was coming apart, but something deeper, something in and of the human spirit. I just could not put my finger on it.

On occasion, I picked up Old Mud and took him to the sofa with me where I had laid my notepad and a pen, and I plucked at him and scratched at it, but they would yield nothing in the way of insight, let alone, let me find any kind of truth. The truth of my singular detachment, the depression that kept the world at bay, and the soft, untroubled life I was living in the bubble Peter had installed me and the children in was not within their ken.

Then as the summer was almost upon us, the summer when Bened and Scola would celebrate their seventh birthdays came near I decided that we would mark their day in a big way, even though their seventh was no more significant than any of their previous birthdays. I got excited about planning a party for them, something in the garden by the pool overlooking the river. Their friends would come, of course, but also their friends' parents and other friends of Peter's and mine. He was exhausted by work and a day like that would be a tonic. Yes, I thought, I will do it, not just for the children, but for him, a happy, family affair.

When I told Peter about my big idea one evening when he was home, he said no, not possible. The annual summit of his top business associates was already scheduled for Castle Forbes and could not and would not be cancelled to accommodate a birthday party for children. In fact, he was cross with me for not remembering his annual event, an event that his father had invented and that had become an inviolable tradition. My office keeps you informed of my schedule, does it not? I hope, he said, you didn't raise the children's expectations and put me in an ill light?

What do you do with that? That kind of slap? All the crockery you have already flung in your husband's face has been swept-up and tossed down the rubbish chute to be pulverized to a fine sand. That which remains is too precious to waste on one more argument you can't win. You turn your back. You walk away. You go to your room and dab the hurt-pride tears that you will not show him. You sit on the side of your bed and you sob a little and pull yourself together.

As low bent as you feel, you will rise into the body of the proud chatelaine you are, hold your head up on your long neck and continue to run your household so your maids and kitchen help and nannies marvel at your undaunted spirit. You will answer the cheerful banter of your children with encouragements and praise. You will stay out of the rooms where your husband makes himself busy, not talk to him, scorn his unfeeling, selfish self, withhold the little dollop of love that is settled like a fat bead of holy water in your bile.

And when he comes to you later, as Peter did that night, to squeak out an apology for being so thoughtless, you will be as surprised as I was because he had never done it before. He knocked on my bedroom door and slowly pushed it open before entering. He put his head in first and asked if he could enter.

- I know I hurt your feelings, Wicla. I...I, um, I want to apologize.

- Thank you.

- Look, I know you had your heart set on doing something for the kids.

- It's their seventh birthday.

- Yes, I know. Well, look, when I had my seventh birthday I was with my father. At the Castle.

- And he forgot?

- No. No. Quite the contrary. He made a big deal of it. He had Mrs. Glastonbury make a huge cake. She cooked up all the things I liked. Then at dinner time, he had the local pipers pipe it in on silver trays. Mrs. G. carried the cake in a big silver salver for later revelation. There must have been two dozen candles burning on it. Then Jock Glastonbury and the grounds keepers and maintenance people and everyone's wives and husbands followed in. They all sang happy birthday and cheered as I blew out the candles. Mind, it took me three big puffs. Then my father stood and poured a glass of good brandy for all – except me of course – I had a soft drink, I guess – and he proposed a cheer. Here's to the birthday boy! And everyone downed their drinks and sang Auld Lang Syne. I think it was the happiest I'd ever been, really.

- So, quite a production.

- Yeah, it was. So, you see, Wicla, all of that just came to me and now I'm feeling quite badly really because I...

- I understand.

- But, I have an idea. Let's see how you feel about this.

We would all go to Castle Forbes two or three days before his summit and spend family time. Even though the birthday party would just be the family, we'd do something along the lines of the party he had when he was seven. Then, the kids and I would go off to our Paris apartment while he stayed at the Castle for the gathering of his clan. Once that was done, he would join us for another couple of days at the seaside.

- I would like to show them the British Museum in

London too. Maybe Westminster and the Parliament buildings and, oh, I know, a tour of the underground where Cora and Paul Munro were kept. I hear they made it into quite an exhibit.

- Of course, whatever you like. All can be arranged.

- The kids would like that, Peter.

- So, we have a deal?

- Deal.

He leaned over me where I lay in my bed and kissed me warmly on my forehead. Sleep well, he said, then left me to deal with the sore feelings that were still holding onto my thoughts even as they succumbed to the pleasant sensation he had planted on my brow.

That's how it came to be that we were all at Castle Forbes that summer. But between the night when the plan was set in motion and the day the children and I left to hydroloop from Clinton to London, word came of one more tragedy and one more sad event.

The sad event was the passing of Cora Munro. She was only seventy-two or three. Something like that. After her last term of office was over, almost two years ago, she had virtually disappeared from public view. We saw news clips of her and Paul on the day they left the White House. She was frail as she walked out to a waiting limo, holding onto Paul's arm to steady herself. He seemed very solicitous of her and walked her with great care to the car where he helped her get in. Only after the door was closed and Cora became a dark shadow behind the tinted window did he step back to the gaggle of reporters to answer questions on his and her behalf. It was no secret by then that he was acting as de facto President, especially in her last year in Office.

- It really is the beginning of a new era. Cora seems to have lived here forever. To the manner born. But it's time for her us to let her unburden herself.

- Will Mrs. Munro remain active in politics, Sir?

- Cora just wishes to retire after years of service to the country, said Paul. I'm taking her to our new home in California. But don't be surprised to see a couple of books emerge out of Casa Munro as time goes by. Cora has a long memory and a few scores to settle.

A few laughs.

- What about you, Sir? Isn't it time for you to retire too?

- I would love to retire, but the Constitutional Convention is deadlocked. The issues seem trivial to me, but they seem to have excited the partisans on the other side who are using every means possible to obstruct the proceedings. So, it's no time for me to abandon the people's work. Cora would rather have me with her, and I would rather be with her, but she knows I have to carry on.

So, you'll have me around for awhile to kick around, to paraphrase a previous resident of this house.

A few more laughs.

- Some people say you are the problem, Mr. Vice President.

- Those are the people who don't want to accept reality. But enough of the negative talk for today. We've got a proverbial plane to catch. I'll be back early next week to carry on the work. Thank you all for coming to see Cora off.

And away they went. Two years later, Cora died. Food poisoning, they said. Cremation, private burial. No media coverage. Her wish, not Paul's, they said.

And guess what? The Constitutional Convention in old Philadelphia has remained deadlocked the whole time. To this day, in fact. The delegates from every state of the Union and all the Senators and Representatives who had been elected prior to its convening still sit there from time to time deliberating the big questions on their collective plate. And Paul Munro, by prior agreement of the convention and the Congress of the United States who suspended all elections until the new Constitution is ratified and adopted, remains our effective Head of State, called the Vice President to avoid having to deal with the fact he was foreign born.

With just about everyone living in hive cities and domed towns, the old Constitution became an unworkable clunker. The heavy hitters of all national parties said a new and different Constitution had to be devised to govern the reality – as Paul

Munro called it - in which we all now live. It was thought it would take a year to write it assuming good will on everyone's parts. The Outsiders' spokespeople and just about all the States raised a ruckus; they said the entire Constitutional Convention itself was unconstitutional and they have been pursuing and pushing a reference to the Supreme Court, but Court says the political people really ought to work things out first if they can.

Dry stuff, right? Yes, for most. So dry that when you ask people what they think about it, they treat these grave constitutional matters and the talking heads who cannot stop nattering about it like they do dust on their furniture. They blow it off. The fact is that almost none of the people who now live inside have cared one way or another about the outcome of the deliberations - or non-deliberations as some wags call them. Politics thrives on conflict, real or manufactured, and anyone who lives on the Inside will tell you that apart from the usual crap that mars people's lives, they live conflict free. Life is good.

I am – was – one of the multitudes when it came to these allegedly profound concerns, but because Cora Munro said what she did when she took me aside after our chat in Lincoln's Bedroom, the longer that Convention met without arriving at a new Constitution, the harder it was for me to not have her words wriggle in some corner of my conscious mind or niggle at my conscience. I will be the last President, she said. America has been killed, she said.

Back then I thought she was a bit mad. In all the time after, I thought, well, she may have been prophetic, but only in the sense that, she would be the last holder of the Office of the President as we had always known it. The world we lived in then did not exist anymore. The office would be redefined and would welcome someone new to sit on the throne newly made.

These thoughts occupied my mind for maybe a second or two now and then over the years following Cora's departure for California. So, let's make that clear. I can't think of one time when I saw her in any news story once she left Washington. Paul, white-haired, dignified, good natured as always, was in the news a lot, however, but hardly ever in any story out of California, so their marriage was a marriage in name only by the time of her death. Last time I saw him was against the backdrop of a new hive being put up to bubble Washington – something Cora never let happen on her watch. This place needs to be preserved, Paul said to the cameras, looking at the plenitude of monuments and buildings around him, all so familiar, but all now sitting heavy as history on the green lawns of a past time.

As conflicted as I remained about the woman, I felt an ineffable sadness when word of her death was announced. I had watched my mother shrink and dwindle as the cancer ate her, and I knew that something had chewed-up Cora too. I knew I must take great care to preserve myself against all the forces that prey on women, because while some of them might be vanquished through an angry uprising or by lashing an offender with an excoriating tongue, and while others might be turned away or even done to death with laughing scorn, still others are cunning, baffling and powerful. They will wait us out. They are hard enough not to feel or worry about our counterblows. Those forces will overwhelm our defences and lay us low.

Where I used to see my mother hiding in the curtains, or shimmering in my own reflection in a window, or floating above me with fingers wagging, I came to realize by the time

Bened and Scola were five, six and seven that she had taken up residence inside me. Sometimes she guided me to do the very best I could be with my children, but other times, when I should have confronted Peter about the way he treated me, and them, she had me beating a retreat, as though I could step up into our van and peel away down some road where he was sure not to follow.

Was that courage or cowardice? I was never sure. I knew I had to find out. But first, I had to deal with the horrible fact of Kaya's murder, of Titus's awful words when I called him to say how sorry I was to hear what had befallen her.

*The tricky tomb tintinnabulates its tick and tock.*

# Song 42

Outsider resistance against the encroachments of the hive cities and domed towns more or less collapsed across the west after the failed attack at Chiriaco Summit. The Outsider Army was finished as a force that could threaten Hive Corp. and so too were the politicos of the movement because the defeat of the OA had cost them the leverage they claimed never to have had.

Peter had seen to it that Hive Corp. had all the money it needed to proceed immediately with the building of five new hive cities, one near Chicago at last, one near the almost completely Asian city of San Francisco, and one on the high ground above destroyed LA. Bakersfield would be left to rot where it stood while its people moved into a hive ten miles to the west. But the biggest hive of them all would consume the slums of El Cajon and would, in the fullness of time, impose law and order on the entire area north of the Mexican border. Another twenty-five towns throughout the west would be domed. The undomed towns would simply fall apart as wind and weather and rust and bugs made a meal of them. Peter bragged that it was the largest single building program ever undertaken since, well, he didn't know since when. Since forever, he declaimed.

All the new works would be connected by hyperloop and a half dozen autodrive highways built on the crumbled roads that still wended there way through the burnt territories and they of course would be integrated with everything already built further east. Within ten years, one could board a hyperloop in Clinton, Obamaport or Miami and travel west to the shores of the Pacific, to Gatesport say, through twenty hives and a dozen domed towns without ever going outside. Hell, if you boarded a hydroloop at Gatesport you could cross the Pacific to Tokyo and never go outside.

And yet there remained an almost intractable problem. The Indians who controlled the Indian lands had not given up the fight and would not give up. And who was their champion but Kaya? She was their Joan of Arc, no longer the timid singer I had first met in Lewiston when Merri and I were making our way east, not just a daughter and niece, but a fiery, passionate leader who almost singlehandedly kept the Indian federation together and directed its operations against Hive Corp.

The great swath of territory they controlled, from the lands of the Nez Perce to those of the Osage, were fenced by emotions so strong that Hive Corp. had been unable to placate them with either promises of plenty or, when those failed and Hive Corps' negotiators were driven away, beaten or killed, with police action. Paul Munro spoke for the Government when he said he was worried that the Indians might bring a legacy of unending famine on themselves and their descendants if they did not give up their Outside ways.

Even those of us who thought the Indians should give up, so they could raise their children on the Inside, knew Paul's words were a not-so-subtle threat to deprive the Indians of the water that was now streaming out of the Yellowstone distillation plant and flowing into the Indian lands and beyond. But Kaya, from one of her hiding places deep in the mountains, released a video in which she sat by a stone pit fire and said that if there were to be a famine, the Indians would not be the only ones to suffer. She meant that her people would blow the Yellowstone plant to bits even if it brought the long-feared monster of Armageddon out of the Yellowstone caldera.

Now and again, a video would appear that would show a large gathering of Indians on one or other of their lands. Though they happened frequently no one outside the Indian lands knew when or where they would gather, and somehow none of Hive Corps' spies among the Indians knew either. So, no opportunity ever arose to arrest Kaya and other members of the Indian leadership.

Kaya took to the stage in front of them but made no speeches. Sometimes she would sing the Outsider songs that had originally brought her fame but as time went by, it was the new, more militant songs she penned that rose in her voice. The song I heard Kaya sing, just after Paul's threat had failed to persuade anyone who mattered to get to the negotiating table, put a chill up my spine.

*When the white man tries to inflict his pain.*
*Beat the drum slowly and pray for rain.*
*Our rain will drown the white man's cries*
*And wash away the white man's lies.*

The words to the song were chilling, yes, of course, and the melody too. But it was really the way she sang so clearly and full throated, the way she stood on the stage above her people, at one with them in that precise, undistracted moment when everyone's heartbeat is one drum beating, where a song that has been born in one imagination suddenly lifts, by some magic, into the invention of a single prayer that is said by all to a common, higher power.

It is that moment when that higher power hears the single supplication, then out of love turns that energy back to all who have raised their voices and fills them with dauntless courage and invigorated hope. And that is what Kaya did with music - what she could not do with mere words. What I used to do when I was Trader Merri Weer's daughter, when I was Wicla the Singer, Queen of the Outsiders, not Wicla, mother to twins, chatelaine of Insider luxury, and Peter Benevolus's fearful and resentful wife.

The betrayal of others always begins with the betrayal of oneself. We all know it. I think back to the last concert I did with Kaya in California and how wonderful it felt to be back on tour and singing to a rapt audience. I thought at the time I had become my youthful self again, that my backbone had grown longer and straighter and that my breasts had refloated upward to where they used to be, and that no one could see the slight pouching under my chin, or the lines of my face. I wouldn't have minded grabbing one of the musicians or roadies and taking him into my bed for a full night of hard fucking. Yes, I thought about it, but I didn't do it because, well, by the end of the concert, I was tired and really just wanted to sleep.

Then the video that showed me for who I was. Then the press conference where all the questioners demanded that I answer for what I did not want to, but had to, recognize as my betrayal of the very people who I was pretending to love and champion. Then the long period immediately following that confrontation, when for months and months after I returned home, no matter how I tried to explain myself to myself, I could not escape the underlying truth. I had betrayed myself long before I had left for that tour before I let Peter browbeat me into going in the first place. But try as I might, I couldn't fix the specific moment when my betrayal had occurred. Was it that night I left the van to go back to Grinder's roadhouse and left my mother to carry out her plan of suicide? Was it that day up at Lolo or Lemhi in the mountains when I became irrevocably committed to going east and did not think to turn around and go back to Ojai with my mother so she could die in peace on her own time? Was it the day we left Portland? Earlier?

I know now that it is rare that we can pin down something as ephemeral and uncertain as a moment like that. Some could I suppose. For most of us it is different. We may never have formed any principles which can be betrayed. That's a tragedy in and of itself. Or we may have had them, but slowly lost confidence in their power to make the world we want to live in, causing us to find other, unprincipled means. We let time and faithlessness erode the foundations upon which we continue to believe we are standing until we implode and fall in upon ourselves.

I loved my mother, but I am willing to concede that I may be one of those in whom a set of lively, live-by principles was never inculcated. I hate to hear myself say it. Yes, she was a tough woman who instilled a kind of toughness in me. She was demanding, and in my way I became demanding too. But I don't remember any lessons concerning the right of this and the wrong of that, lest it was in her trader's credo: give good value for good money. She applied it to the things she sold to all those women who flocked to her van, and later I gave everything I had to those who paid to come hear me sing. You can live life according to a never-ending series of quid pro quos, but what do you do when some sacrifice is required?

But wait. When she was a girl, my mother left Chicago to go west to help with the rescue and recovery efforts that followed the quake there and she worked like a Trojan for months on end, tending to the injured and dying, burying or burning the dead, helping to resettle the refugees who came streaming up from the buckled coastal cities and towns looking for higher, stable ground. So, there we have it: youthful idealism, youthful commitment, youthful energy, youthful work in a great cause. Some sense of the right thing to do. I had it too, at one time. And now I saw it in Kaya and in all the braves, the young Indian men and women, who were holding on to their world against the rising, pushing tide of a progress that was beginning to look like it was not progress at all, but a tsunami pushed upon them by not the not so invisible hands of Hive Corp.

These things were much on my mind when I was at home in Clinton, almost a minute-by-minute preoccupation. Sometime after the passing of Cora Munro I left our compound to go walking in the streets around the market square in Clinton. I stopped at a café and while there, I chanced to look up at the news feed on the giant tron in the main square. That's when I learned Kaya had been killed along with a man who was accompanying her. They were shot dead by an assailant while they were walking into Gaytown in old Portland. It hardly registered with anyone else around me because Kaya's potent fame had never spread east. If she was anything to those Inside, she was just - and only - the shrill voice of a retrograde, almost silly movement that would ultimately be stamped out.

Cut to Portland and a reporter there framed against a dark brick wall. Kaya, the reporter said, was walking along the street that separated Gaytown from The Perly when she and he companion were assailed by a rough looking man dressed in black demanding money and valuables, a drug user probably. I knew she was walking near the place that Titus used to live before he and Arre moved to the Knightsburg hive – the hive that was built right over the lands upon which Fort Ketchup used to sit. So, why was she in Portland?

Cut to Lewiston, Idaho. The streets are filled with Nez Perce shaking rattles and banging on drums. Indians from the other side of the mountains are pouring down the slopes into the town. As they arrive there are handshakes, embraces, tears. Outsiders from Washington, Oregon and California are arriving too, caps in hand, not knowing if they will be welcome to mourn Kaya's death. You can sense the fury that is running through the grief of the Indians and the fretful concern that has overtaken the whites, blacks and Asians who are strangers there.

Cut to Portland, to the ramshackle Police Headquarters with bars on every door and window, an armed outpost in a dangerous place. Looks like someone high on drugs tried to rob them says the Chief of Police. We're investigating, he says. These things take time, he declares, but we'll get our man.

Cut to Lewiston outside the tribal offices. A new chief, not Kaya's father, Ed. But there is Ed, angry and sad all at once, who is seen head bowed in the background with his arm around Kaya's mother whose fists are curled. The Chief says he doesn't for a moment believe it was a random murder. She was assassinated, he says. Someone will pay for this.

Two days after hearing the news I called Titus.

- It takes the death of my niece for you to call?

- I'm sorry Titus. I am so sorry.

- I don't think I can talk to you Wicla.

- Please, Titus.

I hear muffled talk in the background. Titus passed the phone to Arre.

- He's too upset.

- It's horrible, Arre. Just horrible.

He walks away from Titus and whispers.

- She was put down, Wicla.

- Put down?

- Killed. The killer was seen running away.

- Did they catch him yet?

- No. And they won't.

- Why not?

- He's not from here. He was a pro.

- A pro?

- Two shots to the chest. Shot to the head. Coup de grace. Professional job.

- Why was she in Portland?

- Titus hasn't been well. Kaya wanted to see him. But she can't get into Knightsburg There are facial recognition systems all over the place. We kept the apartment in Portland so…

- How did anyone know she was in Portland?

- A spy probably. It's the only explanation.

- A spy?

- Probably on Hive Corp's payroll.

- Can I talk to Titus?

Pause.

- Not today, Wicla.

- I'll call in a few days.

- No. Better not.

Pause.

-   What's going on Arre?

-   Titus thinks you're complicit.

-   Me? Why?

-   Aren't you married to Hive Corp.?

Not in so many words I wanted to say. But I couldn't say anything.

-   Goodbye, Wicla.

Noise of a final and irrevocable disconnection.

The children arrived home from school. They came in through the kitchen door with our driver. I heard coats being dropped, shoes thudding on the tile floor as the kids kicked them off, a race for the living room where I am holding onto my vice, but just. They want hugs and kisses. Me too.

*Cruel is the kick in the kooky keister of a clown.*

# Song 43

Then came that summer. The children, their nannies, our security staff and I would first go to London for three nights of sightseeing. Peter asked to see our itinerary and thought it a bit overstuffed, but he conceded that if the children tired of being dragged around, their nannies could take them back to our hotel and I could continue on my own if I wanted. The children and I, sans nannies and our bodyguards, would then go north to Castle Forbes for two nights where he would greet us and we would spend the first part of our family time together before his summit. Before his colleagues arrived, we would drone over to Paris where the nannies and guards would have already enjoyed a couple of days off on their own. Together we would await Peter's arrival there before going south to our domed estate on the Côte d'Azur. Education for the children first, a little play time as a reward.

Things did not go as planned. I guess I shouldn't smirk when I say that, but it has been thirteen years, and well, laugh or cry, right?

London is an open, Outside city so it was on New Time then and continues on New Time today, although its population has shrunk by three quarters now that the Shakespeare and two other hives have finally lifted their drawbridges. Shakespeare is an extraordinary place I hear because it incorporates Warwick Castle into its town center. The buildings inside its western flank, I'm told, look down upon Stratford On Avon which, no doubt, still carries the whiff of medieval sweat in its French-fry and corndog breezes. I am confined to quarters so I will never see or smell it firsthand.

The first night in London I took the children to the British Museum where we had arranged a private tour that ended in the dinosaur hall. Bened, who had become a dinosaur expert over the last six months, treated us to a dissertation that outshone the prattling of the guide. Scola cowered behind my knees at first, but finally came out from behind to giggle at the botched names that her brother had assigned the monsters. The long-necked herbivores had a friendly, sun-seeking turn of head on their long necks, but Tyrannosaurus Rex glowered down at them like the tasty morsels they would have been a few millennia before.

I asked the guide to show us the Reading Room, where I sniffed the rarified air under its dome (not Crysalinks thank god!) but the children grew restive in its silence and stillness. As Bened pulled me out into the corridor again, Scola pulled my arm and said I think I like books, mother. Do you? When she came into my study at home she always went to my bookshelf and ran her hands down the spines of those she could reach. Mental note made that day: will my books to Scola.

The next night we outdid ourselves: Buckingham Palace, long since vacated by the last of the Windsors when the UK fell apart and England became a republic again, The Tower of London, London Bridge, the crumbling ruins of the Southbank theaters that long ago lost their audiences to the titillations of the new media, past the Parliament Buildings and Big Ben, which still chimes the hours with its mighty gongs. Past all the in-between bric-a-brac of Victorian times where tens of thousands of people, in the years before the new hive cities opened, lived in a squalid despair their monuments could never admit to. We drifted by all of them in our silent limo while I listened to the kids complain that they were getting hungry, or were tired, or begged to go back to the hotel where they could watch the vice.

The next evening the children were falling asleep on the couch, so I asked the nannies to take care of them while I went out for awhile. I wanted to go to Leicester Square and descend into the underground where Cora and Paul had been held captive during those thirty days of The Show. My guards, of course, had to come along, even though I was sure no one in all of London would know me from any other rich American or care that I was in their dank, drab city. If I sprained an ankle and fell to the pavement they would walk on by thinking it was a ruse to rob them of their last remaining valuables.

We purchased tickets and were waiting for the elevator to come back up with a load of sightseers who had done the rounds. As another dozen or so people gathered around the elevator, one of my guards leaned in and whispered.

- I think we're being followed.

- Really?

- I think so.

He nodded his head toward a moustached, swarthy looking young man who had been smoking a vape on the walk outside the elevator lobby. When the elevator dinged its arrival, the man put away his vape and joined us as we waited for the elevator to disgorge its passengers. He was taller and leaner than I had first made him out to be. Once on board the elevator, he made very fleeting eye contact with me then took a position in the back corner just beside one of my men.

His glance was disconcerting because it was so intense, but more for my bodyguards than for me. In the harsh light of the elevator I could see a rising young-man's stubble on his pointy chin, dark circles around tired, furtive eyes. He was the kind of man who would prickle the nerves of trained bodyguards like mine. I admit he put me a little on edge, but I was also intrigued by his look, which was very theatrical.

- First time here? I asked.

- Yes, he answered. You?

- Yes.

The elevator stopped; its doors parted. Everyone to the front of us stepped out and scattered as they entered the main hall. The young man held out his arm to gesture that I should go first.

- Enjoy your visit, I said.

- I will, thank you. You too.

Thick accent. European. Slavic? I couldn't place it. He put his hands in his coat pockets and entered the exhibit area, round shoulders leading the way. I saw him walk over to the front porch of the small, plywood building that was the First's home while they were in captivity. That porch with its overhanging roof and spindled, wooden balustrade was very familiar to all who had watched The Show. It was the only part of the buildings exterior that had been constructed for the camera. That faux porch is what made the building seem like a bungalow just like a million others on a street in a mid twentieth century American suburb.

He stepped up and went through the red painted front door, open to all now, but once a door upon which Haines knocked when he had a delivery for Cora and Paul, a delivery like the fateful Scrabble game that cost Haines his life. We followed in shortly after. When I went into the kitchen, I could see through to the living room where the young man was standing with his back to me in the door to the bedroom, still with his hands in his pockets. My bodyguards kept an equally close eye on him sensing something amiss, and not wanting to report to Peter that they had failed their duty to him by allowing anyone to do anything to the mother of his children. Protecting me was simply an extension of protecting his heir and heiress.

Just as we entered the living room, the young man exited the sliding glass doors at the back of the house to continue his tour. We did likewise a few minutes later, but as we went around the cavernous underground vault he seemed to have vanished. One of the guards had heard the elevator dinging and had vaguely seen a few people get on and off and said he thought the young man had simply ended his tour and gone up.

The other guard was ahead of us, excited as anyone could be to be in the museum. He and his wife had watched The Show avidly and he knew every nook and cranny of the place. But he also knew every bit of drama that had played itself out those thirty days, including every step taken by Paul and Cora as they made their escape, and every last step taken by the three men who had held them prisoner. He was as excited as Bened had been in the dinosaur exhibit at the British Museum.

Over here, he said, and beckoned his colleague and I to the columns of bricks where Cora had been held hostage at their center by the last of their captors before Paul stepped into the breech to put a bullet through the villain's forehead.

This way, he said, and he led us to the opening of the tunnels that led to other parts of the labyrinth that Paul and Cora had to find their way through. We moved down the now dry, well-lit tunnels that fed into the main room. Imagine these tunnels in the pitch black, I thought or with just a little, bouncing hand-held light to guide the way.

We came to an archway that would take us into an open space holding the cages where Cora and Paul had spent their first night underground. They were smaller than they appeared on the video stream. Their smallness made them more poignant because when Paul and Cora were together on their cots separated by bars, they were far closer than we could have known. A heartbeat away.

We went further. We came to the small portal in the side of the tunnel that Paul and Cora had to squeeze through on their way down into underground that first night of their capture. The guards bade me to go first. I put my head through and there was the young man, presumably backtracking. But before I could say anything he put his finger to his lip to shush me, then pulled an object from his pocket and put it in my hand.

He put his finger to his lip again. I took the item, a small metal object that glinted slightly in the dim light of this new room. Then he spoke, loudly.

- You first lady. Please let me help you.

He took my arm and pulled me all the way through as one of the bodyguards behind me stuck his head through, heart beating fast as he wondered what might be happening out of his sight. I slipped the object into my pocket. The young man quickly whispered to me.

- It's from Root.

Then he backed away to let my men come through. They eyed him with deep suspicion.

- It is all very interesting, said the young man. But this is not the way up to the street where they got out. The other tunnel leads there. This is the way they came in.

- Ah, thankyou, I said. Good to know.

He bent himself in double and pushed through to the other side of the small portal. We could hear his footsteps as he moved away.

- Strange fellow, said one of my men.

- A bit too weird for my liking, said the other.

I stepped forward into the room, fondling the object in my pocket as I did. I turned to the men.

- You know what? I've seen enough. I would like to go back to the hotel.

- Ma'am?

- I'm tired. I'm hungry. I want to see the children.

- As you wish, Ma'am, said The Show expert, clearly disappointed.

- You can stay if you want.

- We'll come back another day, Ma'am.

Back at the hotel, the children ran to the door when I walked into our suite and quickly wrapped themselves around my legs. I managed to extricate myself after tickling them, and then excused myself to go to my room for a quick freshening up. I pulled the little metal container from my pocket and looked at it closely under the bright lights of the bathroom fixtures. It was about the size of an old coin – a quarter. It had a small sprung hinge on one part of its edge. I got my long nail between its two sides and flipped it open. Inside there was a round disc of the kind I had seen Peter slip into his table vice from time to time.

Things had all of a sudden got curiouser and curiouser. Maybe Reedl Root wanted me to be a go-between. His revolt was failing. His comrades were being killed by the dozen. I knew that. Maybe he wanted to talk peace. Or maybe not. I would have to find out what was on the data drive before knowing what to do with it. I felt the tingle I imagined people in the spying business must feel every day, and I thought, perhaps now I can prove my worth to Peter. There were a few vices at the Castle. We would be there just after dawn. But as I turned out, I would not find myself alone until Peter's friends arrived for their summit.

After we ate lunch in the hotel restaurant I took the children for a midnight ride on the Thames. Unlike a lot of rivers at home which had either evaporated altogether or were thin ribbons compared to what they were even fifty years ago, the Thames was plumped-up. The damns that were used to keep the North Sea from pushing upstream to the city also caused the royal river to stay high inside London's embankments.

It was a hot, humid evening, so Bened and Scola, like all their minders and me, you enjoyed being onboard the river boat as we cruised from Westminster down to Greenwich and back, faces into the breezes. The children would go from portside to starboard to peer down into the murk as they looked for some sunken object that might denote its depth, or they would stand with their hands on the railings looking shoreward at the ancient buildings, some of them uninhabited shells that would some day, I was sure, fall over into the brown, unreflective water through which we were cutting. We would pass by areas that were illuminated by the glitter of a million lights, and then along stretches where the abandoned hulks of the past sat in profound darkness. What, I wondered, had the city been like at the height of its Empire? I could ask the same question when I was in old New York, or at that time, in Washington if I were to go there.

Later, keeping to the itinerary that I had worked out with Peter, our nannies and bodyguards put us on the drone that carried us north, up and over the rural patchwork of the south, shadowed by trees and hedgerows in the new morning light, over the roofs of villages where the rising sun had driven everyone back to their homes for their daily rest.

We flew over church steeples whose crosses had been bent by time and whose paint had been peeled by wind and rain, whose bells hardly tolled at all, except for those old timers who kept the faith until their last breath had been expelled, and some old codger of a Christian priest did his best to remember the old rites. Try explaining Christianity to seven-year-olds as they rattle off one question after another.

By the time we came to Hadrian's wall, the air had lost the clarity it had further south. The drone descended to fly under the cumulus clouds that were bunching up into thicker, grey piles as we moved northward. Under the clouds the light took on a dull evenness, and the contours of the land beneath rolled-by in shadowless shades of dark greens, purples and blues. We skirted Edinburgh, but even in the near distance it looked foreboding, all dark stone and slithering streets.

Over the cramp of Aberdeen we flew, then over Dundee whose drowned buildings on the shore of the Tay poked up in the currents and made the city seem unrescued, forgotten and forlorn. Scola and Bened were sleeping with their heads against the windows while I twiddled the data disk in my hands, wondering if the message inside would be as clear as the sunny terrains we had just left behind, or as ambiguous as the inscrutable fog that was no longer on the horizon but beginning to surround us.

*I exit in extremis to my exorbitant exile.*

# Song 44

Jock Glastonbury came out to the drone pad to greet the children and me to help us with our bags. Age had crept up on him so I felt a twinge of conscience that he was doing the lugging while we walked empty handed toward the castle. He trudged along behind us, a suitcase in each hand and parcels stuck under his arms, nattering about the fact that just the day before, the heaths all about enjoyed the light of a full sun under a cloudless sky.

- Don't despair, Master Bened, he said, old Sol will return again one of these days. God knows when, but rest assured, m'boy, it will come. Take heart Ms Scola.

Peter was waiting inside the vestibule with Mrs. G. and offered a warm welcome to the children and I, a short hug for each of them, peck on the cheek for me.

- You must be hungry, children. And why wouldn't you be? I've fixed you a plate of this and that, so come along to the kitchen and we'll fill you to the rafters while Mr. Glastonbury takes your bags to your rooms. Will you join us Miss Wicla?

I said I would, but I would straighten myself up a little before coming down. Mrs. Glastonbury bent down and put a hand on the backs of Bened and Scola and ushered them off in the direction of the kitchen while Mr. G. huffed and puffed his way up the main staircase, stopping now and then to put the suitcases down while he caught his breath.

Peter was chuffed that we had all arrived on-time and intact, but all the more so because this was the first time his son and daughter had come to Castle Forbes, which he regarded as the family seat. His son and heir would acquire the same feelings for the Castle as he and his father had. In due course, he said.

- It's a magical place for a young boy.

- And girl, I replied with mild sarcasm.

- Yes, of course. For Scola too.

It goes without saying, he wanted to say, but didn't because he knew that I knew he didn't hold out the same dynastic hopes for her.

Peter and I walked through to the grand salon where a dull light was coming in from the windows facing the cliffs down to the sea. I repressed an urge to turn on a few lights to relieve the dimness of the room. Outside, the fog was thickening in all directions.

- Will your friends be able to make it through the weather?

- I don't see why not, he said, but with a tone of doubt. It will blow off by the time they are ready to arrive.

- It's pretty thick now.

- I can see that, Wicla.

That was a good time for me to go upstairs to the master bedroom and freshen up. That was the room from which Cora and Paul had been kidnapped out of their sleep and transported down to that phony dream world below Leicester Square. I had no trouble imagining the terror they must have felt then, how far they had fallen out of their accustomed comforts and protections. What a shock!

I had stayed in the room on just one previous occasion, sleeping in the big bed myself, just as I slept in my own bed back in Clinton. Peter slept in one of the guest rooms down the hall. My suggestion that in future we sleep together on holidays – including those at the Castle - was meant with a gruff 'perhaps.' He tried it the night I first mentioned it, but we both found it hard to sleep together after having lost the habit of it already. He returned to the guest room the following night, although before going to bed we would lay on the big bed in the master and talk about whatever came to mind. Mostly about the children, really.

One night after a long dinner where we consumed more wine than usual, we went to the salon where he poured brandy into two large snifters. Then another. Once we ran out of things to talk about, but both of us utterly relaxed, I sat with my head back against the sofa and gazed absent-mindedly into the fire. I turned to look at him and found him staring at me, staring but with a soft look. A lascivious look it turned out.

- Let's go.

- You tired?

- No, he said. Not tired.

- Upstairs?

- Yes, upstairs.

And we made love. Well, you know. He was earnest, I was grateful. First and last time he ever satisfied me. But at least, we did it – christened the room that is – and, well, as I said, I was grateful and pleased. After I fell asleep, he slipped off to the guest room again. I would not have minded if he had crept into my bed again, at the Castle or in Clinton, and we'd made love the same way, but it never happened.

Still, that night he raised my hopes. So, the next morning over breakfast I suggested the master bedroom be de-masculin-ized to reflect Peter's change in circumstances (our marriage!). But he reacted badly and swiftly to that idea. He didn't say why, but I knew it was because it had been his father's room. Peter wanted to keep it more or less as it was when Peter Senior was Laird of the Castle. The shrine, as I began to call it, even had a table beside a rickety antique chair into which was carved the adopted family motto, *nemo me impune lacessit*, meaning no one attacks me with impunity, or, as I learned later, touch me at your peril. Not just a warning, but a prophecy.

On the table some of Senior's possessions were laid out as though they were ready for the day he would come out of the *en suite* and dress himself. Senior's silver-plated hairbrush and comb lay there along with a thick gold wedding ring, gold cufflinks and a tie clip with the Benevolus family crest emblazoned on them, a small silver framed picture of him and my Peter taken on one of the battlements above the room, with Senior tickling Junior's ribs to evoke an unaccustomed joy. There were gold florins that he would stick in his sporran if he were to wear a kilt, but in his trouser pockets if not, and, if he should don his kilt his ruby encrusted dirk was laid on a small cradle that made it easy to pick up. Peter had Mrs. Glastonbury dust the setting every day.

As it turned out, the summer fog did not lift during the two days following my arrival with the children. The fog became so dense, in fact, that even with GPS and all the rest of the self-guiding systems Peter had installed in all his conveyances, his colleagues were stuck in London, or Paris, or wherever they might be at the time they were supposed rising into the air for the short hop to the Castle. Nor could the children and I leave the place as per our approved itinerary.

Peter's irritation at the weather gods grew hour by hour. The noise of the children running through the Castle, up and down stony corridors as they played tag, sometimes with old Jock bellowing Gallic curses at them unsettled him. So did the clatter of their feet when they ran up and down the staircases looking for something better to do in some other part of the far-flung place. They banged on mighty doors that remained impregnable to their explorations. They shrieked at one another as they competed for the fastest this and the smartest that, and all the while they wore on Peter's nerves. He kept a tight smile on his face regardless, but an explosive pressure was building.

It was not the first time I had seen it coming.

- You haven't shown them the vault yet?

- They are a bit young for that don't you think?

- I don't think so, Peter. I think they will remember it forever now. They're old enough.

- You really think so?

- I do.

Later in the day, we were reading in the library. Jock had set a fire for us. The house was cold despite it being summer.

- I am going to have The Ten bussed up from London, Peter said.

- Really.

- Yes. They will be here by morning.

- OK.

- We need to meet, so they will make the effort.

The Ten were the top ten men of the companies Peter's bank financed. He could not abide the fact that if the annual summit did not take place it would be the first time since his father had started the tradition almost thirty years earlier. He did not want to disappoint the ghost of his grandfather. Well, I knew those kinds of feelings full well, didn't I? My mother floated above me with disapproving looks and cluck-cluck warnings for years after she died. She may have sunk into my marrow by now, but that had been her way. If Peter Senior were hanging in the rafters of the Castle, so be it.

- If we can't arrange to have you and the children fly off to Paris, you will have to remain upstairs the entire time.

- Really?

- Really. This is not family business.

- You don't want to introduce your wife and children?

- Maybe Bened.

That shocked me. Just Bened. Of course, son and heir. My face flushed, but I remained silent on the point.

- No, he continued. All of you stay upstairs. There will be other occasions for introductions. Not the summit.

I shot a cold look in his direction, but he was, as usual, impervious to it.

- Well, let's hope we can get out in time and leave you to it.

A few uncomfortable moments passed.

- You haven't shown the children the pool or the crypt, I said at last.

- You're right. I should do that.

- You should.

- You're right. After dinner.

- Good.

- Peter?

- Yes?

- If we can't leave and I am going to be upstairs with the children, I want the use of one of the table vices in my room.

- Why?

- Why?

He understood we might be bored without some distraction. And he also considered, I'm sure, that it would be one more thing to reduce the probability of our interfering with the goings on downstairs.

- I'll have Jock set one up for you.

- Thank you.

- Least I can do.

In fact, Peter's rulemaking opened up the chance I had been looking for since I arrived. I was burning to look at that data disk dropped into my hands by Root's man in London. Every time I had tried to find a quiet place to access one of the vices at the Castle, I had been interrupted by Peter or one of the children. One evening when the kids were asleep and Peter was meeting with the Glastonbury's to talk about the plumbing or something, I went to the Library. I had the data disk in my hand and was ready to slide it into the vice there, but Peter walked into the room, and more or less pushed me out of the way, so he could search the Net for some contact he wanted to give Jock in furtherance of maintenance work that needed to be done.

I was not going to tell him anything about the disk or how it came into my possession until I had seen what was on it myself. If there was an opportunity to channel info from Root regarding a cease fire or some such thing, I wanted to be sure it was real. Otherwise, Peter would rage at me for getting involved in things way outside my area of concern. He would do that anyway, even if it was good info and useful for peace-making, but his anger would be mitigated by the chance to put things to rest in the Adriatic States.

After dinner, Peter could not settle. He walked to the window and peered out into the milk of the fog but could find no fissures in it where he might see the sky or the glancing blow of a fracturing sunbeam. He went to the front door and went out on to the porch then down onto the pea gravel in front of the Castle and almost disappeared in the fog himself.

When he came back to the salon I reminded him, again, that he might take the children to see the rock and the crypt. Promising idea, he said, as he pulled his vice from his pocket to check the time once again. We went looking for the children and found them in the kitchen where Jock and Scola were locked in a game of electric checkers and Bened was wrestling with a thick mix of oatmeal dough in a large mixing bowl under Mrs. G's squinty, chuckling supervision.

- Children, your father has something to show you.

- What? Asked Scola as she triple-jumped Jock's pieces.

- Now's a good time, Master Peter, said Jock looking for an escape, a knitted frown on his brow.

- I can finish this up, Master Bened. Don't you worry, said Mrs. G.

Peter led the way while I followed, a child's hand in each of mine.

A look of astonishment came over Bened's and Scola's faces as we entered the covered courtyard.

- Are we going for a swim? Asked Scola.

- I don't want to swim, said Bened. I hate swimming.

- Swim with your clothes on? I don't think so, said Peter, smiling.

He stood by the side of the pool and the children came to his side.

- What do you see down there, he said, pointing at the mother crystal hibernating under the surface?

Scola backed up, but Bened stepped a bit closer while Peter clutched the neck of his sweater.

- Is that the big crystal, father?

- It is.

Scola stepped up too, her hand still in mine.

- The one that grandpa found? Asked Scola.

- The very one, yes. It is the rock upon which our family stands. Every new hive and dome that we build is grown from a tiny piece of the mother rock. An entire empire of towns and cities where millions and millions of people now live.

The children did not say much but I could tell from the way they looked into the water, they way they peered at the rock and the way they looked around the room that they were astonished into silence, even reverence.

- There's something else, children.

Peter took Bened's hand and walked toward the dais at the far end of the pool. I followed with Scola who broke free and ran to catch up to her brother. Peter punched in the code to open the crypt whose doors slid open, and down we went into the dim light where the Lifebooks of the children's grandfathers and grandmothers flickered their constant communication. The children went first to the glass wall and looked through the clear blue water out toward the crystal which looked fatter and more alive that it did when they cast their glances down through the surface of the pool.

My father's Lifebook was in the center next to Peter's father's sitting on his right. My mother's was to the left of Clement Samuels, Peter's mother's to the right of her husband's. The wives' Lifebooks were not as close to their husband's as the two grandfather's were to one another, and the women's were set lower down. My Lifebook was still in my mother's case, and would, one day, I supposed, be set in its own case to the right of Peter's.

- Your two grandfathers were great men, children. Together, they remade the world. One could not have done it without the other.

- Of course, neither your father or I would be here had we not been born. Let's give that one to your grandmothers.

Peter turned quickly toward me, irritated.

- Yes, he said, never underestimate the power of women.

I touched my mother's Lifebook and held my hand there.

- Can you hear anything, mother?

- Oh, yes, Scola, I said.

- What? What is she saying, mother? Asked Bened.

I reared back and put my claws in the air then went for their throats yelling booooo! As they giggled.

- Please, please, said Peter sharply. Remember where you are!

He turned and walked up the steps then waited impatiently for us to follow. By the time we surfaced, he had regained his composure.

- One day I will tell you all about how they did it.

- Tell us now, father, said Scola.

- You're a bit young. But someday soon. One day your mother and I will be here and you'll be telling the story to your children.

We left the sanctuary and Peter went back to the salon where he looked out the windows, not looking for a break in the fog now, but awaiting the appearance of his colleagues who would arrive soon in a bus. As to the children and I, we could not leave. We were told to go upstairs and stay there except for meals. We could come down the back stairs into the kitchen for those.

The bus carrying The Ten – actually eleven, as I was to soon learn - arrived from London. They were ushered into the grand salon for a round of drinks and laughs and the summit got under way. I could hear their voices from the master, but they were muffled by the thick, medieval stonework that separated us and I could make out nothing said, either in seriousness or in jest. I endured the prattling of the children – wished the nannies had come north with us. I took charge of their bathing and teeth brushing, read them stories until, even with the man noise coming from down below, they fell asleep.

I closed the thick oak door to the Master, now ready at last for the spy work I was about to undertake. I felt a bit of a thrill actually, after three days of gloomy, subdued relaxation at the Castle. I even glanced at the fireplace and wondered if it would slide open and allow bad men to enter as it had for Cora and Peter, not to kidnap me but to stop me from carrying out my assigned duties. I retrieved the small, silver object in which the data disk was protected from the pocket of a skirt hanging in my closet, its hiding place for the last while. I booted up the vice and then sat down at the desk Jock had managed to bring up on Peter's orders. Once it was on, I slipped the round data disk into the slot on its side and waited.

A program on the disk immediately announced it was

terminating the system's network connection. Root or his people did not want to be traced by Peter and his people. Root had learned his lesson. Then, suddenly, a short piece of white text appeared on the black screen.

**Statement of Peter Benevolus, II**
**Regarding the Kidnapping**
**Of the President of the United States of America**
**Cora Munro**
**And The First Husband**
**Paul Munro.**
<u>Top Secret & Confidential.</u>
Federal Bureau of Investigation
Washington, DC
June 12-14, 2068

I could not have been less prepared for what I found.

*Vex not the vicious vortices of a villain's vanities.*

# Song 45

It was a long document and Peter's testimony moved back and forward through time making it difficult to put it all together, to know, even halfway through, where he was taking us. As I read, I kept one ear cocked on the oak door, partly to listen for any noise from the kid's room, but more often to check for Peter's footsteps in the corridor beyond. I did not want Peter to catch me in the thrall of the illicit material that had been placed in my hands, because he would, rightly, demand to know, in accusatory and apoplectic tones, when and where I came into its possession.

From time to time the hilarity of the men below ballooned into loud guffaws, or the muffled base notes of drunken toasts that yanked my anxious head in their direction. From the kitchen at the bottom of the back stairs I heard the short, sharp clang of pots banged together and the knock of heavy crockery on service tables. The on-duty Glastonbury's and the hired kitchen staff were kept hard at work, but I knew, once dinner was done, the kitchen would fill with silence as they departed for their beds. After a few hours of precious sleep they would wake to breakfast chores. After dinner, Peter and The Ten would parade into the salon for brandy, cigars, more man-jokes, and the inevitable ribbing of one and then another. Business would be left to the hangover of the following morning.

In his testimony, Peter first talks about the day Cora and Paul Munro burst out of the tunnels and caverns beneath

Leicester Square in London. The memory of it is still vivid in my memory because I watched them with my own eyes on the public tron in CashCarter, cheering with my fellow citizens as the Firsts came up into the rainy square to do their victory dance. Where were you when it happened? is the question everyone asked of everyone else for a few years after, and still do from time to time.

It is all the more vivid because I have just come up out of the caverns myself and know their echoing malevolence, their smells, their dankness. I know their darkness too, even though it is all so well-lit now for the pleasure of tourists. The event has become remote in time, it's true, the fast-built bungalow where Paul and Cora bickered, then found their way back to their common cause of life over death, has become quaint almost. But as I read the transcript of Peter's account, I feel the shivers of an original experience

Throughout his statement, Peter illuminates details of The Show that any of us Watchers could have seen. The Show streamed out of the bungalow every minute of every day for thirty days. But despite how much I watched, I didn't know even half as much as Peter knew about all that had gone on. I was driving Merri through the Indian lands toward a destination that I could scarcely have apprehended before leaving old Portland, or at any other time, as we moved along the roads we traveled. But still, I thought, Peter is a very busy man. Did he watch the goings on below Leicester Square so intently that he too was able to recount so much of it to his interlocutors? Probably not, I concluded, as I read and read.

Peter had been briefed formally by investigators in his employ, informally by contacts in Washington, and thoroughly by Paul, his mentor and friend, whom Peter would have probed until Paul was bleeding information from every orifice. Peter had made it his business to learn as much as he could, because the kidnapping had affected his business interests so deeply and maybe because he learned insights that could be used against Cora and her government in all the dealings that came after her release.

I was rationalizing to stifle the instincts bubbling in my guts.

And I read about my father. For the first time, actually, I began to see him as my father, accept him as my father. My father. It is difficult for me to express what that means now. But Peter's story painted the picture of my father, Clement Samuels, in a way that I had never envisaged before - the whole history of his life from before the time he left Brooklyn to set-out for the ruined spaces of America, until his pitiful death in prison not so many years later. He was still a young man when he died.

His genes are as much in me as those of my mother Merri Weer, and it is from him, I'm sure now, that I received the gift of song. I don't mean that he was a singer, but the gift of song comes from the bigger gift of creativity and that is clearly what Clement Samuels had. But more than that, I could see that he would not permit his vision to be denied, found ways and means to ensure that, even if he should come to a sudden end, the thing he created would live on. Yes, I know, my father's will was stronger than mine and that I will leave no legacy, but when I was Wicla the Singer, all those years ago, I would not be denied either.

Why did I have to read this secret testimony to learn about my living father? Why had Peter withheld so much from me? So, yes, as I read on, astonished anger was tossed like a blind worm's sting into the cauldron of my blood-red emotions.

Merri's words rang in my ears as I read about Clement Samuels. He was a good man, she said. And so, where, in light of the inexorable spread of the Inside world that was born of the crystal he had found in his journeys, I had questions about his intentions, I decided to resolve my doubts by giving my father the benefit of them.

In his testimony, Peter mentions the time when Samuels was flying through the pitch-dark Nebraska countryside and went off the road and injured himself but had found help in the shape of some woman parked behind a nearby barn. Samuels must have mentioned the accident, but not his brief affair with Merri, to Peter's father, who, in turn, passed it along to Peter, stripped of all but its broken-bone data. But that injured man was my mother's Clem and I knew from her, how, as she nursed him from his hurts, they found the heart and soul of one another. I knew the hot moment of sexual entanglement in which I was conceived was shot through with love and the true desire of love – not the orgasmic flash, but the starlight that two lovers move through together as their bodies fall upward, no longer alone. But the height to which my mother was raised induced a fear of possible abandonment so deep she left my father standing in the Nebraska cornfields bewildered, and I have no doubt, with a feeling of inexplicable and devastating disappointment.

I learned as I read, about my father's sudden grasp of a giant opportunity, about how thousands of abandoned malls across the country could be converted to a new purpose by making them our new burial grounds. Heaven's Gate memorial malls yielded gobs of cash that propelled everything else, and still do. I learned too, about the unlikely partnership that evolved between my father and Peter's father, about Samuel's discovery of Crysalinks, about the Tulsa skunk works where he and his team finally figure out the way to build a new world with it, how they begin to do exactly that, and how, in so doing they come to cross-purposes with the government of Cora Munro, and I began to see how all our fates became so intertwined.

But as I read, I detected a schism between my father and Peter Senior that landed the one in jail where he was murdered and the other to the summit of success in the topmost business circles where he was fêted. My father stayed down at ground level, eschewed the limelight, avoided, at all times but a few, the gaze of onlooking cameras. He stayed humble, never ran a comb through beard or hair, kept his busted, dented Tesla Bat miraculously roadworthy and travelled only the backroads with it. He wore a caftan and sandals and only bowed to winter's frigid powers by donning a prairie cowboy's coat and thick socks.

Of all the unwashed he met along the way, he was the least washed of all, an unpretentious Jew who spoke in the barking twang of Brooklyn and laughed at his own hooked nose and gangly ways. And so, Clement Samuels managed somehow to endear himself to those whose paths he crossed so they might hear his wisdom and his insights and see the wild vision that was in his head, a utopia rising on the beautiful landscapes that were the real surfaces of their benighted country.

Peter Senior was the opposite of my father, and it turns out, the more I read his son's words, my husband, was the opposite of me. For the virtues extolled in both Peters' lives arose not from the poetic mysticism of Clement Samuels, but from the rigors of law and accounting and the accumulating and momentous power of Power itself. They are not wise people, no not at all. And it is just that, that made me do what I did, because, that day, and that night, my emotions got the better of me, for the lack of wisdom leaves the force of money, status, authority, and all the rest of the world Peter moved in untempered, its consequences as unmitigated as they were unforeseen by my long dead father.

When it was time for the men below to end their revelries, I heard them shuffling out of the salon into the foyer below the grand staircase. I knew they would be ascending to their rooms along the corridor outside my door, that their belching and farting and last moment jollities might wake the children, which fortunately did not happen. I shut down the vice because I knew, once his guests were behind closed doors, he would enter the master bedroom looking for the comfort of his side of our bed and a few hours of perhaps fitful sleep.

He went into the *en suite* and, as I turned down the covers, returned in his pyjamas, the top buttoned to the neck, which made one collar corner turn up a little. His hair was still parted and combed. He crawled right in.

- Have you managed to keep yourself occupied? He asked.

- Yes. I've been reading, thinking.

- Children behave themselves?

- Mrs. G. brought them coco and it wiped them right out.

- Her special recipe. She used to give it to me when I was their age. It was like a drug.

- I'll have to try it some night, I said.

- Working hard is all I need.

- It didn't sound like you were working.

- For me, being social is the hardest work of all. G'night, Wicla.

- Sweet dreams.

- I should get some sleep, he said, as he turned off the lamp on the table beside the bed. It might help if your light is off too.

I crawled in and turned off the light, but I was wide awake, intensely caught up in the plots that I had now started seeing shuttlecock their way through Peter's long statement.

- You alright? Peter asked, sensing my alertness.

- Go to sleep, dear.

- Mmmm...

And he did. When he had drifted down into the depths of his unfathomable slumber I knew he would be out for at least a few hours. Dusk – our Outside morning - would come fast, but he would awake to it, fully energized, without any prompting from chimes, beeps or buzzes or, if back in Clinton, the gentle shaking of his butler.

I rose in the dark room and went back to the table where I had been sitting earlier. I turned the vice around, then picked up my chair and put it on the other side of the table and turned on the machine so its light was facing away from the bed. I could also keep an eye on the lump of Peter where he lay extended under sheets and blankets, not completely still, but still enough.

And I read and read, consuming its details and trying, as the FBI men to whom he had made the statement, tried to fix them into a make-sense narrative. At time, Peter would venture down some seemingly irrelevant path only to come back to a recollection that was so dense with information you could hardly penetrate its meanings.

But slowly, and even fearlessly, he revealed all. That schism between the two founding partners was hidden in their common purposes for many years. It was assumed in the early days, that Clement Samuels vision was driving all the work, that Peter Senior was following his lead and putting his legal talent, and it turns out, his financial talent, to work in the fulfillment of that vision. The assumption was true, no doubt, at least in those early days.

But then came the election of Cora Munro and the mighty conflict that ensued between her government and Hive Corp. I learned from Peter what a dynamic, forceful woman she was, how sleek and beautiful, how so very intelligent, how animated her temper could be when she was crossed. I learned that her dedication and focus, the exigencies of the work she had to do as President, drove wedges into the fissures that always lay in the smooth surfaces of early love and marriage, and how, as a result, at the White House, Paul became unhappy, and felt his charming, physical, an no less intelligent manhood, unappreciated by his President-wife.

And what I also learned, as I turned from one page to another, was that Peter Senior did, in fact, control the Bank that financed Hive Corp., using money flowing-in from Heaven's Gate at first, then the money that bubbled up from the licensing of the magic crystal out of which the hive cities, domed towns and agricultural structures dotting the country were grown. But he controlled Hive Corp. too.

Reedl Root's words came back to me. My husband's own statement about the kidnapping of Cora and Paul Munro was the proof of it. It was a big shock to me, very big. It made me shiver as I sat before the vice in my night dress looking at the husband who lied to me about that very thing. But did it matter? Did it matter in the great scheme of things? Oh yes. It did.

*The jeer of a Jabberwock will jolt the joker from his jokes.*

# Song 46

What did Clement Samuels want? The same thing that Cora Munro wanted. There was great suffering everywhere and both wanted to end it. People were dying under the poisoning sun, but even more people were dying in the dangerous chaos the country had become, as the seas rose around our coasts, as storms battered, as fires raged, as the desserts grew and our waterways shrivelled. My own experience of the hardships, of the violence, of the descent into self-help was firsthand, but I also knew it from the tales my mother told me, and they were decades old by then. Cora's and Samuel's argument was an argument over ways and means. My father, had he met her, would have said, be patient as we rebuild the country, all will be well, better in fact. But young Cora lashed his patience with her whip and demanded things go faster, much faster.

But they didn't meet did they? My father left the politics of this contest to Peter Senior and by then his brain was, like Cora's, full of law and legal stratagems, offences, defences, moves and countermoves, attacks and tactical retreats, and in all he did, he had the benefit of knowledge and information about his unworthy, female opponent from an inside man with a wounded ego, Cora's husband, Paul Munro. She could hammer away at Hive Corp's recalcitrance with the manifold tools and weapons of government, but Peter Senior could use money, guile, and a plethora of nasty subterfuges to evade and avoid the worst of what she brought to the abstract battlefield.

My father, staying out of the public eye, not wanting to join the battle, confident that there would be an inevitable stalemate requiring sane people to reach a useful accord, seemed to Cora, not a wise man staying above the fray, but a powerful recluse hiding from her authority, and directing the action from whatever cave he had retreated to. She was determined to flush him out, to force him to put Crysalinks into the public domain where she could put it to work on behalf of the people.

Then, the entire dynamic changed. Samuels died in prison and Peter Senior died of a heart attack at his desk. And that is where my reading of the narrative brought me to as the new dusk approached. In the crack of the curtains in the master bedroom I could see the light of day fading. But the light is different, it is brighter than it has been for days. I walked to the window and looked out – the fog was lifting. As I looked out, I heard the whir of copter blades in the near distance. The sound woke Peter too. He started, sat, swiveled his legs to the side of the bed, stood, then walked to where I was, and listened more closely.

- He's here, he said.

Peter dressed quickly and turned to me with a severe look on his face.

- You and the children will stay up here. You understand?

Then he left the room, opening the door with such force that on its return, it banged on the stone wall behind it. He descended to the foyer two steps at a time. Once he was safely out of sight, I left the room too, not to go downstairs, but up to the third floor where I opened the door to the roof. Still in my night clothes I stepped out into the noisy air to watch an American government copter alighting in the forecourt of the Castle.

I ran to the parapet on that side of the building and poked my head through an opening in its crenelated top to see who was arriving. Once its blades came to a near stop, the door to the copter on the side facing away from me opened, and Peter made his way around. I could just see them shaking hands but did not see who had arrived until he walked around the copter. Peter's new guest, hale and well-met, was the nattily-besuited Paul Munro, the both of them laughing at some comment Paul made as they walked toward the Castle door. It is at this moment, I realize now, that things began to spin out of control. For me that is.

When I got to the second floor, the other men were emerging one at a time from their rooms and making their way downstairs. I waited for the corridor to clear before I stepped out from the archway where I was hiding and made my way to the children's room. I occupied myself with them for as long as it took to dress them, get their teeth brushed and deliver them to the kitchen via the backstairs into the over-busy hands of Mrs. Glastonbury, who palmed them off on Jock.

- Get them fed, Jock, for gods sake. Can't you see I'm busy with the big table doings?

- Consider it done, Mrs. G.

Peter, Paul and the other men, The Ten, would sit at the dining table for breakfast but once finished, the table would be cleared away and they would get down to whatever business they had to do. While they were eating I returned to the master and got myself showered, made-up and dressed. Then I went down, got the children and brought them back upstairs and let them watch cartoons on the big vice in the lounge down the hallway – a rare treat for them. It would keep them occupied for hours – so long in fact, I forgot they were there.

I had already formed a plan to eavesdrop on my husband's business meeting by the time I snuck back down, this time via the main staircase because I didn't want to be caught by Gillian or Jock Glastonbury. In his statement, Peter had told the FBI men how he used to stand in the shadows and listen and watch his father and the other men when he was a boy, so I knew where to go and where to stand. As I approached I could hear Peter's voice.

- ...and Paul, I want to thank you for making your way here.

- Not at all, Peter. I've been looking forward to it for weeks.

The arched entry to the dining room is tall and wide so from my hiding place I could see the backs of the heads of some of the men along the side closest to me, the faces of a few on the other side, and the head of the table itself where Peter was standing and holding forth.

- It has been a momentous couple of years, gentlemen, but

things are moving along more or less as we had planned. I wanted Paul to come and address us in person to bring you up to speed on what has been going on in his world, and where we go from here.

Peter sat down kitty corner to the head of the table to make way for Paul. Paul paused a few seconds and looked at the men around the table.

- Congratulations, gentlemen. We have now arrived at the penultimate moment. Our efforts have paid off. Well, yes, they always do, don't they?

Chuckles all around.

- Cora is dead. It took a little longer for her to succumb but, succumb she did and the autopsy showed no sign of the…whatever it was.

I could not believe what I just heard. Thought I heard.

- The book she was writing at the time, the so-called expose of our little cabal, has gone missing. When her publisher called and demanded to see what she had written by the time of her death, I said, well, a lot. Our contract says its ours, he said. A nasty little shit, I have to say. That publisher I mean. Of that I have no doubt, I assured him, but it seems she may have thrown it in the fireplace and burned it to ashes. We found a few unburnt shards of paper from what looked like her manuscript, but, well,

I am sorry, I said. She was terribly unpredictable. It took me a long while to poke that wad of paper so it would go up in smoke, but, well that's done.

My heart was racing. I wanted to run into the dining room and scream.

- I hear the Outsider Army may be on the rise again, Paul. Is that so? Asked one of the men.

- Surely not, I heard Peter say. They're done with, no? Spent force and all that.

- Indeed, they are, answered Paul. Once we eliminated that girl, the singer, what's her....

- Kaya, someone said. Good singer, though.

- She's joined the heavenly choir now, said Paul, laughing at his own joke. Anyway, spent force is exactly right. The OA will trouble us no longer.

My legs buckled.

- Lastly, said Paul. The good people who have sat at the Constitutional Convention have thrown in the towel. The Congress has withered away as we expected. So, that worked out as well as we thought it might.

- The dome over Washington will be finished in a couple of

months and the place will open as a, well, as a museum. It should pay for itself and then some within a few years, added Peter.

- America is no more, concluded Paul.

I could bear it no longer. I held myself back from vomiting, but nearly choked on the vomitus as it came up out of my stomach into my mouth. My head was swimming. I backed out of the hallway into the foyer, and up the stairs, while having to listen to Peter and his friends give three, rousing, horrible cheers to Paul Munro. I went into the lounge where my children were sitting with dull eyes looking at the screen of the vice. I sat down between them and pulled them close.

- What's wrong, mommy? Scola asked.

- Nothing. Nothing.

- Can we go downstairs yet, mommy? Asked Bened.

- No, darling. No, not yet.

These children I knew now, had been born into a world they ought not to live in; a life that is marbled with murderous deceit. I sat with them under the crooks of my arms enwrapped by their childlove, and I thought, I really thought this, that my responsibility, my deep, motherly obligation might be to take them up to the castle roof and throw them over so their brains would be dashed and scattered on the cliffside rocks and their bodies washed away in the cold saltchop of the North Sea until their last memorable molecule had dissolved in it. And did I have the guts for that? And if I could not do that for them, what should I do?

I shook in the horror of those imaginings, forced myself to reason with the despair that had overcome me. OK, OK. I could deal with the vicious metaphor that had just consumed me, forgive myself for disappearing into abstractions I never thought myself capable of. Logic. Logic. Every murder and suicide is formed around the wish to escape the life we have and every sin is grounded in thievery. Mine was to give and protect life, not to take it and exploit its vulnerabilities.

- Time for lunch, I said. C'mon.

Down the backstairs we went, to the kitchen bustling with the rattle and hum of cooking, serving, cleaning-up. Mrs. G. still happy to see the kids, ready to give them a good lunch. She'd rather do that than tug her forelock to the high and mighty in the dining room beyond the kitchen wall.

- There's plenty left from the meal I'm serving the mucky mucks, ma'am.

- In a bit, Mrs. G. I have to do something first. Do you mind if I leave the children?

- Of course not, ma'am. Jock was put on God's green earth, to help me when my octopuses' arms are doing their level best to keep up. He just didn't know it when he came a courting. Jock, tend to the wee one's now and mop up your own drool while you're at it.

Up in the master, I called Tooty in Paris.

- I want you and Muldoon to bring a drone here to pick us up. Mr. Benevolus is still tied-up with events here now that the fog has lifted. I want you to arrive at 7:30 on the dot. Can you do that?

Of course he could, and would. In a few hours we would be airborne, could watch Castle Forbes and all its prevarications shrink as we rose into the unfogged sky and slide eastward on the prevailing winds. Between now and then, I would pack up a few things and, when the coast was clear, finish reading Peter's testimony whose bits and pieces were now shifting kaleidoscopically when I twiddled its trapdoor envelope in the pocket of my dress.

The noise from the dining room where Peter, Paul and the other men summited was a dull murmur from upstairs. They would continue marching through their agenda until dinner time, then they would eat, then all but Peter would depart. These were the barons who ran the various divisions of Hive Corp., the Bank, Heaven's Gate, and the now vast network of Hyperloops and Hydroloops that connected everything in the world they had created. One of them, I feel certain, was the topmost generalissimo of IntFor, nominally a security force, but in reality, I learned later, the most powerful military force on planet earth and beyond. He looked awfully much like Haines, the swarthy man who guarded The Firsts when they were underground and whom Paul was said to have killed during their escape but didn't. Indeed, it was he.

My plan was to leave with the children and once out of Peter's immediate reach, sue for divorce, sue for custody, get what I could to support us, maybe even, come to it, go and live on the Outside. I reasoned the children should know a little of the hardships their grandparents, and even I, endured when we lived out there. Little did I believe at that moment, that those hardships had multiplied many times since I stepped in the door at CashCarter, and that I could not in all good conscience place my children in such mortal jeopardy.

Why should Tooty arrive at 7:30, even if he had to circle the Castle for a good long time to arrive precisely then? Because Peter's goodbye dinner would be in full swing. He, the other men at the table, the Glastonbury's and all the kitchen and wait staff would be fully occupied. We could get away without any interference at all. Simple as that.

I parked the kids in front of the big vice again so they could while away the hours in the lounge down the corridor from the master bedroom. I felt guilty about leaving them there, but I wanted to read Peter's summing-up of what had transpired when the kidnappers came out from behind the fireplace in the very room where I was sitting and took Cora and Paul away. What and why.

Now you must forgive me, because what happened as I came to the last few pages of Peter's statement twisted me into a shape of being I had never experienced before and have never experienced since. What I read lifted me out of my body, which writhed in agony below the stone vaults in which I floated as a disembodied, disbelieving self. I'm not sure I ever came down.

But that day, and for days after, all that happened, happened in a time made of moments my memory continues to move around like the squares of a Rubik's Cube, and that left me pained to think I was not intelligent enough - or brave enough - to solve the puzzle that constituted my husband's crimes.

Peter orchestrated the kidnapping with The Ten's approval and consent. Paul was complicit from beginning to end. That is what I read. That is what Peter admitted to the FBI people who interrogated him. His confession was taken and immediately archived. It never saw the light of day until Reedl's people cracked the encasing codes and began to strategize how best to use the knowledge that had come into their possession. Reedl himself decided to put it in my hands.

Neither Peter or Paul or any of the co-conspirators were ever prosecuted because the FBI had become a toothless agency of a government that had lost its bite. Those who heard Peter were the first to know they had the choice of speaking-up, or continuing to earn a paycheck, of living under the new regime, even though complicit in its coup, or possibly dying at the hands of assassins who were not so scrupulous as they.

I paced. I searched the master bedroom for other evidence. I bounced around the document on the vice and re-read many of its pages and saw how each and everyone of those pages – each word in fact – had been carefully articulated to draw you to a conclusion that was not inevitable until his narrative was complete. Everything that transpired after Cora and Paul escaped their imprisonment was explained in light of Peter's account. These men had killed off a buggered America and killed anyone who might rescue it before the deed was fully done. Peter sat in the interview room, supercilious and smirking-guilty as he laid it out. You know he did because that is his way. Too clever by half; genius son of the genius co-founder of the new State, his father, Peter Benevolus Senior.

I looked at my watch: 7:10. The drone was due to arrive momentarily. I got myself together as much as I could and went to fetch the children. As I passed the grand staircase I could here the men at dinner down below. Conversation, belly laugh's, compliments to the chef, wine paired perfectly with every course, tongues loosening under its accumulating effects. By 7:25, I had the children in their coats, knapsacks on their backs at the top of the stairs. I carried my own small suitcase. Everything else we needed was in our Paris hotel suite. Down we went to the foyer, where I pushed them across toward the huge front door, with Bened resisting, but just out of his ritual obstreperousness. Their small noises were not heard by Peter or his guests.

But, before I opened the door to go outside, I heard words tumbling out of Paul's mouth, then out through the arch of the dining room entry way and into my ears.

- What say gentlemen? Here's to another rebellion put down. To our success in old Croatia.

- To Croatia! said by all as they down a glass of whatever they were drinking.

- Here's to our defeated enemies, may they rest in peace.

- To our defeated enemies!

How brave am I going to be, I wondered. How brave am I?

I opened the door to the outside. Both Bened and Scola love flying, so when they saw the drone descend at 7:30, they were beyond excited.

- Hurry, momma, said Scola.

And now Bened was pushing me. But I had made up my mind. Tooty stepped out of the drone and came toward us. He took the kid's knapsacks and my suitcase and greeted us all. He lifted the kids into the drone and buckled them in, then turned to help me.

- I'm not going.

- Pardon, ma'am?

- I'm staying here another day. I will join you in Paris tomorrow. I'll hop a ride with Peter.

The children were not sure this is what they wanted. But whatever doubts they had rose out of the forecourt with them. I forced a smile to my face and waved them off. But once the drone peeled off over the roof of the Castle heading for Paris, I strode back to the front door of the Castle and into the foyer. A deep breath there, probably. Yes.

Down the corridor to the dining room. I stood in the archway until I was noticed, not smiling, not at all. First one man and then another saw me and stopped speaking, stopped everything they were doing, in fact. Then Paul saw me. He tapped Peter's arm and when Peter looked at him, Paul nodded in my direction. He suppressed his shock, then a look passed over his him as he saw my face, wondering if something horrible had happened to one of the children.

- Everything all right, dear?

I didn't answer.

- Are the children alright?

I nodded yes.

- Is there something you need from me?

I shook my head.

- What is it then? We're...

- I have something to say.

- Something to say?

- To all of you.

I walked further into the room, but toward the opposite end of the table, away from Peter. Away from Paul, too.

- Gentlemen, my good wife, said Peter, trying to lighten the atmosphere. She has something to tell us apparently.

- Well, why not? Paul said. We're all out of things to talk about.

I lifted my hand and pointed a finger at Peter.

- You orchestrated the kidnapping of President Munro.

Peter leapt to his feet, but all eyes were now on me, then him, then back to me.

- And you, I said, pointing at Paul, were in on it from the beginning. You all were.

Peter started moving down the room toward me. I walked in the opposite direction and kept my distance. I had not stopped pointing at Paul.

- Killed Cora.

Peter rushed, I moved again.

- Had Kaya killed.

Paul stood up to block me at his end of the table. Peter quickly closed the distance.

- She is quite mad, gentlemen. My apologies.

He grabbed my arm, squeezed hard into the joint, pushed me up on my toes and marched me out into the corridor into the foyer and then onto the bottom rise of the grand staircase. He was flustered and angry.

- What are you going to do, Peter, kill me?

- Don't think I won't.

He twisted my arm and began marching me up the stairs. I stopped resisting and with his weight below me and hoisting me upward, we went quickly up to the second floor. He grabbed my hand and pulled me down the corridor to the master bedroom and in, then swung me around and sent me on my heels back onto the bed, where I regained my balance enough to find purchase on its edge. The pain of his grasps and twists had brought tears to my eyes. I wiped them off.

- You'll stay here until our friends have departed. I'll deal with you later.

He backed out of the room, slammed the oak door shut with a bang. Then it opened again. He rushed in, grabbed the table vice and carried it out of the room, pausing only to lock me in with the iron key always sitting in the keyhole.

I thought I could escape down the backstairs, but within seconds it seemed, the door at their bottom slammed shut, and I heard a key turn in it. I thought I could open the fireplace and find a way out that way. I knew how to open it from the inside now. But it was a stupid thought. The sea cave below was flooded shut. There would be no submarine there to spirit me away as there had been for Cora Munro and her conniving husband.

Peter said he would deal with me after all his guests departed the following day. He would not chance, he said, the embarrassment of a crazed woman shaking a loud finger at him or any of them. In just a few hours, a half dozen buzzing drones would alight from the brightening air above the castle and Paul and all their so-called friends would go back to wherever they came from and continue to administer the empire created by their fathers and themselves.

But how was I to deal with Peter? We would soon find out.

*The sacramental stone of sanity dissolves in a satanic sea.*

# Song 47

The data disk containing Peter's statement, secure in its silver packet, was tucked into the corner of a little used pocket of Scola's knapsack and would eventually make it back to Clinton where it remains hidden in the greenhouse at the back of the garden. But its possible revelation by an embittered wife would remain a useless threat forever. So, even though Peter, under the anxious gaze of his colleagues, probably considered by what means he might dispose of me before I left the Castle or somewhere along the way home, I obviously made it back to our mansion above the Hudson. But he did not.

The dinner broke up, the men went to the salon for a last round of drinks, but this time, no laughter exited into the foyer or made it upstairs to our bedroom door. I had the sense they had formed a low-voiced council of war for it was apparent from the accusations I flung in their collective faces that I knew of what I spoke and might know a great deal more, that someone had provided me with a plethora of inside knowledge - and maybe a good deal of supporting evidence - that could endanger their project if it should fall into the wrong hands.

I waited. More than three hours passed before, ear against the door, I heard the men trooping up to the second level to bid one another good night - in tones that suggested they were happier than when I had been muscled-out of their presence by my husband. No doubt Peter assured them not to worry about me.

When I heard the last of their bedroom doors shut, I listened for the sound of Peter's footsteps coming up the grand staircase. When I heard footsteps in the corridor outside the bedroom door, I flew back to the bed and turned off the reading lamp just as the key to the room turned in the ancient lock.

Peter stepped in quietly, went into the bathroom, closed the door and turned on the light inside. I was turned in that direction so I could see shadow-movement in the yellow light at bottom of the door. When he turned the light out and entered the room I closed my eyes again. He walked to his side of our bed, pulled back the covers, slipped under and turned so his back was to mine. My heart raced, I tried to suppress my heavy breathing. A slight film of sweat crept down my back. I did not move. His breathing, however, was light, his last breath the subtle shudder of exhaustion. He drifted quickly off to sleep. The anger and fear that had been fermenting behind my breastbone began to burble and froth.

I would not give Peter the satisfaction of a confrontation. Not stir him out of his slumber. Not raise my voice. Not point the finger. Not stomp the room. Not cry, and wail and moan, not tear out my hair by its roots. Not be the demented woman who would be so easily dismissed. Not jump from the Castle parapets to join my children in their imagined sacrifice. So, I clenched my fists, and brought my knees closer to my chest, pulled a lock of my hair into my mouth to muffle any sob that might try to make an escape, to stop my teeth from beating on my perplexed tongue.

I became as quiet as I could. Lay there in the absolute dark, brain turning like a fantastical machine with silent cogs and belts moving molten metal from blasting furnaces into sparking, iron molds. Lay there and came finally to the realization that Peter had no fear of me. He'd put it all together, kissed Paul Munro and all the other members of the fretful Ten goodnight and told them the bedtime story that made me, the monster, flee their heads. I was an irrelevancy. Whoever had spilled their beans was an irrelevancy.

There was no way for the information I had been given to be disseminated to any part of the world. The media was controlled. There were no police forces that would or could investigate the case against them, no prosecutors to prosecute, no judges to sit in judgement. All of them were bought and paid for. I would be remanded to my luxurious confinement in Clinton under his protection. So, drink up gentlemen, and cheers!

Then, when those thoughts had cooled into a fine certainty, into the near silent void came my mother, death mask Merri, a quarter-seen face behind a vale of time. Black and white. Old and wizened but cancer free, free of pain. I wind it all back, back out of the vault in the crypt downstairs where we sit in a box blinking at one another, back to CashCarter where we both lived for a time, back across the Mississippi, through the baking Indian lands, up into the mountains and to the very lineament of the Great Divide. Down, down the west facing slopes, I drive with her along the riverbanks to Portland, near to where the water pours into the sunlit sea, to Portland where she was only really last alive at a table in Erato's mission, snarking at the lost men and women with whom she loved to break bread.

And I see there at the table, the high cheek-boned face of Titus, large, bald head tilted into happy, arrogant defiance of convention. I see him tapped on the shoulder by shy, handsome

Arre newly arrived from the Inside world of the east. They dance in the red strobed club light with other warrior men of their ilk, their leather panted asses and bulging dicks caught in the curve of a safe time and a safe space, their sweating, hairy chests roostering their sexy, fraught togetherness in the toughening world in which they choose to live.

I cannot unsee the men who fathered me the most, Lawrence and Javier, kissing one another by the sink in the cabin after the dishes are scraped of the last particles of good food they cooked together, or where they sit, side-by-side on the plush sofa, one reading and the other singing softly under his breath into the microphone of a brandy glass, sweet smile on his face.

Lawrence, big and black, fierce of eye, graceful in the uniform that becomes him but which he never becomes, how he snarls at the miscreants who would disturb the kingdom of the studios where he maintains a lovely law and diffident order, but how he laughs so loudly out of his white-toothed mouth at the slightest twitter of good will, good humour.

Javier, a witty crème brûlée of a man with sinewy arms and long fingered hands who works a dexterous magic in the arts of all the make-believe that pours out of the movie-making shops that he runs with magisterial disdain while in the employ of the money men in Ojai, and all their reductive power. I do not want to see them die again in a hail of bullets but if they are to expire over and over in my mind, let it be in the flames and rising smoke of that house now a carbonized pile of rained-on ash, or the ash that rose and went loose in the wind of the Outside world.

Goddamn you Peter. Fuck you, Paul. For the world you made is a world of sleek surfaces and a trillion moving, man-made parts, of rarified, but windless air, of perfect, pearly light that casts no shadows, of endless days and nights in which no dogs bark at the howling moon and no rooster crows the dawn, where there is no gunfire, no screech of tires, no motor's roar, where no one stands by the side of a road to watch a parade go noisily by, where no trumpet dares to blast and no pipe or drum will stir the soul, where millions live long and mostly silent lives and have you to deal with should their conflicts burst their banks.

I see out there in the Outside, the elemental truths of its bewildering variety and incomprehensible complexity and I know, as I lay beside your calculating self, Peter, that when you are awake, the all of it baffles you, has caused you to create this other world where things are amenable to your artificial intelligence. I love this cunt of mine, my bleeding womb, these breasts, for I have given birth, have had our babies feed on me and look with newborn eyes into mine where they see in them the wild mother cat, the growling mother bear, the human mother who will do for them what no other life will do, can do.

My mother had it in her eyes too, blessed me by making me understand I was in her care, blessed me more by taking me with her on the roads she went down singing all the while, through the growing deserts and troubled forests, over the dwindled rivers, into the blighted towns and cities of a world that was not Outside when she was born, or when as a young woman she started to make her way. It only became Outside when you threw up that first domed city. Which one was it? I don't know. I don't care.

As Trader Merri Weer, my mother, became a legend she surrendered even that so I could sing. You have no idea, Peter, of the power of motherlove, of the vast, intricate, mystical purposes to which a woman's wiles are put and must be put. Out there in the land of is, as she called it, she drove through the barricades that men erected around their staked-out places, worried not a moment that those men would raise a gun on her or turn her away.

Simple, terse, un-made up, vulgar as any man, she was allowed on the faith of her winks and jokes to drive the van into a thousand, armed villages to their very heart, because the men wanted her to give their women what they could not – a moment's pleasure, a little respite from their constant cares, things that would evoke their feminine selves, pills that would prevent another pregnancy when push came to shove and they had to let their men fuck them. You think, don't you Peter, that the hive cities are different than those barricaded towns? But they're not. You and Paul and The Ten stand at the gates and you believe - to the vanishing point of absurdity - that the protections you guarantee are a gift.

I was in her belly when Merri came down off that hurricane bridge and crashed. My father was Clement Samuels, your saint, her Clem. She knew full well who my father was despite the ordeal she put herself through to rationalize her leaving him bewildered in the yard of that Nebraska farm. So, what happened after she was rescued? The black women of Fort Ketchup took her in, bandaged her, prepared her for the birth of me. Those women had a place in the world because smart, tough Willia made it so, and kept it so, but she did not do what you do, Peter, which is to command, to make your people fear your money and your mind. Oh, no. She raised those women up.

My mother, knelt by the tiny bed in that small log room and labored until I dropped into the hands of the midwife Cladine, who sang to her, and stroked her back through those long hours and assured her that despite her manliness, my mother was a woman, that all her parts were working right, that my mother's pain was a mother's pain, and finally, that she had given birth to a feisty, fat and beautiful baby, that my crying was a kind of joy. No, not a kind of joy, but joy itself.

Over the years, in Cladine's voice I found my own voice and became Wicla the Singer, and always, almost until the last, whether in some roadhouse in the back of beyond, or upon some stage in front of thousands of adoring fans, I could look down in front of the stage and see my mother turning on her toes, hands in the air, her pinned and buttoned vest jangling as she tripped the light fantastic, astonished always by the realization that I had come out of her, come out of her because one hot, sun-filled day she had stopped moving long enough to love a man and let him love her. She doubted that had she and he stayed together they would have stayed in love the way she wanted and needed, but she never doubted the glorious, exalted release she felt when he thrust into her in those final spasms of their sex and flooded her with the seed that gave her me. None of life's tribulations were encased in the egg of that specific moment and as riled, difficult and horrid as things might become, its shell never cracked.

I held the image of the cosmic egg. The black void rushed back in. Suddenly, Peter snorted into the darkness and his body shifted. He turned on his back, and I thought oh god, my imaginings have awakened him. He has heard my dangerous thoughts. His rage will be compounded. But he quickly fell back to sleep. His movement, the slight purring emanating from his mouth in the large silence of the room triggered me to a state of wakefulness. I swung my legs up out over the edge of the bed and I waited a few seconds for my head to settle. I stood and walked to the bathroom door and went in, turning on the light as I did, but closing the door behind me.

In the bathroom mirror, I could not make out my own face. There was another woman there. Who is that? Who is that? Cora Munro. Yes. Behind the tinted glass of her limo that day she left the White House. Paul standing nearby joshing the reporters who came to watch her departure. She was, I remember from the footage, bent over, eyes averted, aged beyond her years. She was mistaken, I was sure, about the cause of her demise. She had surrendered to a profound misconception about why things had gone the way they had. She believed, I knew, that the grind of high office had taken an inevitable toll; that she had been drained by time itself of the energy necessary to fight the unremitting war that Hive Corp. had waged against her people, that the politics of the moment had evolved beyond her meagre skills, that the odds of winning in the time she had left in office were so stacked against her that they had become impossible to beat. She would go to an early grave not knowing the truth: her husband, in league with my husband and the other members of their oligarchy, had betrayed her down to the last molecule, had indeed split the very atoms that had once constituted her vivid, illustrious, determined and beautiful high-heeled self.

Do I enter the mirror to tell her that awful truth?

I went out into the bedroom and pulled the door almost shut behind me with the light still on. I walked to the antique chair just beyond the foot of the bed. Nemo me impune laces-sit. The light from the bathroom fell across Peter where he lay face-up, the black buttons on his night shirt undone, the covers down near his waist, arms to his side, palms up. Supplicant to his strange sleeptime gods, I thought. Ugly man in that light, balding pate on a narrow, long-nosed, thin-lipped head, bony clavicle, sternum sunk, knobby shoulders. Computer ticking behind sunken eyes. Who is that man, I thought?

The light from the bathroom door that slashed across the bed and illuminated Peter also rose vertically on the wall on the other side of the bed, like it was coming through a parted curtain. I looked at it until the light blurred, until through that imagined curtain I could see Kaya on a stage singing. Could hear her voice. Could hear the crowds to whom she sang so clearly, so passionately, so righteously, could hear them cheer her like they used to cheer Wicla the Singer. Me.

Something stirred. Not sure what. I remember thinking the fireplace is sliding open. Men in masks are coming for me. But it wasn't that. Over in the blackness between the fireplace and the curtain on the window looking out at the North Sea from which all fog had been sucked into the mouth of the full moon, I was sure there was a man, a man with a knife. Then he moved like curtains move, shadows folding into shadows. He moved over to the bar of light that I have been looking through and he too sees Kaya singing. As she finishes a song and applause washes over her, he looks at Peter and sees the nod of Peter's assent. He steps into Kaya's impeccable light then crosses the stage with his gun in hand, gun in hand. At the very moment she sees him approach - just at the moment - she knows the devil for whom she has been waiting. He fires two shots into her head and guts. No song now. As Kaya falls into the vortex, her voice falls out of the tower of song.

A dizziness came over me. I leaned on the table where Peter's father's things were laid out. I looked at Peter again. I thought of who I used to be: Wicla the Singer, daughter of Trader Merri Weer. And I knew that If I had remained who I was, brave woman that I was, but I am not now, I would have awakened Peter to bring him out of the dream of all the destruction he had wrought and was wreaking and would continue to wreak while in its embrace.

Thinking, was I thinking? If I had been thinking, yes, I would have shaken him awake and made him listen to me. I would not have tolerated his smirk. I would have screamed to make myself heard – finally heard – by him. I would not have permitted his smug, superior there, there's and the usual, sarcastic comment about my lack of intelligence. My lack of understanding. My lack of insight. Because in that one, clarifying moment I did understand. I understood everything.

So, what I did, with no more thought than one gives to turning off a light, was to take up his father's dirk, walk to Peter's side of the bed and hold it up above my head and wait for gravity to plunge it deep into his heart. And when he let out a short sharp yelp, and his eyes opened, and his arms flew up, I plunged the dagger in again, again, again and again until the dirk was too slippery with blood to do anything but let it drop to the floor between my feet.

Yes, if I had been able to, I would have demanded he put everything right. But I wasn't able to, because there was nothing he could put right, no more in death than in life.

*Awareness of the avoided alternative abuses all.*

# Song 48 - Coda

I washed my hands. I opened the big oak door to the bedroom and walked down the hall to Paul's bedroom and knocked. No answer. Knock then bang, bang, bang again until he and a few other of The Ten opened their doors. Paul saw immediately that I was drenched in blood. Looked at me, like he already knew what had happened.

- He's dead. Peter's dead.

- What?

- I killed him.

The other men started walking toward us, shouting through the doors of those who were still asleep to rouse them. Paul pushed out past me and trotted to the master bedroom. He knows right away that Peter cannot be revived. He pulls the sheets and blankets up over Peter's head.

I am told to stay upstairs and clean myself up. I take a few things from the master and take them to the kid's room where I shower and put on clean clothes. Paul and the other men go down to the salon where they hold a conclave. A scandal now, when they do not know who is in possession of the information given to me about the rise of the Inside world, is to be avoided at all costs. Bened and Scola will one day inherit Peter's wealth and position. Their standing must not be tainted. Peter's legacy and the legacy of Peter Senior, of Saint Samuels, must be protected. At all costs.

During the next two days, I am sent back to Clinton under escort. The children are taken to our estate in the south of France by their nannies and security people. On the third day, a public announcement is made. Peter Benevolus died of a heart attack while staying with his family at Castle Forbes in Scotland. Everyone is deeply saddened.

The service for Peter was held in the sanctuary of Clinton City where his father was memorialized not that many years ago. Paul gave the eulogy. I was there under Paul's direction with instructions to play the grieving widow, Bened and Scola sitting beside me, sad-eyed and bewildered. I didn't have to act my grief too much because I truly did grieve Peter's death, even though I despised just about everything he did.

That was many years ago. The true secret of Peter's death has been kept. As I said, I am still living in Clinton. The kids are at school far away and come to see me from time to time. They do not know I killed their father. I am the dowager empress. The children are under a regency until they are of age – yes at which time they will inherit all that was their father's. This document – my statement – may find its way to Bened and Scola one day, after I am gone. Yes, Scola too, for she has proven herself to Paul and The Ten.

My children, however, are entitled to know the truth. Why did I kill their father as I did? Because I knew, in the moment just before I picked up the dirk, not just how Peter had caused Paul to betray and finally kill Cora, not how he had sent an assassin to murder Kaya, but how he had, in some way or other, killed or maimed everyone I ever knew or loved, and how he had taken my children and would, over time, make them an image of his ugly self. And, I knew also in that singular instant, exactly how, when and why he betrayed me.

Wicla the Singer wrote songs as a testament to the people and places she knew and loved out there in that world now gone. As I read Peter's testimony, I knew for a certainty that my father, the sainted Clement Samuels, did not and could not foresee what the two Peters made of the country he loved. Had he lived, he would have stopped Peter Senior's bending of his vision long before things got into the hands of his son.

Had my father lived he would have done things differently; found a way to save the country, not bury it. The Outside world would have been de-cluttered and revitalized as much as it could have been. People would have had the choice of living inside or out. He and Cora would have found common cause. He was, as Cora Munro said to me while we sat in that White House bedroom, a good man.

Down in the crypt with its window facing into the blue pool, Peter married my father to his father. Even today, they sit there snugly side-by-side, don't they? Peter believed the blink-blink of their Lifebooks represented their enduring partnership in a common enterprise. Just as the crystal my father found is the root stock of the new world, that belief remains the root stock of the Inside world's founding myths. But it's a lie. But even that insight was not what made me pick up the dagger that I used to kill Peter. It was something else, deeper and more invidious.

Peter came to CashCarter with the express purpose of marrying me. He bent bendable me to his will and purpose. The marriage of our fathers' Lifebooks was not enough. His legacy would be carried on the shoulders of his son and heir, in the same way as he had carried that of his father's. I was Clement Samuel's daughter. He wanted to breed with me. He got a son – and a daughter - from me and he was absolutely joyous about the success of our mating, because in them runs the blood of sainted the Samuels, of his father and himself.

More than that, he didn't really care about unless he could use me for other things like getting me to go out on the road to sing with Kaya. He knew, by my hypocrisy, I would draw the Outsider Army from hiding so he could have them massacred where they stood. But at that last concert in California, to a vast Outsider audience, I did, at least, get to sing the last song I wrote before I left the road of music forever. I often think about my mother Merri when I hum its last two verses.

*The Spirit Mother comes to me*
*Says never let your future be*
*Just the product and the sum*
*Of freedom and forever love*
*But all that was in the land of is.*

*All that was in the land of is*
*Was never hers and never his*
*But always was and will always be*
*A god within who holds a key*
*To an inside world where we are free.*

Also by this author

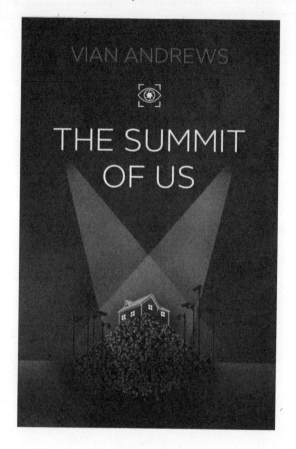

*The Summit of Us*
by Vian Andrews

Published by The Conrad Press
ISBN 978-1-914913-41-9